Superintendent, you've walked into
a delicate political situation."

"This planet belongs to the bezeri, that moon
belongs to the wess'har, and the isenj make territorial claims here. So the wess'har have what you
would call a military presence here to protect the
bezeri, who can't defend themselves."

"Ah," Shan said, "is this military presence
something I should be worried about?"

"See the plain?" Josh said.

She looked around the unspoiled wild landscape. She could see nothing, absolutely nothing,
except the alien scrubland. "Are they out there?"

"It's what's *not* there that matters. There was
an isenj city out there once, coast to coast. Now
there's not a single trace of it. The wess'har
wiped it off the face of the planet. They don't
bluff and they don't negotiate. Be mindful of that."

It was hard not to. Shan stared at where the
isenj town conspicuously was *not*.

Josh carried on walking. "Welcome to the
frontline, Superintendent."

Books by
Karen Traviss

CROSSING THE LINE
CITY OF PEARL

CITY
OF
PEARL

KAREN TRAVISS

An Imprint of HarperCollins*Publishers*

This is a work of fiction. Names, characters, places, and incidents are products of the author's imagination or are used fictitiously and are not to be construed as real. Any resemblance to actual events, locales, organizations, or persons, living or dead, is entirely coincidental.

EOS
An Imprint of HarperCollins*Publishers*
10 East 53rd Street
New York, New York 10022-5299

Copyright © 2004 by Karen Traviss
ISBN: 0-06-054169-5
www.eosbooks.com

First Eos paperback printing: March 2004

HarperCollins® and Eos® are trademarks of HarperCollins Publishers Inc.

Printed in the U.S.A.

10 9 8 7 6 5 4

For the men and women of the Falklands Task Force—for those who came home, and those who did not, and those who still bear the scars.

Acknowledgments

My thanks go to Dr. Kelly Searsmith, whose unerring judgement kept this book on track: to Liz Williams, Charlie Allery, Joe Murphy, Chris "TK" Evans, and Mike Lewis, meticulous readers; to Lyn Graham and Martin Welsford for technical advice and moral support in every sense of the word: to my editor Diana Gill for getting a far better book out of me: to my agent, Martha Millard, for doing the biz: to Greg Frost for his unstinting support and wisdom: and to my mother, Barbara, for instilling in me a lasting sense of wonder at the age of five when she told me just how far it was to Andromeda.

Prologue

GOVERNMENT WOR

The bot was immune to the snow, and so was Aras. He watched it working its way across the surface of the stone with a blind purpose that defied the ice. Words emerged behind it like droppings.

GOVERNMENT WORK IS

A little shaving of ice drifted down as the bot moved. It cut steadily into a block of stone so hard that only an obsessive would have bothered to try to carve it, an odd choice of material in a construction made otherwise of composites and alloys.

But the bot had no passions as far as Aras could see; its single-mindedness must have been by proxy for its masters. As it finished gouging the last letter out of the stone, it executed a 90-degree turn, moved down the supporting column to the ground and plopped into the snow to trundle away, trailing a wake of parallel lines.

GOVERNMENT WORK IS GOD'S WORK.

Aras mimicked the lettering, copying it into the unspoiled snow beside him with a steady claw. He considered it, then brushed it away. What was "God"? And why did it care about government, especially so far from home? They were just words. He was only beginning to come to terms with the *gethes'* language, and many things still baffled him.

"Is that *gethes*?" asked the apprentice navigator. It was his first trip to the quarantine zone, and he was suited and sealed against invisible dangers, those that would never again bother Aras. A slight tilt of the navigator's head steered Aras's attention to a low platform on tracks, rumbling around the perimeter. "They look like *that*?"

"*Bot*," said Aras, using the *gethes* word he had gleaned from transmissions. "A machine they sent ahead of them to build a habitat. Some are fully intelligent. That one is not. It's a load-carrier." Aras stood up and wandered into its path; it paused and corrected its course to avoid him. He blocked it a few more times and then tired of the game. "It cannot distinguish me from a *gethes*."

The *gethes* were definitely coming. They had known that for a long time, from the first signal that was intercepted, but they were imminent now. There had been a stream of data directed to the bots about the first *gethes'* intentions and needs. Now Aras had satisfied his curiosity and allowed the habitat to begin to take shape, and judged it was time to act.

He wandered through the growing compound unchallenged. There were no security measures to keep him out; bots scattered from his path. But there was no damage he wished to do, nor information he could not easily glean from the intercepted data transmissions.

The navigator turned and labored through the drifts until the irregular crunch of his boots vanished. The youngster was from the warmlands and even less able to tolerate freezing conditions than the average wess'har.

But Aras was not an average wess'har. And nor were the comrades he had lost.

Goodbye, Cimesiat. I'm truly sorry. Aras glanced around the landscape. There was no funeral to be held here, no remains of his friend to re-enter the cycle of life, so he simply remembered. In the coming season there would be black grasses as far as the eye could see, the sharp and glossy blades that grew nowhere else on Bezer'ej. If only they had never landed on this island—if only the isenj had never landed here—then Cimesiat would have died naturally at the proper time. Instead, he had been driven to destroy himself, the fifty-eighth of the remaining *c'naatat* troops to take his own life since the last of the wars. Peace made you purposeless if you let it. Aras had found his purpose in another war, a slower and more considered battle to protect Bezer'ej. One day he would win it, and he thought of his comrades and wondered if it was a victory for which he would be prepared.

There were just three of his squadron left, without family, without purpose, without any of the things that made a wess'har want to live. *But I have my world*, Aras thought. *I have duties here enough for another three lifetimes, now that the* gethes *are coming.*

He squatted and dug his claws into the snow, pushing down into the hard-frozen soil beneath as if he were connecting with it in the disposal rite that Cimesiat would never have. "Forgive me," he said aloud. "I should have known better."

There was silence again. It was a crisp and perfect calm, except for the occasional distant clank of closing hatches and the hum of motors. This was a dead homestead, industrial and unwelcoming, without life or community. The gray composite walls curved into a featureless roof.

Buildings always bothered Aras. This one was conspicuous, placed where anyone could see it. Imposing on the natural landscape was a vulgar act, an alien's taste, not a wess'har practice. The arrogance of it nagged at him. He stood up and stared at the horizon north of the island. All the lights on the shoreline had gone; after centuries all traces of isenj building had been reclaimed and erased by the wilderness. It had taken far less time to erase the isenj themselves.

So *gethes* built to be seen, too. That was all he could note. He followed the path churned up by the navigator all the way back to the ship, to avoid leaving any more of a mark than was absolutely necessary on the featureless whiteness.

"We must take it all away," Aras said. "Their construction must be moved from this place."

"And will you erase the *gethes* when they come?" the navigator asked. He had that bright expression—a mix of fear and adulation—that Aras had seen too many times. *You were the Restorer. You can save us again.* "Or will we take them before they land?"

The youngster's eyes darted between Aras's face and his claws. Every normal wess'har—clawless, heirs to death— seemed to stare at those claws.

"I will decide that when we know more about them. If they seek refuge, I will examine their need." Aras paused, and wondered again if he could have acted differently long ago; but he knew he could not have done anything more or less than to wipe out the isenj cities. He had no idea why this question continued to plague him. "If they come intent on exploitation, I will remove them."

"Sir, is it something I should fear?"

"You'll be long dead if the worst happens," Aras said. "But I'll live to see it."

He would live to see it all.

1

I will be honest in all my dealings with others.
I will avoid experiments on feeling life-forms wherever
    possible.
I will safeguard the environment.
I will not plagiarize or hinder the work of other scientists,
    nor knowingly publish false research.
I will put the common good before professional pride or
    profit.

THE DA VINCI OATH,
popularly known as the Scientists' Oath,
amended 2078

Mars Orbital
April 25, 2299

I'm going home.

"Good morning," said Shan Frankland, and held up her warrant card. "We're from Environmental Hazard Enforcement. Please, step away from the console."

She loved those words. They cast a spell. They laid bare men's souls, if you knew how to look. She looked around the administration center and in three seconds she knew the man at the desk was uninvolved, the woman marshaling traffic was surprised by the intrusion, and the man lounging against the drinks machine . . . well, his face was too composed and his eyes were moving just *wrong*. He was the fissure in the rock. She would cleave it apart.

I'm going home. Five days, tops.

"Inspector McEvoy," she said, and motioned her bagman forward. "Over to you." She put her warrant card back in her top pocket and stood watching while her technical team flowed in and put in override codes on all Mars Orbital's systems. The station was temporarily hers.

This is the last time I'll have to do this.

"May I?" She walked across to the station's video circuit. The traffic marshal stepped aside. She settled into the seat and tapped the transmission key.

"May I have your attention, please? This is Superintendent Shan Frankland. This orbital station is now under the jurisdiction of the Enforcement Division of the Federal European Union. There will be no traffic movements or transmissions until the preliminary investigation is complete. Please report to your muster stations at 1600 station time for a briefing from my officers. Thank you for your cooperation. We'll be out of your way just as soon as we can."

She leaned back, satisfied. Space stations were lovely places to carry out environmental hazard audits. Nobody could make a run for it. Nobody could get evidence off the premises. There was only one way off Mars Orbital without a scheduled flight, and that was via an airlock. It was right and fitting that she should have a relatively simple rummage job as her final task before retirement. She had earned it.

McEvoy crouched down level with her seat. "All locked down, Guv'nor. We should have it logged and wrapped in six hours, but there's no reason why we couldn't start carrying out preliminary interviews now."

Shan cocked her head discreetly in the direction of the man she'd spotted at the drinks dispenser. "I'd make a start on him," she said. "Just a feeling. Anyway, I'd better go and pay my respects to the station manager. This has probably ruined her entire day."

And this time next month, I'll be clearing my desk.

Mars Orbital looked and felt exactly as the schematics on her swiss had told her it would. She took the little red cylinder with its white cross from her pocket and unfurled its plasma screen to study the station layout.

"You should treat yourself to some new technology," McEvoy said, and tapped the side of his head, indicating his implants. "How old is that thing?"

"Hundreds of years, and still as good as that thing in your skull. I'm an old-fashioned girl. I like my computing in my pocket." She stood up and oriented herself along the lines of the map on the swiss's screen, then set off down the main passageway. Looking straight ahead, she could detect the gradual curve of the main ring. For a second she felt she might be falling, but she looked straight ahead, resisting the temptation to stare out of the nearest observation area to goggle at a Mars that filled her field of view. It wasn't her first time away from Earth, but she had never been within touching distance of an inhabited planet before. She wondered if she might find time to do a few tourist things before departing. She'd never get another free flight like this again.

The station manager's office was exactly where the swiss said it would be. Its name-plated occupant, Cathy Borodian, was quietly angry. "I thought you people were on a fact-finding mission for the European Assembly."

"It wasn't a complete lie. We're still finding facts, aren't we?" Shan stood before her desk and watched the woman trying to cope without access to her mainframe, hands fumbling across the softglass surface; it remained steadfastly blank, showing only a SYSTEM UNAVAILABLE screen under the coffee cup and half-eaten chocolate brioche. "We'll be out of here as soon as we possibly can. Routine inspection for biological and environmental hazards you're not licensed to manage."

"I don't think Warrenders is going to be happy about this. They have a contract."

"Well, last time I looked, civilian government still just about ran Europe. Not corporations."

"Are you able to tell me exactly what the problem is?"

"So there's a problem?"

"No. Not at all."

"The Federal European Union doesn't ship out forty audit and technical officers unless it thinks there might be irregularities. Does that answer your question?"

"Not completely. What about our teams on the surface? Can they come back inboard?"

"If they need to, they can flash us and one of my people will escort them." Shan understood the woman, even if she felt no sympathy for her. She had schedules and commercial pressures, and shutting down the orbital was a major crisis, with or without a police investigation. Downtime cost money. "I'll be in the cabin you assigned me, if you have any questions—or anything you want to tell me."

It turned out to be quite a pleasant cabin. Borodian must have wanted a good report to the Assembly, because there was a real viewplate and a shower cubicle. Shan dropped her grip on the bunk and stood at the plate for a few minutes, mesmerized. McEvoy had told her she could see the American and Pacifica stations at different times of the day if she followed his instructions, but she was far more captivated by the rusty orange disk that filled the window. It was so vivid that it looked unreal, a projection for her education or entertainment. No matter how hard she tried to see it as a three-dimensional sphere, it remained an illustration on a flat screen.

Movement caught her eye. Along the jutting spar of a mooring boom, two figures in self-luminescent green marshaling suits were guiding a tiny vessel into a bay. No mainframe access meant the automatic navigation was down; they were securing the ship manually, one standing on the gantry above the vessel and signaling with spiraling hand gestures, one alongside on the boom operating the winch.

Odd to think they still used antiquated hand signals. But even Morse code still had its uses. There was a lot to be said for old tech, Shan thought, and toyed with the swiss in her pocket.

She watched. Slowly, slowly, farther astern, then the figure on the gantry held arms aloft, wrists crossed in an X, the signal to *make fast,* to secure the lines. The locking buffers extended to take the touch of the stern, and the vessel shivered to a halt. And suddenly she couldn't see the hand signals of the berth marshals anymore, because she was looking at the leather-glove hands of a gorilla.

The primate was staring intently into her face as it made the same gesture, the same sign, over and over again; rubbing its palm in a circular motion over its chest, then a fist-on-palm gesture. Its eyes never left hers.

Please help me. Please help me. Please . . .

She didn't know what it meant at the time. The animal technician had said it was asking for food, *please,* and wasn't it great that you could teach apes to sign? And she had believed him, right up to the time when a deaf interpreter told her what the gesture really meant.

How could I have known? She didn't sign. But she knew now, and she had gone on knowing every day ever since, and the shame and regret had not faded any more than had the blinding, personal revelation that there was a *person* behind those ape eyes.

The gorilla was gone and lime-green shiny marshals were working their way, hand over hand, up the gantry to the next mooring. Mars was as red as Australia. She had forgotten how much color there was to see in space.

And I'm going home.

For a moment she wondered who would worry about the people behind ape eyes when she had retired, and hoped that it would be McEvoy.

She unpacked her grip almost without thinking. She had

been living out of it for the last ten years, and her life could
fit into it with room for a dress uniform, personal library
and her own steel mug with a carabiner for a handle. Just
running her hand over the grip's taut-stretched navy blue
fabric would tell her if she had forgotten anything, and she
hadn't. She didn't forget things. There was one extra item
wedged in the shockproof section: a two-centimeter-square
case that would have rattled if she hadn't packed wadding
into it to stop the seeds inside it giving the game away.

Technically, the tomato seeds were illegal biomaterial,
but she was EnHaz, and nobody would stop her. Anyway,
she no longer cared. It wasn't a contamination risk. But she
was damned if one more agricorporation was going to tell
her what she could plant and grow and eat. All seed vari-
eties were the patented property of a company; so her own
crossbred tomato plants, reared on a windowsill from carefully hoarded seeds, were unregistered. Technically, it was
an act of theft.

Technically.

She tucked the seeds deep into the folds of her cold-
weather suit at the bottom of the grip. In a few months,
maybe, she'd have the first plants growing in her own plot,
somewhere out of the way where there were no Gene In-
spectorates or patents or licensed crops. She thought of the
hairy green leaves and their pungent cat's-pee scent, and
saw her father carefully tending a straggly plant in the windowsill high above her head. He looked down at her. *Never
lose touch with what you eat, sweetheart. Touch the soil.
Embrace it.*

He never did. The best that her apartment-bound family
could do was visit friends with a smallholding. And then
her father was dead. At least he had finally embraced the
soil.

Oh, Dad.

McEvoy appeared at the open door. "Bingo, Guv'nor,"

he said. "Rummage One's located a grade-A biohaz containment area. You okay?"

She snapped alert. "Well, they couldn't exactly hide something the size of a warehouse up here, could they? Any indication what it's busy containing?"

"It's not a new flavor of soda, that's for sure."

"Ah, joy upon joy unending." She opened the secure link on her swiss, flicked the keypad and gave him a wink. "I feel an order for suspension of government licensing coming on. There." She tapped SEND. "That'll get their attention."

McEvoy sagged visibly against the frame of the hatch. "Come on. You know this is pissing in the wind. They'll be back on agriweapons and god knows what as soon as they've paid the fine and sacrificed a few executives. Companies are bigger than governments."

"Maybe. But this'll cost them in lost production. Put a crimp in their bottom line. Let them know the electorate isn't going to lie down without a struggle."

"There's times when I really understand eco-terrorists."

She paused. "Me too, son. Me too."

Oh yes, I understand them all right. Was McEvoy trying to say he knew the gray areas in which she worked, that she had her deniable connections, and that it was okay by him? He wouldn't have been the first. In a way, it helped to have those rumors flying round. Thwart EnHaz, and you'd find yourself dealing with people who worked well outside the law to express their disapproval of environmental tinkering. Governments had always made use of cheap, effective terrorism when it suited them. It certainly suited her.

"Want a look round?" McEvoy said.

"Okay." Shan slipped on her uniform jacket and pulled on the boots that anyone could hear pounding down a corridor. She waited to follow McEvoy down the passage.

"After you," he said.

"No, you go ahead," said Shan. "Clear a path for me, eh?

Be the ice-breaker." She knew she looked like bad news. It was something you could learn to do. Her old sergeant had taught her twenty years ago to never step aside and never break eye contact, and it worked as well as it ever did. McEvoy swung through the hatch leading off to the containment area, and they were suddenly facing a small group of technicians in pale green lab suits.

The techs were leaning against the bulkheads or had their backsides perched on sills. A couple of them straightened up as she approached. They all looked her over, and she looked at them. They looked away first.

"It's just weed control," said one. "We're working on *Chenopodium* strains."

"I haven't cautioned you, so perhaps you'd like to save it for the interview," Shan said. "But it's useful to know it's *Chenopodium,* seeing as that's also a food staple in some areas, and your organization does have some track record in contaminating crop species."

"Hey, Warrenders wiped out the opium poppy."

"Yeah, and spelt, and non-GM millet. Like I said—I haven't read you your rights yet. Save it for later."

She walked away, leaving a hard silence and then a hum of hushed voices behind her. The word "unaltered" filtered through. She was glad they could see that she was one of the few with plain old unaltered human genes. It would psych them out a little further, that hint of wildness and savagery. It was no more than her mother's Pagan distrust of any medical treatment involving gene therapy, but it had its propaganda uses. McEvoy brushed against her arm.

"Well, that confirms the Foreign Office suspicions," he said. "Maybe they *are* developing a crop killer for some tin-pot government."

"Could just as easily be our own." She found it harder than ever to ignore the closed hatchways flanking her while she walked. To McEvoy, they were probably still just

closed doors. To her, there was always something behind
them, something disturbing and brutal and sickening. She
wondered if she'd ever look at doors and see just openings
again. There were always things behind them and once you
saw what was there, you could never shut them again, not
even with plenty of alcohol. They would always be as laden
with sinister meaning for her as kitchen knives and cleaning fluids.

"Bet you'll miss all this," said McEvoy.

Shan shook her head. *I want to be like other people. I
want to look at ordinary things and not see all the pain that
they can cause.* "I don't think I'll be able to miss it at all."

"You could get a lot more pension contributions out of
private security work, you know."

"I'm not interested in watching anyone else's arse any
longer. Not even for a better pension."

"Not the smallholding thing, Guv?"

"I kept saying I'd get a life one day, and now I'm going
to do it before I'm too old to bloody well enjoy it." She
thought of her tomatoes. It was reassuring trivia—trivia, the
details other people didn't want you to look at, the clues,
the building blocks, the very texture of life. But yes, she
would miss the family of uniform. And getting by finan-
cially was a concern. "Don't forget that, Rob. You think
you've got all those years ahead of you but they get eaten
up fast. And you with them."

She wanted to explain to him about all the corners she
had cut and all the gray areas he would have to make black
and white when he succeeded her, but her swiss chirped in
her pocket and saved her from regret. She flipped it open
and checked the message. "Well, the Foreign Office has a
team inbound. They could have said so before we embarked, couldn't they? I hate joint ops with civvies."

"How long?"

"Eight hours."

It was typical of another department to do this without telling EnHaz. Shit, they probably set out at the same time as she did. She concentrated on the prospect of signing out of the service and made her way back to her cabin. As she walked—and it was a long walk following the central ring of the orbital—she passed the occasional station worker who hadn't been confined to quarters. Sometimes they stared and sometimes they just looked away.

It was definitely time to pack it all in. Staying objective was getting to be a struggle these days. She shut the hatch and loaded her music library into the swiss before flopping onto the bunk the wrong way round so she could stare like an astonished child at the face of Mars.

There was a chirp from the swiss. She opened her eyes, closed them again, and then there was an insistent knock at the hatch. "Bugger," she said. The clock read 2017. She'd slept far too long. When she opened the hatch, there were two men at the threshold. They weren't company security muscle and they weren't police, but they slotted into their plain suits like men who had no other existence beyond their jobs, no messy home lives, no other role as daddy or darling or son. If they turned round, she expected to see voids where their backs should have been. "You're early," she said. "Are you taking over jurisdiction now?"

One of the suits—very young, thinning blond hair— glanced over his shoulder; the older man blocked the hatchway. "This is nothing to do with your investigation, Superintendent Frankland," he said. "Foreign Minister Perault is here to see you."

Perault. Eugenie Perault was a politician she had never met, another familiar two-dimensional player from a newscast without a family or a back to her head. Maybe this was a job offer. "I don't work for the Foreign Office," Shan said carefully.

"This is a *Key Task*," said Blond Suit, somehow adding capitals to his pronunciation.

"As of next month, I don't work for anyone anymore. I'm retiring. I'm going home."

The two men looked embarrassed. Whatever they were, they weren't used to debate. "I'm sorry, Superintendent, but when a government minister travels this far to brief you, I really think you should hear her out."

Ah, McEvoy and his pranks. A retirement joke. "Oh, okay. Funny. Can I go now?"

Older Man ignored her politely. "May we show her in?"

Blond Suit stepped forward; Shan stiffened. He was a few inches shorter, and she was surprised that she had already sized him up for a fight. It had been a long time since she'd had to do that sort of policing. His face was apologetic, bewildered. Something was half hidden in his hand, and it wasn't a gun. It was a sub-Q drug cartridge.

"This isn't a joke, is it?"

"No, ma'am." He stepped back and Eugenie Perault appeared beside him as if she regularly dropped in unannounced on space stations.

"Minister," Shan said. It was funny how the words came. The thoughts weren't there at all. But she kept her eyes on the sub-Q. "This isn't what I was expecting."

Perault, all clipped gray hair and unnaturally uncreased fatigues, stared up at her. "I never leave a difficult briefing to others." She looked over her shoulder at the suits, a silent prompt to leave and close the hatch behind them. The two women stood facing each other.

"Frankland, you're not going to like what I have to say, so I'm saying it as briefly as I can. We need you to . . . shall we say, *supervise* a sensitive mission."

"I'm released from duty next month, ma'am."

"We've had to override that."

"You can't. I was conscripted, and my conscription has

already been renewed for the maximum period. I should have been out ten years ago."

"I'm really sorry about that. But we can. Emergency powers."

"Oh, terrific. Okay. How long is this going to take?" *I want to go home. I need to go home.* "A couple of months is—"

"A hundred and fifty years. That's how long the return journey to Cavanagh's Star will take."

Shan heard the words. But they served only to split her into two parts, one part retrieving information about Cavanagh's Star and intrigued by the invitation, the other part screaming *no, no, no.* It triggered a reaction in her over which she had no control. She heard her other self ask a sensible question while her core being shrieked how unfair it all was. "What's important about Cavanagh's Star?"

"Constantine colony," said Perault

"Constantine was lost." Everyone knew that. It was history now. "At least it wasn't taxpayers' money."

"It might have been lost, or it might not. A joint government and commercial reconnaissance mission is about to launch and I need a government representative there who isn't afraid of hard decisions."

"So they've found it?"

"We have better data now that suggest the planet is economically and environmentally viable for humans."

"But have they found the colony?"

Perault gave a little twitch of the mouth, a reluctant sad smile, and Blond Suit came into the cabin, this time with the sub-Q openly in his hand. "You've experienced a Suppressed Briefing before, Frankland? I know you Pagans tend not to like pharmaceuticals."

Shan stared at the sub-Q, and then at Blond Suit's rapid blinking: well, at least she'd rattled him. "I have." Suppressed Briefings were expensive. The drug cost more to keep under lock and key as an exclusive government resource than it did to produce. Under its influence, she would understand what she was being told, and her compliance with the instructions would be voluntary, but she would not consciously recall what information she'd been given until circumstances triggered its release. The one time she had worked under it before had been unpleasant, frustrating, like having a name on the tip of your tongue the whole time.

Shan didn't like her subconscious holding the reins. But the stuff did the job. She would have to trust it again, and reluctantly.

"It's that serious, then?"

"It's important enough for you to be given extended pension rights."

"How extended?" When retirement meant sixty or more years, that *mattered.* "Until I return?"

"Until you return. But you can make up your mind after you've heard what I have to say. Suppression doesn't remove your ability to refuse the mission, remember."

Shan did not believe in gift horses. She rolled up her sleeve and offered her arm to Blond Suit anyway. The sub-Q popped slightly against her skin and her ears began buzzing. She sat down.

Her swiss chirped: it was 2030.

The buzzing in her ears stopped. She looked up. The display on the wall said 2103, and Blond Suit was carefully wrapping two sub-Qs in foampak. She'd had the stopper, then—the second phase of the drug that brought her into the conscious now, and sealed whatever had been said to her into the retrievable past.

"Yes, ma'am," Shan said. "Of course I'll go." It felt good and right. Whatever had been said, it had persuaded her, and thoroughly. When she tried to recall it—and not trying to recall was like ignoring an itch—it left her tasting worry, determination and a disturbing guilt.

"You have a detachment of Royal Marines, Extreme Environment Warfare Cadre, as support." Perault held out a ten-centimeter wafer of data pack. Shan, numb but still functioning, automatically took it. "The briefings in here are unclassified. The ship is the *Thetis,* and the civilians and EEWC have been embarked in chill-sleep, so I'm afraid you won't have the chance to talk to them for another seventy-five years."

"I haven't got a clue how to command marines. I nick people. That's about it."

"I think your skills are a little more sophisticated than that. Anyway, you'll have an FEU Navy officer as second in command."

"And how are they going to feel about finding me in the luggage?"

"This is the best team of specialists we've been able to assemble. Nobody worries about who's wearing what cap badge these days—they slot in where we need them. The regiments and companies and ships are just there for tribal bonding purposes."

"Even so—"

"You'll join them from here."

Shan sat down on the bunk, weighed down by unfathomable time scales. "I can't go home first?"

"Can't risk that, I'm afraid. We can take care of your home and finances. And there's no family to notify, is there?"

"No." Not anymore. "Nobody I can't live without seeing again, anyway." Suddenly that thought seemed less pressing. Even getting out of EnHaz, even being temporarily robbed of her retirement garden, didn't feel so bad. Whatever had been in the Suppressed Briefing must have been extraordinarily stark.

"Don't forget," Perault said. "The priority is Constantine and its planet. Nothing else."

Shan looked into Perault's face and decided she was one of the few people she could not intimidate, and she couldn't work out why. She now *knew* Perault was not an ordinary politician, but the detail eluded her. She also knew why she had been given the task. And even though the reasons were still buried in pathways of her brain that were temporarily blocked, she believed them with a crushing emotional certainty located somewhere behind her sternum. It was an unpleasant sensation for a data-rational woman.

"Good luck, Frankland." Perault reached out and squeezed her shoulder. Few people dared touch Shan but the gesture didn't feel intrusive this time, even though this was a stranger and a minister. "Thank you. And thank you for Helen."

The hatch closed behind her and Shan sat back on the bunk again. Who was Helen? No, she'd remember when it mattered. This time, she had no lurking suspicions that someone had lied to her or set her up, as she did the last time she had been suppressed. She felt focused and urgent.

Now she'd have to make sure she had a last drink with Rob McEvoy before he returned to Earth. He would be the last friend she would ever see from her own time.

She checked her uniform in the mirror and prepared to step outside again, unable to get the name Helen out of her mind.

2

Aliens are dull. Jellyfish. Bacteria. Fiction gave us such high expectations of what contact would really be like, and the reality isn't what we expected. We didn't expect them to be blobs we could only chat to in prime numbers and wait years for the answer. But now we've got the worst of both worlds—we know we're not alone, but the physics is so unforgiving that we might as well be. As for relationships with aliens—we've had things that have evolved and gone extinct on this planet that are even more alien than the extraterrestrials we've encountered. And there are still things in the ocean, things we know about, that are truly alien and even intelligent. We put them in pet food.

GRAHAM WILEY, speaking on "Science and You,"
BBChan 5682,
April 30, 2299

Eddie Michallat didn't care for Graham Wiley. Wiley was a broadcasting Brahmin, a professor who had the prime science correspondent slot across thirty Web channels. He treated Eddie like a tabloid hack, because, Eddie believed, he didn't regard his Master's in anthropology as serious scientific credentials. It was rare they came this close physically in real life, but this was an important news conference. Everyone worth a byline in the journalistic community was there.

Tech came and tech went, and the dissemination of information and opinion could take place a hundred different ways, delivered straight to the brain and optic nerve of the audience in many cases. But a news conference required flesh-and-blood attendance, because only flesh could enjoy the food and wine laid on afterwards. Eddie was glad there was some respect left for tradition.

"I put in for the docco assignment they're advertising on the Ariel staffnet," he said, by way of a throwaway remark to Wiley. "To Cavanagh's Star."

Wiley, affecting professorial tweeds today, gave him a sympathetic look all the way down his nose. "Well, some-one had to."

"Could be some extraordinary stuff at the end of that."

"Could be 150 years out of circulation for nothing, too."

"Okay, what if the planets around Cavanagh's Star really are habitable long-term? What if the colony made it after all? I'd say that's one great story."

Wiley, gazing up and down the rows of hotel seating in the conference room, said nothing and stayed saying nothing for an irritatingly long time. To a journalist it was the equivalent of a gunslingers' standoff, and Eddie's meta-phorical hand hovered over his verbal gun. Suddenly he didn't care anymore and filled in the silence the ex-professor had dug hole-deep before him.

"Whatever you say, I'm still interested," he said. "I still think it's the most important mission in the history of the space program. The network wouldn't be contributing so much to the cost if it weren't. I'm going."

Wiley blew out a long silent breath through pursed lips. "It's living death," he said. "Living death. Now, where's that bloody lunch?" He looked round impatiently for signs of the caterers moving in with trolleys of delights. "You don't know what audience you'll have in twenty-five years when the signal starts reaching Earth. Or even which net-work. All you need is yet another damn planet being de-tected after you've left and you've wasted your time."

"I thought you'd express some concern about my leaving my nearest and dearest."

"I didn't think you had any."

You bastard. "I don't. The mission's restricted to single-status personnel."

"Well, then, I'm sure it'll be time well spent for you."

It was a very tedious news conference after that. Eddie left before the buffet lunch was served.

He found himself getting angry only when he was halfway through his supper in his favorite restaurant. He hated that habit. He suspected the internal replay of *he said, I said* that was running before his unfocused eyes while he ate was evident to other diners. Perhaps he was even moving his lips. He snatched the wineglass up to his mouth just to make sure he wasn't talking out loud.

Smug little shit, Wiley. He might have been making his money in punditry, dismissing exploration, but he might still be around in twenty-five years when Eddie filed his first reports, and that would show him. This was real drama. There were lost tribes and big business and a new Earth. All right, it was roughly the 67,450th planet detected, but the people factor was immense. It was absolutely logical that he should go, and observe, and report, even if nobody ever got to hear his words. He couldn't believe that instinct wasn't hardwired into everyone somewhere.

After all, facing the unknown hadn't ever deterred the first explorers, had it? How was he different from the Vikings setting off across the uncharted Atlantic, worried about getting close to the edge of the world? On the other hand, perhaps he already knew too much, perhaps more than the sailors of the past had ever created in their imaginations. He knew that even if his journey took months or years, the world left behind him would be aging far faster. Living death, as Wiley had said.

Eddie suddenly found swallowing was hard work. He had always thought phrases like "chill of fear" and "cold anxiety" were clichés, and not ones he would lower himself professionally to use, but that was precisely what went through him at that point—cold. He reassured himself it was the by-product of epinephrine. It was just his body pumping out hormones to prepare him to deal successfully with a stressor. That was all it was, blind physiology, not prophecy, not premonition, not at all. He repeated it to himself over and over.

And he was still cold. But he was still going.

3

First snows, 2374.

It was a hard walk back to Constantine for humans. Aras was mindful of their little legs and their poor stamina, and kept pausing to allow Josh to keep up. The snow grabbed at them and hid obstacles. But it had a clean silence about it, and it reminded Aras of home, the plain of Baral in Wess'ej, which he hadn't seen in a long time.

"You're sure they're coming?" Josh asked. He puffed little clouds before him. "You're sure it's a human ship?"

"Yes. It's not isenj, it's not ours, and the markings resemble yours."

"We don't want them here."

"We haven't made contact yet. At their speed, they'll pass here next season. There's time to discuss this."

"For you, maybe."

"I could prevent it landing."

"No, no more killing."

"My duty is to maintain the balance here. You know I

will, if I have to." Aras felt it was well to remind Josh that however much he regretted his own military past, no amount of exposure to human morality would prevent him doing his duty again. The past was not the present. It was foolish to forget history; but remembering would not change what needed to be done, only how he would feel about it.

Josh reeked of agitated embarrassment. Aras wondered if he did, after all, regard him as a monster for eradicating the isenj from the planet, even though Josh said he understood those had been difficult times. It was as if every mention of the massacre—centuries past, in local reckoning as well as in human years—caused him pain. Aras had moved beyond that. Josh's ancestor had forgiven him; *forgiveness* had been the first human concept he truly understood, even before his body started assimilating human genes and their attendant behavior. He could not change the past; he could only regret it and strive to change the future. That was forgiveness, he thought.

Josh looked up. If he could see anything, the incoming ship would be only an abnormally bright star. "Perhaps we could avoid them," he said, a child's frightened hope breaking through his usually steady voice.

"They're on a direct course. They're coming here, and it's likely they will land unless I prevent them. If they're coming, they're coming to see you. Don't you want to see your own kind again?"

Josh paused and bent over, hands braced on knees, panting. Aras waited for him to recover his breath. He straightened up.

"We had little in common with them when my people left," he said. "And how much will we have in common after all these years? Even less. You probably know that."

Aras thought briefly of the colony's archives. Yes, he

knew what the seculars were like. He also knew what the God-worshipers of all kinds were like, too, and most of them were no better, indistinguishable except for their funny little rituals. Josh and his people at least tried to be different.

"No, I don't think this other human society is compatible with yours," Aras said. "But this isn't society. It's just a ship. A few people."

They waded on in silence. Eventually the snow became more shallow, and Aras felt level ground beneath it, and knew they were nearly at the compound.

Josh was silent. Aras could not tell whether he was out of breath or in the grip of anxiety, because the stinging aroma of the man's eucalyptus oil salve overwhelmed his sense of smell. They crunched above the main street, passing over knee-high roofs clear of snow from which glowed the faint warm light of homes. Over the decades Aras had always wondered what truly went on in the buried village when he wasn't there. He had visited humans but he suspected, *knew,* that they switched into another state when he entered the room, and that he would never see them behaving naturally. They urged their children to behave and offered him their finest foods when what he really wanted was to wander in, barely acknowledged, and merge in with the family.

But he was two meters tall, inhuman and clawed. And every generation took their time getting used to him.

Humans were the only family he would ever know now. He would accept whatever degree of belonging they could offer him. Wess'har society had no place for a male who could not be allowed to mate.

"I'll call the other council members and we'll meet in the church," Josh said. "This isn't a decision I can make alone. You'll attend, won't you?"

"Yes," Aras said. "If that's what you want."

"Sometimes I feel we run to you like children each time there's a problem."

"I have nothing more urgent," Aras said. He meant it literally: the welfare of this colony, the balance of this world, were his calling. But Josh smiled, as if he'd cracked a joke.

"We'll find a solution," Josh said.

GOVERNMENT WORK IS GOD'S WORK

Underground, deep in the heart of Constantine, Aras glanced at the inscription set in the wall of St Francis Church. It was his most vivid memory of the coming of humans, and it had taken him years to begin to grasp its meaning. The saying had originally been the boast of European colonial invaders subduing what seemed to them a less advanced culture. Now it was the earnest wish of a band of idealists struggling to survive so far from home that few of them could even write down the distance in their notation.

Using power intelligently did indeed require a superior being. He had to admit that. The council—mainly male, which still baffled Aras—settled round a table near the altar and looked up at him as if they expected a momentous statement. They were afraid: he could smell, see and hear it. They fidgeted. They gave off pungent acid scents as they shifted position. All their muscles, from shoulders to throat, were tense, forcing their voices a little higher.

"They *are* coming here, right?" said Martin Tyndale.

"Oh yes. It's a ship with cargo space and little armament." For Aras, a trifle; for them, a potential disaster. "You have little to fear."

"How do you know that?"

"The monitor took readings through the hull. There are few people on board, and they're not conscious. I would say they're either intending to stop en route to another planet, where they have items to collect, or they're planning to collect something here to fill those cargo spaces. It's hard to tell when there's no voice traffic."

Martin didn't look reassured. "Perhaps they think we need rescuing. We should never have sent the message."

"We haven't asked for help," Josh said. "We've refused all attempts at contact. I'm afraid they've probably come to collect material with a view to exploiting the planet."

"Then I'll turn them back." Aras knew the rest of the colonists' sensitivities well enough to avoid explaining how. It was a subject they didn't discuss. "There are questions you should ask yourselves. What could they do to you if they were allowed to land? They could infect you with pathogens. They could introduce a way of life you don't like. They could try to exploit the planet, and even encourage others to try to come here. You know I won't allow that. So we will deal with it accordingly."

Josh appeared reassured. "Then we evaluate their mission and take it from there."

"That's sensible. It gives us an opportunity to see if they are an isolated group or the vanguard of something more serious. And we need to know what they are capable of doing."

Aras wondered sometimes why the humans bothered to gather a group to make decisions, because when matters were serious, they looked to him, and they never put it to the vote. Maybe, when he wasn't there, they dissented among themselves and had to count heads to reach a decision. But whenever he made a suggestion, it became the only course of action.

He wondered how they would have reacted if he had told them the safest option was to destroy the sleeping ship before it reached them. He looked round at their faces. They were all worry and fear, and—he sniffed discreetly—a little excitement.

"If I'm wrong," Aras said, slowly, "and they offer violence . . . will you fight?"

The waft of urgency began to take on a stronger, denser scent. "We'll defend ourselves and our work," said Luke Guillot. "And if that means fighting, yes."

Josh was nodding. "We're prepared for any test God sends."

Aras had lived among humans for six generations, and he still found some of their ethics inconsistent. If you were prepared to kill, then why not kill when you not only had an advantage, but your target would know nothing about it? What was the point in letting the situation develop into far more messy conflict? Why was it more honorable to look your victim in the face?

It was no trouble to him, either way. He decided to let them have their way. Besides, he was anxious to see how the other species of human, the Godless, shaped up. It was intelligence worth gathering.

4

Who knew how long the bezeri had been trying to signal to us? We saw the lights, but we failed to understand. And then we saw the bodies and the podships drying on the beaches when the bezeri volunteers died to get our attention. We had no plans to stay on their world, but we spent years trying to chart their language of lights. And then the isenj came, and bred, and we finally understood the bezeri when they said: "Help us."

SIYYAS BUR,
Historian Matriarch

The matriarch Mestin might have had authority to make decisions for her clan stationed here on Bezer'ej, but Aras needed approval from a wider group of *isan've* to justify what he had planned. He didn't like using the long-range link. It attracted the isenj's attention, which concerned him even though their reactions and furies were less than nothing to him now.

He had time to travel back to Wess'ej before the human ship was in range. Perhaps these were things that needed to be conducted face-to-face. But that meant exposing himself to the curiosity of normal wess'har, and right now that was something he didn't feel inclined to do. It was hard to be different, to be a genuine alien among your own kind. He settled for the long-range communications net and asked for an audience with the *isan've,* the matriarch of F'nar, whose opinions on off-world policy seemed to carry most weight across Wess'ej.

"I believe we should let the humans land, or at least some of them," he said to the void in the cockpit of his grounded craft. The vessel seldom flew, but he preferred to live in it or in Constantine rather than in the Temporary City. "There aren't very many and they aren't well armed, as far as the drones can tell. We need as much intelligence as we can gather to prepare us for future incursions."

"That seems reasonable." Mestin's cousin-by-mating, Fersanye, had her clan's genetic pragmatism as well as its feral looks. "I find it surprising that humans share so little in motivation."

"Perhaps it's because they don't mix their bloodlines as much as we do. Either way, the species of human that's coming is as much of a potential threat as the isenj, and even if this mission fails, Joshua believes more will come in the future."

"What are our options?"

"To get to know them and then decide if they're potential allies."

"If they have long-range military ambitions, we'll be stretched very thin handling enemies on two fronts."

"Perhaps. Let me meet them and see."

"We were lucky with the first humans. We might be lucky again." Fersanye's tone indicated she thought it was a genuine possibility. "I still think we might have made a mistake in letting the colony send a transmission."

"Not the first mistake I've made, I expect." Sarcasm was another human habit Aras had picked up, and it still went unnoticed by the average literal wess'har. Fersanye nodded as if she were accepting an apology. "But if the colony had been allowed to die, how many innocent species would have died in their cryo stores?"

"You made the best decision you could at the time," Fersanye said. "You always have. Now is a different time. Let us learn."

Aras closed the link. Fersanye would never have thought he needed forgiveness for killing isenj civilians. She was wess'har, unburdened by rules of engagement, by the differences between legitimate targets and civilians, by fear of causing offense. He had been wess'har once, too. These days he wondered what he was.

He thought of his first human friend, Benjamin Garrod, Joshua's great-great-great-grandfather, dead for more than a hundred years and as freshly mourned and vividly remembered as if he had passed into earth yesterday. Benjamin understood what it was to have pain trapped in your head.

And yet Aras now couldn't recall the face of his own *isan.* It was bad not to remember your wife.

But, as Benjamin had told him, not even a wess'har could be expected to remember things that had happened when the year on Earth was A.D. 1880.

Something went *clack* against the hull.

Commander Lindsay Neville glanced up. Apart from that *clack*, the ship's cramped cockpit was showing normal on every panel.

"Micrometeor impact, Boss?" Sergeant Adrian Bennett had logged more flight time than Lindsay had, and she wanted him to be right. "Shouldn't be."

"Might be." Lindsay checked the hull status panel again. "No, nothing. I'll run more checks. Could be contraction noises."

Their target planet, Cavanagh's Star II, was a couple of days away now, and it had a large moon orbiting it. The forward video feed had shown two small pale disks, and when *Thetis*'s centrifuge turned the right way, you could actually see them from the viewing port. It seemed much more real to watch it with the naked eye, and both worlds had now resolved into a mass of blue, white and green swirls.

For a moment Lindsay wondered if the revive program had malfunctioned and they were just weeks out from Earth, beginning the gradual acceleration that would take them twenty-five light-years. The *clack* might have been a boarding crew, coming inboard to check them out. But it was not Earth. There were two planets, and their polar ice caps were substantial. She watched for a while and realized Bennett was standing—hanging—behind her in zero gee.

"Looks reassuring," he said. There was a flurry of light and sighing noises as streams of telemetry came in from the main planet. The AI was gathering spectrometry and high-resolution images at a frantic rate, and instantly beaming back the raw data. In a couple of decades, others would be marveling at those pictures on the news, unless something more fascinating had cropped up in the meantime.

"Well, I don't think I'll be needing my piloting skills," Lindsay said, and folded her arms across her chest to stop them floating. "Not that we'd have a prayer if this crate ever needed to be flown manually."

"All it has to do is to get into orbit and stay there."

"Yeah."

Bennett looked thoughtful. He appeared to be the standard issue concrete-reliable Royal Marine sergeant, except for the times he gave her those dubious looks. She was lucky—she had a whole detachment of booties, as the navy called them, the best specialist troops she could want. She could easily have been lumbered with a ragbag of army and air force personnel. They said cap badges were just for comfort, a sop to identity in a vast anonymous European defense force of core skills and interchangeable parts. But as far as she was concerned, booties weren't interchangeable at all.

"It's the name, isn't it, Boss?" Bennett said.

"What about it?"

"*Thetis.* You know. Historically speaking."

"I'm no historian."

"*Thetis* was a submarine."

"I'm not going to enjoy this story, am I? Go on."

"*Thetis* sank with nearly all hands and the dockyard civilians on board within sight of land, all because a test drain had been blocked by a fresh coat of paint."

"Thank you for enlightening me, Bennett."

"No trouble, Boss."

Lindsay didn't believe in bad *joss* and all that superstitious bullshit. Bad *joss*, bad luck, meant bad planning and poor attention to detail, as the original *Thetis* had proven. Behind every disaster there was a string of false assumptions and checks not made. Lindsay Neville could plan bad *joss* out of her life, and if anyone called her boring—well, that was just fine.

Drill keeps you alive.

She couldn't plan for the civilian scientists she had in the freezer, though, because she hadn't even met them in an ambulant state. That bothered her. And she certainly hadn't planned to wake up and find her command had been usurped by a bloody civvie, and a copper at that. Shan Frankland's file in the AI's database had been less than informative. But the words Special Branch and "EnHaz" were enough to worry her. That was several lines before she got to the part where she was ordered to "offer full support and cooperation to any instruction" that Frankland issued when revived on establishing orbit. The FEU had hijacked her ship. She couldn't even thaw the payload or the rest of the marines until bloody Superintendent Frankland—confidentially briefed Superintendent Frankland—gave the order.

"Had any feelings about this deployment, Ade?" she asked. "You've clocked more spacetime than me."

Bennett chewed his inner lip as if calculating. "I've never had a payload of civvies embarked, if that's what you mean. But this lot are trained, aren't they? I mean, they've worked extreme environments. They're not tourists."

"And Frankland?"

Bennett shrugged. "None of my business, Boss."

It was time to refresh her knowledge of the civilians. She pulled down a container of coffee and swung for the hatch. "Ought to try to memorize names and faces before they wake up," she said. "They all look the same in chill. I suppose I could call them all Doc."

She curled up against a bulkhead, feeling awkward. Onboard carriers, she had always had a cabin to retreat to, but *Thetis* was designed simply to store unconscious people in transit. There were no cabins or wardrooms or stewards, and the only privacy was the flimsy bathroom where anyone could hear what was going on. Slurping hard on the coffee, she stared at the eight faces that appeared and changed on the smartpaper hanging in front of her.

"Hugel—physician. Rayat—pharmacologist. Mesevy—botanist." She shut her eyes and repeated the names.

"Do we need to remember what they do?" asked Bennett.

"Seems rude not to."

"They all have different specialities."

"That's to avoid fistfights, apparently. The techs told me you don't know a thing about rivalry until you've seen blokes in white coats going at it. But some of them work for rival corporations, and they're all on some incentive bonus or other, so they might slug it out." She shut her eyes again, and felt oddly disoriented. She thought she'd got over that sensation. "Champciaux—geologist. Galvin—xenozoologist. Parekh—biologist—"

"*Marine* biologist."

"Thank you. Paretti—xenomicrobiologist. You've already done this, haven't you?"

"I loaded it into my panel, Boss." Bennett held out his open palm, shimmering with color and text. The living display warped and flexed with the contours of his hand: the graphics weren't perfect because the bioscreen panel was designed for larger areas of flesh. "Just until we get to know each other."

"I might have to resort to that." But it was bad enough taking a shower and finding a shifting display under the soapsuds without seeing a stranger's face as well. Lindsay carried on staring at the smartpaper and repeating the mantra of names.

"Michallat," she said. "Journalist. Anthropologist. What use is he going to be?"

"You can never have too many anthropologists, Boss. Handy for ballast."

She knew what the problem would be: boredom. The payload would be off doing what they did best and she would have six spring-coiled booties looking for something to keep them occupied. There weren't going to be any colonists alive down there. She concentrated on revising those parts of the mission that involved looking for debris from the landing. There would be useful survival data from that for future missions, and it was going to make her an extraterrestrial specialist. It was going to fast-track her career better than a dozen small ship commands. It was worth it.

But she slept badly that watch. There was no need for them to operate a watch system, because the AI could maneuver into orbit without their input, but they did it out of a need to wrap themselves in that familiar comfort of routine. Bennett woke her, looking more relaxed than usual.

"Just established orbit, Boss. Thought you'd like to see it. Shall we—"

A red flash caught her peripheral vision at exactly the same time as the insistent *pip-pip-pip* of an alarm broke the hum and chatter of the AI. Bennett frowned and Lindsay swung into position at the console.

"Last time I heard that sound I had missiles locked on me," she said. They had been exercise missiles, but it still rattled her. "That's got to be a malfunction."

Bennett tapped the console. There was a five-centimeter display almost lost in the rest of the telemetry panels, and it was pulsing red. The AI interface was set to text, and words began pouring like torrential rain down the main head-up display in front of the pilot's seat.

INTERFERENCE IN NAVIGATION LASER.
INTERFERENCE IN NAVIGATION LASER.

"What the hell's causing that?"

"No idea, Boss." Bennett tapped reset panels and overrides. "No idea at all."

The litany changed abruptly. NAVIGATION LASER DISABLED. BACKUP DISABLED. And the lights around them went out. This was a rotten time for a systems failure. For a second they hung in the blackness, not breathing, and then the lights came on again and with them a dozen different alarms clamoring to tell of system failures.

"What have we got, Ade?"

Bennett confirmed her fears. "Life-support and cryo. Nothing else."

"Are we just lucky or have we been shut down deliberately?"

"Oh, God. Look at that."

The sensors that swept for EM frequencies were alive, not with the usual crackling of distant stars but with a clear pulse. Bennett was now leaning over the display with a fixed expression that made Lindsay think he was panicking. Marines didn't panic. She elbowed him out of the way, and realized why he was transfixed.

"We're being targeted," she said. The screen confirmed it; something was delivering EM pulses to key systems and crippling them. She switched to her headset to give her a view of the whole ship in 3D, and saw red pulsing lights covering the whole aft section of *Thetis*.

In a normal combat situation she would have had firing solutions. She would have had a good idea of the weapons ranged against her. A hundred exercises and a thousand drills had taught her that. But this was an unarmed survey ship, and no Thursday war had ever prepared her for an apparent assault from an enemy she could neither see nor even imagine. Unless the colonists had survived and taken "Onward Christian Soldiers" to a new level of understanding, she was dealing with an alien force.

It didn't even bear thinking about. But she did.

"Show me the point of origin," she said to the AI.

UNABLE TO LOCATE POINT OF ORIGIN.

"There's nothing out there," said Bennett. "But if they had wanted to shoot, they'd have done it by now, wouldn't they? They wouldn't just rattle our bars. Not if they were serious."

He had a point. It didn't stop her mouth going dry, or the sweat prickling on her back, though; and in zero gee, sweat just stayed where it formed. "Maybe they're just pinging us," she suggested. "Testing us out."

And maybe not. Three sides of the faceted panel that wrapped around the two pilot seats were now black and dead. Only life-support and cryo panels showed activity.

"Bennett, have we been hit at all?"

"Not as far as I can tell. No hull breach. We'd feel it. Shit, we'd *see* it."

Lindsay was crammed in a cockpit with one other person, in space, with no visible enemy and no tangible damage and yet there was every sign that her ship was under attack. She had nothing to indicate the *Thetis* warranted evacuation—to where, anyway?—and no way of returning fire. She couldn't even make a run for it.

Sheer impotence made them both lower themselves into their seats. *Thetis* was dead in the water, if there had been any water, and Lindsay checked the systems again, pressing the panels. How long before their orbit decayed?

"Bugger," she said. "We can't even land this thing." She

turned to the AI. "Revival and evacuation time please."
There was a *ticker-ticker* noise but no response from the AI.
Damn: a manual job. She activated her bioscreen and began
calculating to see if she had time to revive the payload and
the rest of the detachment and get them into the shuttles before *Thetis* hit the atmosphere. The figures didn't look
good.

"What if it *is* just a malfunction?" she said. "Maybe
there's no external threat." She tapped the AI controls and
waited. It took a second or two more than she expected, a
very long time in her book just then. Its test-and-repair pro-
grams must have been working flat out. "Can you confirm
malfunction?"

NO SOURCE IDENTIFIED, it said again.

"It's screwed," said Bennett.

"Okay." There was nothing she could do: the AI was trying to restore power, and there was no damage that any
emergency team could tackle, no hull damage to seal or
fires to extinguish. "Time to revive Superintendent Frankland, I think."

"If we're seriously in the dwang, Boss, an extra pair of
functioning lungs might be just what we don't need."

"Well, I'm fresh out of ideas, and she's in command. Orders say wake her up on establishing orbit."

"Wouldn't the AI know what was in her confidential
briefing?" asked Bennett.

"You watch too many movies," she said.

On the way through to the cryo tubes, nausea gripped
her and she grabbed a bag from her pocket to throw up.
Odd: fear had never had that effect on her before.

Something went *thwapp* on the bulkhead. It was like the
clack the day before.

Shan Frankland, still disoriented from chill-sleep,
passed her swiss from hand to hand, deriving some comfort

from fidgeting. "That's something attaching itself to the hull."

"What do you base that on?" Lindsay asked.

"Because it sounds like it," Shan said. She regretted her waspishness but felt an apology was out of order right then. Something started tugging at the back of her mind. It was just a hint, a fleeting moment of feeling like an obscure memory. She tried to grab it as it dissolved, but it was gone, behind the inner door, and there were no handles to grasp. She shut her eyes tight for a second and forced the sensation away. "Say our lost tribe made it after all and they've got some interesting tech after all these years."

"No external vid feed, but I could go EVA and check," said Bennett.

Shan shook her head. "I'd really rather have the qualified pilot where I can see him breathing, thanks. Have you tried flashing anyone?"

"The AI's been looking for signals. Nothing."

"Maybe they're not sending. Try calling on a radio frequency. You know, voice traffic."

Bennett swung himself into the seat without a word and plugged himself in to the console. It was nothing as graphic as inserting a jack into his skull, but just knowing he had implants sitting under his skin made Shan feel slightly queasy. He fiddled with the little crescent-shaped receiver that latched on behind his right ear. The AI obliged by selecting a range of frequencies.

"What would you like to transmit?" he asked. In a world where AIs spoke silently to each other to share battlefield data, the art of radio conversation was long lost.

Shan got the feeling Bennett was looking for a line fit to record in the archives. She disappointed him without meaning to. "Just say, 'Constantine, this is Thetis calling Constantine, respond.' If they're out there, it'll get their attention."

Bennett began a nervous monologue. After a few repetitions he appeared to settle into it. Then Shan looked into the face of a woman she'd read about in briefing notes but never really met.

Lindsay Neville was horribly young. She looked like she was wearing her older brother's uniform for a lark.

She was twenty-seven. Shan had spent her own twenty-seventh birthday behind a riot shield, sick from the smell of petrol, conscious of her brand-new sergeant's stripes. She'd needed ten sutures in her calf. But the bloke who gave her the wound needed forty.

"All I can say is that we're probably not in the shit," Shan said. "And that we should wait for a response."

"I know some of this mission is classified, ma'am, but it really would help to know what we're facing here." Lindsay looked irritated. Maybe she shouldn't have made the reference to qualified pilots. "We're on the same side."

"I'm not being secretive, and I'm not a spook. I've had a Suppressed Briefing. You know what that is, don't you?"

"Yes." Lindsay's expression told Shan she rated it marginally below water divining and reading runes. "Not something I've experienced, not at my rank."

"It's not a perk, Commander. It drives you crazy trying to work out what's niggling at the back of your mind, so you just let it drive you. If I seem vague, it's not by choice. It's the only way you can share intelligence without the risk of revealing it at the wrong time."

"It's our job to give you whatever support you ask for, ma'am. But we do work better with knowledge."

"I'll share what I know with you when I know it. And right now I recall knowing that at the time we went extra-solar, there were indications that the colony had survived. Let's assume they also survived our flight time and we can make contact."

"If we don't plummet in flames, of course."

"Has the orbit decayed?"

"No, we're still stable."

"We've probably been immobilized as a precaution. A sort of vehicle stinger on a big scale. That's what I'd do if I were them. Not that I know who *them* is."

Lindsay raised her eyebrows. "Well, that's a handy piece of kit. Some useful tech we can take back."

"Might not be ours to take." Was this the time to . . . Jesus. The thought was suddenly solid in her head, a real memory the Suppressed Briefing had let loose.

There are nonhumans involved.

Her surprise must have shown on her face, because Lindsay spoke.

"Are you all right, Superintendent?"

"Just thinking." No, it wasn't quite the time to mention aliens. She'd have to understand more herself before she could do that. "Trust me. I'm as motivated as you are to make sure we don't land the hard way."

Bennett glanced at her briefly and then at Lindsay. If he was looking for a reaction from his CO, he didn't get one. It couldn't have been easy for them. Shan couldn't imagine any military personnel being reassured to wake up from chill-sleep to find that they were answering to a copper, a copper they didn't know, a copper who was so far out of her depth right now that she almost didn't care if her numb fear showed on her face.

Apparently it didn't. Bennett gave her a quick smile and went back to repeating his mantra.

Something mentally tapped her on the shoulder and reminded her she had a job to do. The SB whispered that doing this job would put something right.

Whatever it was, it was something she had wanted to put right for a long, long time. The fear retreated.

* * *

Josh Garrod flinched in his seat as if someone had let off a charge behind him.

"Constantine, Constantine, this is European Federal Ship *Thetis,* repeat this is *Thetis.*"

The voice was male; the accent was odd, and some of the words were unclear, but it was understandable. It didn't sound as if they were used to communicating by voice. The speaker didn't have the throwaway tone Josh had become accustomed to through entertainment videos.

"We are Constantine," Josh said carefully. "Why are you here?"

"Request permission to land our party, sir. We have a systems failure, we're unable to maneuver and we're not sure if we can sustain life-support."

Land? Could they bring that monster down here? Josh had never made a decision like this in his life. There was no emergency to force him back to instinct and no time to discuss the matter sensibly. He glanced at Aras, who mouthed "quarantine" at him. It helped bring him back to plan.

"We need to discuss quarantine arrangements—we've been isolated from terrestrial bacteria for generations. Wait and we will contact you shortly."

He broke contact and turned to the wess'har. His heart was pounding and he felt sick.

"What now, Aras?"

"Allow them to send down an atmosphere-capable vessel. They'll have at least one. Insist that they bring a blood sample from each crew member so we can screen for pathogens, and that just one representative lands to discuss the next step."

Josh wrote it down carefully on a coarse sheet of hemp paper. If he could see it, he could do it. "Is their ship really damaged?"

"The sentry is programmed to neutralize any system it

detects that appears redundant to life-support. They shouldn't be in any danger. Or present any."

"This isn't what we intended."

"Josh," Aras said soothingly. "If they present any threat whatsoever, I'll remove them. I have to. It won't be your decision or your responsibility, and you need not fear them."

Aras could make anyone believe. A slight rumbling, like a cat's purr but nearer the boundary of hearing, swept away all fear. Josh felt his shoulders relax and his voice returning to normal. He could swallow. He pressed the button.

"*Thetis,* this is Constantine," he said. "*Thetis,* I have instructions for you. Please follow them."

"Are you sure you can handle it?" Bennett asked, floating at the hatch of the shuttle.

Shan checked the panel. The biohaz suit creaked as she leaned forward against the restraints. "No."

"I could come along."

"Wouldn't look good, disregarding their first instruction, would it?" She tightened the restraints round her and gave him a thumbs-up. "Let's trust the automation and South American workmanship."

Her last view of Adrian Bennett was his worried face as he swung the hatch shut and the automatic locks took over. There was a small cut on his chin where he had shaved the old-fashioned way. If she died, she thought, it would be a banal image to take with her. She had always imagined her last sight would be a spray of small-arms fire or at least a half-decent sunset. She decided to trust the mechanics anyway.

Silence surrounded her, pressing on her eardrums. She hoped the onboard AI could fly the thing: trusting its piloting skills was worse than the SB. She kept her eyes shut from the time the small vessel shuddered out of the launch bay to the time she felt the vibration stop.

She opened them again. The viewplate was full of a

blue-and-white planet at an angle that made her feel as if
she were falling forward, and instinct made her raise her
arms in front of her to take the fall that never came. She felt
sick. It was only concentrating on the fact that Perault's
briefing was unfolding on schedule within her that stopped
her stomach yielding to the inevitable.

The planet beneath resolved into finer detail, fast and
overwhelming. She was dropping towards an island in a
clear turquoise sea.

The cryo panel went dead. The biosignals of the sleeping
crew and team were still within safe margins, but there was
no indication that the systems were intact.

"Here we go," said Bennett. "That's all we need."

"Have we lost cryo?"

"Possibly. We have to assume we have."

"Okay. Frankland or not, we have to revive them. Let's
do it."

Bennett tried the manual override and waited. It was a
long five seconds. Then the alarm on the biosigns panel
turned amber. "I'll go and lift the lids," he said. "They'll be
conscious in a few minutes."

It was all turning into a cock-up. Lindsay could feel it.
She braced herself against the bulkhead and let the wave of
nausea peak and subside. She could hear the buzz of conversation in the aft section. At least three of the research
team had revived fully, and she decided that if she didn't
imprint favorably upon them now, she would never have
any sway over them. She pulled herself through the hatch
and tried to float down to a steady position.

"What's happening?" It was Mohan Rayat, the pharmacologist. He kept shaking his hand as if it had gone numb.

"Frankland's gone down to the surface to make formal
contact," Lindsay said. *He's just a rating. Think of him as a
rating. Don't weaken.* "You're only awake as a precaution

in case of cryo failure. We're experiencing some technical problems."

"Oh, great."

"Frankland has the situation in hand."

"And who's he?"

"*She.* Superintendent Frankland is from EnHaz and acting as an officer of the Foreign Office's Ethics Division. She's overseeing this mission."

"Police? What the hell's all that about?"

"She was embarked after your cryo. Political matter. Don't worry about it. She's here to maintain proper procedures in acquisition of novel substances and processes." Well, that much was true. Or at least that was what it said in the file. "You know how it is."

Rayat looked as if he was going to protest but as his lips formed a word, his face paled a little. That was no mean effort in zero gee, with his blood patiently distributing itself fairly round his system. Then his cheeks bulged and he made a fast turn—too fast—to grab a sick-bag. Lindsay heaved herself up through the hatch and let his two colleagues deal with the gently drifting rain of vomit. It was only liquid nutrient, after all.

Back in the forward section of *Thetis,* the EEWC was conscious and checking suits and weapons. The small space seemed full of them; Barencoin, Becken, Webster, Chahal, and Qureshi. They seemed okay. They said ma'am, and saluted minimally: at least they had been trained not to bounce off the bulkheads.

"Everybody up, then, ma'am?"

"Some of them," Lindsay said. "It goes without saying that this is turning into a lash-up. Frankland didn't want them revived until she'd secured an agreement with the colony. That means we'll have to keep them occupied until she says we can disembark."

"I still think we should have sent the sarge down with her," said Barencoin.

Bennett shrugged. "She can cope. No point pushing the quarantine. Anyway, they have access to kit that can stop this ship, so better to defer to them at the moment."

"It's not her safety I'm worried about." Barencoin clenched and unclenched his fist and looked at his palm and the inside of his arm. His face was illuminated by the glow from the bioscreen that was part of his skin. "Have we all got synchrony here?"

Lindsay checked her own palm at the same time as the three remaining marines and saw seven comm lines—her own plus each member of her unit—pulsing on idle above the panel that creased and flexed as she twitched her fingers. It was a spin-off of leisure technology. You could have a living display screen grown into your skin, anywhere you wanted, any size, any shape, as long as you had enough body and money; and while it was senseless fun for the well-off, it was unbreakable, totally portable comms and data tech for the military. She just hoped it worked. "Yes, got you all," Lindsay said, and the others said, "Check."

"No civvie superintendent," said Barencoin. "Not wired?"

Lindsay shook her head. "Couldn't pick up anything from her at all. Not chipped, I assume. The bioscreen would have clocked something if she'd had ID implanted."

"Do we know anything about her?"

"Only that she wants a Pagan rite if we have to dispose of her body before we get back home."

Bennett tightened his webbing. "And she carries a 9mm handgun. Saw the outline, back of her waistband. Old but efficient tech. And a swiss."

Lindsay felt a little shiver of uncertainty. "So she's Pagan, armed *and* gets paid too much."

"What's a swiss?" said Barencoin.

"Very old, very valuable. A cylinder about as long as your hand, and it's got all these parts that fold out of it—blades, adapters, data storage, netlinks, ultrasound probe, you name it. And a dinky little display screen that pops up in a frame."

Barencoin simply raised his eyebrows and said nothing. Antiques used casually prompted a little suspicion in the ranks. Everything they carried or wore was disposable, thin film, quick dry, organic tech, recyclable. Unnecessary luxury smacked of old money and wardroom snobbery.

But the handgun wasn't a toy. Lindsay doubted if Frankland wore it as a fashion accessory. There was something about the woman, even in her slightly unsteady post-thaw state, that suggested people normally didn't answer her knock on the door willingly. Lindsay swallowed back another wave of nausea: she'd have to get that medic Hugel to prescribe something for that.

"Come on," she said. "Let's get to it. We've got a planet to secure."

5

Planting plan, years one through five.

   Primary crops, seed: wheat, rice, oat, barley, quinoa, sorghum; primary crops, legumes: soy, broad bean, kidney bean, haricots, carlin pea, mung bean; primary crops, tuber: potato Charlotte, potato Desiree, sweet potato, Jerusalem artichoke; vegetables: lettuce, kale, onion, leek, garlic, tomato, mushroom, cucumber, carrot, parsnip, beet; primary crops, fruit: apple, raspberry, blueberry, grape (black muscat, Huxelrebe), lemon. In the event of crop failure, any appropriate plant from the secondary list may be substituted, depending on local conditions. Until grape vines are established, it is permitted to use other fruits or vegetables to make communion wine.

Constantine Mission,
agricultural planning document

Shan waited by the shuttle. The sky burned turquoise; the air ticked and burbled with unseen creatures. In a biohaz suit, the beautiful day was just a curse of trickling sweat in places she couldn't reach. She was close to ripping the hood off, filter and all, and letting any pathogens try their luck. It seemed a reasonable price to pay for a good scratch.

But caution prevailed. She visualized not feeling the itches. She concentrated on what appeared to be trees and for a moment the vivid autumnal reds and golds distracted her from the misery of the suit.

She kept herself fixed on the immediate diplomatic task at hand by rehearsing greetings and pleasantries until movement caught her eye. It was a small, battered all-terrain vehicle, growing larger and larger against the amber backdrop. It drew up to her, whirring like an antique friction toy.

A man in late middle age looked her up and down with complete indifference and indicated the passenger seat. She switched off her comms link to avoid interruption.

"Welcome, Commander," he said. It was the style of English she'd heard over the comms system, not so very different from her own, but oddly accented, every syllable clear and separate from the next. "Get in."

"Superintendent Shan Frankland. Police—EnHaz division. I'm not the military."

"Superintendent," he said, as if testing the sound of it. He tapped his chest. "Sam."

"Pleased to meet you, Sam. We thought you were all dead."

Sam looked unmoved. "You were wrong."

She handed him the container of blood samples from the crew and eased herself into the cab, aware that the suit's fabric was making obscene noises against the seat cover. "Now this is what I call a perfect autumn day," she said.

Sam's eyes never left the track ahead. "It's spring."

"Spring's supposed to be green." She attempted to break Sam out of the monosyllabic rut. "And light green at that."

"Anthocyanins," he said. His accent fascinated her, and she had to steel herself against mimicking him, slipping breaths and vowels between every consonant. His shapeless tunic and pants were all of the same buff material. "I'll drop the samples off first and then I'll take you to see Josh Garrod. He's getting ready for the holiday, so he's busy."

"Holiday?" she asked. *Don't put yourself out, I've only been on the road for a few decades.* Discretion prevailed again. This was not an interrogation. "What holiday?"

"Christmas," he said, emphasizing both syllables as if it were a foreign language. "It's Christmas Eve."

The autumnal landscape was alien enough, but Christmas in spring jerked her back out of what little familiarity she was beginning to establish. "Still sticking to the old calendar?"

"Yes. It's slipped out of sync with this place over the years."

"I don't suppose you thought of tying it in with the natural cycle."

"You want to work a nine-day week?"

"I'm not sure I'm even ready for the thirty-hour day."

"Some things we can't reorder. Besides, the Lord labored for six days and on the seventh He rested. You'll be glad of that."

All the way along the route to Constantine, the fresh foliage on the huge cycad-like plants was hot with cyanide compounds. She would have liked to pause and wander among the ridged orange trunks. But she made a mental note to travel this road again in her own time. The cycads thinned out one by one, and they were suddenly on a plain of shimmering gentian blue. Her monkey-brain tried hard to put familiar labels on the utterly alien, telling her *heather, bluebells, lavender.* But it was nothing of the sort. The flying creatures she could see skimming the vegetation weren't birds; and the odd opalescent patches that flared up behind them defied any classification.

Sam drove on in silence. Around them, the plain gave way to gently rolling hills carpeted with what looked like gray ferns. Shan wondered why he wasn't staring at her, or at least showing some sign of curiosity at seeing someone from another world. But he kept his eyes ahead of him as if she were regular cargo, nothing especially noteworthy. It occurred to her that he might be trying to avoid getting into conversation with an outsider.

"Here we are," he said, and began slowing the ATV.

She couldn't see anything resembling a settlement. The

vegetation had become sparse and silver, but that was all.
Sam steered the vehicle slowly, as if he were negotiating
invisible obstacles, and then the track dipped and enveloped them, and they were suddenly driving down a tunnel with a brilliant white light at the end. It blinded her.
She couldn't help thinking how much it looked like a near-
death experience.

They were underground.

"We park here," Sam said. "No vehicles beyond this
point."

He jumped down from the ATV and let her struggle out
of the cab unaided. She stared around her; her eyes adjusted
to the light and she realized she was standing in a large
vaulted chamber like the cellars of a vineyard. There was a
patch of bright bluish light at the far end, and Sam was
walking towards it. She followed him.

"Josh is in the church," Sam said suddenly, and it made
her start. "Have you ever been in a church?"

"No," Shan said. It wasn't strictly true: she'd visited
churches as architecture. She'd walked through the flooded
ruins of Chichester cathedral. But she knew that wasn't
what he meant. "I'm a Pagan."

Sam paused noticeably. "I'll take you there first, then."

The pool of light at the end of the vault turned out to be
a doorway, and she stepped through it into a vision of long-
destroyed Petra. The settlement was carved out of the rock,
Nabataean style.

Terraces of buildings stretched out on either side of her,
but instead of the gloom of caves she walked in diffuse sunlight. Was she back on the surface? She strained to look up
as far as she could, expecting artificial illumination, bewildered at the mix of apparent high technology and simplicity.

"Okay, what powers the lighting?" Shan asked.

"Sunlight," said Sam.

"How?"

"Gathered at the surface, reflected down here." He didn't seem about to go into detail. So they were definitely underground. "It normally suffices."

"Is the climate that extreme?"

"Extreme?"

"You live underground."

"No, the winters get cold, but I would not say extreme."

His silence was sudden and complete. It was all she was getting out of him. Small talk had failed; her alternative interview technique, beating the crap out of the interviewee, was out of the question. She decided to save her questions until she met the community leaders. Sam was just the gofer.

There were no people in the streets, and few sounds except the distant wail of a baby. She wondered if she were walking through an elaborate ruin. But there were lavender-flowered vines crawling up the walls towards the light, and the feel of life. She couldn't smell anything through the biohaz filter, and yet she could almost taste fresh air.

Whatever technology they had, its results were impressive for such a small colony. She stared at the circular windows and arched doorways, imagining a souk of sorts.

And there it was ahead of her.

A church.

In an underground chamber, trillions of miles from Earth, a traditional Norman-style church rose up out of the rock floor with a spire that dissolved into the light above.

"Oh my," she said.

"St. Francis. Out of the living rock."

On closer inspection the huge church was relatively modest. It had no elaborate stone ornamentation, and from the outside its stained glass looked like a craft class' first efforts. A block of stone set in the wall near the doors bore an inscription: GOVERNMENT WORK IS GOD'S WORK.

The entrance was a tunnel of round arches, and along

the walls the space between them was taken up with a narrow wooden bench. She walked through behind Sam, an alien in a space suit, wandering into a church. From outside herself, she could see how bizarre it looked. The cool darkness swallowed her and her eyes took time to adjust again.

What she saw revised her opinion of the glass. The leading, whatever it was, made no sense from the outside, but with the sun streaming in the images and colors were breathtaking. There were curious opal-white areas that looked as if someone had run out of ideas for halos: apart from that, the human figures—out of biblical stories, she imagined—were exquisite. Pools of brilliant emerald and violet and ruby were beginning a slow, majestic sweep across the altar.

"Josh," Sam called out, in a strained loud whisper. "It's the task force."

So that was how they were seen. And maybe he was right. She had a problem: she was here with a handful of aid troops—nominally, anyway—and commercially sponsored researchers, in a world where the inhabitants clearly needed no aid and probably wanted no research.

Josh bobbed out from behind a pillar and stood staring at her. He held a small plant tub in one hand and a bunch of pink and white hellebores in the other. No, they were artificial; very realistic, but they were paper. She noticed that before she truly noticed Josh. He was a broad and very lean man, leaner than most humans she was used to: forties maybe, wiry light hair, very pale blue eyes, a man whom other men would probably have liked to resemble. His clothing was the same utilitarian buff fabric as Sam's, except the top buttoned up like a frock coat.

"Commander," he said politely. He put the tub down and held out his hand for shaking.

She took it as firmly as she could in her glove, and tried

again. "Superintendent. I'm a police officer. Good to meet you."

"I'm sorry we asked you to come alone," he said. "We don't want to appear hostile. But we didn't plan on having visitors from home, and it's a shock to have our first contact with troops."

"I can understand that now," she said, and meant it. All the forces of secular enforcement were soldiers to him. "I apologize. We could have done this better."

"You've come a long way. We need to do some talking."

"If I've interrupted something important, I can wait." She was stepping gingerly from one cracking slab of conversational ice to another, never sure when she would fall in. "Busy?"

Josh held out the flowers for inspection. She put out a hand to touch them but the suit made the exercise pointless. The restriction was irritating her.

"Hellebores," he said. "We have real holly as well, but the trees are too large now to bring them inside. We wouldn't cut them just for decoration, of course."

"They're very realistic." She longed to scratch between her shoulders. "Look, how long will it take for you to analyze the blood samples?"

"We're processing them now. I promise you it won't take long."

At least it proved they'd retained some level of sophisticated technology if they could run a lab. Had they also developed that defense system? They'd had nearly two hundred years to do it. But she doubted it.

"Why don't you sit here awhile?" Josh offered, as if she could have done anything else. "I'll be back as soon as your own samples are cleared."

Shan found herself alone in the church. It would have been a serene experience if the suit helmet hadn't amplified her breathing. She concentrated on the rise and fall of her chest and settled into a shallow rhythm. Colored light from the window edged across her lap, picking out the monitor panels and seals. It was hypnotic.

A saint surrounded by animals hung motionless in light before her. She read the words on a scroll at his feet: "It is Satan and his henchmen who martyr animals." It was almost wiccan. She knew Josh wouldn't have agreed.

Shan woke with a start, heart pounding. Josh was standing over her. He smiled and tapped his head. "You can take that off—you're clear," he said. "Sorry I startled you."

She broke the seal with relief. The air that rushed in was wood-scented and slightly damp, underlaid by unidentifiable smells that reminded her of fruit as they hit her palate. "That's better," she said. "I nodded off. I think my metabolism is still screwed from the cryo. So, no bugs?"

"Some, but nothing we can't handle. Come on. I'll show you the town."

She followed him back down the nave, relieved to be getting out, like a burglar who had lost her nerve. Treading on other people's sacred soil always disturbed her. She paused to look up at the fine stained glass again.

"That's quite a sight."

"I'm told the translucent areas are actually the most wonderful blues and mauves," Josh said. "But not to human eyes." He looked suddenly awkward, and turned away. Was he talking about the vision of angels? Perault's voice intruded from the dead past: *We know they made contact with aliens.* She decided not to ask, not yet.

It seemed indecent to take off the rest of her suit in the church. When she reached the porch she struggled free of it, draping it over one arm. She could feel a slight but steady breeze on her face—artificial, she imagined—and a heady mix of cooking smells that she couldn't quite identify beyond garlic and ginger.

"I'll walk you round the main parts of town, so you get your bearings," he said. "It'll take awhile. We don't use vehicles much. Are you able to walk?"

"I'll get used to the gravity," she said, and noted that Josh was a head shorter when she drew level with him. He could still walk faster, though: it would take her a few weeks to get used to weighing an extra seven kilos. They walked up the long sloping road to the surface, passing windows that spilled brilliant light. There was so much of it. It seemed to burst out from underground, as if there were a sun at the heart of the world. Shan pointed at the sunken dwellings.

"Houses?" she asked, then tried the same question from a new tack. "Why are they like that?"

"Usual reason. Saves energy, lets in enough light," Josh said. "And we do get some ferocious gales round here sometimes. What do you think of our church, then?"

"Very impressive." She recalled the inscription, a boast from the days of the Raj, when Europeans occupied India. GOVERNMENT WORK IS GOD'S WORK. "A labor of love. Especially building it underground."

"Local custom," Josh said, a little awkwardly, and nothing more. He steered up a long ramp to the surface again. She looked back and found she could pick out the tops of submerged buildings catching light but otherwise as buried as missile silos. "Manufacturing plant is down there. The bot gear has lasted pretty well, but we don't use it all the time."

The houses were more randomly dotted the farther they walked, and it was harder to spot them in the landscape because of that. It struck her that it might be a defensive precaution. If it were, then it was a defense against an airborne enemy who targeted by sight or by heat signature. Or maybe it was, after all, just a sensible way to build against the weather in this place.

"No unwelcome visitors?" she asked.

Josh's voice changed again. He wasn't very practiced at deception, that was for sure: she was on to something.

"Most of our visitors are very welcome," he said. "Take a look at the doors when you visit one of our houses."

Shan decided to drop the subject until later. It was the time for tourist questions about flora and fauna and weather. Whatever sore spot she kept touching, this was not the time to pick at it. And it was still not the time to ask about aliens.

She stood and looked out towards the horizon and saw a fertile land with a marbled blue moon hanging over it like a displaced Earth. And she saw a battlefield, too, because now there would surely be those who would want to leave Earth and come here. Not many would be able to make it, perhaps, but there would be enough of them to overwhelm the colony. It wasn't a thought she wanted to put out of her mind. The Suppressed Briefing wouldn't let her anyway. Perault's voice spoke of the need to preserve the colonist's mission.

Perault was almost certainly dead by now. The realization caught Shan unawares.

"The fields are out there," Josh said, and brought her back to the here and now. The land sloped gently away from them, and she could pick out many little beige-clad figures scattered amid random patches of varied greens that abruptly gave way to the wild blues and ambers a long way in the distance. But fields meant horizon-stretching squares, one color per box, and lots of machinery. Her brain struggled to make sense of it.

"You'll have to forgive me. I can't tell what I'm looking at. I can't see boundaries."

"There aren't any. We plant in small patches and combine

crops. We were persuaded against monoculture. There's a lot of soy down there, and wheat."

"I'm impressed that you can grow crops in the open."

"We can now." Again, that slight pause before answering: maybe he had some biotech that he didn't want the commercial team stealing. "We can grow a great deal, some above ground, some below in hothouses."

"Is that a uniform, this beige?"

"No, but we don't bother to dye work clothes. Indulgent trivia." Josh pulled his coat out with both hands like an apron. "It's the natural color of the hemp fiber."

"You're big on environmental protection, then." The Suppressed Briefing filtered into her conscious mind again: *They took the world's most complete archive of plant and animal specimens with them.* "I think we have a great deal in common. Heard of EnHaz?"

"No."

"Environmental Hazard Enforcement. It's a police function. It's what I do. Or at least it's what I do now."

"It's commendable that people from your time treat despoiling the natural world for the crime it is."

From your time. Ah, that stung. Yes, she was dead as far as everyone she had ever known was concerned, killed by the one-way ticket of distance and time. She had a feeling that realization would start to eat at her.

"And I won't allow your world to be despoiled, either." Poor Josh: he had his little paradise and now the secular, grasping, exploitative world had come bursting in on him. He had a right to be edgy. She began wondering how she would contain the research team.

By the time she had completed the circuit of the main settlement, her legs were demanding that she stop. She was wheezing; her eyes and nose watered with the effort. It was going to take some time to adjust to higher gravity and lower oxygen. A rotten combination, she thought, but as habitable planets went it was a remarkably close match to home. It wasn't methane and she was still able to lift her legs. Yes, it was close enough.

Josh led her down steps and into a subterranean hall of sand-gold stone. It was solidly quiet except for distant bird-song. The walls curved round her, and there appeared to be rooms off a hall that was large enough to accommodate seating and tables. It seemed to be the hub of a wheel-shaped house.

Paper chains in muted colors hung in swags round the top of the walls, and there were those paper flowers every-where. Some—less wonderful, less realistic—were evidently the painstaking work of a small child. There was no Christmas tree. But a waist-high plant in a large ceramic pot was decked with tiny glass globes in a riot of colors. Glass-making was evidently the big art activity here.

"I take your point about insulation," Shan said. "This is very peaceful." She craned her neck up to the domed sky-light, which took up the entire width of the roof. It was slightly opaque, and gave a soft shadowless light. "Is this carved into rock too?"

"Part rock, part soil. The facing is compacted earth. We sealed it with a sort of chalk." He busied himself at a side table. "We have wine. Would you like some?"

She bit back her automatic refusal. "Yes," she said at last, concentrating hard on diplomacy. "I'd love a glass. Thank you."

She sat down on a padded bench at the table and watched him pour from a ceramic bottle. Courtesy told her not to examine the wine's color too closely. The glass that held it was shot with opaque swirls and would have dis-guised all visible shortcomings. It smelled faintly of rasp-berries and mint, and although it triggered half-memories that she couldn't pin down she knew they were genuinely distant, not obscured by neurotransmitter markers. She allowed herself a small sip. It was actually very pleasant wine, and the glass was beautiful. She thought glassware would be her lasting memory of Constantine. It was a transparent sort of place.

"What are your plans?" Josh asked.

"If you don't need assistance, we'll just carry out some surveys and perhaps catalog some of the flora and fauna." The birdsong was beginning to distract her for some reason. "With your consent."

"I'll discuss that with the council," Josh said. "I don't think we'll have a problem with your people looking around. But we can't let you take anything that's alive."

Shan paused. Constantine had its own values and rules, forged over centuries of isolation from human society. As taboos went, the request was at the pale end of harmlessness.

"Josh, do you have an ethical problem with native botanical samples?"

"As I said, nothing alive."

She should have expected that. She hadn't. "Okay. Can they use any non-invasive techniques? Scans?"

"You're welcome to look around, and to learn. Stay awhile. But you mustn't interfere with this world, and you can't stay here."

"Don't worry. We're all planning on going home. And we'll respect the fact that this is your world."

"Not our world. Remember, we're all guests here."

"I won't lose sight of that."

"Would you like to stay for dinner? Many people will want to see you. Perhaps you would come to midnight Mass, too. I will understand if you find that inappropriate."

"Paganism teaches tolerance, Josh. I'm not offended by difference. *Ere it harm none, do as thou wilt.*" She gestured with the glass as if she was really intending to drink it. The first rule of diplomacy was never to refuse food and drink; the second was to genuflect to the local deity. She could see no harm in being polite. "Just explain one thing for me."

"I'll try."

"I can hear birdsong. I shouldn't be able to, should I?"

"Blackbirds," Josh said.

"From the gene bank?"

"No, it's a recording. Our forefathers missed birdsong most of all. Now, would you think me rude if I left you here for a while? I have to go and check on the flowers for the service. Help yourself to the wine. The kitchen's over there."

Shan shifted uncomfortably on her seat. "And the bathroom?"

"That way."

Either she had earned his trust or he had nothing worth stealing. That degree of naivety was as alien to her as the autumn-spring trees, but she confined herself automatically to hall and bathroom. It seemed churlish to help herself in someone else's kitchen even when invited.

Thetis warranted a sitrep call, but that could wait until she had a tighter grip on her thoughts. She held the glass up to the light and admired the changing patterns and colors. Shame about the wine. She felt guilty peering down the stark lavatory bowl—opaque white glass, more a urinal than anything—to check that it was a safe place to dispose of the alcohol. Booze didn't fit into the working day, especially with a headful of SB. She found the flush button and watched the wine disappear.

The nonexistent blackbirds trilled. Constantine was beginning to feel good. It was certainly a town of craftsmen and -women who loved their workmanship, and it showed in the furniture and walls. The doors were perfectly planed.

She ran her hand up and down the material—wood or composite?—and smiled at their smoothness.

And she noticed, after a while, that none of them had locks.

6

We protest at arrival of alien ship in our territory. We tell you we not tolerate more colonization of land that is claimed ours. You will remove and allow us to enter.

Isenj legate to Bezer'ej sector,
in a message to Fersanye clans

There had never been any need for maps. The bezeri had them, of course, but the detail was in the waters, not on the land. Aras still had an original bezeri chart, a lovely thing in colored sand pressed tightly between two glass-clear slices of azin shell. The green areas were peppered with swirls of depth markings and the gathering points of clans, named in light and color. But the mass of information ended at the brown areas, the Dry Above, the land masses unknown and largely irrelevant to the water-dwelling bezeri.

Sunlight filtered through the deckhead hatch of his craft and onto the galley table. He turned the azin-shell chart over and over in his fingers, letting the light dance on it. It was ancient: it had been made before even he had been born. He noticed that some of the painstakingly placed grains of sand and rock and luminescent microfossils had started to shift where the sheets of shell were beginning to warp from the dry air, releasing their tight grip on the sand layer. The map was shifting and breaking up. He blew a little puff of regret and laid it carefully on the table to avoid further damage.

It would never be made again. The bezeri had better technology now, knowledge from other worlds, courtesy of the wess'har. Azin shell was a poor substitute for glass and translucent composites. Its gradual deterioration saddened him.

The map is dying, Aras thought. *I'll even outlive the map.*

He was now the last of his squadron, and the last of his kind, and he didn't know if that was a cause for sorrow or not. Two hundred and seven killed outright in the war; sixty dead by their own hand, the only possible way for them to die, a sudden and explosive death a long way from where their tissue might pose a hazard. There was no return to the soil and cycle of life for them. And here he was, alive and resenting it, because Benjamin Garrod had stopped him choosing oblivion by telling him he had work to do, and that his life was not his own to take.

That was the problem with being burdened with scavenged human DNA. He never knew what was his own decision and what was done at the insistence of alien instincts. Humans had a strange relationship with death.

Aras gave the map a last glance, tucked it into his pack and began the journey back to the Temporary City, the garrison on Bezer'ej. It had been a long time since he had last visited but he owed them an explanation of what was now happening to the human enclave. Mestin's grandmatriarch had warned him the human species would take some managing, and so had her daughter after her, and now Mestin herself was quick to point out how right they had been. But there were so few of the new ones. There seemed little damage they could do in the time he would take to assess them.

But the pressure was growing. A temporary respite for thousands of endangered species had seemed a good reason not to let the colony perish all those years ago. Today, though, he had the feeling he had unleashed a tidal wave.

The sun had dropped closer to the horizon by the time he stepped from the human environmental zone and stood waiting by the shoreline for the bezeri pilot. The shallows were already dark, and sharp scents of decaying vegetation and salts drifted on the wind. He walked slowly up and down the pebbles, circling a route between the Place of Memory of the First and the Place of Memory of the Returned, shrines to the bezeri explorers who had beached their craft to explore the Dry Above.

The First had never returned, like many pilots; unable to propel their pods back into the surf, and fully aware their journey was one way, they were prepared to die to acquire knowledge. Aras felt inexplicably sad every time he passed the shrines. There was no reason to mourn that choice, because one thing bezeri and wess'har shared was an acceptance of endings, but their sacrifice had begun to depress him. Maybe he had spent too much time around humans.

These days the bezeri had better propulsion systems as well as a ready source of data from Aras's own people. If they beached themselves, it was through foolish adventuring. As Aras waited, the shimmering lights from the deep became brighter and danced a message of recognition.

Do you wish to travel?

Aras raised the signaling torch above his head and angled it onto the gently rolling waves: red, blue, ultraviolet, then green and ultraviolet together, in a set pattern that danced around the circular rim of the bowl-shaped torch. *Yes, I want to go to the Temporary City.*

Reliable as ever, the bezeri vessel rose to the surface, breaking foaming waves across its back. There was always one around here somewhere at this time of day, patrolling in case any bezeri sightseers wandered out of their depth and became stranded in the shallows away from the sanctuary of deep waters. There were always a few willing to chance suffocation to get a closer glimpse of the Dry Above. The pilot risked air for a few moments to allow Aras to wade out and slide into the soft, translucent hull.

There are new ones here, the pilot flickered, and wrapped his tentacles around the controls that pressed seawater from the propulsion system in a steady jet. *The sea tastes of burning.*

Aras didn't reply until he had suspended his breathing enough to cope with the inrush of water. He turned the torch towards the pilot. *Yes, but not many. Rely on me. I won't allow the balance to be affected.*

The pilot sent a rippling motion all the way down his six arms to the controls. Aras thought it interesting that soft-bodied, fluid beings like the bezeri should share the habit of shrugging with the humans, and with many of the same nuances of meaning. He leaned back as far as he could and concentrated on the sky that was still dimly visible through the translucent hull and the shallow water.

A beautiful pattern of conversational light patterns sparkled above him as a troop of bezeri strolled through the water enjoying the early evening. His was a lonely and frustrating life, made difficult by his parasite, his *c'naatat*, but there were also many advantages to the changes it had wrought in his body.

Concentrating on the ebb and flow of his breathing, he began to lower his rate of respiration, eventually suspending it completely. He could reduce his need for oxygen enough to travel with the bezeri in their own soft-shell ships. No normal wess'har could. It was a unique privilege.

C'naatat had its compensations.

Shan stood leaning against the doorpost of Josh's home. She could hear a growing hum of voices. It was surprising how much you could hear, and how far, when there was absolutely no traffic or heavy machinery around. She had never experienced silence like this, and she thought it almost had a throbbing hum of its own—until she recognized the liquid rhythm as her own heartbeat in her ears. As the sun moved towards the horizon, the settlement began to take on new sounds. People were returning from the fields.

Josh appeared first, with a teenage boy, small girl and a woman his own age in tow. Like him, they were short and wiry, wearing functional work-clothes in varying shades of beige and cream, but the woman was more Oriental, and the children an attractive amalgam of both races.

"Superintendent, my wife Deborah, my son James, and my daughter Rachel," he said, and swept his arm out to indicate them. They simply nodded at her, looking none too convinced that she was harmless, and Shan managed a pleased-to-meet-you nod. "We'll clean ourselves up, and then we'll make our way to church for the Christmas Eve service."

"You're a police lady," said the little girl.

"I am indeed," Shan said.

"You're ever so tall."

"Like my dad," said Shan. She could get tired of this, and fast.

"Do you shoot people?"

Oh, God. "Only when I have to."

The child nodded sagely and skipped off into the house. "Don't mind me," Shan said to Josh, whose expression had set in a carefully composed but shocked smile. "I'll take a walk, if that's okay. I know where the church is."

"We should be an hour," he said. "There's plenty to read in the vestry if you run out of things to do."

Shan assumed the vestry was somewhere in St. Francis. She turned out onto the main path and passed people who acknowledged her but looked nervous. Word got round very fast here; she understood their anxiety. This was Earth as it should have been, at least at first glance. And she was Earth as it actually was. She decided she would not have been pleased to see herself under the same circumstances. The mission and the colonists might as well have been different species.

She wandered into St. Francis and tried two doors—both unlocked—before she recognized a data terminal and placed a cautious hand on the panel to try to activate it. In videos, technology always worked; in real life, interfaces were a lot less universal. She was still fumbling across the smooth surface trying to locate the controls of the archaic machine when the sound of people welled up from the passage.

The colonists were crowding into the main body of the church, and she slipped in behind them. They were pressed into each other, adults and children, yet there was only quiet patience and general good humor. This was not a subway crowd. She turned and saw Josh beside her.

"Is this your whole community?" she asked.

"Yes." He was smiling a distracted sort of smile that was anchored in the event, not a friendly gesture to her. "Nobody would miss midnight Mass."

Shan understood Christmas all too well. Solstice was the same. She thought of the early-setting sun, and the rush to get to somewhere truly ancient to mark it. She remembered the price hikes at hotels near Avebury and Stonehenge, and how everyone said they'd never do it again next year, because Solstice was getting too commercialized and all the wonder was going out of it. They started selling live mistletoe long before Samhain these days.

Or they did, she reminded herself. Seventy-odd years ago.

She settled back in the pew and noted that she had a very definite exclusion zone around her. It might have been that Josh's guests were spared the crush, or that the colonists still feared catching something from her. But she wasn't here to gain acceptance or fit in. It didn't matter. She was just passing through, doing a job.

Carols sprang from nowhere. The singing simply seemed to start up in one part of the church, and everyone joined in, worked through to the end and started on another. She felt able to study their faces; they were too caught up in their worship to mind. The racial makeup of the original landing party was evident, some people showing a single heritage and others appearing of mixed race. Christianity, for all its decline, still got around.

A black teenaged boy walked up to the lectern in the gangly and self-conscious way of growing lads and opened a huge bible of real rustling paper. He began to read aloud into a silence that was perfect. Not a cough or a child's fretting disturbed it. *But the lectern should be an eagle,* she thought. She had seen magnificent gilded lecterns in monuments and books, and they had always been eagles. This one wasn't. It was a winged creature, but nothing she had ever seen before.

The service had taken more than an hour, but she was only aware of the passage of time from the shrinking of two nearby candles. A wavering gonglike sound quivered on the air, then another on a higher pitch, then another, like someone playing a tune on a set of wineglasses. The colonists began turning to each other and embracing, shaking hands and kissing cheeks. "Christ is born," they said. "Praise the Lord." The greeting ran round the entire floor of the church. Midnight, then, and those strange plaintive gong sounds were bells. It was a definite, simple musical sequence. Josh appeared to spot her dawning recognition.

"Not exactly cathedral standard, but they do the job," he said. "Glass. We don't have bronze."

He pointed up, and Shan could see a dark gallery near the top of the vaulted roof where the dim light picked out a faint gleaming surface that shivered every few seconds as an unseen clapper struck it.

"There's something very perverse about glass bells," she said. "Tempting fate."

"Local glass is remarkably robust."

"Well, a happy Christmas, Josh."

"And you." He paused, as if he'd made a mistake. "What should I wish you?"

Shan shrugged. " 'Blessed be' will do fine," she said, and they shook hands hesitantly. She wondered if it had been wise to reveal her Pagan background, but Josh seemed to be taking it like a true liberal. Perhaps he actually understood what Paganism was.

The midnight meal was served in the refectory near the church. Smells filled the air, both richly familiar and foreign at the same time; spice and crisping oil merged with something perfumed and woody. The community sat down at long trestle tables and two adults from each collected serving dishes from a central table. Shan noted that they said grace in individual groups. They were a devout people, but pragmatic. The food was cooling fast, and a church full of people took a long time to seat, even in shifts.

The food was also not what she was used to. It wasn't entertainment; it was nourishment. There were soups and good chunky breads, and piles of starchy vegetables. Beans shimmered in an oil sauce. Most of the food was recognizably of earthly origin. And there was no meat.

She wondered at first if meat was simply a scarce commodity, but then it struck her that it might have been a deliberate omission. "You're a vegetarian community," she said, and felt instantly embarrassed at her naivete. "I should have worked that out."

Josh topped up her untouched wine and slid a jug of water beside it. "We found we could survive without taking the food animal embryos out of cryo. We came to know God intended us to live without killing."

Shan nodded. If that was his rationale, fine. Lots of Pagans felt that way too. She seized the tenuous kinship. "You must have had a tough time of it in the early days. How did you get the crops to grow in the open? Everyone thought you'd fail if you moved beyond hydroponics."

"No, God provided for us well from the start, even in these unlikely circumstances." But Josh didn't elaborate. She had no doubt the answer—if it ever came—would be on the payload's minds as well.

Josh's son, James, hard and square like his father, pointed proudly to a plate of fried burger-like slices. "Soy," he said. "I grew the beans." He seemed like a nice kid, a million miles from the evil little bastards she was used to dealing with.

"Adaptable stuff, soy," she said, awkward, and wished again that she had some talent for rapport with youngsters that extended beyond handcuffing them.

They all ate as if the plain food was the focus of their existence. She reminded herself that there could be no scope for frivolous luxuries here. Anything they needed had to be built or grown or developed by one of their community. There were no shops. In a small group of people, that meant immense hard work and ingenuity. And it meant they cared about each other, because they had to if they wanted to survive.

Shan suddenly envied them.

"I have a lot of questions," she said. "I want to know how you've managed without medical support, for example, and how you replace and repair machinery. That sort of thing. But I'll save it for later."

"Tell us when you're tired and we'll make up a bed for you," Josh said, ignoring her in an oddly kind way. It was another definite steer away from technical matters. "Tomorrow we can discuss landing your team."

Back at Josh's house, his wife showed her to a small room with a futon-type bed and a hemispherical wash basin served by a short length of piping. Deborah pointed to a recess like a wardrobe space. "The lavatory is there," she said, and managed a slight smile as she backed out of the door.

Shan had a sudden worried thought that what she had

used as the toilet bowl earlier that day might not have been one at all. The idea plagued her as she sat down on the futon. Had she used the handbasin, for Chrissakes? The design could have been any sort of receptacle. *Oh, hell.* She might never live that one down.

It was time to update *Thetis.* She flicked open the swiss.

"I thought you'd run into trouble," Lindsay said. Her voice was breaking up over the link. "How's it going?"

"Fine," Shan said. "But we have a few issues to deal with at this end."

"And a few at this end, too. We had to revive all the payload. Potential cryo failure. I'm sorry I didn't consult you first, ma'am, but—"

"That's fine. You had to make the call."

There was a slight, strangled pause. "Very good, ma'am." Lindsay obviously hadn't expected that response. But it wasn't fine at all. Things were running too fast. "It's getting a bit cozy up here. The ship's not built for full life-support for this many people. When can we disembark?"

"I have some talking to do before we can do that."

"It *is* secure down there, isn't it?"

"The colonists aren't overtly hostile, but we aren't exactly welcome." *And we won't be the best thing that's happened to Constantine, either.* "If we disembark the research team, they have to be prepared to accept a lot of restrictions. Will you prep them for that disappointment?"

"Whatever it is, it won't be as disappointing as running out of oxygen. We've got forty-eight to seventy-two hours. The generator can't keep up."

"Understood. Just find the time to tell them they can't take biological samples. Period."

"Says who?"

"The colonists."

There was a long pause, and Shan thought the link had gone down. She could hear shuffling in the passageway outside the bedroom door and wondered if she had been overheard.

"Commander Neville?"

"Yes, ma'am?"

"Let me make one thing clear. I have my orders, some-where in my memory, and they may not entirely meet the aspirations of our commercial colleagues. But your role is to support the civilian administration, which is me."

"Understood."

"If you're telling me that there's a risk to safety if we keep revived personnel in orbit, then I'll ask the colonists for permission to land everyone."

"I do believe that's the situation."

"Stand by, then."

Shan struggled to her feet to prepare for bed. It took her a few seconds to work out that the whole tube above the basin had to be twisted to release the water. It flowed hand-hot, and she stripped off her fatigues and personals and rinsed them in the basin before wiping herself down with a quick-drying cloth from the do-it-all pack zipped into her jacket.

She draped the clothing over the spigot, and the fabric was already drying before she had managed to find the con-trols for the lighting and shut her eyes. *Did I really pee in the damn washbasin?* No, she couldn't have. It was defi-nitely a toilet. It had a flush.

Funny how that sort of thing worried her. She had a crippled ship and a restless crew and—probably—aliens who could disable an entire fleet out there somewhere, yet that toilet just wouldn't take its proper place in the queue of priorities.

No, it was definitely a lavatory. It had to be.

That matter settled, she plunged instantly into an unusu-ally dreamless oblivion.

7

The universe is not here for our convenience alone. If we as-
sume it is simply our larder, we shall starve. If we think that
damage we cannot see cannot cause harm, we shall be poi-
soned. Wess'har have a place in the universe, but we should
take no more from it than we absolutely need. Being as strong
as we are now, we can take everything from other beings. But
we have a duty not to, because we have a choice. Those who
have choices must make them. And the wider the choices one
has, the more restrained one must be in making them.

The philosopher TARGASSAT,
from her Treatise on Consumption

Shan found it even harder to get up off the low bed in the
morning than it had been to lie down on it the night before.
She eventually straightened up and washed in ice-cold water to brace herself before venturing out of her room. She
expected to find Josh's family up and about, but found only
a place setting at the small table and a note telling her to
help herself from the stores.

Of course. It was Christmas morning. They would be at
the church. She helped herself to a few slices of a crumbly
honey-colored bread and a bowl of fruit. There was even
tea—real tea leaves, *Thea sinensis,* smelling of sweet tar
and leather. She inhaled the fragrance from the jar and suddenly felt a little more optimistic. It wasn't going to plan,
but it might be no disaster either; she could land who she
needed to land, give them their restrictions, let them potter
around at a discreet distance from the colony and then

leave. No longer than eighteen months, maybe even a year. How much damage could that cause?

She found a jug of soy milk and was savoring her second cup of tea before she finally accepted the scenario that was playing out at the back of her mind. It was not what the researchers did that would matter. It was the fact that they were there at all. The true consequences would not be felt for centuries, but they would be felt one day, and they were already set in motion.

Constantine was on the most Earthlike planet that humanity had reached so far. Sooner or later, more humans would try to find their way here as the colonists had done.

It was a shame that such an idealistic little community was finally facing the end of Eden. Even without her implanted orders, Shan would have felt a pressing need to ally with them. Perault had known more about her than she had realized.

The name *Helen* surfaced again for a few seconds, and she brushed it aside for the time being.

Josh was not yet sure how to take Shan Frankland. He pondered the dilemma while sowing broad beans. Not even the arrival of unwanted visitors—or Christmas Day—could be allowed to interfere with the business of survival.

The woman seemed straightforward. She asked his permission at every stage, as if she accepted Constantine's sovereignty. But she had that air of having a task to complete, and a way about her that suggested she was wearing a uniform mentally if not in fact. Had Aras been here, he would have known at once whether she was to be trusted.

The secular world was greedy, destructive, promiscuous. He had the colony's Earth archives to prove it. Those in uniforms were its instruments, imposing the will of corrupt and avaricious corporations, and those of their puppets, the federal governments. Now the secular world and its twin demons of commerce and government were walking his streets. If it was a test of faith, it was a hard one.

The contact with corruption might be bad for Constantine. It would be even worse for the beings with whom they shared this world.

He needed to talk to Aras.

"We have about three generations' breathing space to find somewhere else," Martin said. He walked along behind Josh's rotavator, dropping martock beans into the emerging drills at practiced intervals. "That's how long it will take them to decide that this is land worth taking and send more ships."

"We're not leaving," Josh said. "We have a duty here. And the only way we'll find another world is if Aras's people find it for us."

"But the seculars will overrun us. It'll be many years, but they *will* come."

"You have to have faith." A cluster of stones brought the rotating tines to a halt, and Josh had to back up a little and break them apart with a hoe. "Aras and his people stopped the isenj. They can stop anybody."

"We don't want any more wars fought here."

"Martin, you read too many stories. It's hard to wage a war across light-years. It's also hard to lift that tonnage in invasion forces. It'll be a slow process, and slow processes can be stopped without bloodshed."

Josh wanted to believe that. He guided the rotavator, and Martin lagged a little, as if sulking. "We risk losing it all," he said, barely audible.

"We have to stand firm." That was Josh's job, to lead and to be a rock for them all. "Aras will protect us. But we also have to protect Aras. You know how these seculars would exploit him and his condition."

Martin finished dropping the beans into place and walked back to kick the soil over them and to scatter marigolds as companion planting. He shuffled his boots back and forth in a well-rehearsed rhythm, pausing to let a few of the curled seeds fall from his hands. Then he fumbled in the soil until he found the irrigation pipe, and turned the valve until faint gurgling could be heard. The two men stood in silence, watching honeybees weighing down the delicate pink-tinged bells of comfrey flowers. The insects—one of the few species the colony had chosen to revive—seemed to be having no trouble navigating by an alien sun.

"If I explain to the Frankland woman that we're here under the patronage of an alien government, she will see the implications," said Josh.

"And suppose she doesn't?"

"Then I'll be more explicit. She'll understand military superiority. They'll leave."

Josh began ploughing again, and Martin followed him silently. He didn't need to say that Josh's hope was a forlorn one. When he glanced up from the furrow, there was a figure in gray fatigues and a bulky waistcoat moving through the patches of crops. Shan Frankland was picking her way through the fields towards them, zigzagging as she went. She appeared to be keeping to the comfrey and avoiding bare earth, as if she understood what she was doing.

"Happy Christmas," she called as she came within earshot of them. "Deborah told me where to find you. Long time since I've seen dwarf comfrey."

So she had enough sense to recognize where there might be seeds and what was a green manure crop, then. This wasn't his picture of the urban terrestrial human. Either she had done a great deal of homework and was a practiced deceiver, or she had something in common with them.

"Can we talk, Josh? I have a problem."

"What sort of problem?"

"We've had to revive the research team sooner than I had hoped. There's been a failure in the cryo system. We can't leave them in orbit because the *Thetis* isn't designed for full life-support for that many people, and we can't chill them down again yet, not until we can isolate the fault. So we need to land them all, and within the next day or so. Can we do that? Subject to your restrictions, of course."

Josh looked into her face, which told him nothing other than that her height and unblinking gaze unsettled him. If only Aras were here. Josh had no idea what he was looking for, but he knew politicians and their minions lied. Perhaps, though, she was telling the truth. Either way, it no longer mattered. They would have to confront the situation sooner or later.

"Then land them," he said. "How many are there?"

"Eight, plus six Royal Marines and their commanding officer. We can land accommodation modules and our own rations. We're equipped for an unsupported mission."

"But we must connect your camp to the waste-recovery system before you can use it. All waste here is recycled."

"Okay, show the booties how it works and they'll do the rest. They're pretty adaptable, even if they're not sappers." She looked at him as if he hadn't understood her. "Booties. Bootnecks. Marines. Look, this isn't a ploy to get the team down here, Josh. I had hoped to leave them in cryo until I'd decided whether they should land at all."

Was his suspicion that plain to see? He shrugged. "What's done is done. There are things that I haven't told you that you need to be aware of, though."

"Go ahead."

"We're not alone on this planet."

"I assure you we'll respect the environment. No live samples of native species, no—"

"Forgive me. I mean we're not the only reasoning species with a claim to this world."

Her spine straightened sharply: she seemed even taller. "Ah, it *is* already inhabited, then."

Of course it is, he thought. *You've seen the ecology.* But she meant, he knew, that there were aliens here who were *people.*

"There is one indigenous species, and another with a diplomatic presence here."

"*Two* other races?"

"Three, but the third is kept away from landing here by the others."

Josh needed none of Aras's olfactory skills to tell that the Frankland woman was shocked. She looked away, blew a little puff of surprise and stood with her hands on her hips, staring at the soil. After a few seconds she looked up again. "That really does alter the situation, doesn't it?"

"Perhaps you should carry out your survey within our colony and then return home."

She resumed her fixed gaze at the soil again, and neither Martin nor Josh said anything to interrupt it until she was ready.

"May I contact these aliens? Can you arrange that?"

"I'll see," said Josh.

They watched her walk back across the field, still picking out the same zigzag path, and waited until she was out of earshot before resuming their conversation. Josh could hear Martin rattling the dried beans in their cloth pouch, passing the bag from hand to hand in agitation. He nudged him.

"Stop worrying," he said. "Trust in the Lord. It's not the first test we've had, and it won't be the last." He reached and took the bag from Martin's fidgeting fingers, irritated. "Finish up here. I must call Aras."

The bezeri vessel brought Aras up to the rocky coast of the peninsula and bobbed to the surface to let him out. He waded back to the shore and turned to watch the translucent pod fall back below the waves and disappear, leaving broken amber reflections on the surface. The sun was rising again.

When he had picked his way up the narrow path to the top of the headland, he looked back down into the sea. There were a dozen or more bezeri pods visible just under the surface of the water. It was unusual to see that many on patrol at once, an indication of the anxiety they felt about the arrival of new creatures in the Dry Above.

The path up the shallow cliff wasn't visible unless someone happened to be right on top of it. It wasn't the wess'har way to leave marks on the landscape if it could be avoided, and certainly not on someone else's planet. The bezeri would neither have known nor cared. But Aras did.

He kept up a brisk pace across the short silver moss. The roads hadn't moved at all since he had been here a few days ago. At this time of year, before their growth spurt, they tended to be stable; he could easily pick them out from the dangerous wetsands and bog beneath the moss by the way they curved proud of the ground like engorged vessels under skin. He managed a brisk pace.

Everything he owned, or ever would own, was folded into the pack slung across his back, as Targassat had taught. If you couldn't carry it with you, you didn't need it. If it didn't perform several functions, then it was not worth carrying. And if it had no function—well, then it was an un-wess'har thing, a waste of resources and something to be avoided.

Aras had tried to explain Targassat's philosophy to Josh's ancestor, Benjamin. The humans relished frugality. It was probably more out of the enjoyment of self-denial than concern for the world, but their intentions were irrelevant. Only their actions mattered. They took readily to the waste and water recovery systems he demonstrated for them. They'd even got used to the idea of concealing their homes in the ground, although he knew their motivation was primarily to remain undetected rather than not to interfere with the natural order.

Their one sticking point had been the church. They insisted it be a testament to the glory of their God, and that meant grandeur. Aras turned a blind eye to it because it had so many functions. There was no harm in making a functional thing beautiful. He had even made the decorative glass windows for them, with alien and native creatures, and the image of a human who respected all species and had been—if he had known it, worlds and lifetimes away— a fine example of Targassat's philosophy: *Francis.*

Aras still didn't understand sainthood. He had thought he had understood what God was, but it wasn't a species after all. Nor were angels a species, either; but the humans insisted angels could see the blues and violets in the opal glass just as well as Aras, even if humans could not. It was all part of *God's will.*

He thought that it was just as well for the colony that they had come across him first, and not an isenj, or their God's will might have manifested itself a little differently.

The silver moss of the downland gradually thinned out, and he was in knee-high purple-blue brush again. It blended into a single horizon ahead of him, a smoke sea punctuated by islands of trees in their bright orange growth cycle. This was the wild and untouched land outside the controlled environment he had built for the humans. He liked the blue brush best. At every cycle, he brought a few humans out into the wilderness to see the true world, and their awe always delighted him. It was as if it had a universal truth. All species found it beautiful. But the poor bezeri never saw their Dry Above, uniform brown on their maps, in all its variety and glory.

The sun was close to overhead now. He could see a shimmer of light in the near distance, sun dancing on the quartz deposits in the rocks. Benjamin had seen the Temporary City; he had even traveled to the planet of Wess'ej, to the city of F'nar itself, and seemed very moved by the iridescent deposits left on every sun-facing hard surface by the swarms of *tem* flies. He called it the City of Pearl. Josh had wept at the sight of it, too. It was worth taking humans to see it for the joy on their faces.

Aras had stopped reminding them that it wasn't the prophecy in their bible. It was just a city. But they wanted it to be so much more.

The gate to the Temporary City took a little longer than usual to recognize Aras, and dithered over letting him enter. His DNA had probably altered slightly. It happened. The *c'naatat* parasite must have been busy, tinkering and tailoring its environment—him—to fit its needs. Eventually the mesh across the opening dissolved, and he stepped into the filtered light of the interior. There was a youngster waiting there, and from his startled reaction it was clear he had never seen anything like Aras before. Mestin had probably failed to spell out how different her visitor would appear.

"I'm here to see Mestin."

"She waits for you," said the boy. "This way."

Aras tried to recall who the youngster looked like. "You're Tlivat's son. Am I right?" They walked side by side down the passage, a well of channeled light like the subterranean streets of Constantine. "You've grown much more than I would have expected."

The boy nodded politely. Aras needed no reminder that he looked disturbing to the average wess'har. He really had been away far too long. Even his own language sounded foreign to him now, the words inflexible, the rhythms stilted.

Mestin greeted him with restraint. Aras had the feeling she was discreetly checking him for more ways in which his physiology had altered since their last meeting. He was slightly taller than she was, but if being dwarfed by a male bothered her, she showed no sign of it. He kept his hands clasped behind his back to avoid displaying his claws. He never knew quite which host in the *c'naatat*'s past had furnished those.

"*Chail*," he said politely, and waited for her to squat down before kneeling back on his heels on the floor.

"So, have you met any of the new humans? Can they be contained?"

"There are only sixteen of them. Their technology still appears unable to transport them in very large numbers."

"Once we thought that of the isenj, too."

"I didn't suggest abandoning prudence. But our priority is to prevent their contact with *c'naatat*. Josh fears that the most."

"Josh has never tried to acquire *c'naatat*. Why should the others?"

"Josh believes he will be permanently transformed after corporeal death. The godless prefer to put their trust in science, but they still strive for the same thing—living forever. It's a human preoccupation. They all think they're special in some way and have a right to buy immortality." He wondered if she would see the irony in that, but Mestin was pure wess'har, literal and linear. He wasn't even sure she understood the concept of commerce. "Sometimes I wish I could enlighten them."

She got up and took an opaque glass bowl of *netun jay* down from the table. Aras could see the shapes as the light caught it, a nest of eggs, a pod of seeds. She laid the confections in front of him and sat down to face him on an equal level, a very conciliatory gesture that was made even more intimate by offering food. Perhaps she felt sorry for him. The longer he spent among humans, the harder he found it to relate to his own people.

He took one of the egg-shaped cakes in his fingers, embarrassed at revealing his hands to close gaze, and bit carefully into it, releasing the intensely perfumed gold filling. It ran down his chin and he wiped it away quickly with the back of his hand. "Are the isenj aware there are more humans here?"

"Aware enough to lodge a protest."

"I hope they do not see it as a concession that might also apply to them."

"Then perhaps we should remove the visitors now, whatever Fersanye says," said Mestin.

"I am tired of killing, *Chail*."

"The balance, Aras. It has to be maintained."

Aras finished his *netun jay* and considered the last cake in the bowl. Mestin waved her hand at it. "Finish it. I'll give you some to take back with you." Yes, she was right, and not just because she was the matriarch. He knew humans. He had viewed every single scrap of information in the Christopher's archive over the years, and he knew humans were expansionist, opportunist, and brutal to the weak and the different. His humans said they had fled that.

"Make sure that your contamination does not shape your judgment," Mestin said. "Ensure that it is the wess'har voice you listen to, not the parts of you that are *gethes*. And see Sevaor on the way out. He misses you."

Sevaor. The clan was distantly related to Aras, but Sevaor felt like close family sometimes. Whatever Aras did, whatever he became, Sevaor had a fondness for him: he was proud of his living ancestor. The prospect of outliving Sevaor, as he had outlived everyone he knew, never lost its sting. Even losing generations of human friends had not inured him to bereavement. If anything it seemed to be getting harder each time a corpse was left to the rockvelvets.

"I will," he said, and accepted a bag of *netun jay* for the return journey.

Sevaor was monitoring the warning system, walking up

and down in front of a room-width screen that showed isenj traffic between their homeworld and its satellite. The chart was largely static except for the occasional wandering point of yellow light that marked a drone vessel, or a red one showing a defense emplacement. He turned as soon as he scented Aras and held his arms out in greeting, then dropped them. He had forgotten, however briefly, that you didn't touch a *c'naatat.* War hero, Restorer, Targassati— and freak. Aras did not want to be admired and respected at a distance. He longed simply to be touched.

"You should have told me you were coming," Sevaor said. "I would have brought food from home for you."

"Who do I know back home any longer?"

"Your kin, Aras. They worry about you."

"I don't know them." *They care for the idea of me, not the person I am.* "They were born generations after I left home."

Sevaor smelled faintly of hurt feelings. "So they were." He turned back to the screen. "Your colony has left a message for you. The human ship is landing its passengers. Let's hope your colony doesn't tell them about *c'naatat.*"

"Awareness of it is one thing—owning it is another," Aras replied. *Please, Sevaor. The chances of becoming infected are so low. Just a hand. Please.* "Nobody has taken it from me, and many have tried."

"You don't know how they will react."

"*They,* right now, are just sixteen beings, and I can handle them if I need to."

"It takes only one, Aras. If they acquire it, there'll be chaos for them and for us. We don't want another race of breeders like the isenj."

"They're doing very well on their own without any technical assistance from us." Aras eased himself up from his seat, a wordless gesture that told Sevaor he was no longer in a mood to listen to him. It was not the mild chastisement that had irritated him; it was the physical distance between them. "I admit the technique would be worth an immense amount to them. It would be regarded as a wonderful benefit for the wealthiest in their society while the rest starved. That is what they call irony."

Sevaor flicked the long braid of his mane over one shoulder and appeared to be concentrating on the screen. "Just be careful, Aras," he said, and didn't look back at him. "Please, come again and see us, won't you?"

Wess'har were touchers. They embraced. They liked, *needed* to be crowded together. Aras could indulge none of that instinct. It broke his heart every time, and he would make sure the next time did not come soon.

"I'll be careful," he promised.

He found himself walking briskly out of the control room, back up the smooth-worn passage cut into the plain, and up to the fresh air. He was reminded why he avoided Sevaor and why Sevaor irritated him so easily.

He was so like his dead house-brother, and so much like the son he could never have.

But the colonists needed him, and need was a powerful motivation for a wess'har male without children or *isan* to care for. His humans, however bizarre and untouchable, were his family. Aras broke into a sprint and kept the pace up all the long way down to the shore.

8

You can't catalog Bezer'ej from a hundred square kilometers of island. It's like landing in the Southern French Desert and thinking the lizards represent life on Earth. There was so much we could see when we were coming in to land and this place is just a fraction of it. And we've got just this single opportunity to find out what we can from it. But if we don't come across anything economically useful, it won't bother me one bit. I have waited all my life for this.

SABINE MESEVY, botanist,
from her private journal

Shan walked as fast as she could back to the settlement. It was hard going in the higher gravity, especially after cryo, and by the time she got back to Josh's house she was dripping with sweat. She flopped on the futon and caught her breath. Her distaste for Suppressed Briefing surfaced again; if it held any answers, it wasn't yielding the ones she wanted. She had no expertise in alien contact, she was years away from getting new orders from home, and any time soon she was going to have curious and therefore potentially dangerous researchers crawling around looking for novel products and new markets. Where were the revelations from the SB when she needed them most?

She tried to concentrate. No, that wasn't the answer. Let it go, let the memories drift back—or so they had told her the last time. The worst aspect of SB was that you could find it hard to separate real memories from past dreams.

They were both equally faint and confusing, and both snapped to the front of your mind with shocking clarity in exactly the same way.

One thing she was sure of was that Perault knew little about the aliens. There was no ponderous weight at the back of her mind when she thought of them—whatever they might be—and no sudden rush of memories triggered by the stimulus. She concentrated on what facts she had in hand: a territorial dispute in progress, according to Josh, and, as the colonists were alive and apparently very well, humans were tolerated. Or at least the colony was. There was no guarantee of a welcome for what might appear to be an invasion force.

The what-ifs were legion. She needed more facts, and the primary reliable source was the colonists. If they were going to get out of here without a diplomatic incident, she'd need Josh and his people.

She started to call up Lindsay on the comms link, then paused to marshal her thoughts. There was no point telling the commander the full size of the problem until she had more of a plan herself. She would give Lindsay the order to disembark five marines to bring the accommodation down to the surface using the second shuttle, leaving one behind with the payload, and set up a quarantine area. No point, she thought, having armed personnel ambling around and alarming the colonists—or the natives. It bothered her that she had no measure of the aliens, any of them. She felt like she had stumbled into a pub brawl without backup.

"Shall we brief the payload?" Lindsay asked.

"Yes," Shan said. It would pay to make things look as normal as possible. "Warn them they're confined to the camp until I give them clearance."

"Anything else?"

"Yes—I'll take one of the cabin units as my base. Josh and his family need their privacy." *And I need mine.*

"Give me six hours. If we can't prep for landing before then, I'd rather we waited until tomorrow so we have enough daylight."

"Okay. I'll get back to you in a couple of hours with location coordinates."

"The payload's champing at the bit. They can't wait to make a start."

"Tell them they're going to have to."

"Very good, ma'am."

Shan lay back on the bed again. The ceiling of the room was a circle of opaque light. It had lost all three-dimensionality for her, try as she might to make it a concave dome again. She stared up into it for a long time, and held her hands in a frame so that all she could see was the featureless glow above her. Black specks and filaments drifted across her vision. Any doctor could have removed them, but they were part of being wholly human and she tried to concentrate on them, just in case the distraction helped her recall more of the SB.

The colonists held one of the Earth's largest banks of animal and plant tissue. We have to preserve that if it's still intact. There. It was a memory, and a clear one: Perault with hands meshed on the table in front of her, worryingly earnest, not a politician at all. Well, she knew about the DNA bank anyway. Plenty of organizations had assembled similar ones, all banking biodiversity against extinction. It was even in the archives, if anyone could be bothered to look up Constantine.

They've made contact with sentients. But we've been told to avoid the planet. We have no idea why. We've not shared the information with anyone outside my circle.

Again, clear; and nothing hovering behind it, nothing to give her the feeling that there was more to be revealed. Perault knew almost nothing about the aliens, then—so why the SB? Why would they waste such an expensive process—two shots at 20,000 euros a throw and the personal presence of a cabinet minister—to tell her so little? The best explanation she could come up with was that they wanted to avoid even more attention from the scientific community by concealing the presence of new life-forms.

Hell, they were seventy-five years away. Who was going to come running to take a look even if they knew?

Why Perault wanted the mission to be undisturbed was another matter. She would be gone now, whatever *now* was. Shan glanced at her swiss and flashed up Earth time: everyone she had worked with would be dead too, maybe even McEvoy. It was a lonely thought. The nearest she had to a familiar friend was the antique, inanimate machine in her hand.

Shan wondered what sort of funeral Perault had been given. The woman was a Christian—yes, she'd told her that, too. Maybe a belief in the afterlife lengthened politicians' game plans beyond the next election. Maybe Perault thought she was Noah.

Shan straightened her uniform and prepared to have a serious talk with Josh. If Perault had really wanted to play at arks, she'd probably have needed a terraforming team to sort out Earth before she could find dry land. The planet had been in a sad state when Shan had left. What it was like now didn't bear thinking about.

Aras could see the new human encampment growing. From his vantage point on the crest of the ridgeway, he could take in both Constantine and the growing cluster of sparkling green boxes. It was only a temporary intrusion on the landscape. He didn't have to let it irritate him, but it did.

Josh walked up behind him, crushing foliage at every step and sending bursts of sharp wet scent into the air. Aras didn't look round. He waited for the human to sit down beside him, and they sat wordless for a while. Josh smelled calm.

"Matters are under control, then."

Josh nodded, still staring ahead of him. "They've landed. Their commander seems sympathetic and in control. Actually, not their commander—their governor, I suppose. She's a civilian police officer. I explained the limitations on taking samples."

"If they have no capacity to leave the island, then we should be able to avoid any contact with *c'naatat*."

"They had planned to stay no longer than a year or so. But their ship—"

"Their ship can start to restore itself now. Mestin has shut down the sentry system. They can leave any time."

Josh went to put his hand on Aras's sleeve and stopped. The humans avoided touching him too, even though they were at far less risk of contamination than wess'har. This was too much: two rebuffs in a few hours. He would have got up and left had he not realized the aborted gesture was a silent preamble to an awkward question. He had seen Josh do the same to Martin. It would be an awkward question in the sense that Josh would struggle to ask it for some reason. Aras had no such trouble. Humans' hesitation to just say what they meant still disappointed him.

"Did you set out to destroy their cryo systems, Aras?"

"No," he said, without thinking. "The defense net took the data it had from the probes and simply shut down everything it could identify as not being life-support. It was a technical problem." He paused. "If we had intended to destroy the ship, we would have done so."

Josh gave him that wide-pupiled look, the sort that the first humans had given him. It confirmed he was still an alien to them, however much his appearance had changed. "I had to know."

"Whatever happens, Josh, it won't be your responsibility."

"We sent the original message."

"You sent a warning. That's not the same."

"The Frankland woman says humans have discovered other aliens since our mission left Earth, but it's not aliens that bring them here. It's the planet."

"Detected," Aras said, correcting Josh almost without thinking. As if other species had no existence until humans chanced upon them and defined them, *discovered* them. "Have they ever met a species with a more advanced culture than theirs?"

"If you mean technology, no. Culture—well, in our past, humans have discovered other humans with advanced cultures, but with inferior technology."

"I think I recall what happened to them. I will be fascinated to learn how these *gethes* deal with being in that position."

Josh got to his feet and stood staring down at the construction work going on below. "I haven't heard you use that word in a long time."

"No offense meant."

Aras glanced at Josh and wondered what would happen if he simply reached out and touched the man as he had his ancestor. Benjamin had accepted him, every aspect of him, in a way no other human had. Josh, friend as he was, had his limits.

Benjamin had held him while he roared in pain at his exile. He hadn't cared about the risk. In the complex forest of complete recall that was wess'har memory, that event still stood vivid and separate and precious.

"None taken," said Josh, and walked away.

The payload was getting increasingly restless behind the cordon, but not Eddie Michallat. He was busy just sitting there and watching.

The marine contingent, accustomed to long periods of inaction, busied themselves with construction and routine. Most of them had been in operations where there were disputed borders, and assumed long negotiations would have to take place before there was free movement. Maybe it all made sense to them, but it did not make sense to the civilians: Eddie Michallat sat between two scientists from competing corporations who had met each other for the first time less than two days earlier, and soaked up their frustration. At least they had a mess area to sit in while the kit was being unloaded, and coffee to occupy themselves, even if the toilets were of the chemical kind until the plumbing system was hooked up.

Eddie welcomed the lull. He was cooped up with people who had nothing to do but chat and express their frustrations, and in idle chat lay the raw uncut gems of stories. There were no rivals to elbow out the way, either; he could pick them off at his leisure. It was a journalistic chocolate factory, with him as the only taster around. It was bliss.

He hoped there would be enough hours in the day to get it all covered. "There bloody well ought to be," said Olivier Champciaux, the geologist. "This planet's got a thirty-hour rotation."

Every time Eddie wandered outside there appeared to be a new section bolted on to the habitation. It had started with two cubes on low supports, joined by a short section of corridor that slotted together like a kid's toy. Section by section, it grew into a cubist necklace with two strands, an inner chain of cubes for the living quarters, the outer chain for the communal and work areas. All the walls were an incongruously soothing pale green, almost pearlescent. Eddie inspected them carefully, running his hand down the smooth surface.

"Nice pastels to keep us serene in close confinement?" he asked.

"No, the panels are impregnated with solar and chlorophyll cells to give us enough power and even out oxygen levels," said Sabine Mesevy. "But it's a nice color. Besides, we each have a cube of our own. Didn't you read the mission spec?"

"Not all of it."

"This is a sealed unit. If we have to, we can put this down in pretty inhospitable territory and it'd feel like home. But this world is Shangri La by planetary standards. There's almost enough oxygen."

But not quite enough, Eddie decided. The engineer marines found the oxygen adjustments were malfunctioning, and set about re-calibrating the panels while everyone breathed raw air. There definitely wasn't enough of it. By the end of the second day, he felt like a tourist skier, with a throbbing headache and muscle pains that made him think he had flu. He was desperately tired and yet his sleep was fitful, and he wasn't the only one. During the second night he could hear footsteps outside his cabin, and the hum of conversation from time to time. Nobody else was getting much sleep either.

From time to time the EFU's zampolit, Shan Frankland, wandered in to check if they had degenerated into cannibalism. She had looked workmanlike in her fatigues, but when she came in wearing her police uniform it struck him how big she was. Not plump big, lovely womanly big, but tall, athletic, *hard* big, with a set to her shoulders that suggested she would never, ever try to talk her way out of trouble if there was a quick and physical alternative. Her high-collared black coat definitely said get-out-of-my-face, and not very politely at that.

She came in six times in the first day to say she was having "talks" with the local leaders and that she would keep them "updated" on the situation. He could hear her coming each time: her boots pounded on the composite flooring as she walked up the passage. Eddie decided he wouldn't care to cross her. When she spoke to the group, she fixed someone, anyone, with her stare. When she wasn't talking, she was taking in everything round her with the absorbent gaze of a detective. Then the penny dropped, and he recalled where he had heard her name before.

Green Rage. He took out his database and set it to look through the BBChan library download, already seventy-five years out of date, but perfectly adequate for this purpose. He retreated to his cabin—which truly was just a cube—to inspect the results. *Shan Frankland, Chief Superintendent, Anti-Terrorism Unit, and a police enquiry into the collapse of Operation Green Rage.* Yes, that was it. She had been in charge of Op Green Rage six years ago—no, about eighty-one years now, but no matter—and spent millions in taxpayers' money on an undercover operation but the eco-terrorists had got away. She had been found "negligent" and transferred out of ATU. There was a lot of material to read.

He began scrolling through the pages, too engrossed to transfer the data to the comfortably large screen of his editing kit. There was a sudden and steady hunger in him to dig. He took a renewed interest in her tarnished career. By the end of the afternoon, he'd quite forgotten his headache.

9

We never thought this was going to be paradise. We thought it was going to be hard but necessary work, waiting out the dark times until Earth became ready again. So I tell you this: think what you like, hate who you like, because that's between you and God, but you will act as the community requires, or the community will no longer require you.

BEN GARROD to the council assembly,
Constantine, Easter 2220

A new society had been forged in a matter of days, and societies needed rules. Shan set those rules; she was the government. But it gave her no pleasure to pose as governor of Constantine, and she hoped it never would. The colonists had their own ruling structure and she wasn't planning to interfere. Whatever else the SB had in mind for her, her task was to ensure that *Thetis* caused the minimum of trouble.

Trouble, in this case, meant offending foreign governments, and at least one of them clearly wasn't living in mud huts or devoid of its own technology. That meant avoiding trouble very carefully indeed.

Shan had already set up her cabin as an office. The alpha-monkey part of her brain told her the uniformed personnel, if nobody else, needed to see someone in charge sitting at a desk in order to feel reassured. As the work surface folded down from one of the bulkheads it was impossible to fashion the room to look imposing, but it was close enough. It said *stability*.

She made notes on the pullout screen on her swiss. *No contact between the mission team and the colonists except by prior agreement with Josh Garrod.* If he hadn't been the leader before, he certainly was now. *No team member to enter the colony without prior permission from me. Me: only to enter by agreement with Josh.* She wondered if she would ever find a way to replace the screen; it was fragile from a thousand erasures. *Field missions: colonists to be invited to observe if they wish. Alien reps . . .*

She paused.

Alien reps: invite them to set any other restrictions they want. She had no idea what aliens found objectionable. There was no point guessing.

Lindsay Neville came when summoned. She perched on the edge of the bunk, offering as little backside area to the surface as possible. Shan noted that. Her territory had been adequately marked, then, if the commander was that uncomfortable in it. She certainly looked tired.

"Have the colonists expressed a wish to avoid contact with the team?" Lindsay asked.

"No. I just don't want any complicated relationships."

"My people have been selected for self-sufficiency," Lindsay said sharply.

"What the hell does that mean? They knit their own socks out of recycled cartridge cases?"

"They weren't expecting to have any 'relationships,' as you put it, for some time. Most have opted for suppressants."

"Well, I'm glad to see bromide is alive and well in the European navy." Lindsay did seem tetchy about such a minor detail, Shan decided. Maybe it was already a sore point among her detachment. "I'm not doubting their professional discipline. Just not taking chances, that's all. Besides, there's more to offending our colonists than just trying to screw their daughters."

"Or sons."

"Indeed. Or sons. Let's just stay out of their way without being downright rude."

"Very well, ma'am. But remember, they're not police officers. These are very expensive, highly trained special ops troops. Even if they do rig latrines."

At least she had the guts to say it. Shan deliberately took no visible offense. "I stand corrected," she said. Sometimes complete indifference commanded more fear than a strong reaction. "Just make sure they're clear about the rules, that's all. And one precaution—all external comms transmissions are to be routed through your command center. We want to know what's being said, just in case."

"The payload won't like that, ma'am. Nor will the journalist." Lindsay had clearly categorized him as a separate species, neither uniformed personnel nor scientist. Shan suspected he would see himself that way too.

"Michallat can send what he likes as long as I see it. He'll be used to having his stories screened if he's been a war reporter. Tell the payload that I'll be the only one seeing their material and I won't disclose it to another company. Look, does it matter? I can stop them transmitting altogether if push comes to shove. Remind them of that."

"Very good, ma'am." Lindsay took her orders and disappeared. Shan removed a strip of compressed apricot and soya from her pocket and chewed it thoughtfully. It was the only field ration she'd been able to find that didn't leave a tang of metal in her mouth. Some of the marines were suppressed, eh? Well, she hoped that sort of suppression was a more pleasant experience than the SB. It was one of those things about space travel that you didn't think about until you had to, like toilet arrangements or laundry. The rest of the mission team had the edge on her. One way or another, they were all people who were used to living awkwardly and getting by in remote places. Police officers usually went home at the end of the day, however unpleasant the duties were. It made a difference.

She thought briefly of her first commanding officer, her

first "guv'nor," and the rest of the relief at Western Central. They were all dead now. And if any of them were still alive, they were very old indeed, and she was not. She realized she had lost the last people who would slap her on the back and treat her as one of the boys. She took the water bottle from her desk, flipped the cap and raised it to nowhere in particular.

"Goodbye, Guv'nor," she said.

10

Kristina Hugel double-checked the first batch of blood, urine and stool samples. "You didn't realize you were pregnant when you came aboard? Didn't you have a final medical?"

"Yes, but it must have happened after that," said Lindsay. Jesus Christ, contraception didn't just *fail* like that. She'd been so careful. "I would have acted if I had known."

She didn't know whether she meant she would have aborted the fetus or the mission. She hadn't even known the guy's name. It was just a last-minute, final-night-ashore grab at being normal and human before she plunged into the abyss. It was a wartime reaction.

"Well, you're okay, if that's what's worrying you. How you deal with this is up to you."

"It's not exactly the first question I wanted to ask the mission medic."

"What, whether I could fix you up?" Hugel opened her

medical kit. It looked like a mechanic's toolbox, a clean light gray, but there were no wrenches in it. "Here. Effectively you're a month gone, so use this in the morning for three days. Top of the thigh. That should do the trick."

She left the sub-Q spray on the table between them. It sat there as conspicuously as the absence of the word *baby* in their conversation. It was strictly a functional exchange of clinical options between two professionals.

"Thanks," said Lindsay. She looked at it for a few moments and then tucked it into her top pocket. "Do you always carry a supply of this?"

"Always, when I'm working with mixed teams. If you decide not to use it, let me know, because there'll be things we'll need to monitor. Low oxygen and high gee don't make for healthy blood pressure and fetal development."

She didn't say anything else. Lindsay walked out into the compound, but only knew that she had when she found herself there. Her body was moving independently of her. No, she hadn't planned this at all. What-ifs started to crowd in on her and she turned away from them before any had a chance to resolve themselves into solid worries. There were practical things that needed doing in the base, and now was as good a time as any to draw up rotas and busy herself with detail. She turned back towards the mess hall.

"You're looking knackered," Shan observed. She pushed the containers of salt, mustard and ketchup out of the way of their elbows and wiped the table clean with a dry cloth before placing the roster board carefully at the exact midpoint between them. "It sucks you dry, this gravity."

The two women sat head-to-head in the canteen, trying to work out the most efficient use of the two scoots while everyone got acclimatized to the conditions. The marines and scientists had spent a couple of months preflight up in high country lugging five-kilo weights in their backpacks, but it didn't solve all the problems. There was still some gasping and sweating to get used to.

"I'll be okay in a few days." *How am I going to tell her I made a big mistake?* This woman didn't even risk spilling salt. It would be worse than having to tell her marines. "Any thoughts on who we pair up?"

Shan shrugged. "You know your people best."

"Sometimes someone who's fresh to the situation can see the obvious. I don't know the scientists at all."

Shan glanced down the list of names and fumbled in her pocket. She pulled a stylus from the innards of her swiss and began tapping.

"Okay . . . Marines paired with payload: Chahal goes with Paretti, Webster with Parekh, Qureshi with Galvin, Barencoin with Champciaux, Becken with Rayat, and you can pair Mesevy."

"Is there a method in this single-gender pairing?"

"Do you know how many boy–girl patrol teams I've had to break up in my police career? Plenty. Usually after an angry partner showed up at the station with a bread knife."

Lindsay bristled. "Like I said, my people are professionals, ma'am."

"Okay." Shan slipped the stylus back into her swiss with exaggerated precision and rolled the cylinder back and forth in her hand. "Your discipline problem, not mine. You can probably trust Bennett with Mesevy. You can cover Hugel if she ever goes off camp. And you can certainly trust me not to molest Eddie. But in the fullness of time, highly trained professionals in small groups still behave just like real people." The older woman gave Lindsay one of those tight-lipped mock smiles and pushed the roster gently back across the table so it rested in front of her. Lindsay tried to disguise her distaste with silence.

"You did ask me to make the decision," Shan said.

"I did, didn't I?"

"That's okay. I'll just mark up gender as a sensitive area to avoid with you." She glanced at the swiss and stood up. "Time to see the elders of Constantine, I think."

Lindsay watched her ramrod back disappear out the door and swore under her breath. Not a good start. She thought a little show of deference might help build a relationship, but all it had done was make Frankland think she was a wimp. It was her job as CO to sort rosters. She felt the sub-Q spray in her top pocket and wished *that* decision would go away of its own accord. She knew it wouldn't.

And it was another thing she couldn't expect Shan Frankland to sort for her.

Josh had made himself available to Shan for *orientation*, as he put it. He met her outside the church, looking suitably bucolic in a worn beige smock. She got the feeling he wanted to get the questions over with as rapidly as possible, and she couldn't blame him. He had work to do; the new humans were still a threat to his way of life. If she minimized the threat, she reasoned, then he might be more forthcoming.

"How many people?" she asked.

"One thousand and forty-one," he said. They walked a route around the colony by tracking the dome roofs, joining them up like dots in a child's drawing.

Shan looked out across the blistered ground. "You came here with about two hundred people?"

"Thereabouts, and they were carefully selected to give us a reasonable gene pool. No problems so far."

"Dr. Hugel would be interested in seeing any medical records you might have. I think that's one of her areas of expertise, genetics."

"If she finds it useful, she's welcome to it."

A small breakthrough there, then. Shan fought an overwhelming urge to get *something* done. She had less of an idea what her true task was with each day, despite the SB, but that same sense of absolute urgency, even zeal, was still as strong as ever.

They were high enough on the plain now to see for miles across colored patches of fields and farther, to where the orange-and-blue alien landscape began. The borderline of the human world on the planet was striking. There was no gradual blending of the cultivated and the wild, no thinning out of grass or cycad. It was as if there was a wall around Constantine. There were things, too, that she thought she should have been able to see and could not.

"How do you inter your dead?" she asked, and realized at once that it sounded a harsh question. But there was no graveyard to be seen, and if there was one thing she knew about Christians it was that they marked their graves with memorials. The park near her home had been paved with ancient gravestones. One, worn almost smooth by the centuries, bore the name of an Elizabeth Totton, aged forty-three years, who had died of "teeth." She had never worked out what "teeth" was. "Do you cremate?"

"No, we don't." Josh seemed unperturbed by her directness. "We buried the first few who died here, but none after that."

"Sorry to be thick, but what *do* you do, then?"

"When I find one, I'll show you," Josh said.

It was a non sequitur if ever she had heard one. For a while she thought she had totally misunderstood the drift in language, and walked along beside him in silence. Just how different could these people get in a couple of hundred years? If nineteenth-century men had traveled back to the seventeenth century, they would still have understood the language, archaic or not, despite the huge technical gulf. Maybe Josh was a bit deaf: some of the older Pagans she knew were like that, reluctant to be treated for hearing loss or have cell grafts.

And maybe he was just avoiding her crass question after all.

There was only the nearby hum of bees and the distant whirring and clicking of the planet to be heard. Josh led her near to the edge of the colony, where bramble and tayberry bushes crept close to stubby lilac-colored grasses. They stood there in silence for several minutes and scanned the horizon. It struck Shan that as the Earth flora ended in a stark line, so did the bees, as if they didn't want to venture into the unknown either.

"There," Josh said suddenly. He pointed, and she looked.

"What am I looking for?"

"The black patches," he said.

It took her a while to see what he saw. But there they were, three black patches on the sunward side of a rock in the wild lands. They walked up to it. Shan stared.

As far as she could see, the stone was covered with areas of jet black, velvety lichen, perfect and unbroken. The patches had clean edges; the surface was uneven. It was unusual to see any plant that black without some hint of green or purple in it, but this lichen—or fungus, perhaps—was as black as it came.

Then it moved.

Shan flinched back, startled. The black mantle inched away down the stone and onto the ground. The two other patches came to life and began to follow it.

"I think we might have frightened them," Josh said, and stood back to let the things pass. They moved slowly, looking oddly like scraps of fabric animated by some small creature hiding beneath. "Or they've smelled dinner somewhere."

Shan thought she should have recorded them, and reached for her swiss as an afterthought. She held its viewfinder above them and captured a few slow minutes of the creatures' progress. "What are they?"

"Rockvelvets," Josh said. "And that's how we bury our dead."

"I think you're going to have to draw me a picture."

"They digest dead bodies. They're carrion eaters."

"Oh."

"We bring our people out here and let the planet take care of them. Does that disgust you?"

Shan shrugged. "Pagans like that sort of solution. So do Parsis. But I didn't think Christians did, what with all that resurrection stuff."

"I imagine some don't. But when the customs and rituals were first written, people had no idea we would be keeping Christianity alive in another part of the galaxy. We adapt."

Shan toyed with the idea of being nailed into a box or waiting for the rockvelvets to come. The slow black caress seemed benign by comparison. "Don't your people need a focus for grieving?"

"We record the names in the church. If our loved ones have a presence anywhere physical, they'll be there."

Shan walked a little way after the rockvelvets, and then turned round to look back in the direction of the colony. Now she was staring back at a picture, a tableau into which she could step at will. Even the air looked different on the other side of the divide that was marked by the berry bushes, and she was on the outside. For a moment the sensation made her feel uneasy. Josh patted her shoulder.

"You're overdoing it," he said. "Take it easy on the way back. I forget you people aren't accustomed to the conditions."

"It certainly takes it out of you," she said, and stepped back into a more familiar landscape. It was familiar right up to the point where the clouds cleared and she found that the sky was filled with a streaked white moon. She kept forgetting it, and it kept shocking its way back into her vision.

"Wess'ej," Josh said, matter-of-factly. "The other planet. The moon, if you like, but perhaps our twin is a better description."

She knew what his answer would be even before she asked the question. She asked it anyway.

"Inhabited?" she said.

"Yes, Wess'ej is inhabited too. I wasn't sure if you knew that or not before you arrived, but I can see you didn't."

When the *Thetis* had set out, the best data Shan had was that there were planets around Cavanagh's Star and that the spectrography from two of them indicated roughly terrestrial conditions. She had just about started to come to terms with the implications of landing in alien territory, and now she was thrown again by the fact that another complete alien civilization was a few hours away.

She shut her eyes to see if it would summon up something from the SB. There was nothing. She had the feeling that there was very little lost in her memory right then. Whatever detail Perault had given her, it had not been about aliens. So they were a wild card after all, a genuinely new factor to be coped with.

"You knew, didn't you?" Josh said.

"That there were aliens? Yes. At least, that's what's emerging from my SB—sorry, Suppressed Briefing. I was given information while I was in a medicated state so that I'd only recall it under certain triggers."

"Oh, brainwashing."

"No, you're in full control of your responses when you hear or see the information. You just can't recall it without a specific trigger to jog the memory. I'm here because whatever I was told made me want to do the job. But yes, I knew you had made contact with aliens—although I'm sure I didn't know any details."

"We didn't give any. Just that the gene bank was safe, that we had established our model society, and that nobody was to attempt to come here. So it reached the wrong people."

"No, it reached Eugenie Perault, a European government minister. One of yours."

"The name means nothing to me."

"A Christian. You meant it for your own, didn't you? Well, they got it and they kept it to themselves. The reason the mission's here has nothing to do with that. The Hubble Two-Nine just sent some new data about the system that made the place look irresistibly interesting." She tried to avoid tripping as she fixed her gaze on Wess'ej. She hadn't got the hang of the gravity yet and it was unforgiving of careless footsteps. "When I left I don't think they had worked out too much detail."

"Coincidence, then."

"Happens all the time. And I'm along for the ride to ensure you carry on as you were—as far as I know."

"I doubt that's going to be possible."

"I'll level with you if you level with me."

Josh walked on a little ahead of her in silence, head down and hands in the single front pocket of his smock, his thoughts almost visible. The colonists weren't poker players. "Superintendent, you've walked into a delicate political situation. That much I can tell you, and it's quite separate from any other concerns we might have. This planet belongs to the bezeri, that moon belongs to the wess'har, and the isenj make territorial claims here. So the wess'har have what you would call a military presence here to protect the bezeri, who can't defend themselves."

"So where are they? Why can't I see evidence of them?"

"You're looking in the wrong place. The bezeri are aquatic. That makes fighting a terrestrial enemy pretty difficult—without some assistance, anyway."

Shan tried to force some recall but there was nothing.

"Ah," she said, "is this military presence something I should be worried about?"

"See the plain?" Josh said.

She looked around the unspoiled wild landscape. She could see nothing, absolutely nothing, except the alien scrubland. "Are they out there?"

"It's what's *not* there that matters. There was an isenj city out there once, coast to coast. Now there's not a single trace of it. The wess'har wiped it off the face of the planet. They don't bluff and they don't negotiate. Be mindful of that."

It was hard not to. Shan stared at where the isenj town conspicuously was *not*.

Josh carried on walking. "Welcome to the front line, Superintendent."

In the strip of thornbushes that separated the edge of Constantine from base camp, high voices carried on the breeze. There was laughter, occasional singing and the odd shout. The beings she was watching were about as alien as anything Lindsay thought she might encounter on another planet, and now she had one within her.

Those aliens—those *children*—were weighing and recording the boxes of kale and other greens, or at least the older ones were. The very young, who were evidently supposed to be learning to read an analog scale, appeared to lose interest from time to time and wandered off a few yards to poke in the dirt or examine something utterly fascinating in the bushes. Lindsay could hear an occasional rebuke: "John! Leave the flowers alone!" A serious-looking kid of about fourteen laid his board and stylus down on top of one of the crates and hurried over to the bushes to drag the errant John back by his hand. "If you pick the flowers, we won't have any berries later in the year. Now pack it in, okay?"

He seemed to be more able at parenting than Lindsay ever thought she could be. She flipped the long-distance visor up from her face and let the scene and the sound blur again. What the hell did you teach a kid? Where did you start? And was it fair to raise them here? No, of course it was fair for the colonists, but maybe not for her own. On the other hand, these were good healthy kids, and they weren't vandalizing anything or hanging round in gangs or running risks anything like a kid might face on Earth.

She had an inkling for the first time in her life that there might be something she wanted as much as a navy career, and maybe more. Now that the shock had started to subside she was mentally examining what it might be like to have a child.

After all, she wasn't on Earth. Had this all happened before her promotion board, she'd have taken that damn sub-Q and used it right away, as soon as she could, without a single backward glance. Now she was watching nice kids—not at all like Earth kids—behaving properly and doing something useful. Kids didn't necessarily mean chaos.

She flipped down the visor and watched a little longer. Every so often a couple of adults would walk up with crates of something and stack them where the boy was recording the yields. Other youngsters would put the boxes on a sack truck and wheel them away down the ramps, probably to some huge larder. An adult paused to play-chase one of the younger children, sending her running in circles and shrieking with delight before he scooped her up in his arms and hugged her.

No, I don't want you hanging round with boys. You'll end up ruining your life. Her long-dead mother's voice rang silent but deafening in her ears: Lindsay, twelve years old, bewildered, trying to understand why skating with Andrew Kiernan would end in disaster. *If I hadn't had you, I would have been chief executive by now. Don't make the same mistake as me.* The message, repeated often enough, eventually became clear: kids were bad, and, ipso facto, Lindsay was bad, and guilty of destroying her mother's career.

Lindsay never liked the idea of an afterlife, not if her mother was waiting there to remind her how far short she fell of her expectations. She wished she would stay dead instead of popping into her mind uninvited at the worst moments.

And now I'm me, she thought. *I'll make my own mistakes.* Somehow the time and the distance made it much easier to settle on a course of action. She rolled the visor into a tight scroll and put it in her breast pocket, then ambled back to the base.

She could hear conversation in the mess but she walked quickly by the doorway and down the passage towards Hugel's cabin-cum-surgery. The hatch was open; Hugel wasn't there.

That was a relief, anyway. Lindsay took the unused sub-Q from her pocket and left it on the doctor's desk right where she would see it. It was easier than saying aloud that she had decided to go ahead and give birth to a child trillions of miles from home.

11

An' after I met 'im all over the world, a-doin' all kinds of
   things,
Like landin' 'isself with a Gatlin' gun to talk to them 'ea-
   then kings;
'E sleeps in an 'ammick instead of a cot, an' 'e drills with
   the deck on a slew,
An' 'e sweats like a Jolly—'Er Majesty's Jolly—soldier an'
   sailor too!
For there isn't a job on the top o' the earth the beggar
   don't know, nor do—
You can leave 'im at night on a bald man's 'ead, to paddle
   'is own canoe—
'E's a sort of a bloomin' cosmopolouse—soldier an'
   sailor too.

RUDYARD KIPLING,
"Soldier an' Sailor Too"
The Royal Regiment of Marines

There were beetroot chips in a bowl on the refectory table. The greens on the menu were beetroot tops, and there was chilled sweet borscht to drink. If Shan had been in the mood, she could have added beet salad in vinaigrette and baked beets. Even the plain walls in Constantine's communal eating area had a rosy tinge to them.

"So beetroot does well here, does it?" she asked casually, and took a sip of the borscht. The purple earthiness of it was oddly addictive. She stirred in a dollop of soured soy cream. It was better than eating dry rations while the hydroponics caught up.

"Really well," said Sam.

"Amazing what you can do with beets."

"You haven't had the beet wine and the sugar beet yet."

"The versatility of vegetables never ceases to amaze me," Shan said, trying to keep a straight face. Once the earthiness had assaulted and overpowered her taste buds, she could taste all the other nuances in the various manifestations of *Beta vulgaris.*

The colonists wasted nothing and seemed genuinely thankful for what they received, just like they said in that prayer before eating. They were all just so damned *reasonable.* Her copper's gut insisted they really couldn't be as wholesome and blameless as they seemed. Christ Almighty, they were *people,* and people were basically bad, if bad was the easiest route through life. It usually was.

She chewed on a beetroot chip and watched the ebb and flow of colonists through the refectory, all colors, all ages. All they seemed to have in common was that wiry, worn-out-by-high-gravity look and the universal line in working clothes. There had to be some dissent, even in an ordered and closed community like this one.

"Do people here ever go off the rails, Sam?"

If she had thought the question would shake him, she was disappointed. He thought visibly, head slightly to one side. "How do you mean?"

"Sins. Crime."

"Oh yes. From time to time."

"I'm interested. I'm a police officer. What sort of crimes?"

"We've had thefts. Violence. Anti-social behavior."

And that was all? *Pull the other one.* "And how do you deal with it?"

"Death," he said.

"That doesn't sound very . . . um . . . Christian."

"We turn the guilty person out of the community."

"Oh, *spiritual* death. Excommunication."

"No, *death* death."

"How?"

"See how long you can survive off camp without support," he said. "Brotherhood's a pragmatic thing, Superintendent. Rules hold communities together. Especially in a place like this. A thief can put us all at risk of starvation or disease in a bad year."

"I'm reassured," she said.

"And how about your people? What holds them together?"

"I've no idea yet. Maybe nothing at all."

He topped up her beet juice and got up to go, giving her the first smile she'd seen him manage since her arrival. She smiled back. The world was back to the way she expected it to be, with all too few heroes, even in a village of saints.

She glanced at her swiss. Had this been Earth, it would have been New Year in an hour. But it wasn't Earth, and she had things to tell the marines. She walked around the compound, taking in the balmy spring night with its distant backdrop of wild alien sounds, and wondered if she should have briefed the troops separately.

No, they could all hear it at the same time. That way rumors didn't start and nobody would think they weren't getting the full picture. She made a conscious effort to brace her shoulders and turned to walk briskly into the mess hall.

Hall wasn't quite the word. The accommodation had been designed for exploration in places where air and power were at a premium, so the mess area was just enough to seat twenty people plus a display screen. She'd had bigger offices. She walked in on what should have been a party.

They were trying, she had to give them that. Marines and scientists were chatting politely with shatterproof mugs in their hands, forced by the size of the room into unnatural intimacy. It was as good a way as any to break the ice.

"Drink, ma'am?" asked Lindsay. "Just coffee, I'm afraid, until Eddie gets his home brew going."

"I'll pass," she said. "Everyone here?"

"Yes. Glad you could join us."

"I've got something I need to brief you on." She hadn't even raised her voice, but the hum of conversation stopped and faces turned towards her. "Maybe you'd all like to take a seat. This could take some time."

The tables were refectory-style and she stood end on to them so she wouldn't have to talk to hunched backs. She needed to gauge their expressions. *I really ought to make this momentous.* But sometimes there was no ideal way to break that sort of news. She stepped off the precipice.

"My briefing indicated we might come into contact with non-human intelligence here," she said, and leaned against the bulkhead, arms folded. "I can now tell you there are three alien governments with an interest in this planet, and I'm using government in the most general sense." She fixed on a few faces: Barencoin was blank, Louise Galvin and Vani Paretti slightly slack-jawed. Eddie Michallat's lips were already pursing in an embryonic question. "At this stage, any first contact—if we have any—will be through the colony. Until we get better intelligence, just stick to the rules and don't go off camp without an escort. I'll tell you more when I know myself."

The silence was predictable. It went on much longer than she expected, but she took care not to catch Eddie's eye and turn the moment into a news conference. He didn't butt in. Mohan Rayat fluttered his hand for attention. It was as if she had transformed them all into a class of timid and obedient children. She nodded in Rayat's direction, wondering if she had overdone the intimidation.

"Do you know what sort of aliens we're dealing with?" he said.

"One aquatic, for sure. Two probably not."

"Oh, wow."

Eddie finally cut in. "What do you mean by having an interest in this planet?"

Don't hesitate. Was this the time to mention the obliterated isenj settlement? No. "The aquatics are the native species. Another species thinks it has a territorial claim here and the third is here in a peacekeeping role. If you go out and look at the moon when it's up, that's their homeworld." She thought of the wilderness where the isenj settlement had once stood. "I don't know very much about them but I do know that they can and will remove us without a second thought if we offend them."

"You know quite a lot, then." Rayat was already top of her list of annoying bastards. "A lot more than us."

"I know mainly what Josh Garrod tells me."

"Can we request contact?" asked Galvin.

"I already have," said Shan. "If it happens, I'll do it."

"Do you have any contact training, Shan?" asked Hugel.

"None whatsoever." The first-name familiarity rankled for a moment. She was *Boss, Guv'nor, Frankland—Shan* was strictly for friends and lovers, and not all of them at that. "Do you, Dr. Hugel?"

"No."

"I'll just have to muddle through, then, won't I?"

"Can we carry on working as planned?"

"Yes, within the colony perimeter. It's clear enough to see. Beyond that point, a colonist will accompany you when you do eventually go out, and I'll decide when that happens. It's not only about having armed protection. It's also about having someone on board who knows the local conditions and can offer you helpful guidance about what you can and can't touch—advice that you will take, of course. In exchange, we'll do some work for them. They can't afford to lose manpower for long."

"Jesus," said Mesevy, wide-eyed.

"And that's one thing to avoid saying in front of them." Shan turned to Lindsay. "Any problems?"

"I'd like to set up a defense perimeter, ma'am."

"Okay, alarm only." It would stop any unaccompanied excursions. She was more worried about that than the prospect of attack. "No countermeasures."

"I think—"

"No countermeasures. And around the camp only. Take no risk of provoking an incident."

Shan had expected more; more of what, she wasn't sure, but she had expected more of it. The group simply picked up their mugs and sipped distractedly. She had the feeling they would wait for her to go before reacting. She tended to have that effect on people. She turned to leave.

Eddie intercepted her. "I know this isn't a good time to ask you, but you know I'm a trained anthropologist, don't you? So I might be able to help with contact."

"Thank you. I'll bear it in mind."

"Can I file this story now?"

She considered it. "Go ahead. It'll be twenty-five years before anyone sees it."

"Happy New Year, Superintendent," he called after her. She wondered if that last reminder of their isolation had been a little brutal.

Too bad, she decided.

Lindsay briefed the marines carefully. They were not to let the payload take any live samples or damage anything, not even a leaf. Rock was okay. As long as they were sure it was rock, that was.

"How will we know, Boss?" Barencoin asked. He was dark enough never to look clean-shaven; a few nicks on his cheek were witness to a recent attempt to keep the beard under control with an unfamiliar mechanical razor. "We haven't a clue how they do their work. We didn't train for that."

"Well, improvise. If they pick anything up, they put it back," Lindsay said. "Haven't you heard the countryside

code? Leave nothing but footprints, take nothing but memories." The rest of the detachment laughed heartily. "Seriously, they mustn't kill or damage anything. That includes
picking plants. Frankland says they can do non-invasive
scans."

"Yeah, I heard. The payload said she was mad. I reckon
we're going to have our hands full enforcing that."

"I can understand they're hacked off at not being allowed to run loose and take what they like. But the situation's different now. We're in a potential war zone, and two
of the hostiles have space travel and probably know where
Earth is. I don't have to draw you a picture and color it in,
do I?"

"No, ma'am."

"Get to it, then."

If only it had been that simple. Rayat, the pharmacologist, was already engaged in a quiet argument with Sam. He
wanted to try to propagate any pharmaceutically interesting
plant he came across. Sam was refusing. The two men stood
very close to each other, almost head-to-head at the top of
the main ramp down into the colony.

"I don't see how propagating a plant harms it," Rayat
said. "I didn't come twenty-five light-years to take pictures."

"This is still taking live samples," Sam persisted.

"How am I supposed to work? Painting watercolors of
new plants went out with Tradescant. We need to examine
them."

Lindsay made a deliberately noisy approach towards the
two men. It didn't seem to distract them from their con-
frontation. She had to step in.

"Dr. Rayat, perhaps you'd like to gather your colleagues
and meet me in the mess hall," she said. "I'll be happy to
brief you all on the procedures we've agreed to follow."

Rayat gave her a look that said he had not been consulted on any agreement. Civvies thought everything was

up for negotiation. She wanted to disabuse him of that notion very quickly.

"Ten minutes," she said, and withheld the *please* with relish. She didn't care for Rayat.

In the mess hall, all eight payload were sitting quietly at the two long tables with varying degrees of resentment on their faces. Shan was already there, her backside perched on the edge of one of the storage bins, arms folded across her chest. She was still wearing that multipocketed vest over her fatigues, and there was a definite metallic composite object visible from beneath it. She was armed. Given the instruction to be discreet about weaponry, Lindsay thought it was a singularly provocative gesture but said nothing. Shan acknowledged her with a nod.

"We're all here, then," Lindsay said.

"Yes, miss," said Champciaux, and some of them laughed. If he'd had a full head of hair he would have been handsome, she decided. "Present."

"Okay, then, let me outline the agreement to you. It doesn't mean you can't derive some worthwhile data from this mission. The native species and their allies here appear to be very sensitive indeed about taking biological samples, so we have to respect that. You can observe what you need to, and the, er, wess'har representative—that's our alien neighbor—has agreed to supply data on native flora and fauna."

"What sort of data?"

"I don't know. We'll find out."

"Can we go out into the natural habitat yet, though?"

"Soon. But you will have an escort with you at all times."

"For our safety?"

Shan stood upright with a deliberate slowness and walked across to stand near Lindsay, but she said nothing.

"To ensure you don't breach the guidelines and to reassure our hosts," Lindsay said, picking up from the pause. "I appreciate it's a very restrictive way of working, but our safety could depend on it."

Rayat and Hugel exchanged glances. "We've come 150 trillion miles to a unique habitat. Don't you think we need to achieve more than to see a few picture postcards?"

Shan cut in. "Okay, Dr. Rayat, what do you want to find out? The pharmaceutical value of native plants? There's a database of chemical compounds you can access." She took her swiss from her pocket, flicked a pin and a plasma screen spread into life between two cursors extruding from one edge. She read something from it. "I have here a summary of a natural history database that shows you just about everything on the planet that's of note."

Rayat wasn't giving up. "Who decided what's of note?"

"The intelligent species here. No point rushing things." She rocked back on her heels a few times as she spoke, arms folded across her chest. Her forearms were hard muscle, and obviously not acquired by playing tennis. "On this world, the dominant philosophy is non-interference. As I understand it, the surface is pretty much run by the wess'har, so they're the people to humor first. They're like vegans. They make no use whatsoever of other species beyond food plants, and they have no tolerance of anyone who does. The colonists are wholly vegan too. You have to rethink the way you work if we're to achieve our mutual objectives."

"What the hell does that mean?" Rayat demanded.

"I want to get out of here without making new enemies. You want to get out of here with knowledge you can turn into money. I also want to get out of here without having to cart you back in a body bag, Dr. Rayat. Do you grasp that concept?"

"You're talking as if these wess'har are dangerous."

"They are. If you need supporting evidence for that, I can

show you a site where there was once a city. It's not there
now. It didn't fall into ruin. They erased it. Just think that one
over."

Shan had a way of seeming enormously threatening just
by lowering her voice. Rayat dropped his head and Hugel
glanced away, clearly embarrassed. Lindsay fumed silently.
Shan should have told her about the military risk. It wasn't
something to lob into a casual briefing and leave her looking like a fool.

Shan looked around the group. "We're used to life being
plant or animal. It's not that clear-cut here. I don't want you
pissing off the natives by cutting a chunk from what you
think is a radish and they think is a sentient animal. I'm sure
you can see the potential for misunderstanding. Any questions?" There was silence. She turned to Lindsay. "I'm done
here, Commander."

Lindsay managed a nod. And this was the woman she was
supposed to tell that she was pregnant. She watched her disappear out the door and wondered how the hell she ever
would.

The mission party was now ready to venture out, two weeks
after landing. The payload had their plans drawn up and
each was rostered with a marine overseer. The marines were
amused at having to enforce the sanctity of the local flora
and fauna; one of them had carefully stenciled PARK
KEEPER'S HUT on the lintel over the entrance to their quarters. Other than that, they were taking the role as seriously
as if it had been a beach landing. Shan found Mart Barencoin and Ismat Qureshi poring over a guide to biology field
practice. It was disturbing to watch them reading off the
screens embedded in their palms. They looked like earnest
fortune-tellers.

"You'll be a PhD at the end of this deployment," Shan
said.

"Got to know what they're doing, ma'am," said Qureshi, and went back to her studies on headspace capture and non-invasive tissue sampling. "No risks, right?"

"No risks," Shan agreed.

She began walking the length of the perimeter, which was not a fence but had every sense of being one. Even Champciaux, who had plenty of rock to occupy him, had spent the last three days trying to establish how it worked and exactly what it did. Occasionally Shan would reach out her hand to feel a charge in the air. It raised the hairs on her arm, reminding her of the barrier keeping the two ecologies apart.

As she walked, she saw a camouflage uniform in the distance. It resolved into Adrian Bennett. Maybe he hadn't been prepared for clothing that needed to blend into an orange-and-blue terrain. In his jungle camo he was as conspicuous as a flare.

"I thought you wore that chameleon fabric these days," she said.

"Good day, ma'am." He always saluted her. When he raised his arm, she could see the bioscreen in his palm, looking unhealthily translucent in the daylight, and she averted her eyes. Even if it wasn't recording, it felt intrusive. And if you had that much biotech grafted into you, were you really human anymore? She dismissed the thought. "Haven't activated it. Thought it looked a bit aggressive, trying to conceal yourself here." He pressed his palm against his breast pocket and the jungle greens danced indecisively between shades before settling into a random mottling of blue and amber. "See? It's not my color."

The suit faded back into its default green. For a moment he looked uncertain, not quite the invulnerable booty she expected, and stood awkwardly still. Shan broke the silence more out of embarrassment than a wish for conversation.

"What's your speciality, Sergeant?"

"Mountain and arctic, ma'am."

"Out of luck here, then."

"Feels like mountain, though." He gave her an anxious smile and they began walking back towards the camp. "And it *is* extreme."

"How do you feel about serving under a commander of a different uniform?"

"No problem. We've worked with civilian police loads at times. Anti-terrorism, humanitarian aid, evacuation—"

"I meant Commander Neville."

"We always work with the navy, ma'am. Goes back a long time. A sort of miniature ship, if you like. Navy commands it, drives the thing, deploys us. No different here, except we were all selected for multiple specialities on account of the limited logistics. I'm pilot-trained. Qureshi's a comms specialist as well as EOD. And so on."

"E.O.D.?"

"Bomb disposal."

"Lovely. Let's hope that doesn't come in handy. Just how tooled-up are you people?"

"Multifunction ESF670 rifles, close-in defense and a bit of housekeeping ordnance."

"Which is?"

"Grenades and plastic. For blowing holes, really. We weren't kitted for a combat mission. Just general eventualities."

She must have looked dubious. Bennett laughed. He was a totally average man, and you had to look carefully to see just how hard-trained he was under that uniform. His hair was mid-brown and his eyes were dull hazel and he was mid-height, mid-build and totally forgettable. He struck her as slightly nervous, even afraid. But he was a marine, and Extreme Environment Warfare Cadre at that. You didn't get that cap badge for embroidery. She treated him with due respect.

"Must be frustrating. You came expecting to evacuate or recover bodies, right?"

"There's still plenty to do. Maintenance, cleaning, fitness, victualing—we're okay."

"I think we all have to play it by ear."

"Never known an operation to go to plan yet, ma'am. Way of the world. That's why they sent for us. It's what we do. Anything and everything."

He set off down the perimeter at a steady pace and Shan watched him dwindle and disappear. He had his purpose, and so did the payload.

She just wasn't entirely sure what hers was now. She ambled on, letting her thoughts drift in case some SB memories surfaced, but there seemed to be little in the way of a mental itch there any longer. There was something, something important but not colossal in import, and she let it ride. So maybe this was all that had convinced her: Perault had played to her green side, and told her to save the last precious remnants of rain forests and chalk meadows and savannahs and coral reefs, a gene bank guarded by a bunch of religious nutters light-years from home.

As missions went, it was a noble one, and one her parents would have applauded. It beat staying home to grow old. And as god-botherers went, these Christians seemed pretty sensible and tolerant.

All she hoped was that the facts Perault had not known—the complexities of alien politics—would not get in the way. If they did, she would have to find another way to preserve Constantine's legacy.

12

The problem with the gethes, the humans, is that they cannot differentiate between people. They say the planet belongs to the bezeri, yet they know the world also belongs to rockvelvets and udzas and a thousand others: it is as if they have to establish one people who have dominance in order to make sense of life. Their language is equally confusing. Who can believe what they say if every word has several meanings?

SIYYAS BUR,
Matriarch Historian

Josh called at the compound next day unannounced. He could see knee-high structures the shape of old-fashioned skep hives at intervals across the grass, and walked up to one to inspect it. The thing looked like a nest of smooth bronze tubes studded with disks, and there was an opening at the top. As he moved round, it made a faint whirring sound. A rapid flash of light from it startled him.

"It's all right, sir, we've disabled it." Soldiers. He hadn't heard them come up behind him. One of them was a very dark young woman who looked far too slight for combat. She and her male companion had rifles slung on webbing across their chests. The weapons didn't look much different from those he had seen in old videos. "Can we help you?"

"What is it?" Josh asked, glancing away from the guns and back to the machine.

"It's a defense system. It just tells us if we have visitors." She was not relaxed about it, that was for certain. Had he scared them? "I'll take you to Superintendent Frankland."

He tore his attention from the defense hive and followed

them to the collection of square green buildings standing conspicuously alone in the grass. Inside, the corridors were plain and polished, and the translucent walls gave the interior a sense of being under water.

Frankland was on all fours in the mess. She was wiping the floor with a wad of cloth. The woman soldier stared at her, clearly taken aback. The superintendent didn't look up.

"Yes, Qureshi, what is it?"

"Visitor, ma'am."

She knelt back on her heels and looked up at Josh. "Cozy, isn't it?" she said. "Not quite home comforts."

"You clean floors?" he said.

"There's a rota." She put the cloth aside and got to her feet. "I might as well be useful."

"I need to talk to you."

Qureshi and the other soldier disappeared without prompting. Frankland dried her hands on her pants and motioned Josh to sit down. Floor cleaning didn't fit into his image of secular command—or, judging by their expressions, the soldiers'.

"I've arranged for you to talk to one of the wess'har representatives," he said.

"Here?"

"Probably best to meet in my house."

"What do I need to know beforehand? Anything to avoid?"

"He's used to humans. He speaks excellent English. He's a little different from the rest of his people."

"Is there a greeting in wess'har that I can learn?"

"He won't expect that. We're not physically equipped for some of the sounds anyway. We've known Aras for many years, and you can be completely honest with him. In fact, I would suggest that you are. Wess'har are a very precise people." He got up to go; there seemed no point making small talk, although he was now intensely curious about this officer. "When he gets here, I will let you know."

Shan saw him to the entrance, but not before she had re-trieved the cloth from the corner of the room. Josh turned at the doorway. "You've set up defenses," he said.

"The marines want a little security. But it's just an alarm. They disabled the close-in cannon."

"I don't think anyone will harm you here."

"Neither do I. That's why I told them to disable it." She gave him a rueful smile. "It's just that territorial dispute. It makes the military jumpy."

"The isenj? The wess'har would never let them land here again. You have only yourselves to fear."

Go, please go, he thought as he walked away. *Go back home and say that it's too much trouble to try to get a foothold here. Say it's not economically viable. Just let us get on with what we have to do.* Josh walked back the long way, through the patches of crops, picking his way between the newly sown beans that were already breaking through the soil. He could see James alongside his friends, chatting while they planted hemp. In fewer than a hundred days, they would be harvesting it.

At that moment, he feared change more than death. He had never known which generation would ultimately be the one to restore Earth, but he had known this colony was not meant to be permanent from the day he was old enough to talk. Right then he wanted it to last forever. Who needed Earth? You could serve God and his creation anywhere.

But it was the hand of the wess'har and not God's that made it practical for them to live here. Without alien bene-factors, the colony would have dwindled and died and the precious cargo of Earth's species would have been lost. Faith was one thing; and maybe God had ordained the inter-vention of the wess'har. But it was wess'har technology they relied on nonetheless.

Deborah was playing with Rachel when he reached

home. The little girl held up a sheet of hemp paper criss-crossed by blue and green lines. "Look, Daddy!" she said, crowding round his legs and nearly tripping him. "I drew the fields. It's for Aras."

"That's lovely, sweetie. I think he'll like it." He scooped her up in his arms and stood over Deborah, who was packing brushes and paints back into their box. "He called, then?"

"He'll be here tomorrow. He didn't say much."

"Well, the Frankland woman is ready."

"She's all right. I think you should put some trust in her."

"What makes you say that?"

"She cleaned up her room before she left. Very thoroughly, I might add. That tells you something about a person."

Josh laughed. "Yes, I imagine she's someone who always cleans up after herself."

"Why's Aras got claws?" Rachel cut in.

"Because he's Aras," said her mother.

"He says his people don't have claws."

"Well, Aras is very special, even for a wess'har, darling. Don't talk about that when the visitors are around, though, will you? You know it's our secret."

"Yes, Mummy. Is he an angel?"

"No, he's someone who takes care of us. And we'll take care of him, too, won't we? We'll keep his secret."

Rachel put her finger to her lips in a mime of silence. Then she wriggled free of Josh's arms and skipped off with her drawing.

"Whatever happens," Deborah said, "we'll all come through it. The hardest part was staying alive this long."

Josh gave her a weak smile and sat down to the tea and citrus cake she placed on the table in front of him. Deborah was usually right. It was just the "it" they would have to come through that worried him.

* * *

"Take care with the roads," Josh said, striding confidently. "They're alive."

Shan trailed behind Bennett, Becken, Mesevy and Rayat, mirroring their steps along the slight convex curve of the matted vegetation. Ahead of them, Josh picked out the path.

"The wess'har build organic roads?" asked Mesevy.

"No, the firm ground through the marshy areas is made up of colonies of organisms. We just use them as paths." Josh had that patient tone of someone used to dealing with small children asking the same question for the fortieth time. "The tracks move around from time to time. Look out for the darker moss. That's where the boggy ground is."

"How deep is it?" Shan called.

Josh didn't turn his head. "Meters," he said. "Fall in and you'll be gone."

Mesevy and Rayat said nothing, but Shan noted they hitched their backpacks a little as if to make absolutely sure of their balance. Bennett and Becken both carried metal poles in one hand, apparently standard survival kit in treacherous terrain. It wasn't the sort of precaution Shan was used to in urban Europe, although the poles looked handy enough to give a troublesome yob a quick whack round the ear.

"What's it for?" she whispered to Bennett. He exuded soap and tidy determination. "Testing depths?"

"No, ma'am. For getting out of a tight spot."

The bog—or quicksand—looked deceptively solid. In places, it was almost as lush and velvet-perfect as a bowling green, but liquid pooled in places and gave a hint of the real danger there. Without the network of tangled plant-life that formed a substantial but gradually shifting web across its surface, the bog would have formed a natural barrier between the colony and the rest of the island.

From time to time, Mesevy and Rayat paused to place a

probe into the ground and take readings. Josh stood over them, watching carefully: Mesevy unfurled a roll of white tape, tore off a ten-centimeter strip with gloved hands and dragged the tape with slow care across the surface of the bog. "Is this okay, Josh?" she asked. "I'm just picking up surface cells for analysis."

Josh seemed satisfied it was non-invasive. The bog didn't seem to care. "Fine by me," he said, and from then on Mesevy stopped at every color change on the route to swipe her tape across it and bag the samples. Rayat simply followed her, looking unhappy. Then he stumbled.

"Careful," called Becken. "Slow down. Don't want to have to fish you out, do we?"

I wouldn't bother, that's for sure, Shan thought. *Miserable sod.* She reached for her swiss and stood still to check the transmission digest back at camp. Eddie was busy on the line, uploading voice copy. God only knew how he managed to make so much story material simply out of building a camp, installing plumbing and seeing orange grass in the distance: she had to give him credit for ingenuity.

Bennett turned and waited for her. He smiled nervously and let her catch up before resuming his careful progress. The living road was about a meter and a half wide.

"Wow," said Mesevy. She pointed. Ahead of her, flashing out of the surface of the bog like a leaping salmon, was a glistening sheet of something transparent. Shan held the swiss up to catch a few images.

"Aras calls that a *sheven,*" Josh said. "Stay clear of it. They hunt by enveloping prey and they can be big, really big. Then they digest you."

"Like being sucked dry by cling-film," Shan said.

"Does everything here do that?" Bennett asked. Shan had mentioned the rockvelvets to him, and it did not appear to fascinate him at all. He almost shuddered visibly. "Don't they have harmless furry things?"

Josh didn't answer.

They watched the *sheven* flapping around like a plastic bag and then it plunged back below the surface with a slurping noise. It had probably found some unnamed and unknown victim in the depths of the mud. Shan felt a familiar uneasiness at the thought of unseen misery.

"Like you said, Superintendent, we can always use the database," Mesevy said, and seemed relieved not to have to tackle the *sheven* with a swipe of tape. Shan pocketed the swiss. Maybe the prospect of wildlife with nasty eating habits would encourage the payload not to push their luck over samples.

The road began to narrow. Josh paused and looked around. "I'm sorry," he said. "It's moved since last week. There was a path through here before but it's gone now. Turn around slowly and stand still while I pass you."

They tried to present as narrow a profile as they could to allow Josh to retrace his steps and take up the lead position again. Shan could feel a slight bounce as the live road sprang like a rope bridge at every step. Josh stepped carefully in front of Shan and looked around again.

"Sorry," he said. "It looks like we'll have to double back the whole way. Next time I'll use the surface craft. This is getting too risky."

It was only a single yelp that made them turn. And there was no Mesevy, at least not on the path. She was knee-deep in the bog, then waist-deep in a second, struggling but silent.

"Jon!" Bennett shouted, pointing and holding his arm like a compass as he made his way back towards the end of the line. "Overboard—*there*."

Shan wondered where the *sheven* had got to.

Becken shook the pole out into its full length and lay flat to slide it out towards her. Bennett squatted beside him and

drew a length of line out of his jacket. Mesevy was treading
water in slow motion. She had also found her voice.

"Oh, god I'm going down I'm going down I'm—"

"Stay still," Bennett said, very steady and controlled.
"Just stop struggling. Stay still."

"I can't."

"Over on your back. Go on. Just let go and pretend
you're lying down on grass."

"I—"

"Now. On your back."

She managed to twist and lean back, eyes wide in terror.
Becken pushed the pole under her spine. "Try and slide it
under your hips."

Shan stepped forward. She knew there wasn't anything
she could do that the marines couldn't, but it felt odd not to
take control of an emergency. Where was that *sheven*?
Everybody must have been thinking the same thing. Nobody said a word.

Bennett was still trying to get the pole positioned under
Mesevy. "Stop struggling," he said. "Faster you move,
higher the viscosity. You know about shearing forces, don't
you? Talk to me, Sabine. Shearing forces. Look at me. Just
relax." He turned to Shan and handed her the end of the
length of line. "Anchor this, ma'am. Can you tie a bowline?"

"Just about." Shan detached from the reality. She fumbled the line into place round her waist. And the old
mnemonic came back to her, as surely as the SB ever did:
she was suddenly with her dad at the seaside, watching him
show her how to tie knots, studying his hands. *Rabbit
comes out the hole—round the tree—down the hole.*

She tugged on the knot and it held fast. Detached or not,
she also recalled how to release it if she had to. Bennett
paid out the line in his hands and edged down next to
Becken. Mesevy began thrashing around again, unable to

control her panic enough to lie still and float with the pole lending more buoyancy to her hips. She was going under.

There was a plastic-bag flash a few meters away.

"Shit," Bennett said.

If he hesitated, it was for a split-second, no more. He rolled onto the surface of the bog with his pole and let himself float, pushing slowly towards Mesevy and grabbing her hard. The whole sequence was slow and almost silent, except for Mesevy's sobs. Bennett got the line round her and Becken began reeling her in slowly.

"Go limp," Bennett shouted at her. "Go on. Do a starfish. Arms and legs apart. Stop struggling."

And then she was half on the firm ground. Becken grabbed her and rolled her inboard. Bennett, on his back with his pole under his spine, waited for Becken to throw the line back and pull him in.

Part of the *sheven* flashed above the bog again. It might have been a small one. It could have been huge. Shan still held tightly to the rope knotted round her waist.

"That was close," said Rayat. He hauled Mesevy to her feet and steadied her. The two marines stood panting with exertion, coated in more samples than Mesevy could ever want.

"Back to base," Shan said, spotting the point at which they expected her to take control, and relieved by its familiarity. "I think it's *endex* for the day. Follow Josh."

She put her hand on Bennett's shoulder. "Nice job," she said.

He didn't answer. He was staring ahead, white-faced, and his legs looked like they were starting to buckle. It took her a while to recognize terror. When she saw it, it seemed more shocking than watching Mesevy being sucked into the bog. She caught his elbow. She didn't want the others to see him go down.

"You okay?" she said.

"Yeah. Fine."

"No you're not." She grabbed his face in both hands and forced him to look at her. The slime and mud was still thick on him, and his eyes, fixed and wide, seemed startling. "Come on. Breathe slowly."

The others were a little ahead, and Becken stopped to look: then he ushered the others on, seeming to realize Bennett didn't want an audience.

"It's okay. Come on. Deep breaths."

"I'm sorry, ma'am."

"Hey, no problem. Just stand still for a while."

"Okay. Okay." He jerked his head out of her hands and vomited to one side of the path. Abject fear; sheer bloody animal fear. She felt something of his embarrassment. But he'd held on long enough to save Mesevy, and that took more guts than she could imagine. The *sheven* would have meant an unpleasant death, one that she didn't feel like facing to save a stranger.

"I'll never live this one down." He wiped his mouth with the back of his hand, leaving another smear of bog behind it, and walked stiffly ahead. He had lost more than control of his stomach. He'd soiled himself. "Some fucking marine I am. Sorry, ma'am. No offense."

Shan matched his pace and wished desperately that she had a knack for reassurance. "Don't be bloody daft," she said. "I've lost my bottle a few times, I can tell you. You'd have to be a fool not to be afraid out here."

"But I lose it *all* the time. And everyone knows when it happens." He held out his left palm, lit and live with data transmissions that charted spiked heart rate and peak adrenaline. "This bloody thing transmits all the time. I can't fart without it relaying the fact."

"No privacy, then? Ever?"

He shook his head. "Full-body diagnostics and voice. Battlefield fail-safe. I can't disable it without a technician. Except the video, of course."

She took his arm carefully. "There's no shame in fear, Ade." Using his first name seemed nakedly familiar. "It's nature's way of telling you not to be a dick-head."

"No, I'm a panicker. That's why I joined up, to get a bloody grip on it."

"You didn't look like a panicker to me today."

He shrugged, sad and so deserving of a hug that she almost attempted it. There weren't many heroes in her world. Bennett, who could face fear bad enough to make him lose control of his bowels and still function, had just become one of them.

Before they reached the camp, the reality of Bennett's ever-vigilant bioscreen came home to her. Qureshi and Balwant Singh Chahal ambled towards them, grinning.

"Nice one, Sarge," they called. "Waste of time making you breakfast, eh?" Bennett ignored the jibe and walked on.

"Oi, leave it out," Shan snapped. The marines stood frozen. "It's not a fucking joke, all right? Show some respect."

She regretted the outburst instantly, and was surprised to see the two marines snap upright. They stopped a fraction short of saluting.

Bennett turned to her. "That's very kind of you, ma'am, but they know I dumped because I was scared. I've done it before. But thanks anyway."

"That damn thing records everything you do and say?"

"Everything."

"Really *everything*?"

Bennett caught on. "Ah . . . yes. It's not just the medication that keeps you celibate when you're mission-active. Once they switch you on, everyone knows what you get up to."

Their glances met for just a second too long for either

of them to feel comfortable, and Shan was surprised to feel some dismay at the prospect of broadcast sex. She hadn't even realized she found him appealing in that way. Shame. He was a nice bloke, a brave one, but that was as far as it could go. She made him his mug of coffee in the mess hall, not in his cabin, just to avoid thinking those undisciplined thoughts again. It was nothing she couldn't suppress, after all.

"Guess what," said Champciaux. His fine-boned patrician face appeared round Shan's half-open hatchway. Now that he'd shaved off his thinning hair, he looked rather striking. "The AI got the cartography scanner back on line."

"I know," said Shan. "I saw the downlink activate."

"Yes, but I've done some work on the images. Have you got five minutes to take a look?"

She closed the screen and leaned back in her chair, unsure what thrill a geologist could possibly show her. Champciaux had a kind of innocence about him, or perhaps she had imposed it on him because he was funded by less aggressive organizations than the others. He was a pure academic. He just examined rocks. He didn't change genes or juggle disease against profit or defy nature. He just looked at creation.

Now he showed her what he looked at. It was a very vivid image on smartpaper, and somehow that seemed more real than the usual images on screen. She held the sheet and stared at it, not sure what she was seeing. The reds and blues and lime greens were three-dimensional; an image of a landscape like a fly-through, gently rolling land sliced with meandering streams. On top of the miniature world were superimposed yellow and violet lines, very regular, very unnatural, a grid like a wiring diagram. The bizarre tartan covered the whole sheet.

"City," he said.

"I can't get the scale."

"Think Angkor Wat," said Champciaux. "A city of millions. Even if the physical traces like walls and roads have disappeared with time, they still leave depressions and variations in the natural landscape. You can sometimes only see it with sonar or laser satellite imaging."

"Yeah, I've seen the archaeology shows. Tell me where this is."

"These are the islands down the chain we're on. Not only that, but I've got similar images from the coastline all the way down the continent. This was a heavily inhabited planet at some time in the past. Now, I'm not an expert on this, because I'm a rock man, but I can read geophys data like this as well as anyone."

Shan was suddenly standing with Josh Garrod staring out at unspoiled alien heath, being told that there had once been a settlement there, a settlement that had been wiped away—not wiped out, not razed to the ground, but wiped *away,* erased in every sense of the word. She tried to orientate herself on the map.

"And where are we?"

Champciaux flicked the icon at the margin of the smartsheet, and a new image appeared. "Right here," he said. He flicked the sizing icon and the scale enlarged.

Shan could pick out the coastline, the tiny speck of their camp and the barely discernible lace of Constantine's concealed domes. The building was superimposed on a layer of fainter grid lines that covered the whole island like a net. And when she changed scale, there it was again, on the next island, and the next.

The network of traces might have been older than the missing city. The planet's history was one of those blanks she would have to fill in, and for all she knew it could have been just like much of inhabited Earth, building on building, century after century. But she knew in her gut that it wasn't like that at all.

The wess'har hadn't just wiped away a city. They had obliterated a nation.

"May I hang on to this? I want to show it to someone."

Champciaux nodded. "What do you think? I know we're not here for archaeology, but this has got to be a hell of a find."

"It depends on whether those lines really were artificial and not like the organic roads."

And it depended on how the cities ceased to exist. Shan was getting the feeling that wess'har really didn't piss about. Champciaux looked slightly deflated.

"I'll see what I can find out from the locals," she said, trying to look like kindly caution rather than someone who had just had her worst fears confirmed. Civilians—real civilians—didn't generally handle that sort of information well.

But at least she now knew the true scale of what she might be dealing with. She wondered if Josh would be able to help her a little further with her inquiries. People normally did, if you asked them in the right way.

She seldom had to ask twice.

"Have you got a moment?"

Hugel peered round the hatch frame of Shan's cabin. Shan looked up from the screen of her swiss. This was getting to be a steady stream. "Something wrong?"

"Not exactly wrong, but I just wanted to make you aware of a potentially delicate situation." Hugel stepped in and shut the hatch. "I'm breaching patient confidentiality."

"Go ahead. I won't tell the General Medical Council if you don't."

"It's Commander Neville."

"Yeah, what *is* up with her? She's not all there at the moment."

"She's pregnant."

Shan leaned back in her seat and groaned. "Oh great. Terrific."

"Under the circumstances you needed to know. It's not the end of the world—just something we need to manage carefully. The colony women cope, but they're acclimatized to low oxygen."

"She's not a colonist. She's supposed to be the bloody commanding officer of a warship."

"Well, there's no reason why she can't do what she needs to do for quite a few months. It's not as if she's in a combat situation."

"She's going ahead with this, then?"

"Yes."

"Well, her choice. But what a bloody stupid thing to do." Shan replayed their earlier conversation at high speed, tasting a certain betrayal. "She assured me her people were disciplined pros who could keep it in their trousers. I rest my case."

"I believe she conceived before departure, and didn't realize." Hugel looked uncomfortable. "Mistakes happen."

"Sorry. I know it's unprofessional of me to react like that but it adds another complication, doesn't it?"

"Medically, yes. This is a higher-risk pregnancy, even though she's young and fit."

"Well, let me know when she needs to relinquish command. Who else knows?"

"Just us. You won't mention this conversation? Please?"

"No," Shan said. *Let's see how long Lindsay takes to tell me herself.* "Thanks for letting me know."

"While I'm here, Eddie says he needs to talk to Aras about an interview."

"I'll pass on the request."

Hugel gave her an awkward smile, as if unsure how to extract herself from the cabin. "You won't be too hard on Lindsay, will you?"

"I'll remember every last scrap of my man-management training, I promise."

"That's what I was afraid of. You're from a pretty macho and unforgiving line of work."

"You saying I don't understand women?"

"Possibly."

"If girls want to play boys' games and get boys' pay, they have to do what boys do. I'm not allowed to say that professionally, but I'm in my own cabin twenty-five light-years from Central Personnel and they can come out and discipline me anytime they feel like it." She realized she might as well have had NEANDERTHAL tattooed on her forehead. "Teams depend on people pulling their weight."

"People like Lindsay depend on you, too."

"Yes, and I accepted that and all that went with it, personal costs and all."

Hugel nodded. "I thought as much."

Shan bit back a response. If it helped Hugel feel superior to analyze her, that was fine. She knew why she had felt irrational anger now: Lindsay hadn't done what Shan Frankland would have done in the same situation.

So people made mistakes. She thought of Green Rage and it diverted her from Lindsay. That wasn't a mistake at all, and having to play along with the public illusion that it was a cock-up had hurt her, and still hurt. But it had to be that way. Her professional pride came second to getting that job done. It didn't even matter anymore because everyone who had something to lose from that operation was dead or forgotten.

Silly cow, she told herself. *You did it because it mattered, not so you could let everyone know how fucking noble you were.* She still felt cheated, and guilty because of that.

For some reason—and probably a reason connected with the Suppressed Briefing—the name Helen popped into her mind. She chased it for a while, and then let it fade.

How do I broach this with her?

It didn't bode well that her second-in-command—her 2IC, as the marines had taken to calling Lindsay—hadn't seen fit to tell her she was pregnant in the middle of a mission.

Shan couldn't sleep; there was nothing to do with insomnia other than use it for thinking time. Okay, so the kid was pissed off at finding her command had been cut from under her by a politician with no explanation. All the preparatory training she'd been through had been overturned by events. But that was just too bad. She needed to learn that Shan didn't like her bagman keeping information from her. It fed her natural distrust of the world.

But the marines seemed fine about it, embarrassingly so. They gave Shan immediate and visible deference and so did some of the payload. When she walked in, they stiffened as if she'd fired a shot over their heads. *I'm older,* she thought. *I spent twenty-five years perfecting how to look like bad news, and they don't know the first thing about me. I have the advantage for a while.*

But perhaps it was getting to Lindsay. She might have been a high-flier back on Earth, but out here she was having to prove herself all over again on top of having an embarrassing personal problem. It must have been galling. It was time to do some bridge building between them. Shan would do it because someone had to.

She was lying on her bunk staring up at the deckhead and rehearsing how to approach the issue when the ground shook.

A dull *whump* echoed round the compound. She listened: nothing more. She jumped from the bunk and began walking down the passage, then broke into a run. At the entrance to the compound, most of the off-duty marines and half the scientists were standing looking around, blind in the pitch-black. "What was that?" she asked.

"Defense grid," said Chahal, one of the two engineer-qualified marines. "Nothing else it could be."

"I thought we had disabled it. Where's Commander Neville? Get her for me."

Chahal jogged off. Steps thudded fast towards them. Bennett came running, rifle in one hand, and jerked his thumb back towards the horizon.

"Christ, we've hit something," he panted. "The defnet was triggered."

"I'll take the scoot," Shan said. "Can you track the shot?"

"Green 65 from here," he said, indicating subjective zero with a chopping motion and then pointing. "Wait for me, ma'am, and I'll get Webster."

"No. Get Josh Garrod." She guessed what they had hit wasn't from the colony, and that left one possibility. "I think he'll need to be involved."

"I don't think so, ma'am."

"Well *I* think so, Sergeant. He knows the locals a lot better than we do. I promise I'll stay in voice contact at all times."

Shan went back to her cabin to collect her swiss, a medical kit and a jacket. She couldn't wait for Josh. Hugel stopped her in the passage. "You'll need a medic," she said. "Do you have any idea how to use that?"

"I'll call you if I need you." She suspected first aid might have been a little late, even if Hugel had known how to treat an alien.

Shan stepped out into the night, a blackness that came as a shock to someone from a world filled with city lights. Wess'ej, the moon as far as she was concerned, wasn't up yet, and there was no GPS net to guide her. The scoot could map its way back to base, but for the outward leg she was on her own. She started up the machine.

After a distance she picked up a gouged path of soil and debris, visible enough to follow with the hand-light from her swiss. Some of it was metallic. She slowed the scoot down and followed the trail at walking pace until the fragments of twisted metal became larger and she was able to pick out markings on them.

It certainly wasn't the remains of a shell casing. This had to be alien. It was dark and matt, and where her light caught it, there were mid-blue symbols she couldn't decipher.

Somewhere, she knew, at the end of the debris trail, was a dead alien pilot. She parked the scoot and followed the trail slowly on foot. Behind her she could hear the *thud-thud-thud* of someone running as fast as they could. Josh Garrod slowed to a halt beside her, panting.

His face was distraught. He confirmed her worst fear: they had probably shot one of the wess'har peacekeepers. The colonists seldom went off camp at night, and the mission party was checked in for the day.

"You said it wouldn't fire."

"Josh, I can't tell you how sorry I am."

"I thought he would be walking here. I had no idea he would use transport."

Just once, she thought. *Just once, let me fear the worst and be wrong.* She cursed herself for not checking the defnet and not learning how it worked and not shutting it down herself. There were things you couldn't trust others to do.

Josh was running a little ahead of her now, his breathing audible, but it was more a suppressed sobbing than a struggle to breathe. *I will never accept an assurance again.* Her old training sergeant, long dead, was still muttering in her ear that there was no substitute for your own eyes. It was only the second time she had forgotten that advice.

"Oh, God," said Josh. But he meant it.

The small vehicle had largely survived the impact. If she had been able to put it back together again, it would have been the size of a land cruiser. She could see the back of a seat jutting out of the churned soil, and what were probably forward stabilizers. This was the tough bit: the time to check for bodies. She walked back to get a shovel from the scoot's pannier to begin digging out around the wreckage. Josh began scooping with his hands. She could hear herself wheezing with the effort, and her nose was dripping.

Now there was enough room to get in and shine a light around. She braced herself for a shock. It was never pleasant discovering entrails and body parts, no matter how many times you had attended accident scenes, but the worse the picture you conjured up beforehand, the easier it was to face the graphic reality.

She aimed the beam.

"Jesus H. Christ," she said, forgetting cultural sensitivity, and nearly lost her footing.

Reaching out to her from the wreckage was a multifingered, gloved hand.

She set the swiss on the flat top of a piece of cockpit so the light shone onto the body. Josh grabbed the swiss and held it closer for her. If she didn't remove the debris carefully, she might do a lot more damage to whatever was in the seat. Scraping sounds from the tangle of metal stopped her. Pieces of the hull shattered and flew into the air, as if a very large bird were hatching with some violence. A figure out of all proportion to the vessel emerged and tried to step out of the wreckage, managing only to fall to its knees as soon as it was free of the seat.

Josh rushed to its aid. "Aras, Aras," he kept saying. "Aras, are you all right? It wasn't meant to hit you."

The alien was big, really big. Shan stared up at him as he uncoiled from his crouching position. His movements weren't human and his smell wasn't human and his sounds weren't human. He was an alien, a real live alien, something only a handful of humans had actually seen, and the shocking joy of it almost crowded out the urgency and fear of dealing with the crisis.

An alien. Great Lord and Lady, the wonder of creation, and she was witnessing it.

Something right on the lower threshold of her hearing irritated the back of her tongue and made her press her ears in a vain attempt to stop the insistent itch. Then it stopped.

The creature had two upper limbs and two legs and a head where heads should have been. For some reason that made him even more disturbing and wonderful. She moved her hands well away from her body and hoped he understood that it indicated she wasn't going to use a weapon.

"I'm sorry," she said. "It was a mistake. We didn't mean you any harm." Did he understand? His eyes—very dark, white-ringed, like an animal's, like every animal eye she had ever looked into with its disturbing glimpse into another intelligence—were fixed on hers. It was all she could see of his face. Fabric covered most of his head.

"You're *gethes*," he said. "Shoot first, as they say."

If it hadn't been for the underlying resonance in that voice, like the infrasonics that had made her ears itch, he would have sounded almost human. His English was unaccented. He raised gloved hands and began peeling the fabric from his head, and she half-expected to see he was a man after all, but he was not. His skin was bronze with a sheen of iridescence. It was the face of an idealized beast, and shockingly fine.

"You can understand me," Shan said. No need to worry about the responsibility of first contact; he had met humans before. *But he's an alien, a real alien,* her thoughts kept interrupting. *Be amazed.* "You understand what I'm saying?"

"Even with that accent, yes," he said. "You're Shan Frankland. Can't you control your people?"

"I can only apologize." *And I'm going to have some-one's guts for garters.* "Don't move. I'll get medical help."

The alien made a *fuh* noise like a human puff of con-tempt. "I will recover."

"You might be in shock. Let me——" She reached out but Josh put his hand out to stop her. The alien stared down at her, unblinking.

"There's nothing your medics could do for me, even if I needed it." He tested his right arm, flexing it carefully, then his left. "I will be fine."

Josh put his hands flat together in front of his lips as if in a parody of prayer. He looked afraid. "Come back to Con-stantine, Aras," he said. "Stay with us until you're fully fit."

"This is your peacekeeping friend, isn't it?" Shan said.

"Yes, this is Aras Sar Iussan."

Aras nodded his fine head and a thick braid of dark hair slid out of his collar. He tucked it back again rather self-consciously. "*Shan Chail,*" he said. "Not an ideal way to meet, is it?"

"Whatever harm we've done you is my responsibility, and I accept the consequences," Shan said.

She held out her hand. Aras almost went to take it and then appeared to change his mind. "I bear you no ill will. And you're the matriarch, yes?"

It was as good a description as any. "Yes, I am."

"Then I'll talk with you about the conditions of your stay here. Tomorrow."

"Tomorrow's fine by me."

The scoot could carry three people but not if one of them was as big as Aras. Shan offered him her seat. "I can walk," she said. "We'll collect your vessel when it's light and see what's salvageable. Of course, we'll help in any way we can with repairs."

"The vehicle will take care of itself," he said. "And I can also walk."

Josh interrupted. "You take the scoot back, Superintendent, and we'll catch up."

"Okay. I'll let them know you're on the way." Aras showed no signs of trauma. She had no idea how he could have walked away from that crash. But he had. It was weird, and because it was weird she would keep it to herself for the time being. She flicked opened her swiss and called Bennett.

She glanced at Aras. He was completely and unnaturally still, and he was staring intently at her. No, this wasn't something she was going to mention.

"Nobody's hurt," she said. "Just hardware. We're heading back."

"Are you okay?"

She smiled to herself. "Really, I'm fine. Thanks."

She met the alien's eyes. It might have been relief on his face, or it might have been mistrust—she had no way yet of knowing. But she knew they had suddenly reached some sort of silent agreement.

"I'll see you later," she said, and started up her scoot. Sweeping in an arc, she circled the wreckage and saw dark liquid smears on the seat and shattered screen that could easily have been blood. Aras and Josh were already well ahead of her, walking briskly, and she caught up with them from behind, but as she passed them—slowly, so as not to create a slipstream—she noted the dark stains on Aras's light clothing. If that wasn't blood, and plenty of it, she was the Aga Khan.

Yet Aras walked as steadily as Josh. She had seen cars crushed out of recognition in accidents with no harm to the driver, and she'd watched paramedics remove bodies limb by limb from vehicles with just dented door panels. But taking a full cannon round always had one outcome.

And yet Aras walked. And if Josh hadn't expressed surprise at his recovery, neither would she. It was something she felt was better left undiscussed for the time being.

Lindsay was waiting for her outside her cabin when she returned, and she looked far from happy. Shan gestured her inside and closed the door behind them. It was a small cabin, and not the place for a row.

"What is it?" Lindsay asked. "What did we hit?"

"The peacekeeping force. Or part of it. We brought down a pilot."

"Oh shit."

"Fortunately, he appeared to accept that friendly fire happens. Which is just as well, given their capacity for mass destruction."

"And when were you going to tell me about that, exactly?"

"What?"

Lindsay held up her hand like a traffic cop, and the vivid colors of Champciaux's geophys scan shone from her palm bioscreen. "Like someone wiped out a whole seaboard of cities. When were you going to let me know the size of the potential military threat?"

Shan didn't blink. "Probably at the same time you were going to tell me you were pregnant."

There was a silence. Lindsay didn't fill it. Shan paused three beats for effect. *I can still bowl 'em,* she thought. "Let's get one thing straight. We've got an unarmed ship, not enough personnel to play a game of soccer and basic popgun ordnance. They've got an army and they're playing at home. There is no military solution."

"You should still have discussed it with me."

Shan almost found herself explaining that there was no

hard evidence that the trace scan was the result of a war, and braked hard. "I don't need a lecture on procedure from an officer with no personal discipline." It probably revealed more about her than it did about Lindsay Neville. Enough had been said. "We *will* be doing things differently from now on."

Lindsay's voice cracked a little but her expression was set in neutral. "Bennett said nobody was hurt. Either we hit the craft or we didn't. You don't walk away from a direct hit."

"And either they build to last or we aren't the crack shots we think we are. Whatever, we're lucky we're not a smoking heap right now." And at least Lindsay hadn't expressed any curiosity about why the pilot was in one piece. She probably assumed he ejected. She didn't ask. Shan would have. It was another small but significant difference in the way they saw the world. "I have to see him in the morning. We're going to have talks, which probably means he's going to tell me how things are going to be, and I'll say, certainly, sir, whenever's convenient for you."

"At least we're talking and not firing."

"The alien—Aras—speaks English better than you or I do. He's used to humans, but it's clear we're not the sort of humans he finds acceptable. Josh has told him why we're here."

"It's probably not the best time to ask him for some latitude on taking samples, then."

"I'm not even going to think about it. And get me the pillock who primed the defnet."

"With respect, ma'am, it's standard procedure in potentially hostile territory. And it was my call."

"And I told you not to. I asked for the grid to be disabled, and you failed to follow . . . that—" She was going to say *order,* but stopped short. She had to stop this battle right here; it was one front too many to fight on. It was going to eat up her time. "Get me that marine."

Lindsay turned away and mumbled something into her bioscreen. The glow from it was greenish white now, and the thought made Shan shudder. Nobody was ever going to grow one of those damn things in *her*; that was for sure. The more she saw of them the more they repelled her. She'd stay as she was made.

They waited. They said nothing and busied themselves with the contents of their pockets. A few minutes later, footsteps outside announced the arrival of Marine Jon Becken, a stocky blond kid with a scar across the bridge of his nose. Nobody had to be left with a scar these days. He probably thought it made him look hard. It did.

"What the hell were you thinking of, Becken?" Shan said quietly.

"The defnet interpreted it as a threat, ma'am."

"I told you to stand down the automated systems. We didn't need them."

"Ma'am, with respect, any inorganic object that close, doing that speed, and clearly alien in origin, is a threat."

"For Chrissakes stand the frigging thing down and keep it that way until I say otherwise. And in the morning you will personally show me how to disable it so I can check it myself."

If he was unhappy at the bollocking he showed no sign of it. He stood staring at nothing in particular, looking past her at a point on the wall, and waiting. "Okay, dismissed." She jerked her head in the direction of the hatch and was surprised to get a snappy salute from him.

Lindsay gave her a reproachful look. "If that had been the aliens with a grudge about this place, you might have been grateful for that defnet."

"But it wasn't the isenj. And if it had been, we would

still have stood a better chance of survival if we hadn't presented a threat."

"It buys you time."

"It buys you *dead*. Do your sums. When are you going to stop fighting me on this?"

"Very well, ma'am."

"And let's be clear about your orders. Unless an alien comes up, whips out a knife and says in English, 'Hello Earthman, I want to kill you,' then you do nothing except run, okay? Absolutely nothing. Whatever the provocation. Make that clear to your people. We do *not* piss off the landlord round here under any circumstances."

"We're a little rusty on diplomacy. I apologize. But may we be clear about the matter of orders? I command the marines. Your giving them direct orders undermines me."

"I have seniority on this mission, and if that cuts across your navy protocol that's too bad." *You've lost her now. But she should have known better.* "Let's exercise common sense. They're technically advanced and they know where we live. We back off."

"Understood, ma'am." Lindsay was attempting a deadpan expression but her anger—or something like it—was reddening her throat. "Is there anything we can do now?"

"No, let's wait. Don't tell the payload anything just yet."

"Shall we recover the wreckage?"

"How would you react if someone shot down one of your craft and then stole the parts?"

"Perhaps we'll leave it, then."

"It might also be a good idea if your people leave their rifles in the armory."

"Is that wise?"

"Now that *is* an order."

Lindsay's lips tightened into a line. "I still feel it's my duty to advise you that's foolhardy."

Shan had never justified an order, but if she was going to

save the rapidly deteriorating relationship with her second-in-command this was her last chance to rescue it. She swallowed her anger. "Thank you. Noted."

"Ma'am, have you ever been in a volatile situation like this?"

Shan clenched her nails into her palms. She felt her scalp tighten. No, this had to stop, and now. "Have I? Let me think." She rolled up her sleeve and showed Lindsay a puckered and scarred strip of skin from left biceps to wrist. "I have been hit by petrol bombs. I have been shot six times. They had to take a four-inch steel blade out of my leg. I didn't get any of that writing parking tickets, sweetheart." She was close enough to Lindsay now to smell coffee on her breath, face far too close to face. "When you've faced two hundred rioting scum *this* close with just a poxy plastic shield and a baton, then you can lecture me on volatile situations. Just because I'm a copper doesn't mean I'm a fucking idiot."

Lindsay didn't step back an inch. "Apologies, ma'am. Perhaps if I'd known more about your service record I could have avoided asking the question."

A long pause; neither of them moved. Then Lindsay took a pace back, snapped off a salute and walked out. Shan let her shoulders sag and rested her head against the cool relief of the cabin bulkhead. *Well, I played a blinder there, I think.* It was unfamiliar territory, poorly navigated. She hadn't had to explain to anyone for a very long time that she was hard enough to kick down hell's door without a warrant. Most people seemed to spot that without having it spelled out. She felt she had lost something in having to do so.

But she would have to worry about her relationship with Lindsay Neville later. What she did and said in the next few hours would determine if any of them would get out of here alive. No, it was more than that: it would determine the future relationship with at least three civilizations. It was not something she was trained for. The kid did have a point. She'd never dealt with armies. But what were armies other than rioters with a battle plan? And was there anyone at all trained to handle aliens?

It's a case like any other, Shan told herself. *You analyze it, break it down, and sort it piece by piece.* And the immediate problem was to stop the situation getting even worse than it already was. Well, that was a bloody laugh. She was in a disputed territory seventy-five years from the nearest support with just seven military, an unreliable ship, a payload of unwelcome scientists, unhappy human hosts, a delicate ecology and a number two who clearly hated her guts. And now they had just nearly killed an alien on whom their lives might depend. It was just a perfect balls-up.

She lay down on her bunk. The waves of colored fractal patterns that danced over her as she looked up at the deckhead were entirely the product of her own optic nerves. Beyond the deckhead porthole the night was black, pitch-perfect black. With no focus to orientate her she was suddenly unsure if she was lying down or floating upright, and the brief sensation of falling summed up the whole mission.

But she'd talked to an alien tonight, a real alien who talked back, not algae or bacteria or moss. It was a miracle. The SB tapped her on the shoulder again. *The nonhumans hold some of the gene bank. You must make contact.*

"I think we just did that, Madame Perault," Shan muttered at the porthole. "Any further orders?"

As she expected, there was nothing but silence.

13

The colonists keep meticulous if basic records. Excluding infant-mortality figures, which are comparable to late-nineteenth-century rates, average life expectancy is 64. The most common factors in death, barring accident, are melanoma, respiratory disease, atherosclerosis or cardiac failure. The few who have agreed to examination exhibit varying degrees of arthritis, no doubt due to the heavy manual labor they choose to carry out. They are an excellent control population to demonstrate the virtues or hazards of hard exercise and a carefully balanced vegan diet. Personally, I would rather die ten years early with a Scotch in my hand.

DR. KRISTINA HUGEL, notes

The next morning Shan took a scoot and went in search of the crash site, not entirely confident that the marines would leave it untouched. There were no tracks to the site suggesting it had been cleared—yet, once there, Shan found no trace of metallic debris, just piles of granular dust that dispersed when she touched them with her boot.

So that was what the alien meant when he said it would take care of itself. Fast-degradable metal. Handy for some corporation, but if they wanted it they would have to ask for the technology openly. Shan thought it might be a bad idea to let anyone else get samples of that dust. She revved up the scoot and let its air ducts scatter the material to the wind. Satisfied that there was nothing visible to attract attention except the shallow gouges in the ground, she headed back to the settlement.

One benefit of the simplicity of Constantine was that she

never needed to ask where an important meeting was to be held. If it wasn't in the church, it was at Josh's home. Despite the civic importance of the Garrod house, it didn't appear to be any bigger than its neighbors. Shan rapped the knuckle of her forefinger on the satin-smooth door and waited for an invitation to come in.

There was a subtle scent in the air as she followed Josh's voice. It reminded her of sandalwood, very rich and soothing, but it was little more than a sensation at the roof of her mouth. When she walked into the central room of the house—kitchen, family room, workroom—the scent was stronger despite the competition from baked bread and garlic. Josh and Aras were sitting at the table.

"Good morning," Josh said, and Aras simply nodded at her. It was the first time she had seen the alien in daylight, and she could hardly stop herself staring. He dwarfed Josh. His face was all angular planes, like an ancient poster of a Soviet factory hero, as if it had started life as a mythic beast's and then tried to pass itself off as human. The effect was enough to silence her. The last time she had felt like this was when she had come face-to-face with a live Bengal tiger walking on a lead, one of the very last of its kind, an army regimental mascot taken out on special occasions. There had been something almost unbelievable about the creature. The tiger had three dimensions and it was exactly like its encyclopedia picture, yet nothing like it—a life with an agenda of its own, disengaged from human reference and stunningly real.

Aras looked nothing like a tiger. Shan's human pattern-recognizing brain floundered again, trying *dog, cat, bird,* and failed to find anything to latch on to. In daylight his hair was chocolate-dark, neatly tied back from that unclassifiable face and braided over the cream cowl neck of his tunic.

He had gloves on, too. Beige gloves. She couldn't take in the overall picture and settled on grasping the detail.

"Good morning, gentlemen."

He started abruptly. "*Shan Chail*, what's your purpose here?"

Shan Chail. Context told her it was respectful, although he could have been addressing her as *arsehole* and she would have been none the wiser.

She swallowed. "I was sent to locate the Constantine colony, locate its gene bank and oversee the research activity of a party of people representing corporations and academic bodies." But surely he knew that; Josh had told him. "We had no idea there were any sentient races already here, let alone three."

"Two," Aras corrected. "We don't tolerate the isenj."

"Well, however many—we would have made diplomatic contact before attempting to land. I apologize for any offense we've caused. And any injury, of course."

Aras stared intently into her face. The sandalwood scent was noticeably stronger near him. She assumed it was perfume. "Do your people intend to colonize this planet further?"

"I was never aware of any plan to do so."

"I don't believe that's true."

He was challenging her word. *Liar.* It seemed almost conversational.

"I was definitely given orders to complete the mission and return. There's no plan to evaluate this as a habitat."

"Not true."

Right then it seemed very important not to break eye contact with him. He was unnaturally still. Josh, clear in her peripheral vision, was sitting calmly but he seemed a mass of fidgets compared to the frozen alien.

"Are you a telepath?" she asked.

"No, but you're a poor liar, *Chail*."

It made her angry. She tried not to react, but his expression had changed. "Call me what you like, but those were not my orders."

Josh interrupted. "But did you think that might be on the agenda?"

"Yes, of course it crossed my mind. Anyway, we know this planet is spoken for now."

Aras shifted in his seat, overwhelming it. It must have been uncomfortable for a creature of his size. "And so did the isenj," he said. And then there was silence, as if all of them suddenly shared the view that disasters only happened because people did things without thinking them through.

"So, where do we go from here?" she said briskly, and hoped whatever she had done had not sparked another mis-understanding. Josh poured tea into three opaque glasses with substantial ruby handles and slid them one at a time across the table, followed by a tray of bread rolls. Not an-other meal, surely. Everyone seemed to eat continuously here. Maybe it was the result of hard physical labor. Shan offered the tray to Aras, trying to be polite. He froze again, then reached out and took a roll with a deliberate move. He fixed her with that challenging gaze again. Despite his bulk and manner, there was something oddly comforting about him. It was like having a purring cat on your lap, except that this one could turn and take your head off. But there was definitely an infrasonic emanating from him that made her feel almost peaceful.

"I remind you not to take live samples outside the boundary of Constantine. You can observe what you like, of course, if escorted. I will even provide data on the local ecology."

No, they can't take the crops here. There was the SB again, or at least a realization that sprang from it. *Why?* It wouldn't answer.

With eight payload gagging to get on with their jobs, the prohibition filled her with foreboding. The biotech firms were footing most of the mission's bill. On the other hand, it would be at least seventy-five years before she had to deal with that issue, and by then, who would be left back home to worry about it? Who would even remember the mission? Seventy-five years was a damn long time in commercial life, long enough to see whole empires crumble, let alone companies. No, the immediate problem was offending the indigenous population, and containing eight men and women who had come here to *explore*.

And she had to start talking to this wess'har about the gene bank.

"No specimens or samples," she agreed.

"Not outside the human habitat. Within it is a matter for Joshua."

"We won't be taking crop samples." *Why? No, just trust it.* "And the rest is your planet. We understand that."

"No, it's the bezeri's world, among others," Aras said. "And even though they don't use the land, what happens there affects them. We agreed to help them prevent the isenj taking this world, and the same applies to you. I have read enough of your history. You don't have a good record in new worlds."

If I were you, that's just what I'd be saying. She was growing to like the wess'har. He came straight to the point and he seemed to share her dim view of humanity. And he smelled wonderful.

"So why did you let the colony land here?"

"They had nowhere to go and they would have died." He broke the roll into two pieces and ate a fragment. "And with them, many other people would have died. All those different races of people the ship carried in cryogenic suspension."

"You mean the gene bank. The animals and plants."

"Yes. That's held in safekeeping now. Make no mistake about it—without our intervention to create a local biosphere, the colony would not have been able to grow crops in the soil."

Perault's voice nagged at her. *The gene bank. Secure it.*

"You could have wiped them out and saved yourself a lot of trouble."

"They do no harm. They plan to return to your world one day with those species they've preserved and brought with them. They've kept their word so far."

It was the first confirmation she had heard that the colony was a controlled, enclosed environment, even if it appeared part of the landscape. It answered the question she had tried to ask that first day: How *did* they manage to grow food crops here? It took more than the right light and irrigation to create the right conditions for a plant. It took bacteria and the right balance of minerals and acidity, too.

"You terraformed an area for them? How does that fit in with not interfering with the local ecology?"

"The colony has to be contained in case one of your imports manages to get a foothold and affects the ecology here. The barrier does that. When the colony eventually leaves, we will restore the island."

She thought of the geophys scans that Champciaux had showed her. "Am I right in thinking you've restored rather a lot of this world?" She slid her hand into her pants pocket and pulled out the smartpaper to show him. "All these cities?"

Aras tilted his head, apparently unconcerned. "Yes. All of them."

"Isenj?"

"Yes." He took the smartsheet in his gloved fingers and considered it, expressionless. "We can contain ecosystems. And restore them."

She was getting very straight answers. When interviewing suspects, that meant they wanted to cough to everything. She took the gamble that it worked that way with wess'har too. "And were those cities destroyed by war?"

"If by war you mean planned destruction, yes. For you,

war means army against army, yes? There was no isenj army. Only ours. We erased everything."

Was he apologizing for his nation's record or simply stating fact? It didn't seem to bother him. "Okay," she said. It was like interrogating a psychopath. There wasn't even a hint that he thought it was wrong. "What do you want from us?"

"I expect free access to your camp. And I take it the defenses will be deactivated."

"Already done." He probably had the technology to take what data he wanted anyway; he'd certainly been able to render *Thetis* dead in the water. There was no point trying to keep secrets. "I'll brief my people. You'll be welcome."

"Thank you."

"May I ask you a favor, Aras? Before we leave here, may I meet your people and the aquatic species?"

"The bezeri?"

"Yes. I would like to make contact. I really would."

His eyes were still fixed on hers. It was the sort of body language that would have started a fight back home, but she couldn't imagine anyone being mad enough to take him on, not even her. He was 170 kilos if he was an ounce. "I will ask," he said politely.

The meeting seemed to be over. She finished her tea and took her leave of them, feeling a lot more hopeful than she had the night before. She set off up the slope out of the settlement and began walking back to the base, enjoying the warmth of the sun and the smell of damp earth and grass. There was a real chance she could pull off this mission without disrupting the lives of the colonists.

Gene bank. The SB hadn't given up reminding her about that. What did it want her to do now? From what Aras Sar Iussan had said, it was intact. *Secure it.* Why and how? Perault hadn't banked on wess'har and isenj and the whole shooting match.

There was something else, but it wasn't emerging yet. She let it go.

Aras carefully dusted the crumbs from the table into his hand and let them fall back onto the tray. Shan Frankland was not what he expected. For all the apologies and polite compliance, there was a directness and lack of art that he found unsettlingly . . . wess'har.

"I think she's honest," he said.

Josh topped up his glass of tea. "You thought she was lying."

"She smelled as if she was concealing something. She was, but not her orders. It was her opinion."

"Should we trust her?"

"It's not her you need to be wary of. It's the others."

"I hate to think that we've endangered your interests and our hosts' by leading them here."

"You can't unmake history, Joshua. You're here, and they were coming anyway. I allowed you to stay. I will deal with the consequences."

Aras got up and stretched. All his damaged tissue had been replaced and the *c'naatat* had finished the maintenance of its own biosphere—his body. He wondered what little improvements it had seen fit to include in its latest iteration. It might have improved the impact-absorbing qualities of his skull or his spine; it might have tinkered with his circulation again to deal with sudden blood loss. He would find out in due course.

It had frightened him at first, not knowing where it was taking him from one day to the next, but it seemed to have reached the stage of rearranging details, not grabbing so many fragments of other life-forms' DNA to add to his own. He was almost comfortable with being a world.

Then a ball of white flame rolled down the road towards him, leaving charred buildings in its wake. *Where's my fam-*

ily? He shook the thought away. It hadn't surfaced in a long time.

"I should go," he said. "I need to talk to the bezeri. You'll make sure these scientists don't attempt a sea crossing, won't you? I'll have the security cordon strengthened. One of them is a marine biologist, and that means she'll want a vessel sooner or later."

"I can imagine the consequences if they got hold of *c'naatat.* Leave it to me."

"What would *Shan Chail* make of it, do you think? Would she recoil, like you, or would she see it as a boon to mankind?"

Josh sighed. "We don't fear you, Aras. We never would. But we want to go to God in the end. You do understand that, don't you?"

"I think I do now," Aras said. He took the last roll from the tray and pocketed it. He wanted to change the subject. It pained him to hear Josh explaining why he shouldn't mind being a respected leper. "Do you think *Shan Chail* knew what she was doing when she offered me food?"

Josh laughed, smelling of relief. "I doubt it. Are you going to tell her what it means?"

"Perhaps."

Josh was right. She would be oblivious of the significance of the gesture, just as she probably had no idea that she could exert influence over a wess'har male simply by being strong, aggressive and female. The more time passed, the more he found himself vulnerable to the slightest promise of affection and companionship. It was the one thing the *c'naatat* had not improved.

He wondered briefly if the symbiont was deliberately making him crave contact in order to spread itself to new hosts. It was a common mechanism. The terrestrial *Toxoplasma gondii* made rodents reckless, easier prey for cats, which the parasite depended on to complete its life cycle.

Humans often carried the organism too. If his *c'naatat* had come across the parasite in its endless hunt for bargains among other species' genomes, it might have snapped it up.

Good for *c'naatat*, and no harm to him. But an enormous threat to the ecology of every planet and the balance of every civilization he could conceive of, apart from the restrained wess'har.

Aras climbed the stairs from Josh's house and made his way back up the surface. Respectful nods greeted him. Children gave him shy smiles but kept their distance. He wondered what parents told those children to prompt that degree of caution.

They had little to fear. He'd never known a human to become infected; it might have been due to their fixed genes. They had to reproduce to see any change in characteristics. But wess'har, with their easy exchange of genetic material through copulation, their malleable genome that altered in an individual's own lifetime, were far more susceptible to being colonized. *C'naatat* had gleaned bacteria, shed skin cells and viruses from humans and bolted material onto Aras's receptive wess'har genes just as it had collected fragments from every large host it had passed through.

Including the isenj.

Aras walked along the vanished perimeter of the isenj city once called Mjat and down what had been a main route flanked by houses. There was less than nothing left. But he remembered exactly where it was. He hadn't needed to see the *gethes'* clever images of the ghost of a civilization to recall those roads.

He had destroyed them: it was his command. He had strafed the cities with fire and cut down isenj, and set loose the reclamation *nanites* that devoured the deserted homes. It had been nearly five hundred years ago by the Constantine calendar, but he remembered it all.

Isenj, spreading faster and farther than ever before

thanks to c'naatat. *Thousands of them, living indefinitely, their cities spreading by meters each hour. Pollution diffusing into the seas, killing millions of bezeri. From the air, not a single patch of the blue and amber grassland left on the chain of islands. Desolation within one planetary year. If he didn't stop it here, and now, every world within reach of the isenj would suffer the same fate.*

If the isenj had heeded the warning and left Bezer'ej before they stumbled across the *c'naatat* themselves, there would have been no need to slaughter them. Once a few had been infected, it spread like mold on the humans' bread.

He shut his eyes for a moment. Was this guilt? Ben had talked about the human concept of guilt, and Aras had never quite grasped it. No, he would do the same again. He would do it without pity but without anger. It was necessary.

A ball of white flame bowling down the street, sucking air with it. The deafening shrills of dying isenj. A sense of panic and hatred. Where is my family? Hiding under a collapsed door, too terrified to come out and see the charred bodies.

He was seeing through isenj eyes now. It was not empathy. It was real. It was a memory.

There were delights the *c'naatat* had given him, but they were far outnumbered by the agonies. Endowing him with genetic memory scavenged from an isenj was one of the worst.

It was hard to live with your victim in your head.

14

This place is just astonishing. We had an eclipse today and nobody thought to tell us it was coming. Isn't that something? We all stood out in the compound and went crazy. I think we went crazier than the payload. I got a picture, but then I remembered there's nobody I know left to send it to. It got to me then. We keep going when we're on a deployment because there's a normal world to fight for and return to. Without that, it's getting harder to focus on the job.

MARINE BALWANT SINGH CHAHAL,
from his private journal

There was one general-use laser uplink to *Thetis* and Paretti was hogging it. Rayat was making his displeasure clear.

Eddie thought that had started the slanging match in the comms room. He could hear it even in the compound. He wandered in, preparing to referee, because he wanted them both off the link as soon as possible so he could file his latest piece. Time didn't actually matter. The data sat in a buffer until *Thetis* was in line of sight to receive the datastream and—more importantly—until Shan Frankland had cleared it to go. But it didn't feel that way.

"You've been through my data, you bastard. Don't deny it." Paretti was sitting in the chair and Rayat was leaning over him, hand braced on the table. But it was Paretti who was making the accusations. When they noticed Eddie was standing in the hatchway they paused, looked right through him and carried on.

Rayat put his other hand on the table. "What would I want your data for? Not even *close* to my areas of research."

"And Warrenders wouldn't be interested, *of course.*"

"Hey—"

"This is a spoiler. You're giving my data to your employer—"

Eddie banged the heel of his hand on the hatch. "Lads, I hate to interrupt, but can you take this outside? Please. Don't make me fetch the Iron Lady."

Rayat didn't seem worried by the prospect of summoning Shan. "Good idea," he said to Paretti. "She's supposed to be clearing all the transmissions. She'll be able to show you that I haven't accessed your bloody files." He pushed past Eddie.

Paretti, slightly chubby, middle-aged with prematurely gray curls, looked like a cherub who wasn't aging gracefully. He scowled at Eddie.

"Hey, don't take it out on me. . . . what's he done this time?" asked Eddie. Well, it might be a story, and it might not, and anyway he liked Paretti a lot more than he liked Rayat. "Can I ask?"

"Someone had a poke around my data and it's probably him."

"Why would he do that?"

"Because he works for Warrenders and he's on a very meaty bonus scheme. He'll get five percent of any profit made from the data here. What do you think that's going to be worth when he steps on the Tarmac in seventy-five years' time?"

"But you're from different disciplines."

"And if he's on the same deal as I am, which he probably is, he'll get a flat bonus of a million euros for anything he can get hold of that will block HSL or Carmody-Holbein-Lang from patenting anything *I* discover here. Spoiler."

The concept of ruining someone else's exclusive was not unfamiliar to Eddie; journalists did it all the time. It was part of the grand game. But the sums involved were usually much, much smaller. "I picked the wrong subjects at school, obviously," he said.

"That'll teach you to sneer at the nerds."

"So, it's test tubes at fifty paces, then?"

"It's not funny, Eddie. I gave up my whole life to get here. I left behind everyone and everything for this."

So did we all. Perhaps scientists had hearts after all, thought Eddie. He was so caught up in the thrill of novelty that he really didn't miss anyone or anything yet. His life was one of transmission, not reception.

Whump, whump, whump. He knew those boots by now. Shan appeared in the hatchway, winked at Eddie and sat on the edge of the table. "All right, Vani. Give me one excuse to give Rayat a serious smacking. You know I want to."

"I think he's doing a spoiler on my data."

"I so love working alongside Warrenders." She gave Paretti what looked like a genuine smile. "But I've also had occasion to visit your employers at HSL. You know what I think? You're all scumbags, equal under the law."

"You know how much Rayat is on if he screws us?"

"I'd heard. It's not illegal. It's childish, selfish, wasteful of resources and ultimately stops the public benefiting from your discoveries at a reasonable price, but it's not against the law."

"What if I kick seven shades of shit out of him?"

Shan shrugged. "I might be too busy to notice."

"I'm serious, Superintendent. This is industrial espionage."

"No, it's not. Try breaking his fingers. It used to work fine for me."

She stood up and walked back out. Paretti ran his fingers through his unkempt curls and began loading his data. "Ten minutes," he said, without looking at Eddie. "Don't breathe down my neck."

Out in the compound, Rayat was remonstrating with

Shan. Eddie thought she was in a pretty good mood today. He stood and watched, as did Webster and Chahal. Rayat was demanding that she do something about Paretti's allegations.

"Why?" Shan asked. Lindsay emerged from the mess hall; Bennett stopped to join the audience too.

"He's impugned my professional reputation."

"Come on, we're twenty-five light-years from anyone who gives a toss."

"So you're not going to do anything?"

"Well, now you come to mention it, I think I will. You know what? I'm going to let you all have the same privilege as me and take a look at each other's data before it's transmitted. How's that?"

"You can't do that."

"I can. Fair's fair."

"My company paid for this mission."

Shan glanced at Eddie. "Is that so, Mr. Michallat?"

Eddie checked his database and stuck it back in his pocket. "My original report quoted twenty percent of the total cost."

Shan looked off to one side as if she were calculating and walked over to speak to Chahal. He disappeared into the passageway and came back with a laser cutter and handed it to her. "Mind your fingers, ma'am," he called after her. She walked back into the crew quarters.

Rayat looked as puzzled as the rest of them. Eddie was half-expecting to see her emerge with a mangled uplink module, sliced apart to teach them all a lesson, but he could still hear Paretti talking to the AI on board *Thetis*. Two minutes later, Shan came back with an armful of what looked like rubbish and broken furniture and beckoned to Rayat.

"There," she said. "One-fifth of your desk." She dumped a tray-sized slab of composite at his feet. "A fifth of your chair." Two chair legs followed. "And your mattress, your coffee mug and your plate." Pieces fluttered and clattered to the ground. Rayat simply stared at her; Webster was chewing at her lower lip in a vain attempt not to laugh. "And as soon as it's practical, I'll get you the aft section of *Thetis* and you can be on your way. Now shut up and get on with it."

Eddie badly wanted to applaud but thought better of it. Rayat was still standing and staring down at the pile of debris long after Shan had disappeared into the mess hall and Webster had fled, no doubt to guffaw in private.

Eddie followed Shan inside. "I hate to think what you're like after a few drinks," he said.

Shan gave him a smile as she helped herself to some tea from the dispenser. He had a feeling that was exactly the effect she had intended. "One reason why I very rarely touch the stuff."

"Is this about Mars Orbital?"

"No, it's nothing to do with Warrenders. I just hate whiny people, and Rayat never stops." And she laughed. It was genuine amusement, totally artless. "I don't know what came over me."

Of course she did. He didn't believe that any more than he believed that a copper with her record—decorated for valor, head of a snatch team, fast-tracked in the Serious Fraud Office—could misplace a bunch of terrorists after a massive covert operation. History was full of police cockups, but he hadn't believed the story then, and he certainly didn't believe it now that he had met her. For all the apparent caprice, she wasn't someone who left anything to chance.

He thought he knew why, too. Or at least partly why, and the partly bit was eating at him in the way concealed things always did.

"It would be great to do an interview with you," he said.

"I don't think I'll be of interest to your subscribers in twenty-five years' time, Eddie."

"Not even about Green Rage?"

She didn't even blink. "Maybe some other time. I think I've been humiliated enough over that."

"Yeah. Right." He turned to go. She hadn't blown him off completely, and he had every intention of returning to the topic at that *some other time.* "I happen to have a copy of your service record from the BBChan internal database. Do you mind if I share it with the rest of the mission?"

"Why?" A faint hint of acid there: perhaps she thought he was trying to lean on her.

"When they ask who the hell you are, I'd like them to know."

"You could have done that any time."

"I wanted to clear it with you first."

She smiled. She could have taken it as a gesture of genuine courtesy. Or she could have thought that he was kissing arse, and that he knew he was, and that it was all a reflective game of we-both-know-what-we're-up-to.

He meant it as a courtesy. He hoped she knew that.

Aras had made a promise, so he kept it. The bezeri said they would prefer to look at the new ones from a safe distance first. It wasn't that they didn't trust him, they said. They were just concerned. He came to the edge of the camp and looked at the soldiers for the first time, and noted how they stood stock-still as he passed and stared at him. The encampment was a very visible thing, an insult to the landscape, but these people would not be staying long enough to warrant digging down into the rock to house them. Like the first human landing, when the bots came to the last habitat of *c'naatat,* it was just a campsite that could be swept away or moved when it was necessary.

There were males and females in utilitarian dark grays, greens and blues, and all wearing trousers. When he passed them they greeted him nervously. Shan had warned him

none of them had seen an intelligent alien before, a reminder—if he needed one—that they were singularly blind
to all the other nonhumans they had encountered in their
lives. He returned the greetings with a polite nod.

Shan didn't talk much. She followed him in silence to the
shore, laboring for breath, but she managed to keep up with
him despite the length of the walk. She struggled after him up
an outcrop of black rock to get a better view of the shallows.

There was enough cloud cover today for them to see the
shapes and lights very clearly. Dozens of bezeri, rippling
with the color patterns of the seniors, moved slowly around
the shadows, trailing long tentacles.

Silence. And then it was as if she had suddenly spotted
them for the first time.

"Oh my. The lights."

"Can you see the shapes?"

"Oh yes."

"That's what you might call the bezeri council."

"What are they?" Shan asked. She slid down off the rock
and walked slowly down the beach. "Squid?"

She was looking out to sea, hands thrust deep in her
pockets while the wind whipped her black hair about. She
wore it pulled back in a tail; it would have made more sense
to braid it, but perhaps she didn't know how. An odd human, intense and aggressive, frequently distracted by things
he couldn't see but that she seemed to. And her scents normally matched her words and expressions; when they
didn't, he could tell it was a huge strain for her to lie.

She pointed out into the shallows at dark clouds of
movement and the occasional ripple of light. "You've read
about squid, have you? You know what I mean?"

"Not squid, of course," he said. "But anatomically
they're cephalopods, for want of a better word. That's what
their environment makes them—and like many of your marine species, they communicate by light and color."

She raised her hand tentatively and waved. "In the absence of light, I hope they understand this."

Aras took the azin map from his pack and held it out for her to see. He thought she would appreciate it. She took it carefully in her hands, almost as if she were aware of its fragility and rarity, and examined it.

"It's an ancient bezeri map of their western continental shelf."

"They make maps?"

"Yes. These are just the visual maps, of course, not the olfactory ones. They're updated all the time."

"I just didn't have any idea that an aquatic species would make things."

"They were equally surprised that intelligent technological species could live in an air void."

Shan seemed mesmerized by the shell map. She traced the contour lines with her fingertip. For a second Aras thought she was a child he could teach.

"What does it show?"

"Home territories, depths." Aras persisted. "Do humans now consider squid intelligent?"

"As we still eat them, I'd say not."

"Do *you* eat them?"

"No, I don't. Never have." She looked and smelled agitated, but she was telling the truth. He couldn't smell the flat, bitter odors of dead flesh on her skin like he could on the rest of the *gethes*. They repelled him. Rockvelvets ate body tissues too, but they had no other choice. "I don't think you should eat anything you're not prepared to kill yourself."

"So if *gethes* don't eat what's intelligent, where do you draw the line between prey and non-prey? And how do you tell?"

"*Gethes*? What does that mean?"

"Carrion eater."

"Oh." She shrugged. "Probably anything that hasn't got a vote."

"Do you eat unintelligent humans?"

"No. And before you ask, yes, we do eat meat because we can, not because we need to." The black part of her eyes was a lot larger now and he could smell that scent that was part anger, part excitement. She didn't break her gaze and look away, as the colony women did. *This* was a real matri-arch. "Anyway, what sort of society do these bezeri have?"

"Communal, like yours."

"Are they spacefaring?"

"They think they are."

"Not quite with you on that one."

Aras gestured along the beach. "This is the limit of their atmosphere. They try to breach it from time to time." He beckoned her to follow and walked along the shore, hearing her gasping for breath behind him but still managing to keep up. "Look."

There was a large perfectly spherical stone on the shore at the high-water line, set with intricate patterns of inlaid color. Shan squatted down beside it and examined its smoothness with her hand. It seemed to impress her. She craned her neck to look up at him, still balancing in a crouch. "What is it?"

"This is the Place of Memory of the First," said Aras. "It marks the spot where the first bezeri pilot beached himself to gather information about the Dry Above, which is what they call anything that isn't sea."

"Is this script?" She ran a cautious fingertip over the spots of colored shell and stone, as if she understood it was something to be respected. "What does it say?"

"It says that here the nineteenth of the shoal of Ehek launched himself out of the water and told the waiting ones all he could see of the Dry Above before he died an honor-able death."

"He died?"

"At that time their pods had only enough power to propel themselves out of the water."

"And he knew that?"

"Yes. It was what you call a suicide mission."

She was silent for a while and he couldn't work out what she was imagining. "What happened after that?"

"They developed bigger pod ships with secondary water jets that allowed them to push themselves back into the sea." Aras walked a few meters down the beach and patted another large stone memorial, this time a conical one with lines of color spiraling down its sides. "This is the Place of Memory of the Returned. I expect you can work that out for yourself."

Shan spent a long time touching the spherical stone, as if a dead bezeri was more intriguing to her than one who made it back. He was getting impatient for a meal, but she was a matriarch, and—*gethes* or not—his instinct of deference to a dominant female was hard to override. She confused him. One moment she was *isanket*, a little female, an amazed child, and the next she was an *isan* clearly comfortable with the authority of her gender. He had neither *isan* nor children. She stirred needs in him that he thought he had buried under the years.

He was still hungry, though. "The Dry Above is like deep space to them, a realm of risk," he said, and wished she would follow his lead and start walking back to the settlement. "Apart from some scientific interest, the majority of bezeri have no more interest in finding ways of colonizing the Dry Above than humans have of living under water."

"Or in space," said Shan. "How did you come across them?"

"Sometimes we could see their light in the sea from Wess'ej. We didn't know it came from people until we landed here. Then we noticed bezeri beaching themselves.

It was very distressing. It took us many, many years to work out what they were signaling, and that they were trying to attract our attention."

"You assumed they were communicating, though?" A sudden sharp whiff of anxiety rolled off her. What had upset her? "You tried to work out what they were asking?"

"Of course. And once we had established a common set of signals, the bezeri could ask for our help. When the isenj came, they asked us to intervene."

"So you removed them." There was no hint of outrage in her tone. "The hard way."

"We asked them to leave because they were destroying this world. Millions of bezeri died from their pollution. The marine ecosystem is very fragile. I thought that would be something *gethes* understood from experience."

"I'm suitably chastened."

"The isenj breed fast. They've spread across their own world and its moon. But not here." *Not any longer.* "They are excluded."

"Now we're getting into areas I understand. Territorial ambitions. Fine."

"I doubt you do understand, *Shan Chail*." He regretted his honesty instantly. He should have let her think that the wess'har were driven by petty political ambition. But he wanted her to think well of him; it was a moment of stupidity. She missed very little. The *isanket* gave way to an *isan* used to getting answers.

"Then explain to me. Because this is what's going to happen to us if we're not careful, isn't it?"

"There are . . . unique aspects of this world that make it both vulnerable and dangerous, and we will, I promise you, do whatever it takes to prevent incursions here. By anyone."

"I'm not criticizing you for that."

"I don't want to answer any more questions."

She eased herself upright as if it hurt and rubbed her

knees, which made alarming cracking sounds. She just stared into his eyes. He couldn't pick up any scent that would give him a hint of her state of mind, and she didn't say anything. A wave broke close to her boots but she didn't move.

Shan finally shrugged and looked back out to sea for a few moments. "I'm not interrogating you, Aras." She put her hand out as if to touch his arm and he shied away, forcing a scent of embarrassment from her. She pushed her hands deep in the pockets of her jacket. "I'm sorry. You drew away before. If I've broken some taboo, I really didn't mean any offense."

Why did she have to say that? This was the first person who actually wanted to touch him in many, many years. Wess'har were not built to lie. Not even his acquired human characteristics had changed that.

"I'm not rebuffing you. I have a kind of disease."

"Can I catch it?"

"Unlikely."

"If I do, will it kill me?"

"No." Oh, that much was true. It was almost too true.

"You don't like being a pariah, do you?"

Aras had never met a human above the age of six who was as direct, as brutal as that. Shan Frankland was definitely a different *gethes.* Did she know? How could she? "Explain," he said.

"I've seen how Josh avoided touching you when you crashed, and he seemed ashamed of it. You almost shook my hand and stopped. It's not really you that doesn't want contact, is it? And Josh knows it hurts you."

"You notice very small details indeed."

"It's my job. It tells me a lot." She was still staring into his face, direct as any wess'har. "So?"

"It's unpleasant to have this condition. I live with the fear it produces in others."

And she took one hand from her pocket and touched him. It was nothing extraordinary. It was just a casual, familiar squeeze on his upper arm, done with as much simple ease as the colonists did to each other. This was the first time anyone had really touched him voluntarily since Benjamin Garrod had tried to comfort him nearly 170 years ago. She held the grip for five seconds; if she had held it forever, it would not have been long enough.

He hoped that his shock and confusion didn't show. He would not have been able to explain.

"Well, I'm not afraid of you or your illness," she said. "And I'm not your enemy, and I'm not here to pillage your planet, and what you get up to with the isenj is your business. I aim to finish my job and go home with minimum disruption to either of us."

"And what is your job?"

"I'm not entirely sure yet. Have you heard of Suppressed Briefing?" She turned and linked her arm through his, and began walking him back to Constantine, as if they had a friendship that had mellowed into complete familiarity over a long period of time. He was too surprised to wrench his arm away. "Well, this is how it works . . ."

He tried to concentrate on what she was saying. It wasn't easy. The thought that kept jostling for his attention while he tried to take in talk of sub-Qs and stoppers was that, for once, somebody was not frightened or repelled by him.

She almost certainly didn't know what his condition was. If she did, her motivation for contact might have been purely commercial. But for those few moments he had connected with someone again, and he didn't care.

15

Frankland has had a number of contacts with one of the alien species—the wess'har—but we've had no opportunity to talk to them directly ourselves. She simply passes on the odd detail. You can understand how frustrating this is for a biologist. It's like trying to catalog the species in a rain forest by talking to a tourist.

LOUISE GALVIN, xenozoologist,
note appended to her working-hours log

Constantine's school occupied a whole wing of the underground complex. Shan looked for a door to knock, but there was none. She stepped into a bright chamber full of tables and screens, like something out of a history book, where small children were gazing raptly at a woman demonstrating the formation of clouds in 3D. Two kids turned round and gaped at her for a few seconds, then turned back to the infinitely more fascinating spectacle in front of them.

"Don't mind me," said Shan, and wandered round the room, examining the drawings and pictures on the wall. There were Last Suppers and Annunciations and Partings of the Red Sea, lovingly rendered in shaky hands or in confident but eccentric brushstrokes. There were also strange and largely unidentifiable things that Shan thought probably illustrated some of the local wildlife. And there were pictures of a large and alien biped, which were clearly Aras.

"Sweet," she muttered, and turned to watch the class. It was amazing how little she found she knew about clouds. The lunch bell sounded—wavering, plaintive glass notes again—and she was caught swimming against a steady tide of children ebbing out the door.

"Well-behaved little lot, aren't they?" said Shan, recalling kids the same age with bottles and knives, years and worlds away.

"They learn responsibility early," said the teacher. "We have to be responsible for each other." She tied her hair up in a scarf and rolled up her sleeves. "Did you want something?"

"Josh said this was a good place to learn the history of Constantine," said Shan. "May I have the files?"

She held out her swiss. It was old technology, the sort they understood. Nobody had the time or inclination to develop information tech here, seeing as everyone lived within walking distance of each other and there were no other settlements with which to communicate. The technology that supported the swiss did just fine. The teacher inserted it into the data port on the console, letting it swallow text and pictures for Shan to read at her leisure. Then she handed it back and made it politely clear she was going to show Shan the way out of the complex.

It was a fine clear day with a scattering of thin, high clouds, and Shan collected a pack of dry rations from the base camp to eat while reading the data on her swiss.

The history had been written for children, but that didn't offend her. She knew that someone had recorded somewhere every dot and whistle of the crop yields, council meetings and climate, but what she needed right then was something geared to a child's simplicity.

There were pictures of people digging and planting, and pushing barrows of stone and soil from tunnels. And there was Ben Garrod, thin and smiling, standing in front of one of the first crops of soy, beets and potatoes. It had been a hard few years after the colonists landed, a struggle to keep strains of yeast alive and keep the bots functioning, and only the intervention of a race who already lived in the land—described in the history as a miracle, proof of their righteous purpose—kept them from disaster.

Shan was not much given to appreciating miracles other than the kind that involved ballistics missing major blood vessels. And there were no miracles here. The humans were wildlife in a reserve, preserved as much for the future of the non-human species they brought with them as for their own sake.

Shan considered all the colonies on earth that had survived pretty well without a scrap of righteousness to justify their existence. All colonies seemed to thrive on delusion, whether that was how good the new world was, how much better the old country had been, or how much right they had to do what they were doing. Kids needed to be told harsh truths.

She was scanning through the early history when a word caught her eye.

The word was "Aras."

For a moment she wondered if the files were not in chronological order, and she checked more out of habit than curiosity. But they were indeed ordered, and the dates they referred to were more than 150 years ago. And still they referred to Aras.

Her first rationalization was that Aras was a generic name for the wess'har. Then she rethought the premise. Could he be that old? There was nothing to say that human life-spans were the norm. In fact, that wasn't even true of Earth species, so why should an alien not be centuries old? Nevertheless the thought gripped her, and for some reason she began to worry that the wess'har might suddenly become very interesting to the life-sciences people. She decided not to say anything until she had checked out the facts.

She flicked through pictures at high speed. They were mostly of people, with an occasional shot of the fields, and every imaginable view of the building of St. Francis Church. She enlarged the shot and admired the inventive approach to scaffolding they had used when they built the vaulted ceiling. And then she spotted a creature she didn't recognize in the background of one of the frames.

It was hard to see, but it looked bipedal. It was the height of a man and had what looked like a long, tapering muzzle, nothing like the solid and broad Aras. Was this an isenj? Was this the species they wouldn't now allow on the planet? And if it was, why had they accepted its company while they were building the church?

Nothing here was going to be simple, she decided. She stood up, dusted down her trousers and began walking back to the settlement.

She had to pass the open hatchway to the marines' quarters on the way back to her cabin. Words wafted out in an indistinct buzz, and she wasn't listening, but then a few words leaped out with sudden clarity. "You're bloody sweet on her," said Barencoin's voice, teasing.

"Piss off," said a voice she recognized as Bennett's. "I don't want to hear that again."

Shame, Shan thought. But she smiled anyway.

Eddie stepped into the tiny alcove in his cabin that was both toilet and shower and tried to freshen up. Expecting extreme conditions, the designers had allowed for two liters of water per shower. On the six-week familiarization program, granite-faced Royal Marine Color Sergeant Durcan had demonstrated how to cleanse the entire body, hair included, with the artful use of a substantial sponge and the minimum of water. They could, said the Color Sergeant, have done it with a plain pint, but as they were bloody soft civilians, they could have nearly four to lavish on themselves. He wasn't a man who dealt in liters. Eddie was glad he hadn't actually trained with the marines as his editor had suggested. The personal hygiene was tough enough.

So the system was set up for two liters of water, even though there was plenty of fresh water on tap, thanks to the colony's borrowed pipeline. Eddie resolved to find one of the engineer-trained marines, maybe that nice Susan Webster, and persuade them to adjust his shower.

By the time he made it to the mess area, everyone was eating. Rayat sidled up to him while he tried to decide if the reconstituted egg would make him want to throw up again.

"You're going off camp this morning?" he asked, very quietly.

"Certainly am, Doc. First foray."

"You're the only person Frankland is letting out unescorted."

"That's because I won't stray too far. And I only take pictures."

Rayat lowered his voice still further. "If you were to come back with a few leaves stuck to your boots, you would let me know, wouldn't you? I wouldn't be ungrateful."

Eddie looked him in the eye. "Don't even ask. I'm not interested."

Eddie wondered how long it would be before another member of the payload—and he wasn't payload, of course—asked him to sneak something back into camp. Shan would suspect they would ask, and he didn't want to be grounded with the rest of them. Anyway, it was wrong. The rules had been spelled out to them. And he thought of those obliterated buildings and roads and isenj whose only memorial was a geophys scan of ghosts.

He wanted very badly to know what the isenj looked like and who they were. But there was enough to occupy him while he waited for that opportunity to present itself.

Eddie collected his kit and walked with difficulty out to the perimeter of the colony on the east side, to where he could stand in farmland and yet have a backdrop of orange trees and lavender undergrowth. The hike was agony. He didn't care. He set his camera to follow him, and it hovered behind him like a large tame bee.

"Tight mid-shot and pull out on *but behind me*," he told it. He checked the shot on his handheld screen and moved a few meters to the right. That was better.

"This may look like a chaotic cottage garden, a piece of land planted with some everyday crops," he began. "But behind me, there is nothing remotely everyday about the landscape." He paused for breath. "This is the second planet from Cavanagh's Star, CS2, a planet so like Earth as to enable me to stand upright and breathe its air. Yes, I'm puffing a little, because that air isn't as rich in oxygen, and the gravity is slightly higher than we're accustomed to—but this *is* the nearest place to home that humans have found. And here is where an international group of devout Christians has built a colony, against all the odds. It's also a planet with a violent history, a history of wars that wiped out whole cities . . ."

He wasn't at his slick best today, he knew that. He could tidy it up later in editing. It was a long time since he'd recorded anything that wasn't live. Out here, not being fast didn't matter. There was nobody else to beat him to air, nobody to scoop him. The luxury was so heady that he almost laughed out loud. He had a new world to himself. Sod Wiley, and sod the networks: whatever was happening Earthside when his transmission finally reached home, he would still be the first man to report from the surface of Cavanagh's Star II.

He rounded up the camera and reattached it to his headset, turning round slowly to work out the best angle. The orange pineapple-shaped trees were stunning. If anything said alien world, they did. Great flapping sheets of clear stuff flew at a majestic pace between them. What the hell were they? He recorded some voice-over expressing just that sentiment, and then thought about laying down a more scientific commentary later.

By the time he got back to his cabin, he was uncertain whether his priority was to die quickly of his headache or to eat until he burst. All his body's balances were still in disarray. *Tired,* it said. *Eat, lie down, sleep.* He ignored it and set up his edit suite.

Suite was a grand term for it. The screen was a sheet of polymer 20 cm by 15 cm, easy to tack to a wall or spread on a table or lap. Eddie pulled down the flap set in the wall to accommodate a workstation and set the screen to a 45-degree angle, then pointed the bee cam at it and transferred the morning's footage. Things somehow looked more real to him on screen than they did in the flesh.

He already had the shape of the piece in his mind before he shot it. Now he tried the shots together, cutting, fading, deciding where the hypercaps would go, and then wondering how he was going to capture all that second-layer data from a system as archaic as Constantine's. He could have made up all the background if it came to it, but he had his pride. This wasn't just news. This was history. There were duties involved.

And there was another thing missing. The native inhabitants must have had a name for the planet. Cavanagh's Star II, CS2, was a geek's designation, not a world, not a place on a map. He wanted something that would capture the essence of the place. Maybe Aras the Alien would oblige.

The piece was running at nearly three minutes. He'd wanted to get that sub-menu in about the vanished city of the isenj. But maybe that could wait along with the geophys scans Champciaux was dithering over letting him transmit for "copyright reasons"—as if anyone was going to care who had breached it when they finally got back.

It was still too speculative, anyway. And it added forty-five seconds to a three-minute piece, a tad weighty by BBChan standards. So what? Nobody else was going to get the whole story before him. He cut it and dumped it in the gash file.

16

MEMO TO: Supt. FRANKLAND
FROM: Dr. M. RAYAT

I feel it is unwise to continue to allow Aras free access to the camp. I returned yesterday to find him in the clean room emptying the cryo store, and he has removed all the embryos and the stored rats. When I challenged him he became quite aggressive and lectured me on the abuse of other life-forms. While I admire his fluency, I must protest at this unwarranted interference with my work.

Lindsay sat with Shan in the deserted mess hall, driven into the public areas by the sheer confinement of a cabin. The payload were out and about with their escorts. A cube of a room was no place for a meeting, not when you could look out of the front door and see a blue plain that stretched forever. It was a very large island indeed.

"Can't Rayat come and see me in person?" Shan said, and turned the swiss's screen so that Lindsay could read the memo. "If I'd known he had animals in that box of tricks of his, I'd have smacked him one. He knows the rules here. What does he need rats for anyway? Don't we have tissue-virtuality modeling?"

Lindsay sat with carefully clasped hands on the table in front of her. "I gather it's a backup. In case the virtuality is inconclusive."

"He's a wanker."

"Right with you there, ma'am." The two women looked at each other for a moment, locked in a brief but elusive moment of common purpose. "I say we should let Aras smack him one, as you put it."

"So he took the rats."

"Yes. In a packing crate. I didn't think stopping him would be appropriate. Or possible."

"Yeah, he's a big lad. Has it upset the other payload?"

"Parekh was a little concerned, but she said she thought Rayat had it coming anyway. I wouldn't worry."

The brief camaraderie brought on by the unlovable Rayat stalled. Lindsay sat with hands folded and waited in silence. It was as good a time as any.

"We got off to a rotten start, I think," said Shan, conciliatory and not meaning a word of it. "I know it must have been a hell of a shock to wake up and find me aboard. I wouldn't have taken it any better than you. I'm sorry." It was a cheap, easy word. She couldn't understand why so many people couldn't use it.

Lindsay looked down at the tabletop as if taking her eyes from it would undo the fabric of the universe. "I didn't help matters any by getting pregnant. But you're quite a . . . quite a presence to adjust to."

"I'm a complete bastard and I'm entirely comfortable with that. But I do get the job done."

"I've never wanted to throttle anyone so much in my life."

"Not even Rayat?"

Lindsay laughed uncomfortably. "He's quite a uniting influence. That was a nice touch, sorting him and Paretti out. I learned a lot from that."

"But more chief petty officer than commissioned rank, eh?" *Might as well lance all the boils*, Shan thought. "Not what they taught you at the academy."

"I think that's why the booties like you. You can be one of the lads too. I don't think I'll ever be able to."

"Not appropriate for a naval officer. Compulsory for a copper, any rank. Saying *fuck* occasionally does help."

Lindsay's thaw was turning into a flood. "I've got some of Eddie's home brew. Want to try some?" She got up and took a five-liter water container from under the galley sink, and Shan wondered if she should have helped her carry it given her condition. But she didn't. When Lindsay opened the cap, a yeasty sweet aroma wafted up.

She poured the liquid into shatterproofs. "He's getting better at it. This batch is almost transparent."

Shan held it up to the light. Alcohol was a sign of weakness, but Eddie's beer seemed to have a high fiber content, so she relented and touched glasses with Lindsay in a grim toast.

"Should you be drinking this in your condition?"

Lindsay rubbed her belly fondly. "Kris says a little never hurts. And I think you could describe this stuff as self-limiting." She gave her a sad smile. "There was a time when I thought you were just civilian ballast on this mission, but I was wrong. I apologize."

"Don't confuse the art of damage limitation with professional competence. But thanks."

"We're in a tight spot, aren't we?"

"Yes, but we're going home in a while. In one piece, too."

"I believe you," said Lindsay. She topped up the shatterproof and there was a telltale *slop* as a large and unidentified lump slipped out of the container. Shan hesitated and let it sink to the bottom, with no intention of actually drinking more than a few sips. "I think that's what I'm saying, really. We—the detachment and I—trust you. We feel we can rely on you."

Poor Lindsay: she meant it sincerely and she clearly thought she was expressing solidarity. But it made Shan's stomach churn. It was a degree of faith she didn't want to inspire. She felt suddenly angry, and wanted to tell them all to sod off and take care of themselves instead of burdening her with their welfare. She'd never had anyone to make it all right, not her self-centered absent mother nor her day-dreaming, idealistic and ultimately useless father, nor anyone except maybe her first sergeant when she was a probationer fresh out of conscription.

I'm fed up being the only adult around, she thought. *I want to be looked after for once.* Her resentment threatened to erupt with a force magnified by a lifetime of suppression.

She swallowed it again. "I'll try not to let you down," she said.

Josh wasn't at home. Shan skipped her usual courtesy call and headed for the next nearest center of authority in the colony, the school.

"I'm looking for Josh or Aras," she said to the first adult she could find. The woman was sweeping down the banked steps of a lecture theater that were cut into the rock. "Sorry to barge in unannounced."

The woman looked unconcerned and consulted the ancient console in front of the desk. "Second room on your left, that way," she said, and went back to her cleaning. "Quite a popular venue today, I think."

Shan could hear and feel Aras's voice before she reached the room, but nothing more. She was surprised to find herself face-to-face with at least fifty children. They were all gathered round a table in the center of the classroom, listening in perfect silence to Aras explaining the antics of a dozen or so rats that were zipping up and down the surface and pausing from time to time to stand on hind legs and sniff the air.

The kids were transfixed. Their community held the most complete species gene bank Earth had assembled, and yet none of them had ever seen a live creature from their homeworld other than insects. To them, a rat was as magical as a unicorn.

Aras looked up at her and beckoned her in. He cradled a beige rat in his hands and held it for a little girl to touch. The child hesitated, then placed two cautious fingers on the animal's back. It turned to sniff her hand. She giggled.

"Very cute," said Shan. "Sorry about Rayat. Maybe we can discuss that later."

"I've asked the children to care for some of these people and I will look after the others."

"I'm sure ratkind will thank you for that."

Aras seemed to see no humor in the comment. He turned to the children. "I'll be back to check you're caring for them properly," he said, and it was clear his word carried even greater weight than any human adult. The kids nodded solemnly. "Remember, keep them safe. Don't let them out where the handhawks can get them."

Shan walked slowly back up the corridor, arms folded. Aras caught up with her, exuding that elusive sandalwood scent.

"So, are you here to ask me to keep out of your compound?"

"No. Fine by me. I said you were welcome any time, and Rayat knew the rules."

Aras opened his tunic a little and two whiskered faces, one black, one white, popped out and stared at her. "Aren't they wonderful? They have little human hands. Look." He placed a gloved finger under one of the rat's paws. Shan didn't want to think about hands that weren't human: she could see that gorilla again. *Help me, help me please.* She shook it away.

Aras twitched his finger and the rat gripped his glove. "See? Almost a thumb. I've named them Black and White for the time being—I've no idea how they identify themselves."

"You know what Rayat was going to do with them, don't you?" It might have been a test of her attitude. Josh had advised total honesty, and right then it seemed completely obvious to act as an apologist. "One of those little ironies in the word 'humane.'"

"Yes, I know only too well. You think they're disposable. Vermin."

"The only vermin I know has two legs."

"Josh said you would say that."

"Well, everyone knows my every thought. What you see is what you get."

At earlier meetings, Aras had seemed in complete and quiet control, almost intimidating. Now he appeared to drop his guard. He was distracted. "We don't intrude on other races."

That explained why he called them people. His English was certainly good enough for that not to have been a slip of the tongue. She found it inexplicably touching and fought down a blush of embarrassment. Black scrambled back inside Aras's tunic. "They seem to like you."

"I like them."

"May we talk later? Just general stuff."

"More questions? You as well as Eddie?"

"I'd like to know more about wess'har, that's all."

He paused, two rats folded to his chest. White was cleaning its face as if sitting in the arms of an alien was a perfectly natural place for a rodent to be. "Very well."

"May I ask you a very personal question?" If she was about to break another taboo, she would find out the hard way. "How old are you?"

"Old."

"Am I right if I say well over two hundred years?"

"Yes." No hesitation—but he was suddenly frozen still again. "You're correct."

So he was the Aras of the history books. She'd make

sure those history files were off limits to the payload. "Let's keep that to ourselves, shall we? I don't like the idea of the Rayats of this world becoming interested in your longevity. You're not dealing with colonists here." She waited a beat and risked another question, the one that had really been gnawing away at her. "And who is the alien in the construction pictures? It's not a wess'har."

He stood very still again, a posture she was starting to interpret as being startled. The diplomatic ice was thin, and she wondered if she had really fallen through this time.

"I'll explain later," he said.

"Okay." *Leave it, leave it.* She needed him to take her to the gene bank and pushing him wasn't the way to build trust. "And we never had this conversation, right?"

"That's thoughtful of you. Join me in an hour. I'll show you the rest of the island if you want to learn."

Right call, then. Aras seemed not to bear grudges. It was just as well. Shan suspected she had a festering sore of resentment developing among the researchers, and Rayat made it clear where he thought her responsibilities lay. At least the marines understood it was insane to provoke a powerful alien authority on their home ground. But she wasn't going to make the mistake of going native this time.

She had to work round to asking Aras to show her the gene bank. Then the Suppressed Briefing would tell her what she had to do next.

Shan stood at the highest point of the island and caught her breath as she looked down at the gray-blue moor ahead of her. It wasn't a moor, but she was too tired to think up anything better. Her brain could do all the pattern recognition it pleased.

"Time for these," said Aras, and took a couple of pieces of what looked like gray fabric from the pack he always carried across his back. "Boots. Just hold the fabric around your calves for a few moments."

"I've got boots."

"Yes, and they will be in a very poor state after this excursion if you don't cover them."

The fabric, some sort of charcoal-gray compressed fibrous material, fitted itself to her own boots at a leisurely pace. She decided she was becoming the image of wess'har pragmatism. "Rough terrain?"

"Very. And mind the roads."

"Yes, mum," Shan said. She stared at completely unspoilt wilderness. "All that traffic."

"No, I mean mind the roads. Remember that they shift."

"And I thought infrastructure back home was going to the dogs." She thought of Bennett, mastering his fear long enough to pull Mesevy out of the bog with its carnivorous plastic-bag beast. So many animals you could see right through, and all the glass construction, too. It was a transparent world.

But Shan heeded the warning. In places, the living roads were wide enough for them to walk side by side; in others, they were so narrow that she decided to follow Aras step for step as she had Josh. She was glad of the boots, too. The roads here were dotted with a pretty silver-gray plant whose tiny leaves concealed thousands of grabbing, needle-sharp hooks that could shred flesh.

"We are slack here," Aras observed suddenly. He was getting almost chatty. "You haven't seen the Temporary City yet, but it is not how I would have wanted it. In Baral, where I come from, we don't have any surface construction. We put our routes underground. Where we walk, we walk at random so we don't leave paths. We build our homes into the rock. The Temporary City is all very . . . noticeable. Conspicuous."

So he was the architect of Constantine. "Humans care about the landscape too," said Shan. "Some of them, anyway."

"It's not about aesthetics, about having pretty vistas. We do it because we have no right to mark nature any more than other animals can."

"I bet you're not impressed by the Great Wall of China, then. You can see it from space."

Aras made an animal hiss of annoyance. It was very clear. She didn't need to speak his dialect to work out the general meaning.

"And this is Targassat, is it?" she asked.

"Among other things. You've heard of her, then?"

Her? She'd assumed a man, as humans would. "Josh mentioned the name. I'd like to know more."

"I'll teach you."

"I'd like that. Thanks."

"Your bag," he said. "Targassat."

"Sorry?"

"A fundamental. Own no more than you can carry."

"Oh. Well, I travel a lot. Or at least I used to. I just got used to traveling light. Few possessions. It makes sense."

"It does," he said. "Empty your bag."

"Here?" She looked around and stepped onto a broad mat of vegetation, imbued with a new confidence that she could tell the solid road from the shifting bog. Aras caught her arm just before she plunged into bottomless, living mud. Her gut somersaulted and she found herself flat up against his chest, held fast, and his grip hurt. He loosened it instantly.

"Here would be better," Aras said.

Shaken, Shan tried to enter into the spirit of the lesson. She sat back on her heels and took the contents of her bag out, one item at a time, arranged them and began naming them. "Change of clothes in a waterproof bag, three days' concentrated rations, hygiene kit, fifteen meters of microfiber line, and four clips of ammunition—"

"You always carry arms?"

"Habit. You know what a police officer is, don't you? Well, that's why." She indicated the knife in his belt, a lovely shapely blade with a notched curved tip. "Is that just ceremonial? A warrior thing?"

Aras looked blank. "*Tilgir.* It's a harvesting tool. I use it to get fruit without touching thorns."

"Oh."

"And what's this?"

"A swiss. Oh, you'll just love that." She thought she might recover the situation by demonstrating how to open its screen. "See how many things it does." She watched as he accidentally ejected its blades and flashlight. "That panel on the back is the comms unit and you insert data beads in that slot. That bit there houses the stylus and the keyboard. One hundred and two separate functions."

"It's important to you."

"Never been without it since I left college." At least she had bought it herself: there were no painful memories invested in that part of it. "Very old technology, but it still works, and I'm glad it does because there's no way I'd have implants or one of those bioscreens. It's nearly as old as you, maybe as old." As soon as she said it, she regretted it. "Sorry. Won't mention that again."

Aras paused, examined the imaging device and fixed her with that animal stare. "Why do you want to protect me?"

"It's a lot more complex than that. I'm EnHaz. And this is probably not how I was intended to operate, but I see a potential environmental and economic disaster. If there's anything in your physiology that would help humans to live longer, my planet is in trouble. Many of us live too long as it is. If we can turn whatever gives you longevity into a drug or a therapy for humans, the whole balance of the population will shift. I can show you the maths. And I don't think my colleagues would be too fussed how they got it from you, Aras, because life-extension pharmaceuticals is serious money, and always has been, ever since the days of the alchemists. You might look like a biped but you're still an animal to them. So we keep it to ourselves. Okay?"

A *glop* behind her made her glance round. A *sheven* had broken the surface of the bog and its not-quite-there shape reared a meter above it, a fragile iceberg. She had no doubt it would be unimpressed by her egalitarian attitude towards non-human species if it were looking for lunch. And here she was, squatting on a precarious mat of living material in a marsh full of creatures that she couldn't begin to imagine.

Aras started to put the items back in her bag. She hoped he had understood the lecture.

"I think you grasp the basics of Targassat very well," he said. "The rest, as your Hillel points out, is commentary."

And that was Aras. One moment a complete alien, driven by rigid ethics about plants and how to build and not build, the next almost a man, with a better knowledge of Earth's philosophers and religions than most humans. And still untroubled by the destruction of cities.

"I didn't realize you were a teacher," Shan said, trying to start up conversation again. "I thought you were a soldier."

"I do many things. All wess'har do. But it isn't what I am. Do you see a police officer before you see yourself?"

"You think I ask you too many questions. I'm sorry."

"No, you confuse me. You're too many things and you don't know it."

What the hell did that mean? She wanted to tell him things, offer him honesty, but all he seemed to do was to prompt her to ask more questions. He was right. It was all she was, a series of pursuits punctuated by anger. She had always prided herself on her discipline, her tenacity, her complete independence from other people: but it was all about journey, never arrival. She had never once sat down and felt whole, nor lost the urge to get up again and find something else to fill her time.

She tried again. "I'm not interrogating you, Aras. I'm trying to understand you."

"What do you want from me?"

"I want to see the gene bank." *No point pissing about any longer.* "And I want to be friends with you, because I am very, very alone out here. And so are you."

He walked on with his head down and she had trouble keeping up with him. For a moment she thought she would fall so far behind that she would lose sight of him in the dwindling light and slip off the living road into the cling-film embrace of the *sheven.* Maybe that was what he wanted. She had hit a nerve. Then he slowed down and she caught up. The rest of the journey was in silence.

The swiss chirped about half a kilometer out from Constantine and she flipped the screen open. Eddie was still after her.

"Is something wrong?" Aras asked.

She hadn't realized how attuned he was to human reactions. "Not really. Eddie wants to talk to me about something I did that was wrong."

"How wrong?"

"Depends who's telling the story," said Shan, trying to work out if she was relieved or just itching to tell Aras what an unsung martyr she had been. *I'm a good human, really I am. I'm not a* gethes. "I'll tell you one day."

No reaction.

"I appreciate your patience. Thanks for showing me round."

Aras still looked unmoved. She had indeed lost his trust.

"By the way, you should get your people to rig you an

underwater suit," he said suddenly. "The bezeri will meet you. Good night."

And then again, maybe she hadn't. She wondered if she would ever get used to his habit of suddenly changing subjects—and dropping bombshells—without warning. You had to have your wits about you when talking to Aras. She walked down the narrow beam of her swiss's flashlight towards the camp, ready to face Eddie, and so preoccupied with her thoughts that she didn't notice Bennett until he actually touched her arm.

She jumped and found herself ready to take a swing at him. "Sorry, Ade." She screwed her eyes hard shut in a second of embarrassment. "You startled me. I don't react well to sudden movement. Old habit."

"We were getting worried, ma'am. Out on that bog, in the dark."

"Yeah, I know you'd be happier if I was wired up." His bioscreen reflected green light against the leg of his pants as his arms hung at his side. How much embarrassing detail would it really blab to the rest of his detachment? "But I was perfectly safe with Aras."

Bennett walked alongside her. Ahead of them, the lights of the compound formed a misshapen constellation against the skyline. "Have you eaten, ma'am? There's probably some of Qureshi's bean korma hanging around."

"You know, I could even eat that."

"Right you are, ma'am."

"*Shan,* please. You make me feel like Queen Victoria." Being aloof from people on Earth had been a defense, a bunker. Out here, so far from everything she had ever taken for granted, it was a handicap. She really did need a friend.

The mess hall was deserted. To her tired eyes the strip lighting seemed harsh and jaundice-yellow. The green tint, originally so soothing, had begun to look institutional. Bennett slopped two portions of the curry into bowls and heated them up while she made tea, and they sat on opposite sides of the table and ate. Shan forked over the volatile mix with a rueful smile.

"I'm going to regret this later," she said, thinking of her digestion.

"Ah, but I'll still respect you in the morning,"

Bennett laughed. Shan felt her throat flush hot, and it wasn't the curry. It had been a long time since she had known what it was to feel bashful.

"You sure that screen of yours records everything?"

"Pulse, BP, location, temperature, you name it."

"Interesting."

The conversation slowed and stopped. She busied herself in the remaining curry, conscious of the sounds of her own jaw and heart, grinding and pulsing unnaturally loudly in her head. She knew she had to walk away from this.

"I'd better get my head down," she said, and got up to rinse the bowl. She patted Bennett's shoulder. It felt warm and very hard under her hand. "Good night, Ade."

He paused. "G'night, Shan."

Discipline. She said the mantra a few times under her breath as she wandered down the deserted passage that joined the cabins to the mess. *Discipline.* It was a fine thing to live by, but sometimes it wasn't much comfort.

Sod technology, she thought, and closed the cabin door.

17

They are not brethren: they are not underlings: they are other nations, caught with ourselves in the net of life and time, fellow prisoners in the splendor and travail of the earth.

HENRY BESTON, on animals, from *The Outermost House*

"Look what I found!" Surendra Parekh carried a small dish into the mess hall and laid it carefully on the table, although several of the team were eating lunch. They looked, and groaned.

"I hate calamari," said Paretti.

Eddie took notice immediately. The scientists huddled over the contents of the dish, which proved to be a small jelly creature, oohing and aahing as Parekh carefully lifted flaps and tentacles with a spatula to show off her find. Mesevy didn't join in.

"Which part of the phrase *don't take samples* didn't you understand?" Eddie asked. It broke the congratulatory murmurs. "Where did you get it?"

"Hey, it's already dead," said Parekh.

"But how did you get it back here?"

"Didn't you ever shoplift as a kid, Eddie?"

"No, I damn well did not."

"Well, you'd be amazed how little time it takes to pick up something small when someone looks away for a few moments. Marine Webster doesn't have eyes in her backside."

Eddie tossed a mental coin between being the popular kid in the class and doing the sensible thing. Heads said the latter. He stood up. "Jesus Christ, you think this is some sort of game with Frankland, do you?"

"It's dead. What's the problem?"

"What are you planning to do with it?"

"Well, I was thinking of serving it with a nice beurre manié sauce—look, what do you think marine biologists do with specimens? We dissect 'em."

"You put it right back where you found it."

"Oh, come on."

"We're going to be in serious shit over this."

Parekh gave him a pitying look, the sort reserved for the hard of understanding. "It was beached." She went back to lifting tentacles cautiously with the spatula: the poor dead thing had none of the marvelous luminescence that they had seen from the cliffs, so maybe it wasn't a bezeri, with any luck. It was too small, anyway. He put his hand out and stopped Parekh's arm.

"Wait until Shan gets here. Leave it."

She shook him off, eyes all fury. "You don't touch me. Okay?"

There were a couple of muttered comments from the group that he chose not to hear. "Do we have to get permission to piss now?" Galvin said, and the outburst was unusual for her. "It's bad enough having to run every report past her without her supervising our work too."

"Okay, that's it." He opened up his database and started paging both Shan and Lindsay, just in case. "I can't sit here and let you do this."

"No." Parekh squared up to him. "This has gone far enough. I didn't give up everything I ever cared about on Earth just to come here and take pictures."

If it been Rayat or any of the men, he could have—would have—hit him. Everything Eddie had been brought up to accept without question stopped him doing what he should have done, and that was to physically restrain Parekh. *But you just didn't hurt girls.*

Parekh picked up the crate and made a move towards the hatchway that connected the mess with the corridor leading to the makeshift labs. Eddie stepped into her path and Parekh paused for a pace and then shoved past, no doubt reading those primeval signals that said Eddie wouldn't really hit a woman. She hurried down the passage into the cold room and slammed the hatch behind her.

The biohazard seal hissed and the hatch was locked. Eddie hammered on it and swore a few times, but he had lost the battle. He should have tackled her physically in the mess. But he had no idea then that scientists could be so assertive—nor that he would cave in so easily. The bastards didn't follow rules and regs like marines. He paged Lindsay and Shan again, and waited.

It took way too long. It was ten minutes.

Mesevy and Lindsay came running down the corridor towards him. "Frankland's coming," Lindsay said. "I've explained to her over the comm what happened. She's spitting nails. She'll crucify me. What the hell was Webster doing? She was supposed to watch her."

"None of us knew Surendra would go off like that," said Mesevy. "It's not her fault."

"How do we get this hatch open now?"

"It's a biohazard seal. We don't."

Maybe, if the creature had been beached, nobody would care. They might not even need to know. He was still considering diplomatic solutions when the corridor vibrated with heavy, fast steps. Shan, in fatigue pants and a sports vest, strode in and looked at them as if demanding an answer.

She jabbed her thumb at the hatch. "In there?"

"'Fraid so," Eddie said, and stared. There was a long puckered burn scar the length of her left biceps, and she seemed all muscle. She could have made even a fluffy bathrobe look like combat gear. "She's not coming out voluntarily."

Shan struck the hatch four or five times with the edge of her fist, steady and insistent. "Parekh, stand away from that body and open this hatch," she yelled. "Now."

There was no answer. Shan didn't wait or knock again. "Get me Chahal and Bennett," she said, looking more towards Mesevy, who obeyed and sprinted away. Shan glared at the hatch. For a moment Eddie almost believed the door would yield to the force of her stare alone. Lindsay was making a valiant attempt to look as if she could do something, hovering round Shan.

"Sorry, ma'am," she said "I screwed up,"

"Not your fault. She's the one who did it."

"I should have—"

"But you didn't. No point worrying about that now."

"What are you going to do?"

"Get her out of there and then start getting seriously worried. I'd like you to clear a cabin we can confine her in. Restrain her if necessary. When the stupid cow comes out, she's under arrest."

The sound of Bennett and Chahal approaching made them turn. Shan gave Eddie a withering look. He thought she was going to round on him for not stopping Parekh.

"What are you waiting for?" she asked. "A story? Okay. Stand clear and don't get in the way." She turned to Chahal. "Get that door open."

"We can either access the seal controls through the deckhead or blow the hatch," said Chahal, peering at the status panel. He had a belt of tools slung round his waist. "She's activated the central override from inside."

"Which takes longer?"

"I can get at the seal in about ten minutes with a laser cutter or blow it in five."

Shan lowered her voice. "Open it from the roof." She hammered three times on the hatch again, and shouted. "We're blowing the hatch in ten minutes, Parekh. Open up and you don't get hurt. If you don't, the blast might take your face off and right now I don't much care if that happens. Okay?"

There was no response, but Shan had clearly not expected one because Eddie heard Chahal already scrambling across the roof membrane and then a buzzing and faint vibration as he cut through the membrane and into the mechanism beneath. Maybe Parekh would believe the line about blowing the door; Eddie certainly did. Bennett stood with his hands on his hips, staring down at the floor. This was going to end badly.

Shan's face was grim and resigned rather than angry, although she looked drained of blood. "Once it's open, I'll go in and you be prepared to cuff her."

"I don't have cuffs," Bennett said.

"Well, *I'll* have to restrain her, then. Got a secure cabin ready?"

"Webster's on to that."

"Thank fuck she's on to something."

They waited and watched the opening. The hatch's surface shivered from the stresses being applied to it from the top. Then it sighed gently as the seal broke and the reinforcing bolts yielded within their casing. Shan slammed back the hatch and stared in.

Later, Eddie would find it hard to recall exactly what he had seen. It was over in seconds. Shan said nothing, walked up to a wide-eyed Parekh and landed one hard punch in her face. The woman dropped without a word, sending a tray and its wet contents clattering to the floor.

"Get her out of here," Shan said to Bennett. Parekh, stunned, struggled to stand up as Bennett grabbed her arm and guided her out. It had taken about thirty seconds: economical, brutal and definitely not the navy way. Lindsay was standing at a discreet distance, grim-faced, having had the sense to clear Shan's path and let her get on with the job. It was clearly the superintendent's speciality.

Shan stood rubbing her right hand. Yes, she *had* hit Parekh hard. "Oh, God," she sighed, staring at the remains on the floor. "Oh, *God.* I suppose we'd better try to get the poor thing tidied up."

Eddie watched from the hatchway. Shan found a pair of gloves and pulled them on, and then reached for a small plastic board. There was something undignified and desperately sad about scraping the little corpse together like spilled food, but it was the only option. She slid the remains carefully into the tray.

"You think I'm useless, don't you?" Eddie said, not looking up from the body. "I should have taken it off her."

"I don't expect a civvie to handle the physical stuff. I would have been amazed if you had. At least you called me."

"Christ, you really hit her, didn't you?"

"I did indeed. Look, this is serious. It's a juvenile bezeri, and I have to let Aras know. And the really scary thing about this is that I don't know how this is going to end."

"You're sure about this? Do they have to know?"

"Oh yes."

Lindsay laid a cloth across the tray, and Shan picked it up and walked out. In the corridor, Mesevy, Rayat and Galvin were standing like witnesses at a crash scene. They said nothing. But it was clear they had seen Parekh dragged away, nose bleeding, and there was no doubt that whether they agreed with her actions or not, she was one of their own. The first lines had been drawn between payload and the command. Life was not going to be cozy in future.

Shan paused at the end of the passage and turned round.

"I need to talk to you in private later," Shan said to Lindsay. "My cabin, after dinner. In the meantime, make sure

Parekh is secured and keep the rest of them away from her. Oh, and I authorize you to reissue sidearms to your detachment." She glanced at Eddie. "Where's your camera?"

"I wasn't recording," he said.

"Good," she said.

"What the hell did you think you were doing?"

Shan leaned against the cabin bulkhead, arms folded while Bennett stood against the hatch. Parekh sat huddled on the bunk, knees drawn up, arms wrapped round them. She had two spectacular black eyes.

"It was dead already," Parekh said.

"It's a bezeri. A juvenile."

"Well, if you shared some data with us, I wouldn't have needed to take a look, would I?"

"How often do we have to go over this? No samples. And this is why."

"Look, it was dead already. We can explain."

"Whoa. Let's rethink our attitude to species, shall we? This isn't roadkill. It's a child. Do you know what this is in human terms? You come across the scene of an accident. There's a dead baby. So you pick up the body and take it away, because you're *curious*. You don't report it, you don't try to contact the parents, you just take it, and slice it up for a few tests. Do you understand? Is any of this getting through to you fucking academics?"

Parekh said nothing and simply absorbed the bollocking. Shan waited, although she wasn't sure why. There was nothing to be gained by the lecture. She turned to Bennett and he stepped back to let her pass before following her out and locking the hatch behind. He was starting to anticipate her movements, like a good deputy.

"How long are you going to keep her in there, ma'am?"

"Until I've made my point to the rest of them and until I know what the price for this is going to be."

"The others are in the mess hall. We've made them wait for you."

It was getting to be too much of a habit, herding the payload into a hall and barking at them. The small room was uncomfortably full. The marines stood around the perimeter of the hall at ease, but their sidearms were now visible. It didn't feel like the time she walked into the New Year's Eve party at all. Eddie perched on the end of a bench, part of the group and yet visibly separated, probably making the point that he was just observing.

"Right, people." She looked round. *Make eye contact with all of them, make it personal.* Champciaux appeared to be the only one at ease, but he probably couldn't see that he would be judged as a *gethes,* not a harmless collector of rocks who happened to keep the wrong company. "I imagine you've all talked about what happened earlier today so I won't bore you with the details. Dr. Parekh is confined to quarters until I've had a response from the bezeri."

Galvin half-raised her hand. "Is she under arrest?"

"In the sense that she won't be getting out of that cabin until I say so, yes."

"Was it really necessary to use violence?"

"When words fail, yes, it usually is."

"And what about us?"

"Confined to base until further notice. I can't overemphasize the risk here. If I haven't made myself clear, this is a final warning. We are not the lords of creation. It's not our planet. And as I have the authority to impose martial law, I will, and that means I will personally shoot any one of you I catch fucking around."

"I think that's an overreaction," Rayat said.

"You're grave-robbing. How'd you like *me* rooting around *your* corpse?"

"Makes it worth thinking about having a funeral pyre, that, doesn't it?" Rayat snapped, and shoved past the rest of the group to storm out. Webster, hand resting on her side-arm, blocked his way.

"Don't push your luck," Shan said. There were a few glances, but the outburst faded into sullen obedience as quickly as it had flared.

The payload filed out silently past Bennett and Lindsay, who were flanking the exit. Eddie followed them, and glanced back once before swinging the main hatch shut behind him.

"We're buggered." Shan sat down on one of the trestle tables and swung her legs. "I've no idea how the local politics will play out, but I think we're going to have our hands full with our learned friends here."

"We'll contain that," Lindsay said.

"I won't lie to you. I'm really going to need you people to hold this together."

Bennett looked up. "You've got it, ma'am."

"Okay, do whatever you have to do to keep them in here. I've called Josh, he's notified Aras and I'm heading over there in the morning to see him. The body is in the cold room. I know it's unpleasant to have it next to supplies, but there's nowhere else right now and it's sealed in a bag anyway, so just keep an eye on it, will you?"

There was a communal *yes, ma'am* and they all straightened up as if they had one shared nervous system. They were rock-solid and reliable: good, dependable professionals to have at your back. She thought briefly of the "relief," her old shift of officers at Western Central, and the memory stuck in her throat in the way memories did when tears nearly caught you unawares.

Lindsay was the last to leave.

"Are you feeling okay?" Shan asked.

"Pretty good, considering."

"I just wondered. I thought the baby bezeri might have upset you."

"I try not to think of it in those terms. I don't think

Parekh did either. I think she would call it sentimentality."

"It's not me being the sentimental one. It's them using a religious argument as a scientific one."

"You lost me there."

"It says so in Josh's Bible, right there in the first book— that man has dominion. Get scientists in a corner, argue it out with them, and they still use that biblical excuse, except they use the word "sentience" instead of "soul." They can't argue bezeri aren't sentient. But they still see them as animals, and so pretty well anything goes."

"You think all life is sacred."

"Well, let's say I haven't yet heard a good argument for why human life is more sacred than others. That's not quite the same thing." The SB chafed away at a corner of her mind, and the name Helen surfaced again. "Anyway, you don't want a lecture on post-modern ethics. Let's get back to Parekh."

"Look, I'm really sorry about today."

"We've been through that. You can't be prepared for some things."

"Can I ask why you hit her?"

Shan folded her arms across her chest. She felt lost without something to lean on. "Primarily to stop her moving another muscle."

"And secondarily?"

"Because I was angry. Does that appall you?"

"Not entirely. But I wouldn't have done that."

"You're used to an enemy you deal with at missile length. Mine have always been right here." She held her hand flat up to her face. "I had to be handy with my fists. And sometimes the book doesn't have all the answers."

"Eddie said you had what he called an ambiguous relationship with terrorism," said Lindsay.

"You can't deal with animal-rights extremists without being exposed to some of their arguments." She hoped Eddie was talking in general terms. *Just how much did the bas-*

tard know? "The most difficult thing about terrorism is that it's not absolute. There's always a case somewhere at the bottom of it, however distorted it gets. Sometimes a reasonable case."

"I'm glad I never have to make the call on that," Lindsay said.

I did. And I don't regret it.

Shan could hear occasional ticks of the composite bulkheads cooling and contracting as the outside temperature dropped. "You think I'm the archetypal bad copper, don't you?"

"I'd have to be put in the positions you've been in before I'd pass judgment."

"An ambiguous answer for an ambiguous situation," Shan said.

No, Lindsay didn't understand at all. When she caused death, it was nothing personal; it was all neat and sanctioned and under rules of engagement. After you'd killed them, you would stand at memorial parades and say what an honorable enemy they were. Shan got to know her targets far too well, and honor never came into it.

The people who understood her were long gone.

But there was Aras. Now she had to try to understand him.

In a short time, the *Thetis* camp had developed a pulse and a rhythm of its own, like any settlement. It had noises and smells that defined it, a rhythm like a heartbeat.

This morning the backdrop of sounds was somehow different, and it wasn't simply the drumming of heavy rain. Eddie took a little time walking the few yards from his cabin to the mess hall, testing the ambient sound: there was no sporadic laughter, no voices raised occasionally to call for a hand with equipment. There was just a constant quiet hum of conversation. For a moment he felt like a kid again, creeping down the stairs to eavesdrop on mum and dad's hushed argument and wondering what he had done to cause it. He had to remind himself that he was now forty-three and a BBChan correspondent before he could steel himself to open the hatch and walk in.

Most of the payload was sitting at one table, picking at breakfast plates with no great enthusiasm. They had nowhere else to go. Mesevy was absent; Parekh was still confined to the holding cabin. The conversation stopped when he came in.

He considered taking his breakfast and going back to his cabin to eat it, but that would simply have postponed the inevitable. He had grassed up their colleague. Commercial rivalries and spoilers had been put aside. Parekh was one of their own, and he was not, and he had called down the wrath of Frankland on them.

He collected a couple of pancakes from the galley and made a point of sitting down right next to Galvin.

"Everyone okay?" he asked.

Rayat stared straight ahead. "Considering we're under martial law now, I suppose everything's fine."

"So what's happening?"

"We thought you might tell us. Your being Frankland's right hand."

Eddie laid his fork down carefully. "Okay, if you want to have a knock-down drag-out, let's do it properly. You people are fucking crazy. These wess'har, whatever they are, took out a whole civilization not far from here for some slight or other. You don't mix it up with people like that. Parekh could be putting us all at risk."

"You know this for a fact, do you?" Galvin asked.

Champciaux nodded. "I think Eddie's right about the threat. Best dating for that geophys is a few hundred years, tops. Cities don't decay that fast, and they leave more solid traces. They blew them to kingdom come, that's all I can think."

"And whose side are you on?" said Rayat.

"The side that's going home in one piece."

"It's not the aliens I'm worried about," Galvin interrupted. "It's armed troops and a complete psycho copper stopping us doing our work."

"Come on, Lou, Parekh was way out of line," said Paretti. "What she did was stupid. It wasn't even good science."

"Yes, but did that warrant beating her senseless and locking her up?"

Eddie liked accuracy, whatever Shan had done. "It was one punch," he said. "I was there."

"Okay, seeing as you're her official mouthpiece, what *is* Frankland's agenda, anyway? Government going to muscle in on our investment?" Galvin was from Carmody-Holbein-Lang: it was on Shan's list of scumbag corporations. Maybe Galvin had felt the weight of EnHaz before. "I really don't like how this is going. We wake up to find her aboard like some malevolent stowaway, and now she's siding with some bunch of aliens against her own kind."

Some bunch of aliens. How quickly they forgot, Eddie thought. When they had left Earth, the only alien life they had known existed was simple organisms, semi-sentient blobs and moss. Now, in a matter of a few months, the group had reduced at least one remarkable species to an inconvenience, an annoying trifle. Such was the exchange rate when you looked at those who were different to you. One alien was a miracle, two a novelty, a hundred an invasion, and if they thwarted humanity—they were the enemy. It was just like being back on Earth.

"For a group of PhDs, you're having a worryingly hard time accepting that we're not the top of the food chain anymore," said Eddie. "I think we should just sit very still and hope the wess'har don't notice us."

Rayat, who had been tracing patterns on the tabletop with his forefinger, looked up. He didn't appear angry. He smiled, which Eddie found slightly disturbing.

"I have no intention of sitting still and wasting this journey," he said. "I need to get hold of native flora. Novel pharmaceuticals. There's only so much I can get out of looking at adapted terrestrial species. And I can't tolerate those restrictions."

"Not much you can do about it. The colonists are pretty clear about that."

"The natives, as you put it, aren't always at our side when we work. Without our military escort, how would they know what we took? How would they notice? If you hadn't gone whining to Frankland, would anyone have known about her sample?"

There was a silence round the table. It was as if everyone had interpreted Rayat's comment in exactly the same way. *Without our military escort.* There was only one way to achieve that.

"That's pretty dangerous thinking," Eddie said at last.

"I wasn't suggesting we mutiny," said Rayat, but his face said otherwise.

"And did it occur to you that sentient species would notice one of their number was missing?"

"Are they truly sentient?"

"Would it matter if they weren't?" Eddie found himself detaching from his journalist's grandstand seat and abandoning all the distance of his trade. *Jesus, this is real. I'm in this. It's happening to me.* "The locals make the rules. Take it from me. I've been arrested while filming overseas and held by local police with far less weaponry than this lot and it is very, very nasty. They can do what they want with you when you're on their turf and there's no embassy to bail you out."

Rayat shrugged, so genuinely dismissive that Eddie felt a blaze of anger. Maybe he had been immune to challenge and correction for too long to understand that there were bigger kids in the playground. Paretti's glance darted back and forth between them as if he were expecting escalation. Right then, Eddie was ready to swing for him.

Then Mesevy walked in and let an armful of freshly picked cucumbers roll onto the table like logs, and the moment was defused.

"I'd better be getting on with editing," Eddie said, and left the table.

Back in his cabin, he couldn't concentrate on the previous day's footage. Rain spattered against the small window like a hail of rocks as a gust drove it. Eddie let the editing console slide off his lap and lay back on his bunk, and all he could think about was that he had *become involved*. It was professional anathema. Every other story he had ever covered in his life had *not* been like this.

I am a dispassionate observer.

I am a real-time historian.

In the thick of riots, he was almost safe behind police lines; after a chemical fire that killed twenty people, he had caught a cab back to the office and enjoyed a beer after work. He had even spent an evening in a five-star hotel sampling room service while from the window he watched distant shells exploding and wiping out a Greek village.

It had its risks. He could easily have been killed in all those situations, given bad luck. And he had been banged up in a two-meter-square cell in Yemen not knowing if BBChan even knew where he was. But that sense of detachment, of being special and set apart from the messy drama of ordinary lives, was now gone. He was here and he was in it.

He felt himself sliding into something his professional persona had once regarded with disdain. He was starting to take sides.

* * *

There were two things Aras was not planning to tell Mestin.

One was that he feared Shan Frankland knew that he carried the *c'naatat* parasite.

The other was that one of the *gethes* had taken a bezeri child and killed it.

He lay back in the cramped pod as the bezeri pilot brought him back to the surface and the Dry Above. Normally the journey would be whiled away chatting in lights, but today there was nothing but a faint blue glow holding steady across the pilot's mantle, a sad silence in its terms.

Not even the isenj sought us out to kill us.

Summoning the bezeri from the depths with the lamp to tell them their child had been taken was the hardest thing Aras had done in many years. Their sorrow was a vivid blue. It had so many shades to it, so much agony, that his interpretation system had been unable to convey the full intensity.

We want balance. We want forfeit.

It was arrogance rather than cruelty that had motivated the *gethes*, but that was the cause of most brutal acts. Hiding behind lack of intent was a human excuse.

And the bezeri had been correct. Even the isenj, the careless and profligate isenj who didn't recognize the bezeri had rights, had never taken them and killed them. The poisoning of their environment had been a brutal consequence, not an objective.

But wess'har cared only about what was, and what was done, not what was intended.

Aras knew the outrage would be the final justification that Mestin needed to order him to wipe all humans from the face of the planet. He had overseen the destruction of the isenj, but he would not, if he could help it, see his friends in Constantine pay the price for the *gethes'* stupidity.

The very least Mestin would expect was that he wiped out the whole *gethes* mission, but that too was a step too far at the moment. He would talk to Shan Frankland to see if she respected his position and understood that the price of Surendra Parekh's life was a generous one.

The colonists would have understood: an eye for an eye, they said, burning for burning, no more and no less than the sin warranted. They understood balance. The *gethes* would not.

He considered what would be the quickest, cleanest method of dispatching a *gethes*.

The bezeri pilot who ferried him back to the island offered no opinion.

Little Rachel Garrod rushed to him when he opened the door of Josh's home. "Aras!" she squealed. She clung to his legs in unalloyed childish delight. "Come and see my flowers! I've drawn flowers!"

"Later, *isanket*," he said. "I promise I'll look at them, but not today. I've come to talk to *Shan Chail*."

Rachel's enthusiasm dimmed like a light. "Daddy's talking to her. She scared me. She's all black." Shan was evidently in formal uniform today, then. "Can I come?"

"No, *isanket*. We've got very sad things to talk about. It would make you cry. Go and draw me some more flowers. I'll see them tomorrow." He steered the child gently into a side room and closed the door.

Shan was not a wess'har female, but she was female nonetheless and that made confronting her a difficult procedure. She was sitting in Josh's kitchen when he walked in, uniform coat fastened right up to the chin, hands clasped on the table in front of her. Josh got up and patted her shoulder before giving Aras a *go-easy* glance and leaving them on their own.

"Okay, Aras," she said. "What happens now?"

He fought an urge to ask her how she knew what he was

and what he carried in him. But that would have to wait.

"It will be hard for you," he said.

She shut her eyes for a second. "I realize that. Just tell me what you want me to do."

"I have to take Parekh."

"Exactly what do you mean by take?"

"I mean take, and I mean punish."

A whiff of agitation drifted from her. "How?"

"Execution."

Don't disappoint me, he thought. *Don't protest, don't be a* gethes. *Accept it.* The only movement she made was to grip her hands together more tightly. Her face had turned very pale, and those odd round irises in her pale gray eyes were wide and black.

"Is there any other way?" she asked.

"It's what the bezeri want."

"Could we confine her for the duration?"

"There is only one other option, and I won't take that."

"We can at least talk about it, surely."

"It's no option at all. It's Parekh or every human on this planet."

"Oh, God."

He hated to see her so distressed. He liked her. No, he was fascinated by her, in her capacity to be *isanket,* matriarch and even house-brother all at once. He put his hand out to touch her arm, but she jerked it back.

"Explain it to me, Aras. Just explain it."

"Your people took the child and let it die and desecrated the body. I think, in your world, you would do the same and demand a life in return."

"What do you mean, let it die?"

"If you had left it where it was, the clan might have located it in time. They were out looking for it. Bezeri can survive a while out of water, and they could have revived it."

"Are you absolutely sure about that?"

"My colleagues have examined it. Your Parekh must have found it not long after it came ashore."

"She said it was dead."

"You know nothing about bezeri physiology."

"Oh, dear God." She shut her eyes for a second and turned her face away. When she turned back she was under control again, but he could see her breathing was getting more rapid. "Aras, I don't think she intended that."

"The intent is irrelevant. The child is dead and violated. You were told not to take anything. *Anything*. And your people ignored that warning."

Shan braced her elbows on the table and rested her chin on tightly clasped hands. Aras waited. One way or another, he had to finish this today.

"I will carry out the balancing. I will ensure it's quick."

She appeared to take a deep breath and force her shoulders down into a more relaxed position. There were great red welts just visible on her throat where the collar ended. "I'm sorry. I'm not questioning your laws. We've done something unforgivable and I would rather I dealt with it."

"No, there will be no further debate."

"Why aren't I held responsible?"

"If you're suggesting you trade places with her, that's very noble but it will satisfy neither wess'har nor bezeri. This is about responsibility. Hers."

"I wasn't thinking that. Well, one thousand innocent people or one misguided one. I don't really have a choice, do I?"

"No. Accept that there are some things you can't put right."

She lapsed into silence again and rubbed her palm across her forehead, looking as if the effort of maintaining a calm exterior was about to snap her. He could smell it. The *gethes* might have been fooled, but he was not.

"Then at least let me carry it out," she said suddenly.

"No. This is about responsibility. I let the colony stay here and so I brought you here. It's up to me to resolve the situation. I don't let others answer for my mistakes."

"And if your people kill a human, it'll probably cause a diplomatic rift that will never heal. If I do it, it's more or less friendly fire. We needn't involve you."

"Do you *ever* listen? I said it's my responsibility."

"I think you're making a big mistake."

"I've already made it."

He stood up to go and she caught his wrist gently. He wished she hadn't; it made it hard to stay suspicious of her. She was as kind to him as Ben Garrod, kinder than Mestin and his kin would ever know how to be. "I don't know how you plan to do this, but if you are going to do it, at least use this." She took her pistol out of the back of her belt and held it out flat on her hand. "Please. Point blank, nape of the neck. Should take one shot. Perhaps two. Let me show you how to use it."

Aras looked at the small dull metal thing and took it. "I already know," he said.

She would have to prepare her people, of course. That, in a way, seemed harder than what he had to do. He had no love of *gethes,* and this Parekh had destroyed a child. But he imagined the reaction of the others, and he knew even now that they would all turn on Shan Frankland. Their species was paramount. They would not understand her willingness to abide by a different set of ethics.

"Let me have a few minutes to think how I'm going to deal with this," she said.

Aras waited in the hallway, hefting the pistol in his hand and thinking how efficient it seemed. When Shan came out, she was her usual certain self again. She took out her swiss and called her second in command. The woman she called Lin—the one carrying a child, who would surely understand the bezeri—seemed to concern her. Aras listened to a one-sided conversation, Shan telling Lin she needed to hand Parekh over to the wess'har authorities for sentence or every human, colony included, would be punished.

She did not mention the word *execution* once.

"You lie badly," Aras reminded her.

"I know, but I don't want anyone being tempted to let Parekh escape out of some well-meaning sense of pity. I'll tell them when I'm ready." She looked at him as if she felt he disapproved of her. "I can do the dirty work. Believe me, I've had plenty of experience."

He knew humans well enough to almost understand why she was doing it this way. To a wess'har, there was no moral dilemma. Wrong had been done and it had to be balanced out and accounted for personally. But humans were full of rights, and very short on responsibilities.

"I'll hand her over," said Shan. "An hour."

"I'm sorry."

"It's not your fault. We should never have come here."

"I would like to think we would still be able to talk after this."

"Yeah. Sure."

"You're more wess'har than you think."

"I think the team will see it that way too," said Shan, and walked out in front of him without a backward glance.

The payload started out in shocked silence and then got loudly angry. Lindsay had started to think of them as one entity lately. Herding them together in the mess hall had somehow developed a communal intelligence among them, even in Mesevy, who seemed to be the one most distant from the pack. Bennett and Webster stood in front of the exit leading onto the compound, and Chahal and Barencoin blocked the one to the accommodation and laboratory corridor. Their rifles were still slung on webbing round their shoulders, but their hands rested on the barrel and trigger.

There was just one notch of tension to go before the rifles were raised. Lindsay had realized that no exercise, no play war, could have prepared her for taking aim at unarmed civilians.

But the stakes were high. It was never worth risking the lives of all of them, and Parekh had been a fool. Lindsay wondered how bad a wess'har prison could be.

Her bioscreen came alive. Shan was summoning her to the rear entrance to the camp. Chahal and Barencoin parted like wheat to let her pass and she walked as fast as she could to meet Shan.

She had the wess'har with her. He was grim, silent, immense. Lindsay looked up at him and then back at Shan.

"Just give me the keycard," said Shan. "There's no reason for you to be here."

"You sure, ma'am?"

"Quite sure." She reached round her back, took out her handgun and checked the chamber. "I don't want any argument with what I'm about to say. Parekh has been sentenced to death. If I don't carry out the sentence, the wess'har will wipe us all out, even the colony, and they can do it, believe me. Do you understand?"

"I'm sorry . . . ?"

"The bezeri was alive when she took it. And it's her or *everyone*. Okay?"

Lindsay tried to make sense of what she had heard. There was no rule or regulation she could recall that told her what to do right then.

Shan stood and stared at her, unblinking.

"The keycard, Lin. Now. This is not your responsibility."

She handed it over. It was not the time for an impassioned plea for clemency. The wess'har was watching her. She believed Shan completely at that moment.

In the mess hall, Rayat and Galvin were engaged in a one-way stream of invective against the detachment, while

Eddie watched in his usual manner. Each marine stood silent and unmoving. Lindsay listened for another sound, filtering out the tirade.

"You've let them take her. You bastards."

"Christ, can't we even look after our own?"

"I can't believe you're letting them do this."

And they had no inkling what was really about to happen to Parekh. Lindsay could feel events flipping over into chaos. She let the two scientists rage for a few moments and then brought the butt of her sidearm down hard on one of the tables in an explosive *whack*.

"Shut the fuck up," she yelled.

There was instant silence. She regretted the loss of control at once. But she had so wanted silence, just for a few minutes. It surprised her that they obeyed.

The silence continued while she walked slowly up and down the space between the two tables, rubbing the small of her back, suddenly aware that it ached. And the silence was profound.

Maybe two minutes had passed, maybe ten, but then the quiet was shattered by a gunshot, and then another.

Ade Bennett cocked an experienced ear. "Nine millimeter round," he said softly. "Officer's weapon."

Shan stood under one of the compound lights with Lindsay and Bennett, and it struck her there was no mist of small flying things clustering round the lamp as there would have been on Earth. The rain had stopped but pooled water glittered in the light. Nobody asked about Parekh's body. Shan was sure someone would ask who was going to clean up. She would do it herself.

"What do you want me to do, ma'am? Am I supposed to put this in the official record?" Lindsay was staring disbelieving into her face. That was the worst part of all. "I have no precedent for this."

"Yeah, just file it. Just do it." Aras, gentle Aras, had shown no hesitation. Even Shan, who had meted out her own justice more than once, and without the slightest contrition, was struggling to feel that the events of the last twenty minutes were normal.

But it was the bezeri's world and they had a right to their law. If she lost sight of that, she was no better than the technician who was blind to the captive gorilla's misery because it was different and somehow less than him.

"How can we begin to understand these creatures? How can we ever build a relationship with them?" Lindsay asked.

"Lin, remember that the bezeri wasn't dead. She cut it up *alive*, whether she knew it or not."

Bennett muttered something under his breath. At least she had made her point. It was an unimaginably awful death. She shouldn't have felt the need to justify her actions, but evoking a sense of revulsion would help them understand her, and maybe prevent them from turning on her one day.

There was no point delaying any longer. Everyone had heard the shot. They couldn't have missed it. "I have to announce this to the payload, so I imagine things could get a little heated," Shan said. "You might have to do what your lot do best."

"Yes, ma'am." Bennett cut in. "What do we say?"

"You don't say anything. I do. I'll explain that I carried out the sentence of the wess'har authorities and I'll even tell them why, just so they understand that we're not back home any longer."

"So you pulled the trigger," said Lindsay.

"I've got two spent rounds from my weapon that you can use to verify it." She held out the gun. Aras was really a very proficient shot for a beginner, but that was between

her and him, and always would be. "I'll file a full dis-
charge report."

"Frankly, ma'am, I don't believe you."

"What you believe is your business. The incident log
will state that I carried out the execution of Surendra Parekh
under the local code of the bezeri jurisdiction for man-
slaughter. Is that clear, Commander?"

"Gin clear, ma'am," said Lindsay, but she might as well
have said *liar-liar-liar.* "Whatever you say."

"How are we planning to process the body?" asked Bennett. He appeared remarkably detached. Shan imagined he
had seen his share of body bags.

"Bag and freeze," she said. "I can—"

Lindsay interrupted. "No, ma'am, you go and address
the payload, and then we can put them to bed for the night.
We've rostered security watches for the duration." Lindsay
gestured to Bennett. "We'll do the rest."

Lindsay walked off. Bennett hung back.

"You do understand, don't you, Ade?" Shan said. She
didn't want him to think she was a monster. She might have
had her own doubts about that, but it mattered to her that he
didn't. "Someone had to."

He tried to smile but it didn't work. "I do understand
duty. And I understand . . . um . . . diplomatic sensitivity,
too."

"Thanks." So he didn't believe her account of the execution either. "I don't think most of them will."

"*We* will, and that's what counts. Look, she broke their
law and she knew she was doing it. In the end, she even
broke *our* law. This isn't home. The risks are bloody enormous. I'm not a politician—hell, I'm not even clever—but
even I can see what could be coming. No, don't you lose a
second's sleep over it, ma'am."

Some chance. "You know what I've got to do now."

"I do," he said, and saluted.

She didn't watch him go. She walked up to the entrance to the mess hall and rapped on the hatch.

"Frankland here," she called. "Open up."

18

We mourn with the civilians at the research base, but they must learn a new order of creation. Humility doesn't come easily to mankind. I would like to be able to comfort them—as I would wish to comfort the bereaved bezeri—but they have turned in upon themselves. Sabine Mesevy is the exception: she has Superintendent Frankland's permission to attend church, and I do believe she has found some profound spiritual meaning in her time here.

JOSH GARROD, speaking at council

Shan followed Aras down the shingle of the beach with some difficulty. The environment suit that Webster had adapted for diving was cumbersome, and she found she had to swing her legs out to the side like a lizard to move properly.

"I think I'm doomed to have to make my first contact with every species an apology," she said. "Sorry we shot you down, Aras. Sorry we vivisected your kid, Mrs. Bezeri. I really would have preferred to say something like we come in peace."

"You could leave this to me," Aras said. He held the bezeri's body in both hands, wrapped in a thin sheet of some blue silky material. "They would understand."

"No, this one is definitely my shout. I was always the copper who knocked on people's doors to tell them their loved one had met a messy end. You'd be amazed how far you can detach yourself from it after a while, however they react. I can still do it."

They stopped at the water's edge. There were already

lights rising from the depths, violet and gold, and Shan pulled down her helmet and checked the air supply. She had never dived before. She couldn't even swim. All she had to do was walk into the sea, not even to any great depth. Aras stopped her as she put one boot in the water.

"As you're so insistent," he said, "I made you this." He took an oval shape from his tunic and held it up to her face-plate so she could see it: it was a faceted lamp. She squinted against the sudden burst of colored lights. "It clamps to your headset, so you can at least translate a few of your words as you speak. It's very basic. Keep your sentences simple."

"As long as it can manage *sorry,* that'll be good enough." The rasping against the side of her helmet was magnified for a moment as he fixed it in place. When she said "Thanks," she saw a brief flicker of colors out the corner of her eye.

"In you go," he said.

When she was in the water chest-high she started to lose her balance and slowed down. Aras caught her elbow to steady her. She turned once to look at him, and it was the most unsettling sight she had seen: he wore no special suit, of course, just a throat mike for her benefit. He could sus-pend his breathing. She took it as yet another handy wess'har characteristic.

The water covered her head and pressed heavy on her chest, and then the general light became a soothing aqua-marine. She could pick out shapes moving towards her. When her vision resolved them properly, she was facing a dozen or so enormous squid-like shapes that suddenly erupted into almost fractal patterns of changing light and color. They were huge. She estimated three or four meters: the hand-sized bezeri that Aras carried really was just a kid. She held her arms out to him to take the small body.

One bezeri emerged from the group and drifted towards her.

She held out the child. "I'm very sorry," she said, carefully slow. "My people made a mistake. We will never do that again."

Slowly, the bezeri reached out three tentacles and coiled them gently round the body. Its color had changed to a consistent deep blue, the most intense blue Shan had ever seen, as blue as some lobelia blossoms and so saturated that it almost seemed to be outside her range of vision. The pattern within it repeated over and over in a pulse right across the creature's body. Then more tentacles enveloped the body, and the child was lifted from her arms. The bezeri suddenly shot away from her, sending a jet of expelled water that would have knocked her on her back had Aras not caught her.

The other bezeri closed the gap and hung there, shimmering many colors, but none of them that striking deep blue.

"They say the mother is very upset, but she doesn't blame you," Aras interpreted. "The child was keen to see the strangers. He strayed too far."

Oh, God. "I wish we could meet again under happier circumstances." *Was that too complex?* "We don't mean you any harm."

Lights fired off, and the drifting crowd of immense sinuous shapes began moving away from her slowly, and then picked up speed. A final burst of scarlet flared like vehicle tail lights. They were suddenly gone into the depths again.

"They said *maybe*," said Aras.

19

Eddie had left Shan alone for a couple of weeks after the
business with Parekh. He was expecting some retaliation
from the payload, but their response had been complete
passivity. What they said when he wasn't around might
have been different, but they appeared shocked into compliance. The atmosphere in the mess hall was silently hostile,
and none of them spoke to Shan any more than they absolutely had to, but there was no noticeable recrimination.

Maybe they had the sense to be scared.

Shan strode across the compound after Lindsay's morning briefing, fatigues uncreased, boots polished. He wondered how she managed to keep her kit so neat. Galvin and
Hugel glanced at her cautiously, and when she looked their
way they dropped their gaze. A casual visitor might have
deduced nothing more than the fact that Shan was not a
popular overseer.

The marines had established their own mess in a tent in
the compound. At night Eddie could hear the off-duty watch
playing gin rummy under the ice-blue light of a high-
output lamp. This morning they went about their tasks—

maintenance, hydroponics and cleaning duties, the rest of the shared routine that everyone faced in camp—in near silence. The colonists kept an even closer watch on the payload when they went out on field trips. Factions had formed, and the frosty distances felt worse than open warfare.

Shan kept her distance from the payload and spent her time off camp. Was she afraid of a backlash? Eddie couldn't imagine anything that would frighten this woman nor any dissent that she couldn't crush. She attended morning briefings as if nothing had changed and made no apology or excuse. Parekh had never happened. She was erased, as surely as the wess'har armies had made the isenj cities disappear.

"Shan's trying to make it easier for my lads," said Lindsay, all loyalty. Eddie found it hard to think of petite, pretty Qureshi as a lad. "No flashpoint. No provocation."

"You think she did the right thing?" Eddie asked.

"I don't think she had a choice."

"Would you have done it?"

"I don't even want to think about it." She softened a little, her voice dropping in a confidential way. "Do you think she actually fired the shot?"

Eddie shrugged. "She's done it before. Ask her what she did for a living."

So Lindsay thought it might have been the wess'har who carried out the execution. It was an interesting act of self-sacrifice on Shan's part if that were true. On the other hand, she might have reasoned that it enhanced her reputation as a hard case if she claimed responsibility. Eddie wondered how far he might dare push Shan in claiming the promised interview. Whatever she had got up to in the Green Rage debacle was going to look like a parking ticket after the events of recent weeks.

But there were no deadlines here. How he had changed, he thought. Adrenaline junkies loved deadlines. But he didn't much care about them any longer, and it wasn't just because there was no competition around. Eddie's world-view had shifted its focus. He was no longer viewing the world, but in it.

Still, there was no point wasting any more time. Shan had said she would speak to him, and he would hold her to that. He called her on the comms net to check he was still welcome. Door-stepping reluctant interviewees was a fine sport until you met one who had a smoking gun.

"It's pretty frosty on the social front lately," Eddie said. They sat in neutral ground, on the patch of grass at the edge of the compound where some hardy soul had erected a vol-leyball net. It was like having a picnic with Genghis Khan. "Does that bother you?"

"I don't subscribe to that 'happy ship is an efficient ship' crap," said Shan. "It's orderly. The marines do their job and the payload does theirs. They don't have to love each other to make that happen. And they don't have to love me either."

"You realize there's genuine regret for what Parekh did."

"I'm sure there is. Is this the interview or are you just trying to thaw me first?" She glanced at the bee cam and he wondered for a moment if her gorgon's gaze would fry the circuitry.

"You don't like journalists, do you?"

"On the contrary, Eddie. I do. You ask all the questions that hypocritical viewers would really love to ask for them-selves but haven't got the guts to. They devour your output and then vilify you for intrusion. No, I reckon you and I are in much the same line of work. Us and latrine cleaners."

"I'm touched."

"You're welcome."

"Did you really shoot Parekh yourself?"

"Do you really want to know?"

"Only out of personal curiosity. I'm not a fool. I do un-derstand the needs of diplomacy."

"Then you understand why the matter's closed."

"But you're no stranger to use of force."

"You know perfectly well that I'm not."

"Your name rang a bell and I remembered. Green Rage."

"Well, that's all on the record. I faced a disciplinary hearing for screwing up Operation Green Rage. I expect you've read the file, if you're half the professional I think you are." She pulled out a few strips of apricot rations and held one out to him. "Even I don't walk on water all the time."

"Do you want to talk about it?"

"What's there to talk about?"

"Well, I work on the theory that there's no such thing as a catastrophe caused by a single event. There's always a chain of cock-ups, if the disaster is genuine."

"It was my joint op with the regional crime squad, so maybe I made a chain of cock-ups." Shan looked distracted. "Yes, I managed to misplace ten eco-terrorists after a seven-month covert operation that cost the taxpayers zillions and it screwed my career, and here I am relegated to the arse-end of the universe to prove it. If you can polish that turd, Eddie, you're even better than I thought."

"I was more interested in talking about who than how."

"Why? It was my op."

"I meant the tree huggers. You see, we'd heard a buzz at the time that one of them might have been connected to a senior government figure."

Shan shrugged. "No idea."

Eddie concentrated on her face. She wasn't a stunner by any standard, yet she did have a double-take quality. But it was the disturbing luminescence of obsession rather than feminine beauty. He wouldn't have sat down next to her on a bus. "It's history now. Hardly a story, but I'm taking history seriously."

"Sorry. I really can't make the connection. I knew about

six of the names." She really looked as if she was searching her memory: no act there, unless she was a genius at it. "Nobody like that at all. And I think I would remember, because this bloody Suppressed Briefing is like a mental laxative. It's been flushing out all kinds of memories I didn't know were there."

It surprised him she referred to it so casually. But she was probably smart enough to realize that knowledge of the SB had leaked out to the payload.

"You don't strike me as someone who would screw up, Superintendent." Maybe vanity might loosen her up. "Maybe a lapse under pressure, inappropriate use of firearms and so on, but not incompetence. Were you protecting a more senior officer? You were busted at the disciplinary, but you bounced straight into a government-backed post at EnHaz. Was that an apology on someone's part?"

She looked away at the volleyball net as if she were genuinely wrestling with something for a moment and he thought he might have cracked her. Then she looked back at him and it was with the expression of someone who really, really wanted to talk. He knew that look. *Yes.* He was an inch away from it.

"I'll tell you this," she said. "In my life I've done right things and wrong things. I've been a little rough with prisoners and I've shut my eyes at times. I've even managed to not apprehend terrorists who assassinated heads of biotech corporations and torched their businesses. Now, some of those things were right and some were wrong. You tell me which."

"Do *you* know which?" He prepared for the baring of an anguished conscience.

"Yes," she said. "I do."

There was a pause. It went on a very long time and she gazed around idly at the volleyball net and the swaying grasses. Then she simply looked at him. He forgot the primary rule of interviewing and fell into the chasm: he blinked first. It was hard to do otherwise with her.

"Okay," he said, and repositioned the bee cam with a gesture. "But if it helps, the name I really wanted to place was Perault."

Shan laughed. "I really don't think Eugenie Perault's dynasty was into terrorism."

"I meant her sister, Helen Marchant. Long shot, but I thought if you knew, after all this time, you might set the record straight."

And he looked into Shan's face again, and he saw a moment of total revelation before the veil closed. He wanted to reach out and grab it.

"Marchant doesn't ring any bells," she said. "But I'll keep thinking and I'll tell you if I come up with anything. Like you said, it was a long time ago."

That flicker of reaction said something. It said she had discovered something she hadn't ever known, and it had winded her. Everyone on camp now knew she had been effectively shanghaied by Perault, and if there was a cleaner, better method than deep-space exile to remove someone who had substantial dirt on you—and maybe didn't realize it—he couldn't think of one.

It didn't answer any questions about her complicity or otherwise with terrorists, though, and he had rather liked the idea of her as the wayward copper who helped the bad guys against the even badder guys. Should he have said so? No. It wasn't grown-up journalism.

"You were royally shafted, weren't you?"

She actually smiled a little. "You enjoyed that."

"Not really. What baffles me is that everyone, just everyone, thought you had gone native and they couldn't prove it, but even though you're home and dry now you still won't confirm it. It won't even be a confession."

"You really don't understand me, do you?"

No, he didn't. She was easy to admire and hard to love, but he had thought he had at least worked out her motivations. "Tell me, then."

She leaned her weight on one arm and stretched her legs out to one side. Her voice was very low; it was going to be a messy sequence to edit. "You know damn well I wasn't entirely sure Green Rage was the enemy. Actually, that was the police operational name for the case, not the group's, because they never called themselves anything so bloody juvenile."

"So you weren't actually a terrorist, but you helped them out when they were busy."

Maybe she enjoyed the verbal sparring. It must have been months since anyone—other than that wess'har, anyway—had spent a long time talking to her. She had suddenly become animated, as if someone had thrown a switch. "One minute I was leading a covert operation to trap a group that was targeting biotech companies and the next I was questioning who the real criminals were."

"So what did happen?"

"I started seeing things that made me sick to my gut, and I can assure you it wasn't the eco-terrorists."

"That's not really an answer."

"I know."

"But they turned you, these terrorists?"

"I just remembered the gorilla."

"What?"

"Wholly unrelated incident, except in my head I suppose. I visited a primates lab when I was at college. I know they should have stopped using experimental primates a long time ago under European legislation, but they had a few that were exempt from the ban because they were endangered species and they were carrying out what they called benign research on them. You know, cloning for conservation, language development, that sort of thing. Anyway, there was this gorilla that had been taught sign language. I was looking at it, and it looked me right in the eye and kept signing at me, but I didn't understand, and so I just accepted what the animal technician told me. You know what it was saying, over and over? *Help me please.* It didn't stop. And I found out years later what the signing meant and it just knocked the fucking guts out of me, and there isn't a day that goes by that I don't think about that and despise myself. There was a person in that animal asking me for help and I didn't hear. What did it think of me? How hurt and betrayed and trapped did it feel, if it thought I would be able to get it out of there? I could have done something and I didn't. So every time I look at something that isn't human, I have to ask myself who's behind the eyes, not what."

"I think a lot of people feel that way with great apes."

"And squid? And other things that aren't like us and don't look smart?" Shan fixed him with that cold gray I'm-asking-you-a-bloody-question look that Eddie was certain would have made him tell her everything he knew, if a cell door had been closed and he had no way past her.

"So you question that and you end up questioning a whole chain of things."

"Indeed."

"So what form did your dilemma take, then?"

"I didn't put on a balaclava and shin up drainpipes for the cause, if that's what you mean."

"What then?"

Shan looked almost amused. He knew he could neither browbeat her nor cajole her into answering. If she told him, it would be because she wanted him to know, and then he'd have to work out her motive all over again.

But she did answer. "People haven't got a clue about security," she said. "Never have had, never will. And it's not about systems and technology—it's about this ape inside us all. It's not rocket science. Nine times out of ten, if you ask

someone a question they'll answer it and not wonder why
you asked. If the question's innocuous, they'll forget they
even told you. They never ask what other information
you're going to put that together with, or whether you have
a right to know. People have a need to cooperate and you
seldom have to hit them to achieve it."

"Seldom."

"Seldom."

"And you had a lot of information about these companies."

"I was advising them on countermeasures. I was in their
headquarters. I needed to know where their senior personnel lived, what vehicles they drove, what their identity
codes were. I even advised them exactly where to vary their
routes to the office each morning."

"And they poured it all out to you because you were a
police officer sent to save them."

"I never needed to hack a system or pick a lock to get
data. They handed it all over."

"Plus Green Rage knew what your officers were doing
and where they were looking, of course."

"They might very well have known, yes. I strongly suspect they did."

"And evidence went missing."

"I always was a shit-head when it came to filing."

Eddie smiled at her. She smiled back. It was a lovely
game. She was very good at it. He had enough to make a
very interesting piece, but it would be of so little interest to
anyone in twenty-five years—or seventy-five—that it was
more like the technical exercises in figure skating, something you did to show you could but that nobody paid to
watch.

"Why are you telling me this?"

"I've told you nothing, Eddie."

"I think you have."

"Then I've told you enough so that you know the kind of

person you're dealing with. And that I'll still be that person when we get back to Earth."

It took him several seconds to realize he had been threatened. It hurt him: not because she had told him obliquely that she would exact some unspecified revenge if he crossed her, but because she hadn't understood that he just wanted to know for his own peace of mind. He wanted her to be a hero, a courageous maverick, somebody you couldn't buy or blackmail or beat into compliance.

"There's going to be nobody in power left to care what you did when we go home," he said. "But maybe in years to come, what you did will show people that they don't always have to follow orders. A lot of people these days will see you as a courageous individual."

Do I really mean that? Or am I trying to con her? Some chance. The color had risen in Shan's face and he felt almost uncomfortable to see the emotion in her. She was angry.

"Let me tell you this," she said. "If I did anything, I'll keep it to myself because I don't want to be admired or worshiped for it. I don't even want to *think* adulation might motivate me, so as long as there's nothing to worship, I'll know that anything that I did was done because it was right, and not for my own aggrandizement. There are some things any decent human should be prepared to do, without reward and without recognition, because they're the right thing to do."

Eddie pocketed the bee cam and finished his apricot strip. "Ah."

"I do believe I've left you lost for words, Mr. Michallat."

"And you enjoyed *that*."

"Nah. Like you say, who cares anymore? Nobody except me."

"I've made some more home brew if you're interested."

"I won't reveal any more under the influence of alcohol."

"I was being sociable."

"I apologize. But I'm a tea drinker. Maybe we can have a cuppa some time."

"I'll hold you to that. One more thing."

"What?"

"Just a tip. Watch Rayat. He talks about circumventing the restrictions by not having your marines hanging round. He might have rethought his position since they . . . since Parekh was killed, but I know a slimeball when I see one, and I wouldn't even put mutiny past him."

"Thanks."

"Time we got back to cleaning our latrines."

"See you," she said, and winked at him.

No, Eddie didn't understand her at all. He played back the interview again and again, just to see the moment when the name Helen Marchant shattered the ice of her composure. He even started editing the piece.

After a couple of hours he gave up and filed the rushes for later, maybe much later. She was right. Nobody would care anymore, not when it was measured against the dramas unfolding on this planet.

Besides, he liked her. She'd simply become too involved, and that was a failing he couldn't deny her.

The recall to the Temporary City was sudden, and Aras left Black and White with Josh's son, James. Mestin would not discuss the matter by link. That always meant she was angry. He wondered if she had found out about Parekh, and that he was being summoned to receive the inevitable order to finally end his stewardship of Constantine and kill every human on Bezer'ej. It would not only be disastrous for the colony; it would be a disaster for him.

Wess'har didn't lie even by omission. It was just a human habit, genetic or otherwise, that he had half-absorbed in the long time he had lived among the colonists and that sometimes made it easier to be among them. White lies,

Josh called them. Aras hoped Mestin would mistake his agitated scent for fear.

Perhaps she knew he was lying and had finally worked out what punishment she could mete out to a *c'naatat* that would be worse than his exile or his time as a prisoner of the isenj. She would need to be very inventive, he thought.

When the bezeri pilot picked him up from the shore, Aras had the feeling that it didn't want to talk to him any more than the last one had. He wondered if they suddenly doubted his ability—and the ability of all wess'har—to protect them. He had reassured them about the new *gethes*. Now they had lost a child to them, and in appalling circumstances.

Time would tell. But bezeri were no better at forgetting than he was.

"We have some intelligence reports from the ussissi," Mestin said. The ussissi worked for everyone and served no one. They told each other things. Aras wondered how the *gethes* with their obsession for concealment and their greed for information would view the ussissi if they ever met. "There is another human ship inbound. *Actaeon.* And it is in contact with the isenj."

So, it would be *when* they met. Aras felt relief flood his body like a nutrient: this was not about Parekh. But the relief didn't last long enough.

"Aras, did you know of this ship?"

"No. Nothing." He wondered if Shan did. He had so wanted to like her, to trust her. Now he had two fears: that she knew somehow that he carried *c'naatat,* and that she had concealed this second mission.

"This is a fast ship, much faster than the *Thetis,* with hundreds of *gethes* on board. It left their homeworld years later but it will be in our space in a season, perhaps two."

The transmissions back to Earth were monitored and there had not been the slightest hint of expectation that others were coming. Shan might not know that more *gethes* were on their way. "When did it leave?"

Mestin took a long time looking through the screen in her lap, and looked agitated. "What is 2351?"

"A designation for a human year." So Shan could not have known. *Actaeon* had left fifty years after she had embarked. *Gethes'* technology was advancing. "And the isenj?"

"They made contact with the *gethes*. They are making friends and allies, and apparently discussing how they might share technologies like their instantaneous communications, which the *gethes* want very much. They have set up a relay close to the *gethes'* homeworld, the better to demonstrate their wares."

"Earth. It's called Earth." Aras reminded her, and started doing his sums. There was an isenj instantaneous communications node ten light-years out from Earth, so that meant they had detected *Actaeon* fifteen years ago if they had managed to send out another relay and have it on station by now. If the ussissi hadn't known about it—and if they had, then one of them would have talked about it eventually—then the isenj were treating this with extreme secrecy. And that meant that they had started to play a very long-term game.

For a short-lived species, they had an astonishing capacity to think ahead. Perhaps it was a consequence of their trait of genetic memory. They might have imagined that they lived forever.

"They are becoming a problem, Aras."

"Are you going to ask me to remove them?"

"They exist as a glorified *zoo*. That is the word, isn't it? Where humans imprison other species and stare at them? And they exist because you made a mistake in not enforcing the blockade, and let them live. And that is why the other *gethes* are coming. Because of *you*. We cannot relive the past, but how much easier things would be now if you had saved their gene bank and let them perish in their first season on Bezer'ej."

She was right and he hated her briefly and instantly because she had dismissed the hardest part of his life in a single sentence. "And if I had, we would have learned nothing about a potential threat that we would have faced sooner or later. And we would not have potential hostages." He had tried to explain how that kind of negotiation worked with humans, but wess'har did not negotiate and did not take prisoners. "I think you should let me advise the matriarchs on this, seeing as I am the expert on *gethes*."

It was very bad form to argue with a matriarch. But Aras had no mating favors to lose. It was wonderfully liberating.

Mestin sat back in her heap of cushions. He knew what she wanted to do and she wanted to do it now, but she was clearly outgunned by the matriarchs in F'nar on this one. He had a little more time.

"Prepare your plan to cleanse the island, and wait for instructions," she said. "In the end, you will do as the matriarchs say."

Helen.

Shan's head was clearer now. The niggling half-thoughts like items you hadn't written on your shopping list were evaporating as the Suppressed Briefing played out, triggered one instruction at a time by events.

But it was just *Helen.* And Helen was a Perault, married to a Marchant apparently, and Eugenie had told her so in the briefing.

And thank you for Helen.

No wonder Helen had been so grateful. She hadn't ended up in court on charges of conspiracy, murder, arson and membership of a banned organization, because Shan had known so much about counter-terrorism that she could

cross the dividing line herself as easily as moving from
pupil to teacher. Helen was washed clean. And no wonder
Perault had been so grateful; dumb idealistic Shan, feeding
security intelligence to them because she thought it was
right.

What was the difference, anyway? What was the difference between that and punishing the companies that slipped
through the courts by setting the extreme greens on their
CEOs and shareholders? A leak here, a detail there. Her political masters had been perfectly comfortable with the latter tactic. It was one of the things that gave EnHaz its teeth.
Without it, she'd have been no more than an armed forest
ranger.

Helen. Helen had been chief of IT at one of the biotech
firms, someone Shan needed to know. She knew about
Shan's recurring waking nightmare of the gorilla because
Shan had told her in an unguarded moment; she had been
stupid enough to reveal it because she suspected Helen
might have been a security risk and she wanted to test her
attitude to research. Well, she hadn't been wrong about Helen, but the woman suddenly knew her for the potential ally
she was. And then it began.

Helen had been the only person who had ever managed
to turn Shan's skills back on her. No, it wasn't stupidity.
Shan knew she was the best at her job and never doubted it.
But on that one day, Helen had been better.

*This is your chance to make amends for that animal, Su-
perintendent. Get to the gene bank if you can, and . . .*

Perault's next instruction refused to come. Shan had
wanted to make amends for a very long time.

Perault was probably dead by now and so was Helen,
and it didn't matter anymore. No wonder Perault thought
she was the woman for the job. She knew exactly what
would make her break the rules and how far she would go to
do it.

It was a hard realization, and she put the screen on pause. *I'm black and white. I can't see gray areas even when I'm right in them.* And what motivated Perault? Was she like her sister Helen, or was she just a typical politician, doing whatever it took to keep herself out of a scandal? If so, this seemed a massively extravagant way to do it.

Shan would never know now.

She found it hard to concentrate on the reports on her screen. The light in her cabin was too harsh and there wasn't enough room to stretch her stiff shoulders without hitting her hand against the shelving that Chahal had fixed on the bulkhead for her.

She shook herself out of the speculation and went back to scanning the research data. Champciaux's geological surveys were the most interesting in a dismal selection.

Her eyes were starting to prickle and water with the effort when she smelled sandalwood and Aras simply appeared in the cabin.

"Jesus, don't creep up on me like that," she said. "I was miles away. Make a bit of noise."

He appeared to take no offense. "Did your talk with Eddie upset you?"

"That obvious, eh?"

"I could smell you down the corridor."

"D'you know, that would have been *such* a handy sense to have had when I was interrogating suspects."

"But humans prefer being lied to. I think you would tire of inescapable reality very fast."

"Maybe." She gestured to the bunk: he was too big for the folding chair. "Take a seat. Let's just say Eddie told me something I didn't know that made me wonder why I was sent here."

"I can see why you would prize a developed sense of smell. Have you been tricked?"

"Possibly."

"If you want to unburden yourself, I can keep secrets as well as you can."

She patted his arm. That always prompted a rumbling subsonic. "That's really sweet of you. Thanks, but later."

"What's that?" he said, changing the subject as fast as a child. He pointed to the pen on the makeshift desk.

"A pen. Here, try it."

Aras examined the glossy black tube. His total absorption in the object was hypnotic, like watching a cat confronted with a new toy, and it distracted her from the pain of the day.

"It's just a pen," she said, and instantly regretted dismissing the importance of it to him.

"It's beautiful." He gave it a final look and replaced it on the desk exactly at its original position and angle. "Is it very old?"

"Certainly is—liquid ink. You won't find many humans back home writing manually, let alone using an instrument like that. It's all vox and neural text these days."

She picked up the pen and uncapped it, and held it out to him. He took it and stared; so she made the gesture clearer, relinquished her chair and moved a sheet of the colony's textured hemp paper to a position where he could write on it.

"Can you write?"

"Of course I can," he said. "The colonists make glass pens. I showed them how. Their ink is made from fungi."

"Ah. Silly me."

Aras settled into the chair and dwarfed it. He braced his arm on the table, as no doubt he had seen Josh do, and began writing with slow care. Shan watched from a discreet distance, anxious not to look over his shoulder, and waited while he made apparently random movements with his arm. Eventually her patience faded and she found herself standing beside him, looking at the paper. He stopped and turned to her: he wasn't exactly smiling, because there was no display of teeth, but he beamed. She couldn't define it. But the fast-learning social monkey in her had picked up those basic nuances from the start, and he was *happy*.

Exquisite Arabic script swept along the top of the page. Beneath it, there was a passage of something Asian—Sanskrit?—and Hebrew.

"Oh wow," she said.

From a human, she would have taken it as a show of conceit, a demonstration of expertise at her expense. But this was Aras. For him, it was what it was, and performed for the joy of it.

She capped the pen again and handed it to him.

"Here, it's yours."

"No, it's yours."

"I meant I'm giving it to you."

Did he understand gifts? He was from a race that set little store by possessions, and living with an ascetic human community. She knew that if he didn't accept the gift with the same joy he had shown in using it that she would be inexplicably hurt. For a few moments he was absolutely, completely still. She had never seen such a total absence of movement in a human being. He held the pen in both hands as if aware there was some kind of social ritual at work. She waited.

He suddenly beamed. "You are always unexpectedly kind," he said. "Thank you. I'll find ways to use it."

No fripperies: worthwhile things had a use. She took it as the approval it was and didn't care that he was surprised by generosity. She took the paper and admired the handwriting again. "May I keep this?"

"But it's yours."

"I meant that it has significance for me, and I would like

to keep it because you've made it into something beautiful. One day I'll take this out and look at it and remember you when I'm . . . well, a long way from here."

As soon as she said it, she knew that she could never bear to look at it again once she'd taken her final leave of him. She slipped the paper into a folder on the desk. "So where have you been?"

"The Temporary City. Do you know what *Actaeon* is?"

Another leap off into a topic that interested him, no doubt. Fine. "I think he was a hunter in Greek mythology who was turned into a stag by some angry goddess and then his hounds tore him to pieces. Serves him bloody well right."

Where was he going with this? She enjoyed the rambling discussions she sometimes had with him. He liked knowledge. She thought a long discourse was just what she needed to shrug off Helen and Perault and the nagging memory of Parekh.

"No, it's a ship," he said. "A *gethes* ship. And it will be here in a few months."

You had to hand it to wess'har. They could floor you with just a few well-chosen words.

It was dusk and the horizon shaded through from amber at the skyline to a dramatic purple where the first stars were becoming visible. There was not a constellation Shan could recognize. That was a shame, because she had never been able to see more than the brightest stars in the hazy sky of home, and now that she finally had unimaginable clarity, she couldn't see what she had strained to observe all her life.

She wandered along the perimeter where the barrier cut a visible boundary between a surrogate Earth and wild Bezer'ej. Aras matched her pace.

"I need to see the gene bank," she said.

"Why?"

"It's in my Suppressed Briefing. I have to secure it." She strained for further definition: nothing came. "I'll know more when I see it, but right now I know that I have to get to it. And having *Actaeon* showing up soon makes that urgent."

"And was *Actaeon* in your briefing too?"

"No. Couldn't be. Perault couldn't have known about events that far in the future. She might have set me up for something she had planned a year ahead, maybe a little more, but she'd have to be frigging Nostradamus to slip that one in."

"I don't like this SB."

"Well, it's not a bundle of laughs at this end, either."

"And you say it must be a benign purpose she has for you, because you accepted it gladly when she revealed it."

"Yes."

"And I should believe you."

"I don't really care if you do or not," she lied. "I just know what I have to do."

And that was a lie too. However much she had been told and however valid it had seemed at the time, events had been unfolding from the moment the SB was sealed chemically into her memory.

Things had changed.

They had changed in ways that even Perault had not imagined, and suddenly having reliable instantaneous communications—something that had always seemed just an impractical and costly trick in a lab—was the most frightening. It was even more alarming than the apparent coziness with the isenj. The real-time Earth, whatever that was, would be on her back in a very short time and she would be as adrift from it as a time traveler. There were no guarantees that what had made sense then would make sense now. Out here, her view still shaped by the world of 2299, she knew too little for her own comfort.

She paused at a convenient outcrop and sat down on it, legs braced.

"Aras, just show me the bank. Just the door if it has one, anything that can trigger me. Then I'll have some chance of knowing where all this was headed."

"Very well, I will show you, and that is all. And you will need to explain this to Josh."

"Fine."

"And what do you think will happen when you tell your people about *Actaeon*?"

"Are they likely to find out by any other route until the ship's in range?"

"Not unless they have entangled photon communications."

"Then I don't plan to tell them anytime soon."

Aras gave her that look of head-tilted, almost canine bewilderment. She imagined it meant he was suspicious rather than baffled. It might have been unwise to show a wess'har that you would deceive your own people when you were trying to convince him that you would not lie to him.

She pressed on. "I wouldn't trust any of the payload as far as I could spit in a force ten. I don't know how Lindsay or the detachment would take it, either. And I don't know how much home has changed politically in seventy-five years. So I'm taking it carefully. If there's anything that reaches you that you think I need to know, I'd be grateful for the heads-up."

"Heads-up?"

"Information, advice, warning." Did he believe her now? "Look, you're the walking polygraph. I'm telling you all I know. And I'm scared, because I'm more out of my depth with every day that passes. I'm scared of *Actaeon*'s reason for dropping by, and I'm scared of what your people are going to do when it does. And I'm scared that I might fail. There. I've spilled my guts, take it or leave it."

Aras stood in front of her, staring. In a human it would

have been an aggressive stance. But Aras was just taking things in.

"Fail in what?" he asked.

"I don't know. My self-appointed duty to save the environment, I suppose." She tried to smile and lighten the moment. "I don't like humans much more than you do, Aras, but I'm one of them, and that makes life very lonely sometimes."

Aras parted his lips as if to say something and then glanced around discreetly and appeared to think better of it.

"Tomorrow," he said. "We will go to Constantine, talk to Josh, and then you will look at the gene bank. And then you will consider your position again."

"It's a deal."

"Come on. We haven't finished our walk yet."

Questions kept queuing up in her mind and it took all the restraint she had not to start asking them. What else had the ussissi told the wess'har? Was it third-hand, or were they listening into voice traffic? And how were the matriarchs taking the suddenly blossoming friendship between humans and isenj? She could probably guess that one without too much trouble.

So she would have to trust Aras. It seemed easier to do that now. For all his personal and military strength and the ease with which he carried that, there seemed to be an awkwardness about him, a sorrow and vulnerability that she found disarming. She had not forgotten how grateful he seemed for a simple touch of the hand.

Yet, she might have been misreading alien body language for human.

"May I see Lindsay's baby when it's born?" he asked.

That was the kind of thing that convinced her there was a core of him that was not two meters tall and unmoved by death. Shan stifled a primeval urge to protect him. "I'm sure she'll be delighted. It'll be a few months yet. Kris says it's a boy."

"I can't get used to females carrying babies to term. Not even now."

It was another of those non sequiturs he often tossed into conversation. Some of them made sense days later, like the way he used the term *people* to describe any species. Others were just mysteries. "You'll have to explain that to me," Shan said cautiously.

"It's a male function."

"Not getting used to it?"

"Nurturing embryos. It's a male role."

"Not where I come from." She tried to avoid the immediate urge to stare at his body and wonder how and where. "Are you serious? Males conceive?"

"No, we gestate. Females conceive. Then the embryo is transferred."

"Ah. Sort of like seahorses." No, this wasn't the time to ask more. The vision was becoming too graphic, and there were no more seahorses left on Earth. "You don't have children, do you?"

"No. I regret that."

"Is it too late to have them?"

Aras made an odd little gesture that might have been a shrug. "I think so. And you, will you have babies with the sergeant?"

"Where the hell did that come from?" She hated the thought of the detachment ribbing Bennett about their non-relationship. It was almost worse than catching them sniggering about her. But Aras was a wess'har, and very little of an emotional nature escaped his senses. Maybe the others had dismissed the idea.

"When he talks with you the sexual signaling is very clear," he said. "Have I spoken out of turn?"

Shan shook her head. Aras really could be a child, appealingly open, embarrassingly frank, delighting in the moment. And then he could put two shots through Parekh's head and not turn a hair. She reminded herself he was an alien, a real alien.

"Let's just say it's not possible right now. It's bad for team discipline. And he has this damn bioscreen network thing built into him that records his body functions and all sorts of stuff I really wouldn't like broadcast to his comrades. Do you know what I mean?"

"Yes," said Aras. "That's very sad."

"Maybe when we're back on Earth." Like Aras, Bennett struck her as a hard man nursing a great deal of pain and uncertainty that he never allowed to get the better of him. She liked that in a man. "But I'm not good at relationships."

"What a lonely pair we are," said Aras, pointing up at the darkening sky to indicate the streaking sparkle of a meteor.

Like a child, he had an uncanny ability to say the things adults preferred to leave unsaid.

20

TO: All *Thetis* personnel
FROM: Supt FRANKLAND

You should be aware that there may be some wess'har traffic movement in the next few weeks. This is in response to diplomatic contact between the wess'har and the isenj. Please ensure you notify the duty officer of exact plans of movement and estimated return times when you travel off camp.

Behind the cool room where the colonists kept the last of the autumn onions and pumpkins, there was a dull gray composite cabinet about the size of a restaurant refrigerator. It could have held sides of bacon. But that was out of the question here.

Shan touched it and looked up at the frame that stood a little higher than her head. The Suppressed Briefing said nothing. "Is that it?"

Josh was agitated. He hovered in her peripheral vision, glancing at Aras and getting no reaction from him. "It's *part* of it," he said.

"Open it up, please."

"Now?"

"Josh, I need to know. We have a ship inbound from Earth and a very real chance that we're *all* going to have our trip cut short rather violently if the wess'har think we're allying with the isenj. I was sent here for this. I am not leaving without knowing why."

Aras put his hand on the door and pressed the recessed

panel. It edged open with a *whomp* of lost vacuum, and mist tumbled out into the cellar. When Shan stepped forward and pulled the door towards her, she found herself bathed in an incongruous red light that said *hot, danger,* when all she could feel was a chill.

"It has switched to internal power," Aras said. "You have an hour. I don't think you need take that long."

No, she didn't. As soon as she saw the layer upon layer of very shallow shelves, stacked a few centimeters apart, and the docking points to accept a data-transfer jack on each layer, the SB kicked in. It felt like she had remembered she had left a tap running. There was a jerk of realization and panic.

Inventory. Download the inventory and check the integrity of the following specimen groups: wheat, rice, maize . . .

It was simply a long list of commercial crops. There was no mention of rare birds or endangered orchids or any of the precious cargo that could re-create paradise. But it was a shopping list worth billions.

Dead Eugenie Perault was standing at her shoulder, telling her what plans the Federal European Union had for those specimens.

Shan knew. She knew it all now, and she knew why Perault's argument had been persuasive enough not only to stop her invoking her right to retire from the force but to commit herself to a bizarre and uncertain mission from which she had no guarantee of returning.

The specimens were a testament to the diligence of a biodiversity team long dead. Every strain of cereal and plant was unpatented, unengineered, and belonged to no agricorporation; each had disappeared from Earth long before, forced out of circulation by transgenics and other modified crops that had a trademark on them.

The plants were anyone's to grow and propagate.

The FEU will take those strains and patent them itself to

break the cartel of the corporations, blocking any attempt to restrict availability and giving them back to farmers and allotment holders across Europe. Perault was right there again in front of her. *It will be the first time in over a century that any man or woman can grow what they please without license or restriction.*

Perault knew her very well, it seemed. It was a project she would have given her life to see succeed. She thought of her contraband tomato seed and shivered.

"Are you all right?" Aras asked.

"I'm fine," she said. But she wasn't. She should have been exulting, punching the air at the realization that she had finally beaten the agricorporations she detested so profoundly. With enough of this seed made available, and cheaply, agribusiness would be stripped of much of its economic power and influence on the actions of governments.

Perault had given her a treasure map to a past. The problem was that Shan had no idea to what present government she might have to deliver this booty.

"Is there more of this?" she asked. There had to be. There had to be tens of thousands of species and strains, and that couldn't fit in one big fridge. Josh looked at Aras again for some cue and it was starting to irritate her. "For Chrissakes, I am *not* compromising this stuff. I need to protect it. Now, is there any more of it?"

"There is a great deal more and it is on Wess'ej," Aras said.

"Okay, that's fine for the time being."

"You know now what your objective was."

"Oh yes, indeed. I certainly do." There was no harm telling them. In fact, the only way she was going to get that material shipped back to Earth was with their cooperation. She could hardly lug that fridge back up to *Thetis*. It was going to require some planning and hardware. "Back home, every crop is patented and belongs to some corporation that makes a lot of money out of it. Farmers can't develop their own strains like they used to or even save seed for the next season. We just let this happen a few strains at a time, year on year, and then it was too damn late to do anything about it. None of the strains stored here are patented. My government was going to patent them itself and make them freely available to bust the agricorp cartel." She spread her hands as if she had completed a conjuring trick, and wished more than anything that she could have rejoiced. Aras was staring at her as if he had seen something he hadn't noticed about her before.

He put his palm against the cabinet door and pressed it shut. "That presupposes your government would not behave as badly as the agricorps."

"That's the problem," said Shan. "Who's my government now?"

Eddie realized just how close the wess'har camp must have been to the colony when he saw the first of the fighters.

A *whiissshh* overhead made him look up from his notes. The craft was small and narrow and, apart from the *whiiissshh*, silent. He knew nothing about wess'har military technology, but he knew a fighter when he saw one. It flew east and disappeared in seconds. Either they were checking out the mission base en route, or they were showing the monkeys they meant business. Still, it was an impressive sight. He made a mental note to have the bee cam permanently active in the future, just in case he missed another chance of good footage. He closed down his note file and went back to his cabin.

On the way he passed Qureshi. "Did you see that?" he asked, thinking she might have a finer appreciation of flying machinery. "Very neat."

"Just caught the tail end," she said. "You going off camp?"

"Thought I might."

"No straying near the wess'har, and mind the roads," she said. "You ought to have Frankland or someone with you. Ade's free."

"I can manage. If I fall in, the camera can make its own way back, so don't rescue me."

"Wasn't planning to," said Qureshi, and smiled.

Both scoots were out and the wess'har base was probably way too far on foot anyway. So there were just the shifting, living roads to watch out for. Eddie arranged his pack to rest comfortably on his back and set out at a steady pace.

He set the bee cam to focus on any movement and enjoyed the day around him. Who would have thought he would end up doing wildlife documentaries? God, that would have pissed Wiley off no end. It was a shame the bastard was probably dead now, but maybe he wasn't. Eddie was comfortable with the prospect of gloating at an old man. When he got back to Earth, there might even be an award waiting for him.

He was wondering how he might make use of such an award upon the thawing of his frozen career when another *whiisshhh* and then another stopped him in his tracks.

This time the bee cam got the shots. Eddie need not have worried: a further five of the sleek craft passed over him in the next hour. They weren't the mail run, that was for sure. He ate his rations in slow contemplation while the bee cam settled its gaze on him, but he waved it away. This, at least, was probably real news material, and it would keep him going until he broke down the colonists' reserve and got some more solid, gutsy human interest *meat* to chew on. Shan didn't mind him visiting Constantine once a week even if she tailed him like the copper she was. But the colonists seemed different now: they were even less communicative than usual and seemed uncomfortable. Eddie wondered if they knew something he didn't, something connected to the sudden appearance of the fighters.

Eddie waited another hour. There were no more craft after that. When he wandered back into camp in the mid-afternoon, he found a small knot of marines and scientists gathered around Shan and Lindsay. Whatever she was saying, it was significant enough for the payload to suspend their hatred of her and stand around to listen. Shan caught his eye, and carried on talking to the group, but Qureshi broke away and came jogging up to him.

"There you are," said Qureshi. "You didn't walk into a firefight, then?"

"I fought off two ten-foot monsters, if that's of any interest."

"Nah. Boring. We have a situation." She said it as if the word had a capital S, and a military capital S at that. "The boss is briefing us."

Eddie thought Qureshi meant Lindsay at first, as Royal Marines would, but when she rejoined the group she was staring intently at Shan. Eddie tried to blend in at the back.

". . . so there's no immediate need for us to evacuate, but let's be sensible," Shan said. "Stick close to base and wait until things calm down a little."

Shan struck Eddie as the sort of policewoman who would usher people away from the corpse of a unicorn, telling them there was nothing to see. The knot broke up. Shan stood there and stared back at Eddie.

"I've missed something, haven't I?" he said.

"A little local difficulty," she said.

"As in hostile difficulty?"

"As in the isenj are reasserting their territorial claims and the wess'har had a major sense-of-humor failure. It happens every so often apparently. Like Gibraltar. An isenj ship was shot down in disputed space. If down is the right word, of course. I'm being colloquial."

"That would explain the air traffic."

"We're not in any danger. There's just a touch of nervousness in the wess'har camp."

"I'm more interested in why the isenj thought it was worth trying again after the kicking they got the last time. Maybe they have short memories."

Shan silenced an insistent beep from her swiss with a flick of her thumb. "Perhaps our landing sent out some confusing messages to them. They might think there'd been an unofficial relaxation of restrictions."

"Wouldn't be the first time that's happened. History is full of such misreadings." Eddie followed Shan across the compound; she seemed to be heading for Constantine. "You would have thought they understood wess'har well enough to know they're not that subtle. On the other hand, human governments play dumb. Why shouldn't aliens?"

"The wess'har cut us an unusual amount of slack in letting us land. Their normal response would be to blow trespassers to kingdom come. Let's hope they didn't seriously misread the situation themselves."

"Even the gods make mistakes."

"We all do." She paused. She cast a dismissive glance at Rayat, who managed to return it for a full five seconds before withering away and disappearing back into the mess hall. "Filed your piece on me yet?"

"No," said Eddie, slowly. He didn't want her to think he was afraid of her, but he couldn't bring himself to say he admired her either. "I don't think it's network material. Do you?"

She had that look of bright and fleeting revelation, the same as when he had bombed her with the name of Helen Marchant. "Understood," she said, her expression closing down again, and walked off.

21

You are to offer every assistance short of military support to the isenj. Your priority is to establish a diplomatic understanding with them under the guidance of my office. I fully understand your concern that you are neither trained nor equipped for either a first contact or diplomatic mission, but an opportunity unparalleled in human history has presented itself and future generations will not forgive us if we squander it.

BIRSEN ERTEGUN, Undersecretary of State,
FEU Foreign Office, to Commander Malcolm Okurt,
CO CSV *Actaeon*

Life went on in Constantine regardless of global politics because it had to, and Aras was glad of it.

He snatched a few moments' respite in the kitchens while he waited. The air was damp and smelled sweetly earthy. An avalanche of soybeans, fine pale beads, roared down the chute from the store and pooled in the pan at the bottom of the hopper, waiting to be transformed into tofu, one of the colony's few staple proteins. Half a dozen children scooped them up in pails and ferried them to the benches, where Ruth Djenaba and two other women poured them into opaque glass bowls the size of the ATV's wheels and covered them with water. Farther along the bench, soaked beans were ready to be ground.

It was as near to a factory process as the deliberately bucolic colony was ever likely to get. They had mechanization available to them, but they often chose to do jobs manually for the pleasure and dedication of it, and Aras understood that need.

The first time Aras had watched tofu being made, one of the craftsmen had pointed to the curdling stage and said, "This is just like making cheese." Later, when they explained to him exactly what cheese was, it turned him off tofu for a long time. He recalled that every time he watched the curding stage. The human predilection to consume matter ejected from animals' bodies revolted him only slightly less than their tendency to eat carrion.

One of the children brought him a bowl of his customary treat—warm soft soy curds topped with grated ginger root and tamari sauce. It might have been his imagination but the boy seemed hesitant, as if he were afraid of him, and there was the same sort of slight tension that he had noticed about Josh in recent weeks. They all knew about Parekh. He understood that killing another human was a sin for them, but it disappointed him that they mourned for a child-killer. You could take this forgiveness thing too far.

And humans were so easy to kill. He hadn't expected that. Fragile bodies, quick to break. Parekh hadn't suffered. It wasn't the wess'har way.

The ginger tingled against his tongue and the tamari was sweet and the curds melted against his tongue. It was a perfect silent moment, a spiritual haven that even the arrival of the *gethes* could not spoil. While he ate, he watched the children patiently rounding up utensils and pans and piling them in a sink to be washed in the yellow whey left over from the curding.

For Aras this was not just a diversion. It had become an affirmation of faith in his own judgment. This activity, this transformation of the unassuming soybean into the foundation of a community, reinforced his belief that the humans could be good neighbors. It harmed no being and it created no waste. Every part of soy had a use: it was a vegetable worthy of Targassat herself, and in that he saw meaning. Growing, it was a green manure; harvested, it became fuel, fertilizer, oil, soap, vegetable, beverage, flour, condiment, and meat. It seemed more a product of design than of natural circumstance, and utterly wess'har in its utility. The colonists would have said it was all part of the great plan.

If only all human activity had been like this, Aras thought. *We might have been able to live together.* He finished his bowl of curds and waited for Shan Frankland to appear.

He had learned a lot about her in recent months. When they went walking around the island, she answered his questions and volunteered much more. She worried about the fate of her houseplants left behind in her apartment when she was plucked from her own time without warning. She worried about another humanoid, a gorilla, that she felt she had failed to protect. She worried about getting old and not having made a difference to the world. But not once had she expressed any self-pity. She had, she said, got the life she deserved.

He couldn't stop liking her more and more.

But there was one thing he needed to know and that was whether she had worked out the true nature of his disease. If she had—and he was wrong about her integrity—then she was a risk.

She asked questions. She knew his great age, and she knew about the image in Constantine's library. She was a professional investigator: she would find out sooner or later. And while he felt she would not betray or misuse that information, he needed to separate fact from hope.

He checked his *tilgir* was in its sheath and leaned back in the alcove to be absorbed by the soothing rhythms of *efte* utensils and sighing water.

When Shan eventually walked into the kitchens she stood looking around as if she hadn't seen him. The colonists acknowledged her with nods and then turned back to their tasks, talking and laughing again, and for a moment he saw her do what the shyer colony children did when they couldn't join in the older ones' games. She dropped her shoulders a little and looked down at the floor, as if for a few seconds she was trying to disappear from view. It was just a moment, a lapse of control, but he saw it and he felt her isolation. When he finally stood up and came forward out of the alcove she had become the matriarch again.

He hoped they might still be friends by the end of the day.

It was a clear sunny morning with high, wispy clouds. Out on the rolling blue-gray plain beyond Constantine, they weren't likely to be followed or interrupted.

"Anything new?" she asked.

"The isenj are in very frequent contact with *Actaeon* now. I would say they are becoming allies."

"How are your matriarchs taking it? I bet they're dusting off the best china right now."

"I don't understand."

"I meant that I don't think *Actaeon* will be very welcome. Do your people perceive it as a serious threat?"

"Of course we do. Hundreds of new *gethes*, all making friends with the isenj. What else would we feel?"

"If it's any comfort, it scares the shit out of me too. It's the payload I'm most concerned about. Once they know *Actaeon's* coming, I think all bets are off."

He understood that from the context. "Concealment is hard."

"I'm not very good at it, either."

But she might be better than he imagined. He had to know. It was more than his growing attachment to her that was at stake: it was the weight he gave to her analyses, the political intelligence he derived from her. He had to know for certain that she had no ulterior motive in her apparent concern for him. If she could feign that, she could also be misleading him on everything else.

An *oset* circled them, and they stood staring up at it.

Shan seemed astonished. He looked at her face, all art and control gone from her, and saw someone he could care for like the child he never had.

"What is it?" she asked. She held up her hand to shield her eyes from the light and she must have seen its long jointed tail, serrated like a knife. "Is it dangerous?"

"*Oset.* Your people call it a stab-tail," he said. "It hunts small prey, pierces it and lets it bleed to death."

"You have such cute wildlife. A better pet than the killer plastic bags, though. Why is it following us?"

"It might be an old one, too slow to catch its usual dinner. I think it might be indulging in wishful thinking."

A stab-tail was a rare sight even on the higher ground. He watched it making slow passes, sizing them up. If they had been *udzas*, it would have fallen on them and rammed its tail into them like a knife, hanging on with grim claws until they weakened from blood loss and lay still enough for it to eat.

"If you don't take specimens, how do you learn anything about other species?" Shan asked, her eyes never leaving the circling stab-tail.

"By observation and by occasionally finding corpses."

"That must be pretty limiting."

"Why? We don't need to know any more than how to avoid interfering with them."

"Good point," she said. "Have you ever seen an isenj? Up close, I mean. Not through a gun-sight."

"Yes." *More of them than you can imagine*, he thought. "And before you ask, yes, they are to be feared. For the time being we might have the edge in technology, but they have numbers. And in war, numbers count."

"You were a soldier. Have you fought them?"

There was no reason not to tell her. She already knew he was exceptionally old. "I was one of the senior commanders when we erased them from this planet. I not only directed the operation, I took part in it. I have killed thousands—personally." The white fire came rolling down the street again like a rebuke, trailing screams, but he ignored it. "You would call me a butcher, a war criminal perhaps. Are you appalled?"

It was as if she had expected it. "I think we're very similar, Aras. There are more than a few deaths on my record too. I don't regret any of them."

"Then you're not like the rest of your kind. Even Josh finds this part of me uncomfortable to accept. His ancestor was kinder. He said if I repented I would be forgiven."

"And did you?"

"No. If I had not removed them, would the isenj have repented for killing all the bezeri?"

She gave him a sad smile. "Are the isenj monsters?"

"I'm not the person to ask. I was their prisoner of war."

"I'm sorry. I didn't realize."

Shan made those tuneless humming noises under her breath that humans reserved for moments of awkwardness. They watched the stab-tail for a few more minutes. It was still wheeling above them, riding a thermal. Shan tried again. She was a persistent woman.

"What's your government doing right now?"

"Preparing for conflict."

"Can we sort out the gene bank before the shooting starts?"

"I will help you select plant species but no animal life."

"Fine by me. That's all I came for." She walked on a little farther, still watching the stab-tail as if the conversation she was having was a casual one. It was clear from her scent that it wasn't. "And what will happen to you and the colony if there's fighting?"

"That depends if the isenj try to fight here."

He looked up.

One moment the stab-tail was swooping over them and

diving round behind them, the next he felt it thud hard against his back as if it had punched him. He looked down and a thin cone of wet bronze had appeared from his chest, draining out his blood and his energy. He was aware of Shan shouting, and the flurry of wings, and the weight on his back as he pitched forward.

It had stabbed him. It had latched onto him with its claws and thrust its armored tail deep into his back. He could see blood speckling the ground as he knelt on all fours. It would stop very soon, but it was not a display he wanted Shan to see.

"Oh, Jesus." She was trying to mop at the wound with a piece of cloth, perhaps a folded glove. He batted her hand away to stop her getting blood on her skin. However much pain he was in, the risk of contamination was uppermost in his mind. "Aras, hold still. I'll call base. Don't worry."

"No. It's not serious."

"It's serious, believe me. I'll get help. Don't move."

"I said *no*."

The pain was receding now. He slumped back on his heels and caught his breath. He glanced over his shoulder and saw the stab-tail crumpled on the ground, trying desperately to right itself, flapping weakly. He scrambled over to it to check that it hadn't broken the skin of its tail. An open wound would have been disastrous.

"Did you hit it?" he asked.

"I pulled it off you." Her face was white and she smelled of panic, but she was going through the motions of controlled calm. "What have I done? Have I made things worse?" She was peering at his chest, then his back. "Christ, that thing's done some damage. Don't move. Here, hold still."

"Don't touch it."

"Sorry. Look, put some pressure on it. You'll bleed to death."

"No, I won't," he said. He made a grab for the stab-tail and held it by its neck. Its tail flicked back and just missed his arm, but he managed to get both hands on it and held it still while he searched for wounds. No, the blood was his own. The stab-tail was an old, weak creature and the effort of the attack had all but killed it. It was dying of exhaustion; its flight membranes were dry and lifeless and its fang-ringed little mouth opened and closed pathetically. After a while it stopped struggling, and he took his hands off it and left it to die. At least that was one problem he had been spared. He couldn't afford to infect something so predatory.

He stood up, relieved. But Shan's eyes were on his chest, fixed on the bloodstains left by the wound, her expression all astonishment and suspicion.

"I've seen enough stabbings to know you should be starting to lose consciousness by now," she said quietly. "Does it hurt?"

"Of course it hurts. Resilience is not the same as feeling no pain. Far from it."

"Resilience? Is that what you call it?" She made as if to touch the wound again and he raised his arm in warning. "Okay. Okay. I'll back off."

"I don't need help."

"You're not even hemorrhaging, are you?"

"I don't. Not for long."

"But that spike went right through you."

"It will heal. Believe me, it will heal."

The immediate crisis was past. He looked at the blood on his clothing: so what had the *c'naatat* decided to borrow from the stab-tail, if anything? Would he notice the changes? Experience told him he would be aware in a few days if the parasite had taken a liking to any of the predator's features. He didn't relish the prospect of wings again. The colonists had reacted to those in the most extraordinary way.

Shan sat down beside him so that her shoulder was resting against his, and said nothing for a while. She smelled agitated.

"You heal bloody fast."

"I think you already said that." The pain was faint now. He shifted slightly.

"I thought as much when we shot you down. Kris Hugel keeps asking if I can persuade you to give some tissue samples. She was really fascinated by how you walked away from that crash."

Under his tunic, he felt discreetly for his *tilgir*. The blade was good and sharp. He didn't want to use it. *Please, Shan Chail, don't disappoint me. Don't be a* gethes. "You know, don't you?"

"Know what?"

He tightened his grip on the blade and dreaded what he would have to do. He had not felt that about Parekh. He had not felt that about the isenj. But this was his friend. "You have calculated my age, and you have seen the images in Constantine's records, and you have seen me survive fatal injuries. Somehow you know about *c'naatat*. Now answer me this: Did you touch me to try to acquire it?"

Her expression was one of genuine and total bewilderment. "I haven't got a clue what *c'naatat* is. What the hell is this about?"

He had gone one word too far. "No matter."

"No, don't you bloody well 'no matter' me. You've accused me of something and I don't even know what it is. Come on. What's the problem here?"

The *tilgir* was still there. He could silence her if he had to, but it was the last thing he wanted to do.

"If I tell you, it must stay with you. Or I will have to kill you. I mean that."

She pulled a hard and unamused face. "Don't take the piss. I'm not in the mood."

"This is far from a joke. I am infected with a native parasite called *c'naatat*. It has colonized my body and does whatever it sees fit to keep me alive as its host."

"Does what, exactly?"

"Repairs injury, restores cellular degeneration, neutralizes pathogens and toxins. It assimilates useful gene sequences from other sources to improve its host's survival capabilities."

"Let me guess. You don't look at all like a normal wess'har, do you? That was the long gold thing in the picture. It was you." She made an embarrassed face, screwing up her eyes for a second. "Sorry. I didn't mean thing. Person."

"That was in the early days of my exposure to human DNA. *C'naatat* seems to like *gethes'* features."

Shan made that *mmm* sound of a human pondering something serious and said nothing. He wondered if she were playing Eddie's trick of sitting in silence and waiting for the other person to weaken and start talking.

"Could it infect a human?"

"I have no idea. But it's a very adaptable organism, and it seems to favor large, mobile hosts."

"So this is your disease."

"Yes."

"So what can kill you?"

Aras knew she had finally worked it out. "Only catastrophic injury like fragmentation. I could starve to death, eventually, or asphyxiate in the right conditions, but my body's ability to adapt makes me wonder even about that. I have no idea just how many survival mechanisms it has collected over time."

"Oh, *shit*," said Shan. "Shit."

"Not your idea of a miracle, then."

"I'm ten paces ahead of you on this, Aras. Do you want me to tell you how we'd make use of this if we got our hands on it, or can you imagine?"

"Only too well."

"You better stay clear of the payload. Like I said, they'll have you chopped, diced and on slides in no time if they find out."

She was silent again, looking out over the plain with her lips moving slightly every so often as if she was going to say something. He could feel the warmth of her through his tunic. It was some comfort.

"How the hell have you coped with this?" she asked.

"Sometimes well, sometimes not."

"This is a nightmare."

That much was reassuring. She had not become wildly excited; she had not started to talk of *c'naatat* being a boon to mankind. She had not asked how it might benefit *her* or discussed the parasite's value. She was frightened for her world and for him, but he hoped she would not become afraid of him as the others had. After a taste of real comradeship, that occasional precious touch, he felt he couldn't face a return to isolation.

"So you've watched everyone you know die. You don't know what new feature you're going to wake up with. Jesus, I'm not sure I could cope with that."

"Ben—Josh's ancestor—said it was my punishment from God," said Aras.

"Well, Ben was a sanctimonious bastard. Have the colonists ever shown any interest in it?"

"And keep them from their God in heaven? They reject it totally. It terrifies them."

"So why did Ben think it was punishment? For being a heathen alien?"

"For slaughtering isenj. I caught it from them here when I was their prisoner of war, you see. Open wounds are an ideal vector. And isenj have genetic memory. So now I have some of their memories, memories of me and what I did to them. I can see why Ben thought it had been designed to teach me a lesson."

Shan's face crumpled for a second or two and she looked away, angry. "Aras, I'm so sorry." She took his hand and he knew for certain that it wasn't to grab a sample. "Is that why you wiped them out? To stop this spreading further?"

"Isenj breed rapidly anyway, but with the *c'naatat* reducing their death rate they became a plague. There were a billion or more bezeri before the isenj came, and now there are just a few hundred thousand. It has taken centuries for their population to recover even to that level—and that is what pollution really means, *Shan Chail*. It means the death of other beings. As I said, I would do it again."

She linked her arm through his and they sat on the slope for a long time, watching a rockvelvet creep up on the dead stab-tail to leave the world tidy again. A few *cusics*, crablike things, began edging closer to it, eventually taking a few nips of flesh and then swarming over the body. The black velvet continued its approach, draping from rock to rock in a relentless flow towards the carrion.

It slid up over a leg. A *cusic* froze, claws raised in defense of its prize, but then beat a retreat. Gradually, mechanically, the rockvelvet forced the *cusics* away with its persistence and enveloped the corpse, shrouding it like a black drape. The mound slowly flattened as the creature beneath was digested, and the shroud eventually gathered itself and flowed off to a sunny rock to bask until its next meal. The whole quiet destruction had taken about fifteen minutes.

Shan made that sighing sound again. "What about your own people?"

"I am in exile. A war hero, admittedly, but no *isan* would copulate with me, not with this condition. You transmit your genetic material vertically, to your children, don't you? We share ours horizontally as well when we copulate. Consider it the worst possible venereal disease."

"Surely *someone* would be curious what it would be like

to live that long. Humans certainly would. We wouldn't
give a toss how much havoc it wreaked with world ecology.
We're halfway to hell with an aging population as it is."

"Wess'har don't share your attitude towards death. We
are far more aware of our genetic survival than our individual ones."

He stood up and helped her to her feet. If he had sought
a demonstration of his powers of recovery, he couldn't have
staged a more impressive one. But at least she still took his
hand when he offered it and didn't recoil. If anything, his
revelations seemed to have stirred a gentleness in her, a
concern that was obvious from the way she had dropped her
voice and softened that rigid posture. She walked slowly in
pace with him, arm through his, occasionally rubbing her
hand on it in that comfort gesture he had seen the colonists
use so many times.

He couldn't expect the *gethes* to ignore the military potential of *c'naatat*. His own kind hadn't, for all their discipline. It had given them a hope of redressing the imbalance
against a far more populous enemy, creating reusable
troops who could survive terrible injuries and still fight. But
recovery was a design flaw if you fell into enemy hands.
The matriarchs never planned for that to happen. And they
never planned to rescue hostages, either. He was just un-
lucky.

His isenj captors taunted him about it. His people didn't
give a damn, they reminded him, when he'd finished
screaming. He didn't matter anymore. He was a monster, a
murderer of children and the unarmed. He deserved what
he got.

Looking back, Aras was unsure what had been worse:
the physical torture or being force-fed carrion. The isenj
knew how particular wess'har were about other life-forms.
It was the heart of their belief and self-respect. He wondered if Shan would understand that. It would have seemed

ludicrous to a *gethes*. The pain faded, and *c'naatat* didn't
scar: but being defiled in that way, defiled to the very heart
of yourself, was far harder to forget.

In a way it was easier to scream. Sometimes they could
make him scream for days.

Shan squeezed his arm.

"Promise me something," she said.

"What?"

"If there's the slightest risk of this getting out through
me, if I catch it, if I might let something slip out . . . you
know what to do, don't you?" She tapped her fingers
against the *tilgir* under his clothing. He had forgotten she
would be able to feel the hard metal handle against her hip.
Her expression was earnest, grim. "Do what you have to.
But make it quick."

Ben had told him all about guilt and repentance. So *this*
was what guilt felt like.

It hurt.

22

You should be within communications range of Thetis *in the next 72 hours. Their comms fit is not compatible with your encryption and you will need to use plain voice to establish contact. According to the isenj, you are also likely to attract wess'har attention at a range of approximately 750,000 kilometers. Please maintain an open channel with the isenj relay at all times for instructions. You are not to land on Cavanagh's Star II, regardless of what emergency might present itself. You are not to take any action that the isenj might interpret as an act of aggression towards them, whatever the provocation.*

AIR MARSHAL XAVIER RONQUILLO MORALES,
FEU Chief of Staff, to CO *Actaeon*

The sky shook.

That was the only way Eddie could describe it. The subsonic throb had woken him before the alarm went off, and he had stumbled out of the camp to see what was happening. On his way out he saw Chahal and Paretti huddled under a table, and stopped.

"What the hell are you doing?" he said.

"Earthquake," they answered in unison. Eddie didn't come from earthquake country, so he ignored them. Earthquakes shook the ground. That wasn't what was happening now.

Outside, there was only one place to look, and that was up. And above him was a sight that stopped him breathing.

Two great slow-moving craft were passing over the fields, casting cold shadows. They were smooth and curved like blue bullets, and he had never seen anything quite like

them. At first he couldn't grasp their scale. Then he realized
they were flying much higher than he imagined and so—so
they were immense beyond his comprehension. He couldn't
hear them, but he could feel them in his mouth and in his
bones. Primeval fear overwhelmed him.

Someone tapped his shoulder. Startled, he spun round to
find Shan standing beside him, looking as if she had been
up all night. He could chart the shadows under her eyes almost to the hour now.

"Isenj?" he shouted over the vibration.

"I can hear you okay," she said. "No, that's the
wess'har."

"What are they doing?"

"Reinforcing the garrison again. I think we have a
problem."

She looked scared. It was an odd expression. He had
seen angry, and he had seen contemptuous, and he had even
seen shocked, but scared was new. It didn't seem the right
time to ask. He stared up again, watching the huge ships
pass majestically overhead and fade into the glare of the rising sun.

Eddie didn't watch where Shan went, nor was he even
aware of her leaving. He squatted down on the ground for a
few moments and tried to regain his orientation. The experience totally shattered his perception of the world. A year
ago, by his conscious reckoning, he had been a member of
the most advanced species in creation. Now he was a small,
isolated speck on an alien world, watching truly massive
ships—ships that seemed beyond the skill and technology
of humans—sweep over him on business he couldn't com-
prehend. *Humans didn't matter.* He wasn't part of the
game. He had stood amid running street battles in Italy,
oblivious to genuine danger, feeling immune from the
events around him because he had a camera. The headset
and the eyepiece were a shield against all perils, and a num-

ber of reporters thought that way right up to the moment they got killed. He wished he could feel that way now.

Then he was angry. It was one of the few times in his life that his first instinct had not been to run for his camera. He had missed the shot.

"Bugger," he said.

Sabine Mesevy passed him. He turned to look, and noted she was in her best fatigues, smart and clean, with her chestnut hair pinned back in a pleat. She seemed not to be alarmed by the military activity.

"Where you off to, then?" he said. "You scrub up well."

"Church," she said. "It's Sunday, in case you've lost track. Why don't you come?"

"No thanks. Heaven might rejoice at a repentant sinner, but its jury is still out on journalists."

"Shame." She smiled at him. "Lovely stained-glass window. It would make a great shot."

For the matriarchs, the unthinkable had happened. The blockade of Bezer'ej had fallen after 495 years.

Aras strode through the passages of the Temporary City, now crammed with extra troops. They had been deceived by scale. The isenj had somehow landed three tiny craft within thirty kilometers of them. The defense grid was set to detect and neutralize much larger vessels to defend against a mass landing. And there was only one reason for landing a small force, and that was to carry out a covert action on specific targets.

The isenj had learned something from the wess'har after all. They had learned that winning wasn't entirely about numbers.

"*Mestin Chail* is busy," said one of the new males fresh in from F'nar, not looking up from his screen, and Aras cuffed him hard round the head. He stumbled but he didn't fall. He gaped at Aras.

"You must be new here," Aras said. "But you know who I am. I will see Mestin now."

It was one of the privileges of being Aras Sar Iussan, the Restorer of Bezer'ej, the last of the *c'naatat* troops. He could see anyone he damn well pleased, even a commanding matriarch. In a social hierarchy where age and experience created rank among males, Aras was very nearly as respected as a female. He planned to use that advantage.

Mestin was standing in the center of the control chamber while her husbands and cousins and older children went about the tasks of organizing supply lines and setting up accommodation for the incoming clans. She glanced at Aras and beckoned him over.

"Are you certain they landed?" he asked.

"Ussissi information is very reliable. They say the isenj timed the incursion to coincide with the arrival of *Actaeon*. They thought we might have our minds on other things."

"We did."

"The ussissi also say the isenj have sent in two teams to infiltrate the Temporary City and destroy our defenses." She brought up the local-scale chart of the area with a movement of her hand and pointed out a constellation of colored points of light, two blue, twelve amber: she had deployed a number of foot units in the hunt already. "We will find them the slow way. I have no intention of using destructive weapons in this environment yet. And if we fail, then we have enough troops and materiel in place to deal with an invasion."

"And the third team?"

"On your island, Aras. They have come for you."

Aras thought it was a foolish waste of military resources to commit troops to settle an ancient grudge. It was the kind of gesture he would have saved for a quiet moment, if wess'har had been the kind of people who cared about revenge. They weren't. But Aras's genes were at least a fraction human, and another fraction isenj; and these invaders were in his protectorate, near Constantine, within striking distance of both his friends and the unpredictable new *gethes*.

"Then they shall find me," he said. "I will see their journey isn't wasted."

23

THETIS THETIS THETIS
THIS IS WARSHIP ACTAEON ACTAEON ACTAEON
THETIS THETIS THETIS
THIS IS WARSHIP ACTAEON ACTAEON ACTAEON
CALLSIGN 67XBN. I HAVE CHANNEL 175.
ENTERING CAVANAGH SYSTEM 15758659
RESPOND CHANNEL 175

"I know you all hate my guts," said Shan. "But, with immediate effect, you're all confined to camp until further notice."

The mess hall was quiet. Lindsay had expected at least some muttered expletive, but the payload were silent. The last time Shan had assembled them in this room, she had announced that Surendra Parekh had just been handed over to Aras. They seemed to know her next announcement was going to be equally unpleasant. Lindsay propped her backside on the edge of a table. She hoped Shan would excuse her lack of military posture, but her back was killing her and her legs ached. And it was still two months before the baby was due.

"I've had two messages today," Shan continued. "One was from the wess'har command post on the mainland to warn us that an isenj armed unit has landed on the island. The other was sitting in the buffer, and it was from a European federal ship called *Actaeon,* which has now entered the Cavanagh system. We've got company."

Lindsay had to hand it to Shan. She had a sense of understated drama. Or perhaps she had just given up wondering about the best way to break bad news to people.

"Is that it?" said Galvin. "Another ship? What are they here for?"

"I thought you might be more concerned about having a commando war going on in our backyard," said Shan.

"But *Actaeon*?"

"We've been gone a long time. New propulsion systems, faster ships. They set out fifty years after we did and they caught us up."

"Are we going home?" asked Rayat.

"I don't know. I sent a standby response. I'll flash them as soon as *Thetis* is in position again. Until then, no outgoing traffic, okay? I want that link kept clear."

"Aren't we pleased to see them?"

"Okay. Let's get the finger paints out. *Actaeon* is chummy with the isenj. We're in a wess'har protectorate, and the wess'har and isenj are still at war. We need to evacuate but we can't as long as there are isenj troops around. So we wait and see. In the meantime, we sit tight and get ready to leave at short notice."

"How do you know they've been in contact with the isenj?" asked Rayat.

"The wess'har told me so, and they're pretty pissed off about it. I imagine they're questioning which side we'll be on."

Rayat raked his fingers through his hair. "Shit."

"For once, Dr. Rayat, I agree with you entirely,"

Lindsay followed Shan out into the compound. She slowed down to let her catch up.

"You okay?" Shan asked. "Don't you think you should be resting?"

Lindsay didn't want to give in. It was bad enough having to dispense with her uniform and wear the shapeless beige shifts the colony had given her to accommodate her growing belly. She didn't feel much like an officer at all. Shan looked at her with an expression that she couldn't help feeling was pity, and not the positive kind.

"Bad time for a rest," Lindsay said. "My blood pressure is fine. Honest."

"If I were you, I'd make my way over to Constantine's infirmary and sit this one out. I don't have a good feeling about this."

"You might be in overall command but the military side is still mine, Shan." She had leave to call her that now, but the familiarity still felt odd in her mouth. "I promise you I'll do it all from my chair. As of now, shuttles are on standby maintenance, the detachment is rostered for hostilities, and Hugel will establish a field hospital in the biohaz room. We're ready."

I'm not ill, she thought. *This is a temporary inconvenience.* But she knew what happened when women had babies, and she wanted to do her military thinking before her body was totally hijacked by hormonal turmoil and a far narrower focus. And she had overseen evacuations before. This, for all its exotic location and combatants, was no different.

"Perimeter set?" Shan asked.

"Yes, but I'd still be happier if we primed it."

"I don't want any own goals this time. Besides, I don't think we're a target. Not for the isenj, anyway."

"How's your friend taking all this?"

"Aras? I haven't seen him since before I heard about the isenj landing. My guess would be that they're just going to take out the Temporary City. If it was a mass invasion, we'd have known by now."

"If we don't get sucked into this, the wess'har might not see us as potential hostiles."

"And what about the colonists? One thing's clear, if we need to evacuate, there's no quick way of moving a thousand people with two shuttles." She looked distracted for a moment, than snapped back to the here and now again. "That's assuming they wanted to go, which I don't think they will. I'm heading over there now."

"Will you be okay on your own? I could get Bennett to—"

Shan hitched up the back of her waistcoat and indicated her hand weapon, stuffed in the back of her belt. "I might be an amateur when it comes to military matters, but this won't be the first rough neighborhood I've walked through. Don't you worry about me."

Lindsay watched her stride off at a pace she could only envy, then turned and walked carefully back to the mess hall. Rayat and Galvin dogged her steps as she approached.

"This might be our last chance to get some field study in," said Galvin. "You sure that the curfew needs to start now?"

Lindsay was starting to get very tired of civilians. She straightened up as stiffly as a seven-month pregnant woman ever could.

"It's already in force," she said, and stared at them in silence until they walked away.

Aras had never seen Josh with a weapon in his hand before. He was sitting at his kitchen table cleaning a rifle so old that Aras wondered how he would ever get it to fire again.

"You won't need that," said Aras. "The isenj are coming for me."

"But I could stop an isenj with a 7.62mm round, could I not?"

It was such an odd thing for Josh to say. Aras doubted if he had ever fired the gun. It surprised him that he even knew the caliber. "They're flesh too," Aras said. "But I would make that three or four rounds, if I wanted to be certain."

Josh wiped lubricant over the dismantled parts with all the care of a human mother washing an infant. "Good. It's a thirty-round magazine."

There seemed little point arguing with him. If the weapon made him feel safe, that was fine. Aras watched him reassemble the rifle with a little assistance from scribbled instructions on a very old scrap of linen paper. That meant it had been Ben's.

"We have ten of these that will still fire," said Josh. "And there are how many isenj, you say? Ten? Twelve? More than sufficient to deal with them, then."

"You're not going hunting. If I don't find them, they will come here for me. I won't expose you to that."

"Aras, we don't always approve of or even understand the things you do, but we do know two things. It's because of you that we're still here, and you're part of this community. We can defend ourselves. There will be no act of self-sacrifice."

"I wasn't planning one."

"Who isn't?" Shan asked. "Bugger me, isn't anyone looking after security here? I walked straight in. I could have been the isenj."

Aras hadn't even heard her come down the steps and neither had Josh, judging the way he flinched at her voice. She looked at the rifle and raised her eyebrows.

"So who's that for?" she asked.

"They are coming for Aras," said Josh.

Shan turned to Aras. "I was wondering if we could have a word. In private. No offense, Josh."

Josh went back to the reverent assembly of his rifle. Aras wondered if they had thought about calibrating the Earth-made weapon for local gravity. At point-blank range, that wouldn't matter, but he hoped he could resolve matters before they had to find out. Once clear of the galleries, out on the surface, Shan rounded on him.

"You're taking your faith in your invulnerability a little too far," she said. "Are you seriously going after them? Where's your backup?"

"Nobody knows the terrain like I do."

"I don't think this is about getting your tracker badge, Aras. If they've got serious artillery of some sort, you won't survive that."

"They won't have."

"This is intelligence from your ussissi pals, is it?"

"They have come to find me and kill me for what I did to Mjat. They will try to bring me down and cut me to pieces. They haven't forgotten just how hard I am to kill."

"And I thought only humans nursed tribal grudges that long."

"It's much easier to keep your hatred fresh when you have genetic memory. Shan, either I find them or they find me. What would you do? Would you live your life looking over your shoulder, or would you go out and seek the threat and finish it?"

"I can't argue with that."

"And I would rather that took place away from Constantine. That is the first place they will look for me, and they will regard the colony as wess'har regardless of what deal they have struck with *Actaeon*."

There were no workers in the fields today, although it was early autumn and there were the first winter root crops to lift. Everyone had gone below, into the depths of the colony.

"I had come to ask about the gene bank," said Shan. "What you've told me makes that a little more urgent. This might sound callous, but if the colony takes a direct hit, I'd hate to lose that material."

He understood completely. There was nothing brutal in her priorities at all: she had her mission, and there was little she could do to protect Constantine with a handful of troops. It was very wess'har of her not to attempt a meaningless gesture but to concentrate on what she could achieve for the future. And it was very human of him to feel a little uncomfortable to hear it.

"I will arrange for the ussissi to transfer it to F'nar," said Aras.

"Thanks. Are you seriously going out after those isenj?"

"I said so."

"I'm coming with you, then."

"No. Take sides now, and you could compromise your people."

"And the matriarchs will cut us some slack despite *Actaeon,* will they? We're screwed either way."

"Shan, you make this judgment without knowing the isenj."

"But I know you. And I know the bezeri don't want them here. That's all I need to know."

It was what he wanted her to say. He didn't need her strength and he didn't need her expertise, but he needed to hear her say she would take the ultimate risk for him. It was enough. Josh was prepared to defend his people; Shan was prepared to defend him. He had not been wrong about her at all.

But he wondered if she fully understood what he had done at Mjat. Humans were squeamish about such things. His one fear was that one day Shan *would* understand, and that she might see him as a monster too.

Her pocket made that chirping sound. Someone was calling her on her swiss. She ignored it, looking into his face for a response.

"You're a good friend," he said. "But the isenj are in more danger than I am. Go back to your people and wait." The swiss was still *eeping* insistently. "You're being summoned."

"Hang on." Shan pulled out the swiss and flicked open the tiny screen that hung between two filaments like a bubble. He walked a few paces away to give her some privacy, but he heard her side of the conversation all too clearly. "Jesus Christ, when did that happen? Didn't anyone try to keep an eye on them? Oh shit. No, wait until I get back. Have Bennett and Qureshi tool up and I'll meet them at camp."

She snapped the swiss shut and shoved it hard into her pocket with that tight-lipped expression that told him she had run out of expletives. She didn't talk at all like the colonists. He had learned a lot of new words from her, words that made Josh recoil.

"Sorry," she said. "Two of my payload have gone walkabout. Rayat and Galvin, like I couldn't guess. Last chance to grab something live in case they're evacuated."

"Too busy trying to stop people getting in rather than getting out."

"I suppose you have to admire their persistence. Personally, I don't care what happens to them—I'm more worried about another bezeri-level incident."

"And you're going out looking for them?"

"If you're going out looking for isenj."

He wondered for a moment if she had set it up. But she couldn't have known his plans. No, she had proved she was as good as her word. He was wrong to doubt her.

"You know nothing about pursuit in this terrain," said Aras.

"I'm sure you'll teach me," she said. "First, though, I'd better pay my respects to *Actaeon*."

With Rayat and Galvin loose on the plain, Shan resented waiting the extra thirty minutes for *Thetis* to reach a point in its orbit where she could route a call through it. Aras waited patiently in the compound: Qureshi had orders to keep an eye on him in case he decided to start without her.

It took four minutes for the comms operator to patch Shan in to the *Actaeon*'s commanding officer. He introduced himself as Captain Malcolm Okurt, and his voice was completely devoid of emotion.

"Good evening, Superintendent," he said. The audio was

clear but the video link was shimmering. Okurt's fatigues were the kind of average gray that any force could wear, and his badges were indistinct. It was remarkable that the tech was still compatible enough for them to see any image at all. "We were relieved to hear from you."

"We're terrific," Shan said, as flatly as she could manage. "And it's late morning here. Now you've found us, could I ask you which government you represent? You'll have to forgive us. We've been out of town a while."

"This is a joint mission of the Federal European Union Foreign Office, the Confederation of European Industry and the Sinostates consortium."

"And you're FEU Navy? A warship?"

"Someone's got to drive. No commercial sponsorship, no warships."

"My. We *have* been away a long time, haven't we?"

There was a pause. If Okurt was offended by her tone, he wasn't about to let her know. "We've had contact from what appears to be the wess'har government, so we're aware of the local difficulties in this sector. We'll be keeping a low profile for the time being. When we get clearance for landing a shuttle, are there any supplies you need?"

"I don't think you're going to be landing here any time soon. Didn't the isenj explain the situation to you?"

A pause. A very long pause. *Gotcha,* Shan thought. Okurt could now sweat over how she knew he had been communicating with the isenj.

"I understand they don't enjoy good diplomatic relations with the wess'har," he said at last.

"I might like to evacuate my people if you're minded to head out of wess'har space. Just to be on the safe side."

"How many are we talking about?"

"Anywhere between twelve and one thousand."

"Say again?"

"There's a colony here."

"We have nowhere near that capacity."

Shan consoled herself with the thought that the colonists would not leave anyway. It was just a test question, a copper's trick. "Can you accommodate seven military personnel and seven civilians, then?"

"We can do that." He had probably dismissed her request as self-interest. She didn't need to explain herself. "Thank you for your advice, Superintendent. It's very helpful indeed. We'll stand off and await your evacuation plans."

"*Thetis* out," said Shan.

She nodded at Bennett and he closed the link. The three of them looked at each other. "So what salient points did he leave out?" she asked.

Lindsay folded her hands over her belly. "Well, if I were *Actaeon*, I'd probably say why I'd come twenty-five light-years—to rescue, to explore, whatever. They weren't just passing by."

"He had no reason to assume we were lost or dead, either, seeing as nobody would have been expecting to receive transmissions from us for twenty-five years after landing. They're not here for a rescue."

"I note you didn't ask Okurt that."

"I didn't need to. It's an industry mission, and he's just the chauffeur. Besides, I always found out more from what suspects omitted to tell me than anything else." Now she took a gamble: Lindsay would find out about the isenj comms link soon enough. She would rather she heard it from her. "If you had the ability to send instantaneous messages to Earth, no time delay, pronto, would you mention that when you made contact?"

Lindsay and Bennett stared at her. After seventy-five years neither had anyone at home who might be waiting for a call. But it was potential contact with home regardless, and it had enormous emotional meaning beyond the scientific amazement value.

"I hope I've understood you correctly," Lindsay said. "If they can do that, why didn't they flash us before they left? Now that's spooky."

"It's not their tech. It's isenj."

"I get the feeling we haven't been invited to the party," said Bennett. Shan wasn't sure if he was referring to *Actaeon*'s withholding of information or to hers.

"What do we tell the payload?" Lindsay asked.

Shan shrugged. "Tell them the truth."

"And have you told us everything you know, ma'am?" Lindsay asked.

"No," Shan said.

"Do you want to elaborate on that?"

"No. I've told you everything you need to know to stay alive. The rest wouldn't help you one bit—far from it in fact. I said I'd get you back in one piece and I meant it."

"What about the gene bank?" asked Bennett. "Shouldn't we be making arrangements to get that shipped out now?"

Shan ran her finger over the console and wiped a trail through the sand-colored dust, briefly distracted by poor housekeeping and wondering why a bored payload didn't get on with some cleaning duties. "I won't be handing anything over to any government that has to work that closely with corporations," she said. "It's one more thing Perault didn't bargain on when she briefed me."

It was hard to blow out a mission that had taken her on what was effectively a one-way trip. Home seemed to have vanished. She now had no idea what she was going to do with that gene bank. Maybe leaving it with the wess'har was the most prudent option. The only thing she knew for certain at that moment was that the matriarchs could be trusted not to misuse it.

"Time we got going, ma'am," said Bennett. "While we've still got the light. Wouldn't want Dr. Rayat and Dr. Galvin to fall into a bog, would we?"

"Wouldn't we?" said Shan.

24

While your wish to support your comrades is understandable, I must ask you to exercise restraint. If they find themselves in difficulty because they are now seen as allies of the wess'har, that is unfortunate: your priority is the continued development of an understanding with the isenj. The isenj see the wess'har as an occupying army. Without isenj cooperation, we will never establish a base on CS2. I think the conclusion is clear. Fortunately, the isenj are prepared to accept that the Thetis *mission does not have the backing of the current Federal European Union.*

BIRSEN ERTEGUN, Undersecretary of State,
FEU Foreign Office, to Commander Malcolm Okurt,
CO *Actaeon*

It was mid July, just hinting at autumn, and the bone-colored *efte* trees were still four meters high and sprouting great silver plumes of sticky floss that trapped unwary flyers. Even creatures the size of *alyats* and handhawks avoided flying too close. It was hard to think that those trees, seeming solid as the Earth oaks in the colony, would shrivel to nothing in weeks and leave a flat terrain scattered with sheet upon sheet of dead bark and fiber. Autumn was papermaking time for the colony. *Efte* was even more useful than hemp, strong enough to be felted and formed into laminate.

It was an annual routine Aras didn't want to see interrupted. He checked the charge indicator on his *gevir,* not wholly at ease with using a firing weapon again. Wess'har didn't forget what they learned. He feared a little human fallibility had crept up on him.

"Will the isenj be able to track us?" Shan asked.

"I hope so," said Aras. "I want this settled."

They were walking with Bennett and Qureshi along the wake of the missing scientists, detectable by the recently crushed groundcover that showed up as a bright track on Bennett's bioscreen. The marine had a device just behind his ear that he tapped every so often before checking the readout on his palm. His battle-dress danced with broken gray-blue patterns of camouflage. And even to an isenj's senses, he would appear the same temperature as everything around him. Aras thought that was a clever touch.

"You have implants," Aras said.

Bennett tapped his device again. "They're crap. I ought to be able to see that track up here." He indicated his eyes. "Organic head-up display. But it's so unreliable I've got to view it on the repeater here. God bless defense procurement."

"And you serve royalty?"

"Haven't had a monarchy anywhere in Europe for centuries, sir. Royal is just a very old title. We like tradition in the services."

"Don't even try to work it out," said Shan. "Come on, Ade, they can't have got that far. Not carrying their gear."

"They could be ten kay from the camp by now."

"They'll be in the bloody sea, then."

"Well, at least we haven't come across any body parts yet. That's always a good sign."

Aras wasn't sure if that was a joke or not. "*Alyats* don't leave any debris from their kills. Nor do *sheven* or *esjen*. They envelop and absorb *everything*."

His comment silenced them. Shan kept close to Aras. He found that rather touching: he needed no protection. But she did. She put a great deal of faith in her ballistic vest, but it was only designed to stop human weapons—a knife or a bullet. He had no idea if it would stop an isenj projectile.

"Bugger," said Bennett.

He stopped and tapped his implant again.

"What is it?" asked Shan.

"Looks like someone drove an industrial floor polisher through here. Either that, or it's vehicle tracks."

"Show me," said Aras.

Bennett held out his hand and Aras adjusted his perspective to the multicolor 3D representation of the landscape. *Champciaux's geophys scan, showing where Mjat had once stood and then fallen at his hand.* Two broken lines of regular swirling patterns snaked into the tracks of Rayat and Galvin at an angle, then the walkers' traces ended. It was a good guess for someone who had never seen isenj transport before.

"I hate to jump to conclusions, but I reckon Rayat and Galvin either got a lift from the isenj or were taken by them," said Shan. "And neither scenario fills me with confidence."

Bennett and Qureshi glanced at each other.

"Let's follow the tracks, then, shall we, ma'am?" said Qureshi. "Or would you rather we waited for backup?"

Aras considered the possibility that the isenj had chanced across the two *gethes* and decided they would make excellent bait for him. He had no intention of disappointing them, and he wanted no more of Shan's group to put themselves at risk.

"We go on," he said.

Lindsay heaved herself into the seat at the comms console and answered the hail from *Actaeon.* On the screen was the image of Okurt's second in command, Nichol Valiet, a lieutenant who didn't look much older than Becken.

"*Thetis,* officer commanding," she said wearily.

"Sorry, ma'am. Did I disturb you?"

"No, just a heavy day." He probably hadn't realized she was pregnant. Of course: he couldn't see her from the chest down. "Go ahead."

"Is Superintendent Frankland available?"

"No. She's gone off camp after a couple of the payload who've broken curfew."

"What curfew?"

"Ours. What did you want her for?"

"I just wanted to check where she was. This is an awkward subject to broach, ma'am, but we've had a communication from Dr. Rayat."

"Yeah, that's one of the morons who decided to go walkabout during an armed incursion. How the hell did he manage to flash you up?"

"He relayed his message from an isenj mobile unit. He's with them."

Oh, God. Get off the link. I need to tell Shan before this goes pear-shaped. "And?"

Valiet lapsed into silence. He was way out of his depth; Okurt should have called her himself. Lindsay used the trick she had learned from Eddie, the sleight of hand worked by simple silence. She waited. It was much harder than it looked.

"He's made some disturbing allegations about Frankland and we just wanted to verify some facts with you," said Valiet. Silence was pretty effective. Lindsay was getting used to wielding it. She waited and he went on. "Dr. Rayat claims your skipper killed one of your party, Surendra Parekh."

"Rayat hasn't been entirely comfortable with the restrictions placed on him by the indigenous government."

"Is he lying?"

"Dr. Parekh was executed under local law for causing the death of an alien child." She had, hadn't she? It had been so clear-cut at the time, so completely wrong, and so utterly important that the native species was appeased. Now that she was being lulled back into the Earth way of doing things, Lindsay had a brief pang of doubt. It dissipated almost at once. "You should understand that the rules are very different here. You're under wess'har sovereignty. Forget that, and you're really going to get a nasty surprise."

"If Superintendent Frankland has exceeded her authority, we *will* have to take action against her, you realize that, don't you?"

That was her boss he was talking about. You rallied to your commander. You rallied to your *friend*. "If you try messing with Frankland, you'll have to answer to me, so realize *that*." The poker face and silent trap were thrown aside: this bastard needed to understand he would have to take them all on if he wanted Shan. "You have absolutely no jurisdiction here. If you think for one minute that you do, you're endangering every one of us—and that includes my child. So keep your nose out of this, Lieutenant."

Lindsay hadn't planned to drop her guard. But Shan was the pack leader, the alpha female. Nobody had the right to criticize her for doing what she needed to do to avoid disaster, least of all some jumped-up lieutenant who had never even set foot on this complex world.

"Child?"

"I'm pregnant. And no, don't even try to exchange pleasantries with me. Give me Rayat's last known position. It might seem smart to make friends with the isenj from where you are, but we're about twenty kay from a wess'har garrison."

"We have orders not to cause offense to the isenj, ma'am."

"I'd be more worried about causing offense to Superintendent Frankland if I were you, or the wess'har, whichever gets hold of you first."

"Ma'am, can I request that you file your official report

on the incident now? You've logged one, haven't you? It's regulation."

"You can discuss it directly with Superintendent Frankland when she returns." She wasn't going to get the position out of Valiet. No matter: Rayat had probably moved on by now, and the booties could track him with or without the information. She switched topics to disguise just how keen she was to avoid discussing Parekh. "Now, if you want to make yourselves useful, Eddie Michallat from BBChan wants to know if you can set up an interview down the line with the isenj, seeing as you're such good friends."

"Isenj. Yes. They even have an interpreter who can speak English." Valiet affected sudden chatty good humor, although his voice said otherwise. "It looks like a mongoose and the isenj look like—well, a pile of spiders. Is that what's known as good TV?"

"Eddie would probably like a real-time link as well, seeing as you've been so kind as to mention you have one."

"Okay. We'll patch through the links. Have a good day."

Lindsay keyed the end command. "Bastard," she said.

Eddie had gone walkabout again and he wasn't answering his comms link. Vani Paretti happened to be the closest to hand on the way to the mess hall. Lindsay caught his arm. "Could you tell Eddie his audience awaits? Or at least his interview link-up. He'll have to negotiate the rest himself."

"Feeling all right?"

"That tosser Rayat made contact with the isenj and he's using their comms link."

"I hope he's not transmitting data home—"

"Don't. Just *don't.* I'm not in the mood."

Lindsay walked out into the compound and looked up to gauge the thickening clouds overhead. It had started to spit with fine rain, and that usually meant a heavy downpour wasn't far behind.

She wondered whether she should get Becken and Barencoin to have a word with Rayat in their highly persuasive way when Shan brought him back. *Foul little shit,* she thought. It was a cowardly, sniveling thing to do to whine to the *Actaeon* about Shan. It was almost a shame that the ship had shown up. Rayat could so easily have been dealt with and nobody would have been any the wiser.

The violence of the thought caught her unawares. Bezer'ej had changed her; Shan had changed her. She understood now why sometimes you had to bend the rules, and wondered why they had never taught her that at the naval academy.

She checked her bioscreen and alerted Qureshi and Bennett. She didn't fancy being in Rayat's shoes when Shan found out what he'd done.

Ceret—Cavanagh's Star—was setting. Aras judged that they had a half-hour of good visibility left, and he wondered if the marines' implant-enhanced vision could cope with low light as well as his eyes could. Time would tell. He walked in Qureshi's wake. Bennett marked a zigzag path between *efte* trees ahead of them, staring ahead to pick up images.

He stopped and glanced down at his palm. "Six-fifty meters, dead ahead. Significant cluster of targets."

"How many?" said Aras.

"Eight, nine."

Aras checked his *gevir* again. He had come to kill isenj. Most of the landing party was probably ahead of him and that meant he had to locate the others soon afterwards. It was more than his responsibility towards the bezeri. He wanted to send a clear message: he was still here and he would deal with them as he had dealt with Mjat.

"Whoa there," said Shan. "This is my shout."

She gave Bennett a look that made him fall in behind her

and went striding ahead. Aras decided that if she put herself in danger he would have to intervene even if it offended her. She didn't know isenj at all.

She disappeared among the *efte* but he could still hear her boots brushing through undergrowth bent flat by the isenj vehicle. The sound stopped. Qureshi glanced at Bennett and they both took a more positive grip on their rifles. Then they caught up with Shan and saw what she had seen.

Aras had forgotten how very odd an isenj would look to a human. They weren't remotely humanoid; a *gethes* would have mistaken them for what they considered an animal. But these isenj stood clustered round their small vehicle, crossbow-like weapons in their oddly jointed arms, and Rayat and Galvin were sitting on the equivalent of the running board. They looked simply bewildered.

Shan indicated *stop* with a carefully extended arm. "Let me see if I can talk to them," she said. "They must be able to understand us if Rayat talked them into linking him up to *Actaeon*."

"We're right here, remember," said Bennett. Aras could smell that acid human tension rolling off him, but he showed no outward signs of fear. Neither he nor Qureshi had quite taken aim, but their readiness to fire would be visible even to an isenj. Aras hoped their weapons were accurate in this gravity. All his instincts told him to shoot now. He couldn't understand why Shan felt the need for discussion.

She stopped fifteen meters in front of the vehicle.

"I command this group," she said. "Are you holding my people?"

There was a long pause. An answer came, but it was from some communications kit in the vehicle, the small raspy voice of a ussissi interpreter relayed from some remote station. "We have talked with them. We have no argument with men and women."

"Then perhaps Dr. Rayat and Dr. Galvin can come back to camp with me."

Qureshi reached in the pockets of her webbing, took out a hand-sized round object and began attaching it slowly and quietly to her weapon. "Might need to take out that vehicle," she whispered to Aras. "If we can get Rayat and Galvin clear, that is. It's times like this you wish Frankland was wired so we could direct her."

The isenj had moved forward. Rayat got up. Galvin looked afraid, her gaze darting from isenj to isenj. Shan stood calmly and clasped her hands behind her back.

She's going to fire. Aras hoped she was as sensible as he thought she was. It wasn't her war. She should have walked away from it.

"We want only the wess'har," said the disembodied interpreter. "We hold the doctors until we have the destroyer of Mjat."

Shan hesitated a beat. "He's not mine to hand over. And I imagine you want continued good relations with humans, so if you harm my team, we will consider that an act of aggression."

Aras could smell her tension even from here. *Don't open fire.* Qureshi had a grenade aimed at the vehicle. Bennett was kneeling down and his rifle was not quite against his shoulder, but only a movement short of full aim. Aras decided somebody would get hurt if he didn't bring this to an end.

He stepped forward out of the cover of the *efte.*

"And I have come for *you,*" he said. "I drove your forefathers from this place and I will drive you from here too, because this is not your world, and you will destroy it." And he raised his *gevir.* "Don't hide behind the *gethes.* Come out."

Humans said that terrible events moved in slow time. He understood that now. The isenj surged forward, weapons aimed. Then Shan cannoned into him and sent him sprawling. He could hear Qureshi yelling, "Clear! Clear!" and the *atta-atta-atta* of gunfire from behind him.

"Stay down," Shan said, squatting over him, reaching for her hand weapon, but Aras sat up and saw a puff of vapor as a projectile smashed into her chest. She was thrown backwards with a great *uff* of breath as if it had winded her.

His world froze for a moment and then he turned to return fire and hatred.

A great explosion of air silenced everything for a few seconds and heat and smoke rolled across the clearing. Aras could see Qureshi was down, clutching her thigh, and Bennett was now moving from isenj to isenj, turning the bodies over with his boot, his rifle aimed at them.

"All clear," he called. "Oh *shit*. Galvin's down, Rayat's okay, I think. Izzy, you okay? Izzy? Hang on, I'm coming."

Aras could care nothing about Ismat Qureshi's plight, nor Galvin's, nor Rayat's. Shan was sprawled on her back, eyes staring up at the darkening sky. Aras leaned over her.

She's gone. His fragile world slipped away from him. *Stupid, stupid, unnecessary.* He could have survived whatever they fired his way. She knew that.

Then she inhaled a huge gasping breath and propped herself up on her elbow.

"Christ, my ribs," she wheezed. Her eyes were watering with pain. She inspected the area of fabric where the projectile had struck her and tapped the now rigid material with her finger, taking deep irregular breaths. "Don't tell me this stuff wasn't worth the money. And when I take you down, stay down, will you? Jesus, I think I've busted my shoulder."

And she was looking up at him with a relieved grin when the second projectile hit her above her left ear and sent a plume of bright blood and bone spraying into the air.

Bennett took two seconds to release pressure on Qureshi's

hemorrhage, shoulder his rifle and swing round to take out the isenj sniper they had overlooked because he was behind them.

He sprinted across to Aras and looked down at Shan. "Oh Jesus," he said. "Shit. *Shit*."

Aras knew little about human medicine but he knew head wounds were invariably fatal. He checked Shan's pulse. She was alive. But there was a five-centimeter wound in her skull that was leaking dark blood, and he could see through the shattered bone and into the soft tissue beneath.

Bennett called base and summoned both scoots. "We've got to get her back to camp," he said. He looked at Shan's shattered skull again. "Look, I'm not sure even Kris has the kit to deal with that. But I know you need to keep head trauma cases as cold as you can. At least the night temperature's on our side."

"She's dying," said Aras. *And she didn't need to, not for me.*

"I'm sorry. Qureshi's losing a lot of blood too. Sooner we get them back to camp the better."

Not even Dr. Hugel can help her.

The isenj transport was still burning: Qureshi's grenade had done an efficient job.

But you can do something, Aras.

The colony had reasonably competent surgeons. But this was damage to the brain, not a shattered leg or a mangled arm. And even if *Actaeon* itself had the medical facilities to cope with this injury, it would probably take hours to negotiate with them and transfer her.

Shan doesn't have hours.

She was his friend. She could have stood back and let him take the isenj, as he had done before, but she tried to protect him. Nobody else ever had.

She's dying for you. You have a duty to her.

And then 500 years of isolation overwhelmed his obedience to wess'har law, and he reached for his *tilgir.*

I will not lose this friend.

"Go look after Qureshi, Sergeant," Aras said quietly. "I'm not without some medical skill." Bennett hovered. Aras glared. "I said go."

He didn't want Bennett to see him do this; he wouldn't have understood. Aras pulled off his right glove, took his *tilgir* and skinned a slice off his palm. He needed to get his infected blood into her system and after that it was up to the *c'naatat.* He pressed his bleeding palm over the wound and felt her blood welling up against it.

It's a very adaptable organism.

Cuts stopped bleeding fast. He had to keep slicing into his flesh anew every minute or two to maintain a flow. Bennett was busy with Qureshi, packing dressing into her leg and keeping her talking about nothing in particular. Aras waited.

Perhaps it wouldn't work. Perhaps *gethes* weren't to *c'naatat*'s taste after all.

Aras had the very clear sense of having stepped into a different world, one he could not now escape. It was why he and his comrades had slaughtered every last isenj on Bezer'ej—to stop the parasite getting loose into the wider isenj population and beyond. Now he had willingly, knowingly, infected a *gethes.*

He'd pay for that, sooner or later. But right then all he cared about was that Shan Frankland had not thrown away her precious life in a conflict of his making.

Her eyes were shut, her face slack and suddenly very much younger for the loss of expression. Ten minutes, blood to blood: if it hadn't started colonizing her now, it never would. He folded his overjacket and placed it gently under her head. If he had stood by and done nothing, he would have regretted it for the rest of his life.

And that would be a very long time indeed.

"Scoots in range, Aras," Bennett called. "How's she doing?"

Aras smoothed the sticky, blood-matted hair back from Shan's head and checked the wound. It had stopped bleeding and so had he. He felt for her pulse: stronger, more regular. Her scalp was hot to his touch. He recalled that sensation of fever every time his gold skin darkened and his face reshaped itself and unseen cells metamorphosed deep inside him.

"She's still breathing," he said.

"Where's Rayat?"

"Over here, with me. Bit shaken. Galvin was hit in the crossfire."

Aras spat on his fingers and wiped emerging debris away from the wound as best he could. Small shards of bone and blood clots plopped out, cleared by a microscopic army. A splinter of something metallic glittered in the clots.

Yes, the wound was changing. The shattered edge of the bone looked smoother. He adjusted the makeshift pillow under Shan's head and turned her to a more comfortable position. Then he stood up, pulled on his gloves and walked over to Bennett.

Qureshi looked ashen and confused but she was conscious. Bennett was supporting her shoulders.

"I was telling her it was a bloody good shot," Bennett said. "It was, wasn't it, sir?"

"It was indeed," said Aras. He leaned over Rayat, who was sitting against an *efte* hugging his knees to his chest, and dragged him to his feet by his collar.

Rayat's fear-scent was overwhelming. "Get your—"

Aras hit him hard across the face, backhanded. "If *Shan Chail* dies I will kill you. I may kill you anyway. You caused this and I don't forget easily."

Rayat wiped blood from his lip and wandered off in silence to sit one tree farther away. He had got his precious leaves. Aras hoped he thought it worth the price. He returned to Shan's side and sat with her until the scoots arrived with Webster and Becken.

Webster was dubious about taking Shan back to the colony, but like most *gethes* she found it hard to argue with Aras. At least she'd brought a body bag for Galvin. She enlisted Rayat to help her zip the body into it while Bennett loaded Qureshi onto Becken's scoot.

"We'll walk," said Bennett. "I'm sure Dr. Rayat will take his turn carrying Dr. Galvin."

Aras decided he liked Bennett. He checked Shan one more time before lifting her onto the vehicle. The wound was about the width of a grape now: the bone was closing and the skin was creeping across it.

It was healing well. It was healing *c'naatat*-fast.

25

July 12.
    *To Commander Lindsay Julia Neville, European Fed-
eral Navy: a son, David Christopher, 3.8kg, in Constantine
infirmary wing.*

EDDIE MICHALLAT, BBChan,
note to all personnel

Shan felt good. No, she felt *great*. She woke up with
just a suggestion of a headache and an overwhelming urge
to eat.

It was as if she had woken after a wild party, forgotten
how she ended up on someone's sofa, and skipped the
hangover. She had never succumbed to drinking sprees, but
she'd heard enough excuses from those who had.

And she was in Constantine. The walls of the room were
smooth, soothingly gold, the light from overhead filtered
and gentle. It was Josh's home.

Oh shit. Someone had undressed her. She didn't remember getting undressed. The last thing she recalled was seeing the isenj raising weapons and then launching herself at
Aras to get him out of the line of fire. Yes, she'd brought
down a 170-kg alien from a standing start. She could still
do the business. The thought was as reassuring as a pat on
the back.

That was it. She had crashed into the equivalent of a
brick wall, and maybe she was here because she'd come off
worst from the collision. She felt her shoulder cautiously.
And she knew Aras was unharmed, because she could re-

member one more thing: he was standing over her in this room, fringed by the gold light, fragrant with sandalwood, and he said, "You're awake."

The memory lapse made a change from the Suppressed Briefing, which was still dusting memories out of neglected corners of her brain and tutting about the mess. Still, she had survived. Breakfast would taste extra good this morning.

She washed thoroughly in the small basin, holding her head under the spout to rinse her hair. Someone—probably Deborah—had left a few towels for her and some working clothes. What had happened to her fatigues? She cast around and saw her swiss and the contents of her many pockets arranged neatly on the nightstand in the corner. Someone had sorted out her kit so perhaps they had taken care of her clothes too. She fretted about the ballistic vest—extra-lightweight, flexible, very expensive—that she'd paid for out of her own pocket. It wasn't police issue. She wanted it back.

And what had happened to Rayat and Galvin?

The smell of breakfast beckoned through the door, and she followed it, rubbing her hair dry with one of the drab, thin but very efficient towels that were standard issue in Constantine. There was no sign of the Garrods but Aras was sitting at the kitchen table. He stood up when he saw her and began laying food and tea on the table.

"You read my mind," she said. "God, I could eat a scabby cat with piles."

"This is a joke, yes?"

"Just a figure of speech to show I'm ravenous."

"How do you feel?"

She shrugged. "Terrific. Now tell me what happened. I have a few blank spots." Tea, porridge and a heap of fruit made an appetizing landscape in front of her. She plunged in. Aras watched her.

"You have been unconscious for seven days," he said.

"Commander Neville has produced a premature male child. Dr. Galvin is dead. Marine Qureshi is recovering and Dr. Rayat is confined to quarters."

It took a lot to stun her. This news did the job very well. She took it in slowly. "I've missed something important here, haven't I?"

"What do you recall?"

"Everything up to when I brought you down."

Aras paused as if measuring his words, which was a very unwess'har reaction. "You were shot in the head."

She put her hand to her damp hair instinctively. She couldn't feel any sutures. "Minor, then?"

Again, a pause, and it bothered her. "Relatively."

"And Galvin?"

"She was hit by Sergeant Bennett in the crossfire."

"Oh Christ, poor Ade. I bet he's taking that badly."

"Not as badly as Galvin."

"Don't expect me to feel sorry for her. She could have got us all killed. Can I assume the isenj didn't walk away from it either?"

"None from that party. There are some others I need to find."

"Have we had any further contact from *Actaeon*?"

"Commander Okurt has been in touch to express his regret at the skirmish and to remind us that he has orders not to offend the isenj."

"Hang on, they effectively kidnapped two of our personnel, arseholes or not. How does that not qualify for some practical sympathy?"

"Because the ussissi tell us that the isenj see the *gethes* here as wess'har allies, especially now that shots have been exchanged. What is the word? Disavow. *Actaeon* has *disavowed* our actions."

At least that settled one thing. Perault, the SB and the grand mission were irrelevant now. "Is the gene bank secure?"

"All material is now on Wess'ej."

"Thanks. I owe you."

"I don't think so," said Aras.

"Have I done something to piss you off?"

"Nothing." He pushed a basket of rough bread rolls in front of her. "But please don't attempt to return to your camp yet. Promise me you will stay here. Or I will lock you in."

"They don't have locks here," she said, and was comforted by his concern. She cared what he thought of her. That was a novelty in itself; nobody else's opinion mattered a damn. "I ought to see Lin, though. How's the baby?"

"This is a difficult environment for a human child," Aras said. "The first generation of the colonists lost many babies the same way, but they adapted fast."

She knew he wasn't being callous. He simply had a long-term perspective that sounded brutal. Shan wondered if it was any more brutal than her expecting Lindsay to terminate her pregnancy.

But that was emotional stuff. She skirted round it and continued eating, wondering where her appetite had come from.

You worry too much, Lindsay told herself. Deborah Garrod knew more about caring for babies than Kris Hugel and all her qualifications laid end to end. *Let her get on with it.* But it was difficult to concentrate on a diplomatic crisis when her body was telling her that she had a much more pressing priority. As soon as she'd finished with Bennett, she'd head over to Constantine and sit with David.

"Okay, let me get this right." She had recorded this incident report four different times now and it still seemed a mess. The only hard evidence she had was Galvin's body in the freezer with five FEU standard rounds in it. At least Parekh had company. The dead isenj had vanished under efficient rockvelvets, which were much faster off the mark than she had imagined. "Who fired first?"

Bennett adopted a fixed I'm-remembering look. "I would say the isenj did, but that was only because they were quicker on the draw than Aras. One round from the isenj took Frankland down and we returned fire. Qureshi launched a grenade at the vehicle and I neutralized the remaining isenj. A second shot from behind us hit Frankland in the head and I located the position and neutralized the sniper. Galvin—"

"Galvin was a stupid cow who compromised your safety. Don't beat yourself up over it. Shame it wasn't Rayat, too."

"Bit harsh, Boss."

"I'm fed up putting my people on the line for civvies who don't heed warnings. Screw them."

"How is Frankland?"

Lindsay shrugged. "Josh says she's conscious and mobile. But they're keeping her in for the time being."

"Bloody miracle."

"What is?"

"She had a hole in her skull you could put three fingers in. I've never seen anyone recover from that sort of injury without major neurosurgery, and then they're not much use afterwards. Except as a doorstop."

"If the wess'har have better surgical technology than we do, maybe that's the answer. I'm sure they do."

Bennett seemed gratefully amazed rather than suspicious. He dismissed himself with a sharp salute and Lindsay thought better of sending the report to *Actaeon* until she could concentrate properly.

In Constantine's small infirmary—a maze of well-lit tiled rooms, nothing more—Kris Hugel and Deborah Garrod leaned over David's cot. Lindsay watched them quietly for a few moments before making deliberately noisy steps, just in case they were discussing some aspect of her child's health that they didn't want her to hear. They weren't. They were silent.

"Hi, Lin," said Hugel. "How are you?"

"You could do with a rest," said Deborah.

Lindsay didn't want a rest. She wanted David. She leaned in and picked him up, cradling his head in her hand and still utterly astonished by him, as astonished as she had been when she had seen Aras or the isenj or the bezeri luminescence. He was so far beyond the world she was used to that she was almost afraid. He made rhythmic, wet sighing noises.

"He's still having problems breathing at the moment," said Hugel. "He's thirty-two weeks. On Earth that's no problem, but given the oxygen levels here and the lack of neonatal specialist care, I'm not taking any risks. That means I've got him on antibiotics, because his immune system isn't fully developed, and Webster's rigging an oxygen tent from the reactive greenhouse sheeting. I'm sorry it's such crude medicine. But I don't even have surfactant drugs."

"Has *Actaeon*?" But Lindsay knew it was a pointless question. Warships were equipped for trauma, clap and substance abuse. "I suppose not."

"He could do with some more milk, if you're up to expressing some."

Not more tubes. He was too weak even to feed properly. She laid him down in the cot again with a breaking heart. Every instinct in her body said she should forget common sense and take him somewhere quiet to comfort and nurse him. But Hugel was a doctor, and knew better. And Lindsay was an officer, the ranking officer now that Shan was out of action.

"I'll get on with it," she said.

Hugel walked with her to the kitchen area. Lindsay

didn't need a spectator or company, but Hugel wasn't accompanying her to be supportive.

"I've asked to see Frankland but Josh Garrod almost threw me out," she said. "Perhaps she's worse than they're letting on."

"Bennett says she really took one."

"Exactly. So if you're in command now, can I ask you if we can evacuate? We've lost two people now. Enough."

"I think we're going to do that anyway. But Shan isn't dead, and she isn't incapacitated."

"Well, maybe you can talk to her."

"Of course I will." *Now leave me alone.* "Time to check up on Qureshi, I think."

Hugel looked as if she had taken the polite hint for the dismissal it actually was, and stiffened slightly.

"Qureshi's doing fine." Hugel moved towards the door and rested her hand on the latch. "But if Bennett described Frankland's injuries accurately, then she shouldn't be alive, not with the level of care available here."

Lindsay resisted getting into a conversation. It was speculative. If Hugel was thinking of wess'har surgical superiority and how she might acquire it, she couldn't have picked a worse time. Maybe she was like Rayat, making her last dangerous bid to wring some worthwhile results out of this mission.

"Miracles happen," said Lindsay, and hoped there would be another one along shortly for David.

"You have to tell her," Josh said.

"I will," said Aras.

"I mean it. What if she decides to go back to the camp and that doctor wants to check her over? You can't stall her forever."

Aras fixed Josh with a warning stare. Deborah was at the infirmary and Rachel and James were at classes. They could now shout at each other without fear of being overheard. "You have no idea what *forever* means."

"I'm sorry. But what were you thinking of? You spent lifetimes keeping *c'naatat* isolated."

"I don't have your heaven in my head. When the people I care about die, they're gone, no eternity, no second chance."

"But you've condemned her."

"To what? Life as a freak? Life like me?"

Josh was as unafraid of Aras as Shan was, or perhaps he was more afraid of his god's wrath than the wess'har's displeasure. "She will never be left in peace now. Sooner or later, someone will find out and she'll become a commodity. And you had no right to do that."

"Do not lecture me on rights or responsibilities."

"But why *now*? You've known her seven months. You've lived with us for generations and never been tempted."

"Because she cares about me."

"*We* care about you too. We always have."

"No, you care about the idea of me, the icon. There is this communal respect for me, but at the end of the day you go back to your families and I'm alone again. You won't even touch me. I'm an idea. I'm not a man."

"I think that's very harsh."

"Would you give up your life for me?"

"That's unfair."

"Your fables say that a man should lay down his life for his friend."

"The word of Christ is *not* a fable."

"It will remain a fable as long as you don't live it as a reality." Aras stood up and made a move towards the door. His anger was getting the better of him. "*Shan Chail* risked death for me without thinking, foolish or not. And I stopped that death, maybe foolishly too. But I will look after her because she is my responsibility now. If she can live with the consequences, then so can I."

"That's selfish."

"Yes, it's about *me*. However I appear, I am a wess'har male. I am bred to need people to care for and look after. I need to belong to someone. After five hundred years without that, one act of unconditional kindness reminds me what I truly am."

"You still shouldn't interfere with the natural course of things."

"If I had honored that tenet then none of you would be here now. If I had stood back and let your forefathers die, there would be no *Thetis* or *Actaeon* here now. Think on that, *gethes*."

Aras swept out. He was halfway up the steps but he still heard Josh calling after him. "What will you do if she can't live with it, Aras? What will you do then?"

Humans often said by way of apology that they hadn't meant to say cruel things. Aras had meant every word. Every human was *gethes* to him right then, except Shan.

Back in his chambers, Aras took Black and White from their nest of shredded linen in the alcove and held them in his arms. They were warm and sleepy: White yawned and stretched luxuriously with both paws, then arranged himself across Black and went back to sleep.

While Aras was fond of them, he didn't want the *c'naatat* to scavenge any more interesting DNA. He kept his gloves on. He knew very little about rats.

He wondered now how much he knew about humans, too. There was no way of telling how *c'naatat* would express itself in a human host. It might just repair damage or it might indulge in grandiose, never-ending genetic reconstruction schemes, as it had with him. Whatever it did, *Shan Chail* now shared with him a common genetic ancestry, and he with her. All the creatures that had hosted his *c'naatat* before it encountered him were now part of her: all her lungfish-lemur-monkey ancestors were his.

She was even closer than friends, than family. She was in his blood.

Lindsay peered round the door of Josh's spare room.

"How are you doing?" she asked.

Shan looked up from the screen of her swiss and got up to greet her. "Bored shitless. Hey, it's good to see you, I—"

Lindsay stepped back, hands held out as a barrier. "Josh said you might have an infection. No offense. But David. You know."

Shan felt instant regret. Deborah had kept her informed of the infant's lack of progress. It reminded her how very far they were from Earth and the safety net of hospitals. "Sorry. Yes, I'm still running a temperature. Is there anything I can do? That's pathetic, I know. I'm not very good at this sort of thing."

"The longer he survives, the closer he gets to forty weeks. No change isn't bad."

"I don't know how I'd cope if I were you."

"You'd cope. Believe me. Anyway, you look pretty good for someone who's been shot in the head."

"Nobody's more surprised than I am. I'd really like to get back to work."

"And have Kris Hugel crawling all over you? No, stay here as long as you can. She's mad with curiosity about wess'har medical techniques since Ade Bennett said how bad the wound was."

The faintest grumble of an inner voice—a copper's instinct—made Shan feel uneasy and she wasn't sure why. Maybe it was her Pagan background, her mistrust of unnatural science, that was talking. "If she comes anywhere near me with a probe she'll be wearing it for a suppository," she said, and smiled. "Tell her that from me."

"Anything you need?"

"Has *Actaeon* responded on the evac request yet?"

"Consulting. I imagine they're trying to work out how they convince the isenj we're not wess'har mercenaries."

"I bet Commander Okurt would still like a word with me about Surendra Parekh."

"I told him to piss off."

"Thanks, but I can face that one myself."

"And Eddie sends his best. He did a live real-time broadcast from Constantine, and he's as pleased as a dog with two dicks."

"Yes, I got the live news feeds, thanks. Earth doesn't look like home anymore, does it?"

"Things change in seventy-five years. I'd better be going."

It was a strange kind of quarantine. Shan took a walk round the perimeter and decided she was indeed remarkably fit for a woman with a hole blown in her head. If it hadn't been for the constant hunger and the mild fever she would have pronounced herself fit, but Lindsay was right about Hugel. If Aras had employed wess'har technology to treat her injuries, it was a good reason to stay clear of the doctor. There were too many things to be unleashed here. And they were probably days away from being evacuated, just days from withdrawing from this world without her very worst fears being realized.

Days away from leaving Aras for the last time, too. The thought had upset her before and it disturbed her now. She had become too attached to him. He was all the things that had kept her in the police when she could have left: belonging, loyalty, family, purpose. She wondered where the next meaning in her life would be found, if anywhere.

For a moment she wondered about *c'naatat*. No, that was crazy. She knew Aras too well. He would never go that far. *Kill me if I might lead them to it,* she'd said. And he would, too.

She watched a group of rockvelvets sunning themselves and thought that it wouldn't have been so bad to have spent a little longer here. It struck her how beautiful they were; despite their eating habits, she found their slow black progress hypnotic. A couple of them lounged on a nearby rock, overlapping slightly as if they were holding hands.

She had never noticed the concentric pale rings on them before. Maybe it was their breeding coat, or gender, or age. And then there were the *alyats*. There was one hanging from a tree like a discarded but glamorous plastic bag, a fabulous peacock-blue sheet of gossamer waiting to drop on an unsuspecting meal walking beneath to smother and digest it.

She had never seen one that color before.

Bezer'ej was full of things you could see right through and yet not see at all.

26

PRIORITY MESSAGE TO: Cdr Lindsay Neville, *Thetis* ground station.
FROM: Cdr Malcolm Okurt CSV *Actaeon.*

Stand by to embark remainder of landing party at 1100 ST August 28. EFS Thetis *will be reactivated to transfer personnel opting to return to Earth at this stage of the mission. An isenj delegation, interpreters and accompanying officers from* Actaeon *will also be embarked. Those personnel wishing to remain in* Actaeon *may do so for the duration of the ship's deployment.*

Ensure Superintendent Frankland makes herself available for embarkation pending a formal inquiry into the death of Dr. Surendra Parekh.

It had been years since Aras had gone hunting isenj with quite this degree of anger.

"You don't have to do this," he said.

Bennett was keeping up with him remarkably well, barely breaking a sweat. "No problem, sir. I have to assume they're a risk to our personnel now, whatever *Actaeon*'s decided."

"But you leave things to me. Is that understood?"

"As long as you're upright, sir, it's your call. If they drop you, all bets are off."

"I think that's fair."

"Shouldn't we be keeping silent, sir?"

"I want them to find me. Even more reason for you to leave me to do this."

Isenj weren't stupid. The first party had tried to lure him with human bait and got it badly wrong: the others would not be so rash. He had hoped he could rely on the bezeri to tell him if they detected traces of isenj waste in the shallows, but the pollution from three or four of them would have been too scant and too slow-moving even for a bezeri's sensitive biology to detect.

Besides, the bezeri had gone deep. There were hardly any lights visible now.

"What is the name Eddie calls me?" Aras asked, eyes fixed on the skyline. A flight of handhawks had caught his attention. Perhaps they had been disturbed by isenj.

"I don't think he means it, sir. He certainly didn't use it in his broadcast. In fact, he didn't mention you at all."

"The name."

"The Beast of Mjat."

"This is how you refer to war criminals."

"It's just journalists, sir. You know how they are."

"You know why the isenj want me."

"It's none of my business."

"Do you know how long ago this was?"

"Does it matter?" Bennett was a man who stuck to his own business, which was soldiering. Aras respected him for that too. "We'll never understand it and you don't have to explain yourself to us."

"You have a commendable grasp of diplomacy."

"I'm just a bootie, sir. They load me with kit and point me in the right direction and I do whatever needs to be done."

The handhawks had settled again at a distance. Aras stopped to listen. So did Bennett. The marine checked his palm to read the living light grown into it, as magically illuminated as any bezeri.

"There you go," he said. He held his palm out. "Three targets heading our way, fifteen hundred meters. On this heading, we should intercept right *there*."

"Find some cover."

"If you're planning an ambush—"

"No. I just want you safely out of the way. Don't die here. I would rather see you live to go home and find a female and raise offspring for her." Bennett stared at him, clearly offended. Of course: this was the *gethes* who needed to defeat his fear afresh every time.

"What if you have to take prisoners, sir? Wouldn't you like a hand?"

Aras transferred his *gevir* to his right hand and pulled out the knife from his belt. For a harvesting tool, a *tilgir* was extremely adaptable.

"I am wess'har," he said quietly. "We do not take prisoners."

The church of St. Francis seemed as good a place as any to sit and think. Nobody asked what you were doing there, and nobody looked at you. Shan sat in a pew right at the front just letting her mind wander. She checked her swiss. There were still no messages. Sooner or later she would have to get back to camp, Hugel or not.

And *Actaeon* or not.

She wouldn't have blamed the resident god for ignoring her, especially as she hadn't wholly—or even partially—accepted he might exist. So if he wasn't going to do it she would judge herself.

She felt no regret for Parekh. She couldn't allow herself to. The moment she started thinking that humans were special and anything they did was okay, then she was no better than Parekh or any colonial governor who counted a native's death as less serious than a white man's.

Shit, she had only come for the damn gene bank. And now she couldn't recover it and return it to the government of the day, because there were no Peraults left to defend it, just men and women who couldn't even maintain a defense force now without relying on the largesse of corporations. It had waited centuries. It would have to wait a few more.

I could have retired after this. I could have gone home.
But what would be happening to the bezeri, and Aras, and
Josh while she lived out her days 150 trillion miles away?
*When I look up at the sky and try to find Cavanagh's Star,
how will I stand not knowing what's happening there?*

There would be consequences to face for the business
with Parekh, and although Shan had never walked away
from responsibility, that just didn't seem fair right then.

Staying here was crazy, a fantasy. *Go home and face
what's coming to you.* And home—home would be no less
alien than here. She would be more than a century out of time.

Oh shit.

It was chilly in St Francis's. The plain's notorious wind
had come up suddenly, poking angry cold draughts under
the doors even at this depth. It was probably going to be a
bright, blustery day.

Shan pulled her coat round her and noticed for the first
time how uncomfortably tight it was becoming. *That's what
you get for stuffing your face all last week.* Early light was
beginning to illuminate the stained-glass window, picking
out a black-lined coloring-book image of a lean man in a
bronze-brown robe. It was a very fine window and it had
lost none of its majesty from the first time she had seen it
and stood amazed before it.

Around St. Francis creatures that she recognized and
creatures that she did not were gathered at his feet and
seated at his side. This time she felt it was important to
commit them to memory. She would never see them again.
There was a European robin, very skillfully rendered, and
an *udza,* a rockvelvet, and a handhawk. And there were
things she had only seen in Aras's library.

Aras, she thought. Of course: Aras showed them how to
make better glass. He would have added images of creatures from home, too.

That made her smile, and it hurt. The light was brighter

now. People would be waking, and she would have to go even though right then she would have been content to stay there for eternity. She allowed herself a few more moments to drink in the now vividly transparent beauty of the window.

She'd never studied it like this before. She wished she had, because it was calming, beautiful and timeless. It transcended faiths and divisions. It had meaning. The more she stared, the more detail she found: the shaft and vanes in each feather, the pale rings on the rockvelvet, the slightest gray-blue border to the robin's red bib. The shading and detail was in the glass itself, not in the leading. It was breathtaking. The rainbow of light cast a distorted ghost of the window at her feet and draped itself across the altar.

And St. Francis—there was real compassion in that lined face and more than a little weariness. He looked every inch a man who had turned his back on privilege and comfort because nothing mattered more to him than what he believed in. He would have had no trouble understanding why an alien life counted as much as a human's. It was a damn shame he wasn't commanding *Actaeon* right now.

As she stared at the figure of the saint, she wondered why she had never noticed that his halo was such a fabulous blue. It wasn't just a single color. It was peacock and cyan and violet, every blue she had ever seen, and she felt she could actually taste the colors pressing at the roof of her mouth.

She moved her head, taken by surprise at the intensity of the synesthesia. The colors flooded into gentian. She was sure the halo had been plain milk-white before.

It had.

Her memory for detail had been honed by a hundred crime scenes, a thousand interviews. *The most wonderful blues and mauves, but not to human eyes.* That's what Josh had said. And she had thought of angels, nothing more.

Now she knew whose eyes he had meant.

And anyone who could see those colors was no longer wholly human.

"Oh *shit*," she said.

Shan was built to cope. She liked crises: they were clean and fast and she didn't have to spend time planning and justifying and persuading. She acted. It was what her brain was wired for.

Even so, this new crisis—for she was certain it was one—was moving too slowly for her. She walked as briskly as she could without breaking into a run along the passages of Constantine and up the ramp into the raw day. She was on the main route out of the settlement, staring at the sunlight as it made brilliant blue bubbles out of some of the home domes visible on the surface.

Oh yes, they were blue. And they had never been blue before.

The fields were south of her; she headed north through the bio-barrier and out onto the plain.

She kept looking at her hands. She had no idea why *c'naatat* should have manifested itself there, but if there was anything of her that spoke of humanity, it was her hands. She understood why medical students said they were the most disturbing parts of the body to dissect. They were more familiar than your own face, unique in a way that organs and muscles and bones didn't seem to be.

Her hands still looked pretty average.

Maybe she was jumping to mad conclusions. There might have been a perfectly banal explanation, but as soon as she thought that she knew it wasn't true, she broke into a stumbling run.

About a kilometer outside the perimeter there was an *efte* in mid-collapse. She needed seclusion for a while. She sat down in the lee of its trunk and listened to the clicks and squelches as the core of the plant slowly deliquesced and sank back into the soil. In a day or so only the discarded eggshell of bark would be left.

Even the grasses and scrub around her seemed more blue. When she looked up into the sky she could see haloes upon haloes round Cavanagh's Star as it edged up over the horizon. There was a flock of *alyats* skimming low across the plain.

They were all blue. The colorless ones she had first seen were a limitation of human eyes.

Aras couldn't have done this. Sharing his *c'naatat* was too much of a risk; he'd slaughtered whole isenj populations to stop it spreading. Whatever had happened to her, whatever had healed her injuries and altered her eyes, had to be a drug or surgical technique.

There was one way she could settle the question. Her hand went to her pocket and felt the outline of the swiss.

Now? Did she really want to know right now? "Stupid cow," she said aloud to herself. "Do it."

She eased the swiss from her pocket, its case familiar and use-worn. She had carried it all her adult life. It was one of the few devices she could operate without looking, and she flicked her thumb over the end of the cylinder. The blade eased free.

She drew it diagonally across her left palm and it hurt like hell. Blood flowed, because she was suddenly clutching stickiness, and the smell of filed metal made her gasp.

Maybe it was her cycle. Maybe the old human female rhythms of fertility were making her sense of smell more acute. Unaltered women always developed heightened smell at certain times of their cycle, didn't they? *Didn't they?*

She wiped her palm on the leg of her fatigues and waited a few seconds. The cut had stopped bleeding. She flexed it a few times just to be absolutely sure there was a wound there at all. Then she got to her feet and began walking with no particular sense of purpose.

She was calming down now. The dispassionate part of her mind, the one she trusted most, was listing prioritized thoughts before her eyes in the reassuring, common sense way it had. First: wait and confirm it. Second: if contaminated, keep away from the research team. Third: ah, third wasn't an order. Third was a concern. What useful little additions was it going to make to her?

It was a parasite as far as she was concerned. Knowing that it was colonizing her made her feel nauseated. She decided she would not have been happily pregnant. Eventually she stopped and found herself a little too far from the settlement, although when she turned she could still see it. What she needed to do more than anything was to stop and take a look at her left hand.

Not yet, though.

"Yes, now," she said aloud. She stared down at the back of the hand, balled into a fist, and turned it over and opened it.

Her palm was unmarked. "Oh, God," she said. She looked again. The redness was fading. She checked to see there were still rusty smears of blood on the gray of her sleeve and leg, and there were. When she took out the swiss again, there were pungent-smelling bloody fingerprints on its casing.

If it was an hallucination, it was marvelous in its detail.

27

Hello Guv'nor.

Long time, eh? I hope you're okay. It's hard to think of you still on duty out there somewhere. They're all gone now: Bob, Ali, Dave the Ginger, Dave the Bald. I'm the last of the team left. I made it to Deputy Chief Constable of Wessex Metro. I saw CS2 on the news and none of the nurses here believed I'd served with you. If they have beer where you are, have one for me.

Look after yourself, Guv'nor.

Message to Supt. S. Frankland from Robert McEvoy.
Please route via CommsOp *Actaeon* soonest.

"We had a colony here, long before the fur-things came," said the isenj. His damning tone didn't appear to faze the ussissi interpreter, translating patiently on another screen while Eddie recorded. "We will not give up. This is ours."

The isenj was probably very old, Eddie decided. A patriarch. He had neither the animal charm of the ussissi nor the striking looks of the wess'har. He folded his long paired arms all around him like the skeleton of an umbrella, reminding the journalist of a dead spider in a bath, except spiders weren't radially built, nor did they move in quite the same bizarre way isenj did. Eddie stared at the image. The creature's jerky movements made it appear as if it were a film jumping frames.

"Who are the fur things?" Eddie asked.

"The wess'har. The ussissi. And you."

It was sobering to be on the receiving end of a blanket stereotype. "Tell me about the wars."

"Wars?" Patriarch shifted his weight, making rustling sounds. The superimposed frail voice of the ussissi translator made the image even more disorienting. "Isenj come back here from time to time to see if we can take back what is ours. We will not forget, ever, which is why we hold out. We need the planet. We are crowded. Why should we obey wess'har rules?"

"What is it about the wess'har rules you don't like?"

"Easy for them to live generous lives and protect plants, animals, lands. They breed slow, they are few. They force their views on us. Why should we die to save plants?"

The interpreter was doing an even-handed job, right down to conveying the stark syntax of the isenj language. This was television. This was what Eddie lived for. "What difference will humans make to all this? What do your people think now that we're here?"

"We may like you better as neighbors. We hear you breed faster than wess'har."

"That's probably true."

"How many humans in your world?"

"When I left, eight billion."

"You have more in common with us."

"We were looking for ways to stop our population growing."

"Yes. You did not have others choose that for you."

"Do you think the wess'har are trying to wipe you out?"

"They try to stop us traveling and make us like them. Static. We are colonizers and explorers. If we could spread, no conflict."

"I didn't think the wess'har carried out police actions other than on Bezer'ej." He was careful to avoid the word *peacekeeping*. "Do they attempt to confine you to your homeworld?"

"*C'naatat.* Hard to kill. Live forever, they say. Their killing forces. They will use them again."

"A myth," the ussissi interpreter told Eddie after the interview was officially over. "The wess'har had small numbers but were—are—technically superior to the isenj. They killed millions. There was a story about wess'har who could not be killed, but that is the sort of propaganda you put out about yourself in time of war. And if you lose badly, sometimes you need to tell yourself the odds were unfair."

"It did the trick with that old boy," Eddie observed. "He really hates them, doesn't he?"

"Yes, isenj pass on memories. Hate is very abiding."

"Yet you can live there with them."

"We do not take sides. And the wess'har are still capable of coming to our aid if we were to ask for it."

Eddie thought of the immense, sky-blackening ships that made him feel as impotent as a caveman with a rock in his hand.

"Are the wess'har a pain?"

"Pain?"

"Interfering. Annoying. Trouble."

"No. And if they are, it will not be because they have not warned you. What they say is what they do. There is no excuse for misunderstanding them."

"But they do carry out police actions to control isenj movements around Wess'ej and Bezer'ej."

"And sometimes beyond that in the past, yes."

"That implies a pretty aggressive policy."

"They do not interfere with other species unless they are threatened—or they want to stop others from being threatened. They think they have a duty to restore balance. Balance is their soul. Balance and responsibility."

Eddie was searching for a one-liner out of habit. He was enjoying talking to the ussissi and trying to reconcile that appealing, thin little voice with the mouthful of tiny needle teeth. The creatures were furry but they were not at all cute. "Humans have rights, wess'har have responsibilities." He laughed. "We had a man back home many years ago who wrote speculative books, a man called Wells, and he said journalism curdles all your thoughts to phrases. It's true."

"I still do not fully understand the journalist. You are not just data interpreters."

Eddie thought of some of the worst excesses of his brief infotainment days: *hell, no.* "I like to think of us as real-time historians. No benefit of hindsight and the better for it."

After the link with the ussissi was shut, Eddie wished he had meant it. Historians didn't have any responsibility other than to the truth. Everyone they could damage or destroy by their revelations was usually dead or past caring, and they could pick through a luxurious mass of information at a leisurely pace. Journalists made that ethical call on the fly, without the benefit of the full picture, and they could hurt the living. He'd done it often enough himself. Sometimes he had even regretted it.

He thought again about the *c'naatat*. However bizarre life could be on an alien planet, this had to be a myth, and myths did not deserve to be propagated. If it wasn't a myth—well, he hadn't thought that one through.

He continued packing and wondered about two things.

He wondered if his first real-time report from Constantine had been screened yet. He had scooped himself, because the original was still heading home at light speed. It was a deliciously bizarre concept.

And he wondered if Graham Wiley, a venerable 114 years old and in a care home, had received his greetings and the news that a greatly enlarged BBChan was rushing to schedule a prime-time Eddie Michallat series.

Life was good. Weird, but good.

Aras could hear Shan coming a full twenty seconds before his door burst open and she filled the doorway.

He braced for a tirade, maybe even a blow. It was as bad as facing Mestin in one of her rages. Shan had a remarkable capacity to trigger all those primeval instincts that told him to submit to a female.

She slammed the door shut behind her and took out her swiss. "Look," she said, hoarse and shaking. "Look at this." And she cut into the palm of her hand without flinching and held it in front of his face.

Aras looked away. She grabbed his hair and yanked his head round. He froze because that was what the wess'har in him told him to do in times of danger, to keep very still and assess the threat. Before his eyes, the cut in her hand stopped bleeding and began to close.

"Now tell me this was an accident," she hissed.

"You were dying, *Shan Chail.*"

She let go of his hair. His scalp still hurt. "Did you even stop to think this through? Did you think what it would do to me, to my world?"

"I have thought *c'naatat* through, believe me."

"What's it going to do to me?"

"I have no idea. But it *will* keep you alive." He didn't mean it to sound patronizing. She was torn between rage and terror, and he didn't need to smell that to know what she was going through. "I'm sorry. I am truly, truly sorry."

"Just tell me why. The truth."

"Your injuries were so serious that you had no chance of survival."

"Don't give me that crap. You've watched hundreds of humans die over the years and never intervened once."

"Perhaps that's because no other human ever put their life at risk for me."

Shan sat back on the *efte* bench opposite him and stared down at clasped hands.

"I'm never going home now, am I?"

She was crying. There was no sound, no change of expression, but her eyes were glazed with tears that threatened to spill down her face. Aras suspected she was not the sort of human who wept easily.

"No. You can never go back, *Shan Chail.*"

"You know what I am now? The most valuable tissue sample in history. Pay dirt. Why didn't you just let me die?"

"Because it's my fault that you were hurt, that you came here, that *any* of you came here. I won't have you pay for my mistakes."

"Then what's this?" She held out her hands. "What's this if it's not another of your bloody mistakes, eh?"

"I'll look after you. You needn't be afraid."

"You bastard," she said. "You stupid bastard."

She got up and walked out. It must have been scant comfort for her. At least his realization of what had happened to him had been gradual, at first just rapid recovery. He had already treated a cohort of wess'har troops with it before he noticed the changes his parasite was making, reshaping him with whatever genetic material took its fancy. He knew then that it needed to be kept isolated.

But it was only when he realized how many of his contemporaries were dead that the full impact of it struck him, and he knew he had condemned his comrades not only to a sterile exile from their families but also to a lonely infinity.

They had been angry, too. But at least they had known why it was necessary, and had had time to get used to it. You had to make sacrifices in war. They hadn't recovered consciousness to find that someone else had made the decision for them in full knowledge of the consequences. No wonder she was angry as well as scared.

It was getting warm in the chamber. Aras leaned across and opened the baffles of the ventilation grille, grateful for a draught of cooler air. It wasn't the usual degree of fever that accompanied *c'naatat* activity, nor was he as hungry as usual, but something was happening in him.

Whatever it was, however it was reshaping him, he had acquired it from Shan.

Shan pulled on her gloves and fastened her jacket right up to her chin, careful to expose as little of herself as possible.

The garment was definitely tight across the shoulders. And it hadn't shrunk.

She switched the swiss' screen to the mirror setting and stared at herself, looking for telltale traces of alien appearance. There was nothing so far, other than that she looked— to herself, at least—more healthy than she had in years. But she knew how *c'naatat* behaved: it was only a matter of time.

Tapeworm. She shuddered. No, it was more like being pregnant, except that she would never be free of this. If circumstances had been different, she would have asked Lindsay how she coped with something else living inside her. It was hardly the question to ask now.

I could do something for David.

The thought lasted less time than a blink. She recognized it for the sentimental insanity that it was. A pity that Aras hadn't had that revelation too. And now she was scared, as scared as when she had first walked into a riot with a transparent shield that didn't look as if it would stop the bricks and petrol bombs. She had a ritual for those times now. *Ten deep, slow breaths. See yourself cutting a swath. They're more scared of you, much more scared. Now walk.*

It worked for kicking down doors, buoyed up on a flood of adrenaline. For lying to people who trusted and relied on you, it was useless.

She made sure Josh's spare room was clean and tidy and began the walk back to camp.

"Hey, you should have told us you were coming," said Lindsay. She feigned cheerfulness but she didn't look as if she had slept for a week. By the number of half-finished cups of coffee around the comms console, it seemed she had spent most of her time in the ops room. "You look a lot better."

"How's David?"

Lindsay's mask slipped. "Not progressing as I'd hoped."

Don't you start crying, Shan thought. It was a brutally selfish wish. She couldn't do a damn thing and so she didn't want to even think about it. It was bad enough being ambushed by the possibility that she could. Not that easy, then: and she suddenly regretted her outburst at Aras. He had made no choices that she hadn't made herself, a very hard choice when both options on offer were bad.

This was what it felt like to be on the receiving end of someone else's morality. *I've got what I deserved.* She'd bloody well have to deal with it.

"What else?"

"Payload's quiet, resending data home on *Actaeon's* link." A breath, no more. "Are you going to talk to Okurt? He's *that* far from ordering us to detain you."

Shan's stomach rolled over in panic before she realized that this was about Parekh. Relief—and relief was always relative, she thought—washed over her.

"So what are you going to do?" Shan asked.

"What the hell am I supposed to do? I know as well as anyone that you had to do it. And who's going to believe me if I say you didn't, and you were just covering for your wess'har friend? You were, weren't you?"

Shan ignored the question. "I've put you in a tight spot. I'm sorry." There were many times when she didn't like herself very much and this was one of them. The opportunistic side of her, legacy of her long-absent mother's greedy sense of her own priority, surfaced and told her what a great break this was, what a fine piece of timing. "Tell him I've gone to see the wess'har matriarchs to try to open talks."

Lindsay began collecting the cups of cold coffee. "Right."

"I'm serious." Yes, she was. She was going to do it, but not for talks. She was going to ask for asylum. Nobody could take her from the wess'har. Whatever happened to her as an individual, the *c'naatat* would be safe from human greed.

Lindsay considered the idea. "He might buy that. I have to keep reminding him to call this planet Bezer'ej if he has any voice contact with the wess'har. He's stopped calling it CS2 but he's using the isenj name for it now, *Asht*. Not very diplomatic."

"As long as he doesn't call Wess'ej CS3."

Lindsay put out her hand as if to touch her. Shan stayed out of range. "You take care, okay?"

"It'll all get sorted," Shan lied. "Don't worry."

The shot on one of the monitors was live from Jejeno, in the southern continent of Ebj, one of the four capitals of the isenj homeworld Umeh. For a moment, Eddie thought the camera—if that was how the images were being transmitted—was set facing a building.

Then his brain suddenly comprehended the scale. There was nothing *but* building in Jejeno. He was looking at miles of matt gray and cream material speckled with apertures and crossed by filaments. This was a high aerial shot. *Actaeon* was now in orbit around Umeh, as far away as Mars from Earth.

Eddie adjusted his external earpiece. He disliked implants as much as Shan, but only because the BBChan ones were notoriously cheap and unreliable. "Could you possibly give me a pullout, please? Is there a more distant view I can take?"

The tech aboard *Actaeon* obliged in silence. The plasma screen snapped to a very long shot indeed, the sort of shot an incoming orbital-launched missile might have seen. Ebj was nothing but gray and cream constructs right up to the rust-red coastline. And Ebj was not unique, because the orbital shot showed every visible scrap of land was that same mix of non-color.

He wondered if he had misunderstood. Isenj could adapt to oxygen and temperate climates, but they weren't primarily oxygen breathers: their world was colder and bleaker and sulfur-rich, so there was no reason to look for greens and blues and assume them to be the natural planet.

But his first fear had been right. The world was completely covered in buildings. What kind of ecology that supported he couldn't begin to imagine.

"You can see space is at a premium for us," said the voice of Ual, the isenj minister. Eddie glanced to the other two screens, one with a mongoose-faced ussissi translator who did not appear to be needed, the other filled with— well, a piranha on a spider's body. Isenj weren't cute either. Sometimes you had to draw crude brushstrokes just to be able to cope.

"I'm astonished," said Eddie.

"Now you know why we must colonize." Ual's voice was distorted by a gulping, breathy delivery, but the words were discernible. "You will understand that need, as a human."

"And the wess'har—the *c'naatat* forces—stopped you."

"You think this is a myth, do you?" Ual challenged. "You think we don't know enough to evaluate military risks? *C'naatat* are real. They were made for the sole purpose of fighting us and keeping us from our rightful possessions. The high-minded wess'har, who care so much about not crushing flowers and killing animals, swallowed their principles long enough to make monsters of their own people so they could do the fighting for them. And then they turned their backs on them."

Eddie felt a pang of triumph that he'd had the right

hunch. Some things were very reassuring. "It was a genetic engineering program, am I right?"

"Possibly. We don't know how they achieved it, because we have no expertise in that area. But I can assure you the *c'naatat* were—are—real. We captured one. You could burn him, cut him, infect him, poison him, and still he wouldn't die. He healed and recovered, often very fast indeed. It's not a part of our history of which I'm proud, but everyone has their war crimes, do they not? Wess'har made those poor creatures to do their dying for them. So think of that when you judge us."

"These *c'naatat* were wess'har, though, weren't they?"

"They were. Just altered."

Eddie heard pieces drop into neat holes in his thoughts, perfect and obvious.

"No myth at all," he said. "What happened to the *c'naatat* prisoner? Did he die in the end?"

"He survived an aerial assault on our camp and now lives on *Asht* with your fellow humans. The destroyer of Mjat is your neighbor."

For some reason, Eddie didn't experience that usual rush of pure adrenal triumph that marked a landmark story. He felt slightly sick. He had chased a tiger and caught it, and now had no idea what to do with it.

When he edited the interview with Ual, he decided it needed a lot more editing—a *lot* more. He was left with a few sound bites. He secure-filed the orbital views of Ebj and the discussion about the wess'har shock troops under GASH FILE, and erased the rushes from *Actaeon*'s buffer.

It was a great story. A show-stopper. Back home, under the same circumstances, he would have run that interview without a moment of doubt. Now he had a sense of what his exclusive could mean—could do—out here.

It was a rotten time to discover a sense of responsibility. He wasn't even sure he was right.

He consoled himself with a glass of home brew and the knowledge that in a few hours a very elderly Graham Wiley would be wheeled out in his chair to watch *Michallat Reports.*

The colonists were polite as Shan walked down through the galleries of Constantine, but they gave her a much wider berth than usual. News traveled fast. She was suddenly grateful for their insularity and distance from the *Thetis* team. Josh met her at the door and redirected her with a courteous but brief observation that Aras was still in his chambers.

She knocked this time.

"I came to apologize," she said.

"I understand how upset you must be."

"Maybe I could have thanked you for saving my life."

Aras pulled up a chair and pushed a plate of okara cookies in front of her. "They're stale. Sorry."

"I could eat anything right now." And she could: her appetite hadn't relented for a moment. "Is this part of it?"

"Yes. *C'naatat* uses a great deal of energy when it's adapting an organism."

"That's me we're talking about."

"Us."

"Yes, sorry. Us."

"You seem more at ease with the situation."

"I find it easier to deal with what's right in front of me. Right now, that's removing me from circulation. I need to ask you something. Would your matriarchs let me stay?"

Aras busied himself with stacking more cookies on the plate. "What reason would you give?"

"*This* reason."

"I would suggest you ask on the basis that you have been identified as an ally of the wess'har and are hence at risk from the other *gethes.*"

"You haven't told them, have you?"

"No, because they would almost certainly execute both of us for such an insane breach of quarantine."

"Oh shit."

"I have learned so many new words from you, *Shan Chail.* Shit indeed."

Any insults she was considering heaping upon him for being selfish, for being rash, for ruining her life, suddenly seemed ungrateful beyond belief. He really had taken a huge risk for her benefit.

"This just gets worse and worse," she said.

"I don't fear death. But it seems unfair to commit you to this existence and then not be there to help you through it. It can be very lonely indeed."

She reached out and took his hand and squeezed it hard. *Nobody could imagine what made me break the law to protect terrorists. So how can I judge you?* The only thing that mattered right then was that Aras cared about her welfare more than anyone else had, even more than her fellow officers, and plenty more than her family.

"Ask them for me," she said. "Please."

28

TO: Research Support BBChan
FROM: Eddie Michallat, CS2

REQUEST: *All accounts and assets held by Superintendent Shan Frankland within FEU and banking zones 2,3
and 4. Special note: she's ex Commercial Branch so she
knows the ropes—do some digging, call in favors. Seeking
unusually large sums, transfers from biotech corps, government agencies. I need this soonest.*
  *P.S. Good to know you're still there. God bless isenj
comms. Do you still need a budget code for this?*

Eddie's mouth was dry and his pulse was racing. It always did that when he was beside himself with excitement
at the prospect of a seriously big story, and in all his life he
had never come across anything this big, let alone had it ex-
clusively to himself.

Nothing was proven. The isenj could have been indulging in self-deception, as the interpreter had said, explaining away military defeat at the hands of a numerically
inferior foe.

But there was the detail. No wonder Aras had walked
away from that crash.

Eddie couldn't quite remember how he'd arrived in the
mess galley and started making coffee. He stopped to stare
at the mug and the spoon in his hands and shook himself
out of the speculative frenzy that had gripped him.

There was something else bothering him—Shan Frankland. He thought he had the full and frightening measure of

her—hard, calculating, but oddly idealistic—and now he wasn't so sure.

Everyone knew she'd had a Suppressed Briefing. It was almost a joke among the marines, a silly political spy-game that they clearly despised. The general view was that it was about aliens, because that was the sort of thing that politicians thought people shouldn't know about. Nothing more.

Eddie was starting to have doubts.

Not even Shan Frankland could get up and walk away from a round in the head. And when had she last gone through the ritual of producing samples for Hugel? It was a camp joke—pee, blood and shit. A sudden cold spasm in his gut made him stop dead.

Maybe this was all about *c'naatat*. Maybe *that* was her order from Perault: secure the biotech for government use before the corporations got their hands on it.

No, that was insane. Shan was EnHaz. Shan was sympathetic to eco-terrorists to the point of self-destruction. He couldn't see her acquiring this sort of technology for patriotism or hard cash.

He didn't *want* to see it.

It was probably just a coincidence, one that was blinding him to the real story of an alien who possibly had the most extraordinary power imaginable. Cock-up over conspiracy theory, he reasoned.

But where was Shan now?

"When did Frankland last give samples?" Eddie asked Kris Hugel.

"She never has," she said. "I didn't fancy forcing the issue, given her sunny and tolerant disposition. Why?"

"Just curious."

"As curious as I am how she's walking around now with no brain damage?"

"Possibly."

"I don't think it's unconnected with the way our

wess'har friend survived that crash. Is there anything you want to tell me? Think how much medical techniques like that could achieve back home."

"Nothing, not yet," said Eddie, grateful that Hugel was still locked into her own narrow area of expertise.

Medical techniques, my arse.

He wasn't sure what had wounded him most—the fact that Shan Frankland might turn out not to be the hero he imagined, or that she had actually managed to dupe him.

Where was she?

It was a hard climb, and it seemed a strange route to take when there was flat terrain ahead. Wess'ej gravity was even higher than on Bezer'ej: a route like this one was taking its toll. Shan jerked the pack higher on her back to relieve sore spots and put one leg in front of the other, mechanically, painfully.

"Are you all right?" Aras paused and looked back at her. "Shall I carry your pack?"

"I can manage," she said. "I'll adapt."

"I have a reason for bringing you by this route."

She didn't have the wind left for a reply. She drew level with him and kept up her clockwork pace. *Discipline,* she said to herself. *Discipline, discipline, discipline.* The mantra had always worked before. They moved up the slope with no further conversation, only her rhythmic gasps punctuating the quiet.

Aras drew a way ahead. She plodded on. She could see him skylined against the light on the top of the ridge. She hoped it *was* the top, anyway.

"There." He had his back to her, staring down at something beyond that ridge. "Do look at this. Wasn't this worth the pain?"

And she looked.

Beneath them, a town was dotted across the basin and

walls of a great caldera, part wreathed in morning mist.
Faceted circular roofs shimmered. Everywhere she looked,
there was iridescence. She couldn't tell if she was looking
at the tops of high buildings emerging from fog or at a
much lower scale of architecture. But she knew she was
looking at pearls—thousands upon thousands of pearls,
pressed into the roof of each and every fairy-tale building,
for as far as she could see.

"Jesus H. Christ," she said.

"I know how humans love sparkly things," Aras was all
pride and delight. "Do you like it?"

The cold burning in her nose and throat as she struggled
to breathe had started to ease: the *c'naatat* was busy equip-
ping her for this foray. Shan sat back on her heels and simply stared.

Sheer glory was spread out beneath her. She could suddenly see through the eyes of the colonists, even though she
believed none of it. This was a vision from their bible. She
opened her swiss and the screen danced with text.

And the twelve gates were twelve pearls: every several
gate was of one pearl: and the street of the city was pure
gold, as it were transparent glass. If F'nar was not the new
Jerusalem of Revelation, it was doing a very good imper-
sonation. She made a conscious effort to dispel awe. This
was a city grounded in pragmatism, and God had played no
part in it.

"They'd go crazy if they saw this place," she said,
mostly to herself.

"F'nar?" asked Aras. He looked at the swiss display over
her shoulder, and the dry sandalwood scent of him jerked
her back to the mundane world. "Yes, you all react like this
to it. The City of Pearl."

"Is that what you call it?"

"No, it's what *you* call it. Or that's what Ben Garrod

called it. I have brought a few colonists here. Not many, but some."

"It's very pretty. How long did it take your people to coat those roofs?"

"Coat?"

"The pearl layer. The coating on all the buildings."

Aras assumed his canine-bewilderment expression. "We gave up trying to remove it," he said. "We found it made the roofs more weatherproof."

"It's natural?"

"It's the secretion of *tem*, small things like your bees. They swarm here and leave little bubbles on the tiles. Billions of them."

"Bugger me," Shan said. "Insect shit?" She regretted her cynicism instantly. This view was beautiful beyond belief. She owed it a little more reverence. The wind had shifted, fresh against her face. Suddenly she was aware of a voice on the breeze, a long, single unbroken note like a singer rehearsing. It held for minutes, and stopped. When it picked up again, another—a different pitch, with a slight tremolo effect—overlapped it. Shan stopped.

Aras glanced back at her. "Matriarchs."

"Singing?" She was looking for a slot, a human slot into which she could put the extraordinary voices. Perhaps it was like muezzins calling the faithful to prayer, or perhaps not, in this place of no prayer. "Is that it? Are they singing?"

"They're declaring," Aras said mildly, as if it were the most obvious thing in the world, and carried on walking. She broke into a trot to catch up with him. After a few paces he stopped again and the expression on his face was unreadable. "They're declaring their territories," he said again, as if he was explaining to a child.

This was getting harder for her. Aras was an alien, but she had grown used to his conveniently human details. Now there were unknown creatures singing over a landscape of pearls, as foreign and strange as the bezeri had been, and her fragile points of reference were crumbling away.

She had not expected anyone to come to meet her. She was begging favors from them, asking for refuge at a time when *gethes* were a sudden and potentially serious enemy. But a wess'har was waiting for them at the gateway on the top of the ridge.

In the flesh, they looked far more intimidating than the picture in Constantine's library. She had looked at that only once since realizing it was Aras, unable to equate the man she knew with that alien—and now unable to come to terms with the idea that some of that creature's characteristics were within her.

She came within a few meters and fought the urge to stare at what now was clearly a female in a shimmering opal coat.

Shan had no idea why she was so certain about that. She looked for the signs of womanhood, from body shape to facial bones, and saw absolutely nothing that confirmed this was a woman, but she was certain it was a female. She could smell it was so.

"This is the matriarch Fersanye," Aras said.

Fersanye stood more than a head above Shan, an exotic Valkyrie with hair braided down her neck. They weren't just plaits. The hair—the fur—grew out from her neck in long stiff strips. Her eyes were almost wholly iris, but light amber and translucent. The fast-changing pupils were a cross, a star, one moment horizontal, the next vertical, and then a star of teardrop shapes again. Shan had never noticed that in Aras's eyes. Would she end up looking like that? Shan stood absolutely still and stared back at her.

The matriarch emitted a stream of rich notes—no, *two* streams—as she spoke. There was another sound simulta-

neously beneath like overtone singing. The effect was
breathtakingly weird. Shan was entranced.

"*Fersanye Chail* says she wants you to explain yourself
to all the matriarchs of this region," Aras translated.

"Tell her I'll do my best," Shan said.

Aras relayed the reply. She had never heard him speak
his own language before, except for the odd word. Listening to that fabulous and bizarre double layer of sound reminded her what he was: an honest-to-god alien. And now
she was alien too, and maybe several aliens for all she understood of *c'naatat*. The two wess'har conversed and some
agreement appeared to have been reached.

"Fersanye has arranged rooms for us in Chayyas's
household," Aras said. "Have something to eat, clean yourself, and then we await your audience with the matriarchs."

"Can I eat wess'har food?"

Aras patted her shoulder. "You can eat *anything* now.
But let's not mention that in front of Fersanye."

"Can she understand English?"

"Not until she bothers to learn it. Some wess'har can,
though. Don't assume otherwise."

There were times in Shan's life when she had the uneasy
sensation that something of great importance was taking
place and that she really ought to have been standing outside herself to observe it. This was one of those times. She
walked beside Aras into a wide colonnaded terrace lined
with buildings that could easily have sprung from the Earth
as living objects. Doorways twisted slightly; windows—if
they were windows—were irregular, one a teardrop, the
next a jagged slit, and there were beings paused in their
daily lives and looking at her. She tried not to stare back at
them. They all looked like Fersanye, and none like Aras. As
she passed, a double-toned burble wafted on the air behind
her, no doubt a discussion of the strange human who had

been brought to explain herself to them. Most would never have seen a live human before.

Their gaze was easy to follow. But they weren't staring at her.

They were staring at Aras.

They gazed at him down long muzzles that were neither human nor animal; Shan tried not to stare back, but it seemed rude not to at least acknowledge them in some way. When one caught her eye, she nodded as she had seen Aras do, but she couldn't gauge their reaction. Aras was still no reliable guide to wess'har behavior.

F'nar spread round the entire bowl of the caldera, an amphitheater of terraced streets punctuated by trickling water courses, twisting steps and brilliant foliage in carmine and gold

"So this is what you meant by noticeable building," she said.

"I come from the north. We build *into* the world. They're soft down here—they just disguise it."

She said nothing more until they reached a building at the bottom of another flight of steps that promised to be treacherous in wet weather. It looked ordinary, if anything in this city could be called commonplace. Aras indicated the door with a spread hand and waited for her to enter. It was just a screen across an irregular opening.

"Is this it?" she asked.

"It's Chayyas's house," Aras said. "Are you disappointed?"

She had expected the grandeur of a government building, a statement of power or past or empire. Once through the door, the building seemed to be the size of a small hotel, a maze of interconnecting chambers that didn't correspond to anything that resembled human architecture or layout. She found herself walking through occupied rooms where wess'har youngsters and small males with their distinctive

long manes paused to stare at her and then glance away
again. She could see no doors to close.

"Am I using the tradesman's entrance?"

"No," said Aras.

"Don't you have corridors?"

"Not in a family home. All rooms connect." He paused
in front of an opening partly covered by a swath of ornate
green and blue fabric and pulled the curtain aside. "We
don't share your need for seclusion. This is the most private
they can make your accommodation for the time being."

A doorway led into a chamber decorated with the same
fabric. There was an alcove with a shelf cut into it at waist
height and filled with bolsters, and several more openings
revealed other smaller rooms.

"Bed," said Aras, pointing at the alcove. "Washing facilities through there. Library in there."

"Library."

"*Everyone* has a library."

"Right."

"I'll go and see what's to eat," Aras said, and slipped out.

Shan unfastened the top of her fatigues, feeling the heat
of the *c'naatat* still at work, and wondered what it was up to
in the quiet microscopic backwaters of her body. Her
clothes were at the limit of their expansion.

She waited for Aras to come back and fetch her from her
room. She didn't relish the thought of wandering around a
wess'har home on her own, not knowing when she might
cause offense or look foolish.

"There's a meal ready when you want it," he said.

"Is this formal?"

"No. You eat with whoever happens to be around.
Mainly the males and children at the moment. The matriarchs are in discussion."

Expect nothing in common with aliens, Galvin the xenozoologist had once told her. Shan thought briefly that it was

a shame Galvin didn't make it this far, but that was danger-
ously like sentiment. She hadn't. It was tough.

Shan watched for a few seconds before venturing into
the room. The aromas were odd, some familiar and dis-
tinctly foodlike, some more chemical, but whatever the
smells were she didn't have the olfactory receptors to pick
them all up. Perhaps the *c'naatat* would add those in due
course. Long tawny wess'har males were chopping vegetables and stirring pans. They glanced up at her and then
looked away, intent on their cooking again.

The difference between the genders was clearer now: the
females were much larger than the males, with tufted manes
rather than long soft braids. There also seemed to be very
few of them. This was a predominantly male society, even if
the matriarchs did have control. Shan was immediately surrounded by a small group of wess'har children. They stared
up at her totally unself-consciously and made little double-
warbling sounds.

"I'm not going to learn to speak the language, am I?" she
said, turning to Aras for support. She tried to smile reassur-
ingly at them for all the good it would do. She was alarmed
not that they were aliens but that they were children. "I
can't do that overtone thing."

"I think you might," Aras said. "Trust your little colony."

Aras dispersed the children with a brief sound and led
Shan to the table. One of the other males laid out plates in
front of them with the quick ease of a card dealer. The
plates were every shade of colored glass she could imagine,
some shot with swirls like the glasses she had first seen in
Josh's house, others speckled with bursts of contrasting colors. Even the serving spoons, broad curved scoops like
overblown sticks of celery, were dazzlingly colorful glass.
The food, at least, would be safe. There would be no entrails or unidentifiable body parts to negotiate.

She gave the bowls of food a cursory glance, searching

for shapes she might recognize. There were some odd
dishes, but one was immediately recognizable. A bowl was
filled with glistening purple shreds.

"Oh boy," she said. "Beetroot. My favorite."

"It's popular here," Aras said. "Our one import. An
honor."

Shan decided to risk breaching etiquette and dug a serving spoon into a plate of brilliant orange cubes that yielded
like sponge. She speared a cube on a single-tined fork and
bit off a piece. *Rosewater, cardamom, salt.* It was slightly
chewy and left her mouth tingling.

"*Evem,*" Aras said. "And *that* is *lurisj.* I would normally
advise caution, but I doubt it will have any effect now."

She took a piece and chewed. It felt like Turkish delight
in her mouth but its flavor was fungal.

"*Lurisj,*" Aras repeated. "It's recreational. Like beer."

"Really?"

"A few pieces will affect your perception."

"You can get legless on this?"

"If your little colony allows it. Which I doubt."

"What do you mean, if it allows it?"

"It's a toxin, as is alcohol."

"Yes, mum, I know that."

"And your new body ecology will neutralize it and ex-
crete it."

Shan stopped chewing. "I can't get drunk, then?"

"No. But you said you despised drunkenness, so that
would be a bonus, wouldn't it?"

He was right. She was puritanical about drinking, even
more than the colonists, but knowing she could never experience its release again left her feeling bereft. She could no
longer get drunk, and she couldn't go home, and she could
never screw Ade Bennett or any other man—and *never* now
translated as an unimaginable time stretching ahead of her.

Tears pricked her eyes. She changed the subject.

"I'm not going to cause offense by serving myself, am I?" She piled more *evem* onto her plate.

"Nobody would seek to serve you food," Aras said quietly. "With the exception of some of the more remote clans, wess'har would only serve food to a sexual partner or their immediate relatives. Or someone they wanted to be their sexual partner."

He beamed to himself as if he were remembering a private joke. She was going to ask him what was so funny when one of the wess'har males stopped what he was doing and came to sit with them.

"I speak English," he said, all musical tones and shocking gold eyes. "I am Cekul. Do you like this food? Is it strange to you?"

"It's very nice," she said weakly, and smiled, trying to reassure him. She bit into a meatball-shaped cake, like the *netun* that Aras seemed fond of: it was overwhelmingly sweet and scented. The center popped and yielded a burst of tart fuchsia-pink filling. "This is very good."

"I make the best *paran jay,*" he said flatly.

Aras gave her a glance that warned her she was on contentious territory. Skills, he had told her, were one of those status things that took the place of possessions.

"It is all safe for you," said Cekul. "Nothing disgusting from creatures."

"I realize you don't use animal products. Lots of humans don't, either. I do understand."

He leaned forward a little, all curiosity. She could suddenly smell—no, *taste*—the most delicious scent of sandalwood rising from him, just as with Aras. She inhaled it involuntarily. It gave her an indefinably pleasant feeling.

"Is it true you eat a substance made with insect saliva?" Cekul asked carefully, as if it were a disgraceful perversion. "A viscous yellow liquid?"

"Honey?" she said. "Oh. Yes."

"And eggs, out of creatures'—backsides?"

Human food habits seemed suddenly embarrassing. Rotted animal lactation laced with mold or curdled with stomach enzymes. Intoxicants made out of yeast-piss. Raw bivalves, eaten alive. No wonder they called humans *gethes.* "Yes," she admitted.

The master chef stared down his muzzle at her and his sandalwood scent shifted a little into citrus. "Oh, *gethes,*" he said. "How will we live alongside you? I think we never will." And he stood up and went back to his pots and knives. For a few moments she couldn't speak. Aras fumbled nervously with the *paran jay.*

"We tend to speak our minds," he said at last. "I have lost something of the habit."

"I think diplomacy is going to be a challenge here."

"I've not prepared you properly for this."

"Should I be that rude to the matriarchs?"

"Yes."

"I spent half my working life learning to keep my big mouth shut. That's what we call irony."

Shan retreated to her room and awaited the call of the matriarchal assembly, and tried not to visualize it. She had been summoned, not invited, and they weren't about to seek her views on F'nar's economic future as a tourist center.

How hard could it be? She'd given evidence enough times in court. There wasn't a lawyer alive who could make her nervous or browbeat her into expressing doubt about her evidence. This time was no different.

Aras appeared at the doorway. "They're ready," he said.

Wrong. This time *was* different.

He led her down buff stone hallways that were punctuated by skylights every few meters. Dust motes danced in the shafts of sun as she passed, and when she looked to one side or the other, she spotted hallways within hallways. There were still no doors. *And nothing terrible waiting behind them.* She still didn't like doors.

As they walked she caught snatches of warbling voices and the scraping of implements on china. No, glass: it was probably glass. These people were obsessed with transparency. She paused and looked up at one circular skylight, and caught her breath with a yelp when she saw a mass of wess'har faces crowded above it, arranged round the margin like flower petals.

"Kids," said Aras helpfully. He gestured through the glass and the light bloomed again as they scattered. "I did try to create some privacy. I'm sorry."

Eventually they reached the end of what had begun to feel like a tunnel and came into an octagonal lobby faced with polished stone. It was a startling contrast to the honeycomb passages and chambers of the family quarters, and if it was meant to inspire reverence and fear in the face of government, it was doing a pretty good job.

I remember this, she thought. *I've been here before in a way.*

She recalled a courthouse built in the nineteenth century, a magnificent Victorian criminal court where the accused were brought up from the cells through the bridewell to ascend steps and find themselves in a vaulted courtroom of intimidating beauty. The judge sat on an impossibly high platform at the front, the jury on extravagantly carved benches to one side and the press on the other. It was a victim's entry into the arena. It was bowel-loosening grandeur. But it had never been her bowels at stake before, just her prisoner's. Now she understood.

Aras led her to the side of the room and picked up a long pole from a bundle propped in the corner. He flicked it and it snapped into a frame.

"Seat," he said, and showed her how to make herself

comfortable on it by kneeling and slipping it under her backside, so that she was almost but not quite taking her weight on her heels. It reminded her of a meditation stool, but wess'har obviously had knees of a more heroic construction than humans'. She shuffled uncomfortably. In so far as her buttocks were on something that was taking her weight, she was sitting. But she had no idea how long she could maintain the position. Her *c'naatat* hadn't yet seen fit to equip her for the furniture.

She glanced around. The lack of seating had now begun to obsess her, and she noted that there were no tables or work surfaces at the heights she expected. The hall she had entered was uncluttered, with absolutely no furniture whatsoever. Then she watched a wess'har male wander in and look briefly along the walls for something as if he were reading a notice. She couldn't see what it was from where she was sitting. It was hard to skew round on the stool, wedged as it was, without popping a vertebra or making obscene scraping sounds on the flooring. The male took a cylinder like a large pen from his tunic, snapped it out into a longer shape about fifty centimeters long, unfolded that into a strip about fifteen centimeters wide, and then folded it into a triangular form to make—another stool. He slid it under him with unconscious skill and knelt. As he touched the floor before him, a flat ovoid surface rose up at a slight angle to meet him at the optimum height for a work surface.

All he had done was pull up a chair and sit down at a desk. But it had dazzled her, just as firearms and cameras had once shocked native peoples on Earth, and it served to remind her of humankind's new place in the pecking order. She laid her hand on the floor in front of her, just to see what would happen, and nothing did. The pastel terrazzo flooring yielded nothing to her. Aras glanced at her and said nothing.

A sound of rustling movement came from another corridor leading on to the lobby and Shan looked up, expecting to see a matriarch bearing down on her. What emerged from the passage looked more like a meerkat or a mongoose: it was smaller than a human, standing upright and moving with a brisk swaying movement that made the fabric bandoliers it was wearing swing dramatically. It pressed the wall and stood staring at it until a screen appeared. Then it took a pole-seat from its garment and sat down, apparently to read. It seemed to be having as much trouble getting comfortable as Shan had.

She turned her face slowly to Aras. "And that is?"

"Ussissi," said Aras. "Are they what you expected?"

"You let them wander around in your state buildings?" All her faith in the wise might of the wess'har was crumbling. "Are they security-cleared?"

"What would they find out about us that the isenj don't already know? They take no sides. They like to live alongside other species."

"Aras, military and technical strength might work for you now, but if you ever mix it up with humans, you'll have to be a lot more canny."

"You can explain 'canny' to me later," he said, and got up, indicating a doorway opposite them. "You're summoned. I will follow."

Fersanye—she assumed it was Fersanye, anyway—stood in the entrance and simply motioned her forward with a single gesture like a parking marshal, and it was a gesture that expected to be obeyed. Whatever chamber was on the other side of that doorway behind that veil of yellow and amber fabric was going to be immense. Shan swallowed. If there were brilliant lights, she would keep her eyes down. If there were rank upon rank of hostile alien faces, she would concentrate her gaze on one at a time. She could do it. It was just a day in the witness box.

She stepped through the opening and glanced round the chamber.

It was slightly smaller than the kitchen in which she'd eaten earlier, and there were nine wess'har females sitting there, some on benches at a table, others in individual chairs. A mongoose of a ussissi with a text pad scuttled up to her side. The anticlimax almost forced a sob from her.

"Shan Frankland, I shall translate for you, although the matriarch Siyyas and the matriarch Prelit and the matriarch Chayyas do speak some English." The mongoose was talking to her in an odd, sibilant little girl's voice. Did they really need an interpreter? Didn't they have software? "They apologize for making you wait in the library for so long, but they had other items to discuss that they thought might bore you."

It was as eloquent a lesson in cultural misreading as she had ever received. *A library*. It wasn't a court lobby. Nothing here was what she took it to be. Its apparent familiarity was deceptive and dangerous.

"You have a function that defines you," Prelit said. "What is it?"

"Your job," the ussissi prompted.

"I'm a police officer," Shan said. "I enforce the rules of my society. My speciality is preventing environmental hazards."

"Can you prevent your fellow *gethes* working with the isenj?"

"No. What they can offer humans in terms of technology is probably far more persuasive than anything I can do or say to them."

"So you have no authority."

Shan made a conscious effort to remove the automatic tendency to edit what she thought before it escaped her mouth. It had taken many, many years to learn to do that. Now she had to unlearn it.

"No," she said.

"So are you of any use to us?" The matriarch Chayyas

was a linguist. She displayed a certain pride in dismissing the services of the ussissi. "Why should we allow you to stay?"

"I understand the kind of human in *Actaeon* better than you do, better even than Aras. But I didn't come here to bargain with you. I came here to ask you to let me stay on Bezer'ej. In the eyes of the government I'm now expected to serve, I've collaborated with you."

The wess'har sniffed. Maybe she was testing for honesty. "You don't smell unpleasant at all."

"Thank you," said Shan carefully. "I don't eat carrion these days."

Aras's assimilated manners had ill prepared her for wess'har directness. If they thought something, then they said it, and they meant it. They liked their truth so plain and unvarnished that it was raw timber, and some of it still had the bark on.

Chayyas stared. "We're not inclined to make a treaty with *gethes*," she said at last. "But what if we did?"

Shan shook her head. "What would you ask for?"

"Peace? An understanding?"

"Unless there was something in it for them, they wouldn't bother. You know what that something is. Commercial exploitation, more humans, technology exchange— so unless you can think of anything else you would want from us, I'd forget it."

Chayyas inhaled as if someone had made coffee in the next room. "Your absence, perhaps."

"Look, you don't like us and I'm not here to tell you what great neighbors we'd make. There are some good humans, some great ones even—like the colonists on Bezer'ej. But the sort of humans you're likely to see out here in the foreseeable future won't be like that. This is business, research and expansion. What else do you want to hear?"

"You want to hear things from us, not us from you."

Chayyas inhaled again. Could she smell *c'naatat*? "We could simply destroy the ship, and you too. All of you."

"Yes. And if I were you, I'd do it. Now. And maybe send a message back to Earth warning the rest of us off. In fact, I have a man on my team who can do just that. You can broadcast it on BBChan, worldwide." She had their attention now, and not simply because she was a strongly scented and exotic curiosity. "But if you do, it won't stop further contact with the isenj, and it probably won't stop humans coming again in the future. If humans have instant comms technology, they can explore and colonize much more easily. They're not likely to walk away from this. Learn from me while you can."

Chayyas glanced at Fersanye and the others. There was no visible reaction other than that, and Shan suppressed a shudder, because she really had meant that they should open fire. It was exactly what a small nation with a lot to lose should have done. It stunned her that she had actually said so. She folded her arms while the Valkyries trilled and warbled among themselves.

Chayyas eventually turned those star-centered eyes on her and spoke. "We have decided. *Gethes* are now barred from wess'har space. Your mission will leave immediately, but you may stay on the understanding that you now serve Wess'ej."

"Understood," Shan said.

"By serve I mean that you will do what is asked of you without question. You work for us. You have the duties of a citizen of F'nar. Is that clear? Ignore your past, and so will we."

"Thank you, ma'am."

She almost said *guv'nor*. Chayyas certainly had some presence. The matriarch leaned forward as if getting one last good sniff of her.

"I hope you understand what is at stake here."

The test. There had to be one. Shan raised her chin just a fraction. *"C'naatat,"* she said. The matriarchs were suddenly very still and her heart sank. She had nearly pulled it off. Then she'd been just one fraction too clever.

"The isenj have told you, then," said Chayyas.

Isenj? *Think, think, think. Don't lie. They'll know.*

Shan concentrated. Maybe there was a God after all.

"It has to be kept isolated. My people might decide they want it, but they will abuse it, even if they start out with honest intentions."

Had Chayyas bought it? It was true. She had to. She tilted her seahorse head and looked down at Shan.

"They are no longer your people," she said. "We are."

29

David Christopher Neville
Born July 12, 2375
Died August 11, 2375
Cause of death: acute pulmonary failure

Shan had never been good at bereavement. It had been a professional thing, just a technique for gauging how to break bad news to next of kin in as economical a way as possible.

Her first time as a probationer copper was awful. She recalled the disbelieving face of a wife who had waved her husband off to work at the monorail without a thought that it might be the last time she'd see him. After that it got easier each time, and in the end she was an accomplished breaker of bad news, as detached as an actor reading lines. It didn't pay to grieve with them because it ate you up, and anger just made you make mistakes if there was an investigation to be done. Shutting down was the sensible thing to do.

Even so, this was the second death of a child in her very small world in less than a year. The first had confirmed that humans and wess'har were on a collision course. The second was a personal conflict, even if Lindsay never found out why.

"I can do this on my own," Shan said.

"I can't take that risk," said Aras. "You should have stayed on Wess'ej."

"I can't just abandon her without an explanation. Wait here."

Shan found Lindsay in the mess hall. She looked like

hell, but she was working on inventories with her gaze fixed rigidly on the board in her lap, ticking items with a stylus and waiting for the confirming *eep* from the database.

"Lin," Shan said.

She looked up. "Hi."

"I'm so sorry."

"It's okay. I'm fine. Kris fixed me up. I'm not going to fall apart."

"I wish I could have done something."

"You can't work miracles. But thanks."

"How about getting some rest?"

"That's the last thing I need right now. We'll be back on *Thetis* inside a week. Funny, isn't it? Right back where we started, like none of this happened."

Shan thought of telling her she was here for her if she wanted to talk. But the idea disgusted her. How could she offer comfort after standing back and letting it happen? Right and wrong weren't going to carry much weight with Lindsay at the moment, and Shan had to admit to herself that she probably couldn't cope with the strain of lying to her.

You can't grieve with them. You'd be no use to anyone then, her old sergeant used to say. She'd taken an EnHaz decision so she would deal with it as an officer, and put a good safe distance between the event and her emotions. That way she'd be ready to deal with whatever came next.

"Lin, I've decided to stay on."

"When are you going back, then?"

"I mean permanently."

Lin looked blank. It might have been whatever mood-blocker Hugel had given her. "I can't say I blame you. Okurt's very anxious to talk to you."

"Then I've saved you the problem. I work for the wess'har government now."

"What?"

"Don't ask, and say you never saw me."

Shan debated how she might take her leave of someone she'd almost counted as a close friend in this enforced intimacy, and decided it was probably better to walk away right then.

Lin looked up. "Shan, I want to have David buried here. You know Josh better than anyone. Will you ask him?"

"Of course." *Hypocrite, hypocrite, hypocrite.* "I'm sure there won't be a problem."

"Buried, Shan. Not left for the rockvelvets."

"No, I promise."

Shan wanted to ask why. But it didn't matter. She wandered back up the passage to her own cabin and opened her locker. Then she took out her uniform jacket and picked off the fluff that had gathered on it, and opened the dark blue grip. As she moved it, something rattled.

The seeds. Of course. She had opened the sealed pack of tomato seeds she had smuggled from Earth, but she had never got round to planting them. It seemed too much like establishing a permanent connection with a world she would have to leave. Now she could have at least a piece of her dream, even if she could never retire.

She made a conscious effort to uninvolve herself. She had real EnHaz work to do now and even if EnHaz no longer existed on Earth, it would live on here, in her.

She picked over the seeds, wondering where she might plant them. As she examined them, her own hands caught her by surprise for the first time.

She could have sworn she had the beginnings of claws.

Aras was proud of his skill with glass. Glass needed making, and there was no reason not to make it well. He put everything he knew into the headstone for David Neville's grave.

He sifted through fragments of pink and gold glass and laid the best pieces out on a cloth to plan the image. Josh had said flowers were appropriate.

The workshop was normally busy with colonists repairing and recycling items, but they left him to his private task with their usual silent diplomacy. He was glad of that. No matter how many deaths occurred around him, he could not inure himself to bereavement: he simply became more adept at it, and recognized its stages, and knew that like pain it would peak and ebb away in a certain time.

But this time was different. There was another sensation struggling inside him. He turned the cutting tool over and over in his hand, trying to pin down the thought.

It was guilt again.

He had the *gethes* to measure himself against now, the kind of humans who would not have shied away from using *c'naatat* to keep the infant alive. He had done exactly what they would have done. He had defied the natural order of things in a single, irrevocable moment because he *wanted* to. Shan hadn't. He wanted to know why.

He finished the panel just after first light and carried the memorial to the edge of Constantine's perimeter where Josh had dug a deep hole and a slot for the headstone. It fitted as he had planned. He stood back, and not so much admired it as noted it. On bright days the sun would slant through it like a disembodied church window and it would throw brilliant colors onto the grave. Real flowers would have been a poor substitute for that display.

He sat back on his heels and wondered just how many of his unshakeable beliefs would crumble in the years to come. He wasn't sure that he knew who he was any longer.

"That's lovely," said Shan.

She had followed him. Or maybe she knew him well enough to know where he would go and what he would do these days. Either way, he was glad she was there, and as she knelt down beside him he patted her shoulder automatically, as if she was a house-brother he was greeting.

"I wanted it to be right before Commander Neville comes," he said. "Will it take some of the pain away?"

"It's—well, you're a good man, Aras." She looked resigned. He couldn't scent anything. "Decent thing to do."

"Shan, is Josh right? Is there life beyond this?"

"The rational me says no, unless that's how quantum physics shapes up. The other me?" She looked around the landscape as if there was some answer it would give her. "I don't want there to be an afterlife. There are some people I couldn't face a second time."

"But almost every human culture has stories of an afterlife."

"But you don't. And the isenj don't either, do they?"

"No. I've never come across another culture that does."

"Every miracle's got a mundane explanation. Your city of pearl is actually insect shit. Eternal life is a parasite. The bubbles in champagne are the farts of yeast colonies. Even that wonderful smell that comes from the ground after summer rain is a bacteria, *actinomycetes*. That's just the way the universe is. And you can choose—you can look at the wondrous surface or you can look at the crud beneath. I want to see the wondrous, believe me. I just know it isn't going to be there when I've finished looking."

"Are you depressed about the death of David Neville?"

Shan shook her head. "I wish I could be. I think I was more saddened by the bezeri, because it was senseless."

"Were you at all tempted to save the child as I saved you?"

"The nearest I got to that was thinking how sad it was that I could but I wouldn't."

"I'm sobered to know you have more resolve than me."

"Wrong question," she said. "I never knew David. The real test would have been if it were you who were dying. If you're berating yourself for breaking the rules and infecting me, move on. I have."

Aras took a last critical look at the grave, determined to reach perfection. Another human was gone; and there had been hundreds over the years, and hundreds of wess'har, too. It had never eaten at him like this before. He wondered if this was some of Shan's biochemistry at work in him, or if it was simply a product of time and events.

He wanted to think of them as meaning more than a cycle of component atoms ebbing and flowing through the world.

For once, he wanted Shan Frankland to be wrong.

The changes were beginning to pick up pace, and Shan's mornings were taking on a pattern. On waking, safe in Constantine, she had approximately three oblivious seconds before reality crashed in. Her first conscious thoughts were to dread what changes the *c'naatat* were making in her body.

She thought of them as creatures now. She had never felt that way about bacteria or viruses, which existed as a corporate entity called Illness. There were no personalities involved: it was strictly business, cause and effect, supply and demand. But she didn't feel ill, and she knew there was no cure. The *c'naatat* would go on with their ceaseless home-improvement tasks for all eternity.

They were terraforming her. Her survival was their survival. It struck her from time to time how very unlike humans they were, realizing she was a resource to be preserved rather than exploited.

She washed her face vigorously in the warm water from the spigot and started brushing her teeth. The swiss on the cabinet *eeped*.

"Eddie, you do pick your moments."

Eddie's voice was different, less chatty, less intimate. "Where have you been?"

"The moon," she said. "Seriously. I was summoned to

F'nar. I want to stay on and the ruling matriarchs like to interview refugees."

"Oh."

"What can I do for you, anyway?"

"Is that how you see yourself? A refugee now?"

"I don't fancy going back just yet. Is there something bothering you?"

"I don't think you're bottling out of facing an inquiry over Parekh, that's all."

Shan spat foam in the basin and rinsed her mouth again. "Go on."

"Do you mind my asking what was in your Suppressed Briefing?"

"Nothing you don't already know. Just to make sure the gene bank was safe for posterity."

"So who's paying you?"

"Sorry?"

"Who's paying you for the wess'har biotech? I can't believe it's a corporation, although you'd be a bloody good cover for that. So I'm thinking government."

Shan was shocked into silence. She was not so much stunned that he had worked out the wess'har connection, but that he thought she was trading biotech for her own ends. There had been no point leveling with him about Op Green Rage at all. He didn't understand. She should have known better.

"What the hell makes you say that?" she said at last.

"Aras takes a shell up the tailpipe and dusts himself off. You bounce back from death's door. And I've been talking to the isenj foreign minister about Mjat. I can add up, you know."

Shit. *Shit.* But Eddie was out there, and she was here. They couldn't take her or Aras. Even so . . . she had hoped it wouldn't get out.

Everything gets out in the end. The longer it takes, the more it looks like a cover-up.

"Then I think you've got your sums wrong, Eddie."

"I hoped I had, Shan. I really did."

"You have no idea. I know what this looks like, but you really don't understand at all."

"A straight answer would help. Who are you playing mule for?"

"You know the potential of the story you're sitting on?"

"I'm right, then."

"It's not for sale. At any price. I know you won't take any notice of this, but stop digging."

The line snapped into static again. *Stop digging.* It was the worst possible thing to say to a journalist.

But it was still better than telling him the truth.

The tayberries were chest high, trained over frames in little domes that were dotted around the fields. Shan took the secateurs and began cutting back the long shoots, holding the ends carefully in her fingertips and dropping the severed shoots into a pile in the barrow beside her. It was a soothingly repetitive task.

Every so often she would find a berry someone had missed from the harvest and eat it. It burst against her palate, sweet and velvety, and right then she couldn't imagine a more pleasant way to spend the day. She was completely caught up in the rhythm of it. When Kristina Hugel walked up behind her, she wasn't even aware of the woman's footsteps.

"Earning your keep?" Hugel said.

"Clears the mind, gardening."

"You ought to wear gloves for that. Look at the state of you."

Shan glanced down at her hands, and then examined her arms. There was a long scrape down her right forearm, oozing pinpricks of blood; it was the sort of scratch thorny bushes gave you and that you stopped noticing when the weather was cold enough. She tutted and rubbed at it.

"Ought to get that seen to," Hugel said.

Shan rolled down her sleeves. Eddie had been talking to Hugel. She knew it. Checking facts, bouncing ideas off her. Or maybe she just looked alien now and didn't notice.

If Hugel did know, it wasn't the end of the world. They had to get samples out of her first before they could make any use of the thing. "No," Shan said, and began clipping again. "It's nothing. Anyway, were you looking for me for anything?"

Hugel shrugged. "You're not coming back with us."

"I like it here."

"I've never concerned myself with what your objectives might have been on this mission, but there are some pretty wild stories going round."

Shan found herself taking an instinctive step back and lifting the double handles of the barrow to put it between her and Hugel as a barrier. Could they recover anything of the parasite from blood on the bush cuttings? She would burn them. She couldn't take chances. "I never took you for someone who listened to wild stories, Kris."

"You know what I'm talking about?"

"You tell me. Eddie's tabloid musings about indestructible aliens? I've heard." She felt bad as soon as she said it. It was unfair to discredit Eddie. He'd done his job, and done it too well. "And if it's true, are you going to be the one to walk up to them and ask for a few subjects for vivisection?"

"Do I need to? Is there a source nearer to home?"

Shan started to walk away. She was prepared to drop the barrow and make a run for it, if need be. And she could run in this environment, far faster than any of them now that Aras's motley collection of genes had started rearranging hers.

"If it exists, you won't get anywhere near it," she said, and began walking back towards the settlement.

"Is that the deal you did?" Hugel called. She was walking briskly behind Shan. "You got the tech the hard way, didn't you? Who's paying you for it? The Americas? The Sinostates?"

Shan could hear Hugel's footsteps stumble into a jog every so often. "You don't know me, Kris. Don't make judgments."

"You're carrying it. You're worth a whole economy and you know it."

Shan stopped and turned. Her sidearm was out of her belt before she knew it and she was aiming it two-handed at Hugel. Both of them froze and the horror and surprise seemed mutual.

"You stay away from me," Shan said. "I'm not going back, I'm not in any deal, and I'm not handing out samples. Now piss off."

Hugel stared. "Think about what you're carrying."

"A plague, if anything."

"And you're going to pass up the chance of developing it, eh?"

"Please, Kris, don't, *don't* make me fire. I am *not* bluffing. Just go."

Hugel hesitated for a moment and then turned and walked briskly away, eventually breaking into a stumbling run. Shan lowered the weapon. For once, she wasn't shaking afterwards. *C'naatat* appeared to smooth out the adrenaline cascade: or maybe she was just less stressed about shooting people dead these days. At least it was out in the open now, and all she had to do was to stay clear of contact and get the mission off the planet as soon as she could. She had one last card, the card that told them where the parasite could be found, and that was the card she had to hold on to regardless of the cost.

She had never considered herself a principled person. All too often lately, her sleep was disturbed by dreams of the rules she had bent and the lives she had bent even further. She blamed it on the slow afterburn of the Suppressed Briefing, but at times she wondered if it really was a dawning realization that she had gone too far too often.

But it was that ability to go too far—or the inability to stop herself at the edge—that had brought her to where she was now. She could have been like the rest of them. She could have done the right thing because it was personally expedient. No, *that* was the real corruption of the soul. Real evil wasn't about bending the law to suit justice: evil was acting out of small, intensely personal expedience and losing sight of the bigger picture so often that you never got it back again.

Perault, she thought. *Perault knew me even better than she thought she did.*

Shan looked down at her hands, which had developed retractable nails, only subtly different in appearance but claws nonetheless. They were red with tayberry stains and some of her own blood.

She knew it would wash off in time, all of it.

30

They prosper, who burn in the morning
The letters they wrote overnight.

ADMIRAL RONALD A. HOPWOOD, CB,
"The Laws of the Navy"

Eddie thought of the aerial shot of Umeh, building on top of building and the total absence of anything that was not an isenj or their construction, except rust-red sea. It made his scalp prickle.

"Wow," said Becken. Webster had rigged a makeshift screen in the mess so they could watch live news from Earth, courtesy of *Actaeon*. The marines and payload were crammed round the table with all differences and dead colleagues forgotten for the meanwhile. "They're out of the league altogether? Jesus. They were premier league when we left."

Sport. Soccer, in fact. The grim news of growing tension between the Pacific Rim and the Sinostates had silenced them at first but then life got back to normal. Even the payload, who Eddie had judged to be less laddish than the marines in their viewing choices, seemed far more interested in the European Premiership than in current affairs. He wasn't so much disappointed as insulted.

Soccer, soccer, soccer. Well, it never changed. It was a haven of familiarity in a now-alien Earth.

"Can we have the interactive banking on, please?" said Champciaux. "Just the icon in the corner. I want to see my money again."

There was a huge whoop of laughter. Once the novelty of instant contact with Earth had worn thin, they had all moved swiftly from reminding their employers they were still alive to checking on their bank accounts.

Seventy-five years' interest was a great deal of money. So was seventy-five years' basic pay. They were all very wealthy, and the euphoria evoked by checking their balances had not worn off yet. Eddie noted he had not had any seniority increments since 2299: that, said BBChan Human Resources, was because he wasn't any more senior in his time frame, and the unions had conceded that time displacement was outside the scope of the negotiated pay structure.

No, some things never changed.

Shan Frankland didn't.

He took out his screen and unfurled it enough to check the message again. It hadn't been what he was expecting.

FROM: *BBChan Research Support to Eddie Michallat CS2. Sorry, no joy. All Frankland's assets are attached. (Please don't circulate this: totally unauthorized access, serious crap if we're caught.) Just her salary in her current account and pension fund. Not even a savings account. Anything else we can do for you?*

He had been so sure. It slotted together as neatly as hindsight; it was enough circumstantial evidence to get a warrant. But he was *wrong.* He had applied normal probability to a woman who wasn't the norm and ignored the obvious— that Shan Frankland cared more about what she thought of herself than making money or even the admiration of others.

I'm going to have to apologize, he thought. *I owe her that.* And he wished more than anything that he had never discussed her with Kris Hugel. But his revelation couldn't be erased like Mjat.

Mesevy sat down next to him. "You look miserable. Not looking forward to going home?"

Eddie pinned his professional bonhomie face back on. "I'm staying on with *Actaeon.* Wouldn't miss the chance of being the only journo in town."

"Me too."

"Not much for a botanist to do on *Actaeon*." *Or Umeh*.

"No, I meant Constantine. I found things here, things I don't think I would have found back home. So I'm staying."

Eddie wished for a moment that he could have slipped so easily into that archaic, ideal world. He'd liked the place. But it was separate, distant, not at all involved with the real ebb and flow of human affairs. In fact, it was waiting for them to end—messily, no doubt—before sweeping over the floor and starting again.

"Didn't you have to get permission from the wess'har?"

Mesevy looked baffled. "No. I just asked Josh Garrod."

He knew the botanist had caught a dose of religion, but not that it had gone this far. But why not? There was real work for her to do here, work that didn't involve making agribusiness richer. And she would be among relatively kind people who would value her and look after her. No, it made perfect sense. "I'm glad," he said. "I hope you're happy here."

It wasn't as if he needed any more reminders that whatever Shan had done had been something desperate and reluctant, not part of a selfish plan. Rayat thought she derived a savage satisfaction from enforcement, that she reveled in intrigue and politics. But Eddie now had a glimpse of a much sadder, lonelier woman who was just desperate to do the right thing.

He might never know why she wanted to put the universe right. In some ways he didn't care. He just wanted her to be a hero.

Everyone needed heroes. He certainly did.

31

The night of November 4 turned out to be a typically mild one, according to Josh. Shan spent it lying on her bed in Josh's spare room, listening to the agonizing sound of her closest colleague screaming in the distance.

Lindsay had called at least ten times that day asking to talk to her, but Shan had nothing to say. *Bloody Eddie Michallat and his big mouth.* It wasn't the fact that he had exposed her deceit that angered her; it was that he had given Lindsay the idea that, if time could be run back, there would be a chance of saving her son.

Lindsay's voice was faint. But Shan could hear it, with or without any enhancements the *c'naatat* might have made to her hearing. If she could hear it in the upper level of chambers in Constantine, then so could much of the colony.

"You can't hide from me, you bitch." Shan picked up the whole sentence that time, and nothing was lost to the breeze. "Was it too much to . . ."

The rest was indistinct. She estimated that Lindsay had to be standing near the first cluster of roof bubbles to the south, almost overhead. Her voice was failing by now: she had kept it up for nearly an hour.

Over the next half-hour, the longest of her life, the only sound Shan could pick out was sporadic sobbing. It was easy to be harsh with the strong and the evil. It was far harder to stand firm against pain, especially the pain of a friend.

In the end it was too much to bear. It was stupid, and it wouldn't help, but she had to go out and face her. Shan slipped on her coat and made her way out of Josh's home and through the maze of buried galleries to the surface. On the way out up one of the exit ramps she felt the slight fizz of the security shield as it tested her: it was the first time she had noticed it in scores of passes in and out of the subterranean village. It had not reacted to her before. But she had been wholly human in the past. Now she was not, and it was simply making sure she was not isenj.

Up on the surface the night was pleasantly breezy. She saw Lindsay a few moments before the woman noticed her. She was on her knees in the short grass, sobbing weakly.

"What can I say to you?" Shan called. "Sorry? Will that really make it right?"

Lindsay stopped and slowly knelt back on her heels. "Is it true?" Her voice was cracked and hoarse. "I just want to know if it's true."

"I imagine Eddie told you."

"Eddie hasn't told me anything. Kris said you had some sort of wess'har biotech that could have saved David. I just want to know if it's true. I need to know if you stabbed me in the back for a deal with some drug company or government. Was that what was really in your Suppressed Briefing?"

It was harder than she thought. *This is a job, and I have no feelings about it,* she reminded herself. *I have no choice.*

"Lin, I never did any deal. I've got an infection that enables me to survive biological hazards and injuries. I have no idea if it would have saved David." *Liar, liar, liar.* "But it would run riot in the general population."

"I know what Kris and Eddie talked about. It keeps you *alive.*"

"If there had been a way to make use of it safely, I would have offered."

Lindsay got to her feet and walked towards her. "You bitch!" she screamed. "You pious, self-righteous cow! How could *you* do it to *me*? Doesn't personal loyalty mean anything to you?"

"It's nothing to do with loyalty. It's about responsibility."

There was no question of Shan being in danger. She could see Lindsay wasn't armed, but even if she was it would have made little difference in the long run. All she could do was scream abuse at her. But that hurt more than any high-velocity round.

There was no point listening to any more. Shan turned and walked back to the entrance, telling herself the things she told herself when she was a young copper. Abuse was just words. It wasn't personal. Words couldn't do you any damage. Only weapons and fists could.

The sound of Lindsay's sobbing and cursing ebbed, leaving Shan to slip back into her room in Josh's home and shut the door.

The *c'naatat* might have been good at dealing with organic damage, but it had no idea how to heal a broken heart.

Her swiss told her it was the next morning and that there was a call waiting, just the one. Shan washed in the small basin and checked herself carefully against the previous day's appearance. There was nothing extra that she could see, but she was definitely getting broader in the shoulders and she felt she was looking at a changing face in some indefinable way, like trying to focus on your reflection when a migraine was starting and disrupting your vision. As long as the thing didn't give her those weird wess'har pupils, she could cope. She returned the waiting call on audio-only.

"What do you want, Eddie?" she said.

"I wasn't sure you'd call back."

"If you've called to berate me—"

"I haven't."

"Okay."

"I'm sorry about what happened, Shan. I got it wrong."

"I told you so."

"But most guilty people do. I'm just not used to people telling the truth."

"Neither am I."

"If I could undo what I've done, I would. You have no idea how much I regret this."

"Did you tell Lin, Eddie?"

"No. I didn't have the guts. Kris Hugel probably gave her the impression she could have isolated some of the *c'naatat* characteristics to create immunity. Without messing with life span."

"Do you seriously think that, given a whole sample, some biotech firm would take the gene sequences that stop bleeding, or create novel antibodies, and throw the anti-agathic uses away? You know *nothing* about life science corporations. I'm EnHaz. Don't even ask me what I've seen."

"I know. You don't have to spell it out to me."

"No, you *don't* know. Human cloning and chimera bans didn't work. Crop terminator genes are still traded despite a worldwide ban. If it's doable, it gets done. I just bloody know where this will end."

"Shan, I've seen footage from Umeh. That's without *c'naatat*. I think I can do the maths."

He sounded like the old Eddie again. Shan wondered why they still called digital images footage. "So what did you want, anyway? An interview?"

There was a hiss of breath. "I just called to say I think Rochefoucauld was right." And the line went dead. The swiss chirped and reset itself.

She had no idea who Rochefoucauld was and put it on

her growing list of things to look into. In twenty-four hours, the *Thetis* team would be heading home, or at least to the relative haven of a human ship. There would be plenty of time for dissecting Eddie's motivation later.

Nevertheless, she set the swiss to monitor outgoing transmissions routed via *Actaeon* just to see what he was going to tell the world about her, or more precisely about the *c'naatat* parasite. He only had myths. But myths were very credible in the right hands.

From time to time, she looked at the swiss and noted that today Eddie had filed features on *alyats,* ingenious ways to use 100 percent of a soy crop, and local craftsmanship, but nothing about her.

But then he had never filed any of her revelations about Green Rage, either. Even his recently broadcast interviews with the isenj had not directly picked up on the significance of the *c'naatat,* as far as she could see; his voice-over had referred to "a long-standing war with as many legends, propaganda and misinformation as any on Earth." It was as if he were playing it down for the time being. But what material had he edited out?

She flicked open the swiss and keyed ROCHEFOUCAULD into the database. The plasma screen, strung like a child's soap-bubble toy between the filaments, disgorged a long biography and selected passages from the man's works.

French seventeenth-century classical author known for epigrams expressing a harsh or paradoxical truth in the briefest manner possible. La Rochefoucauld saw selfishness, hypocrisy, and weakness in general in human behavior.

Well, she didn't need a dead French intellectual to teach her that. She read on anyway. It was when she was scrolling through the selected quotes that she began to realize just how little she knew Eddie Michallat. She was also reminded of the time that she had told him they were in the same line of business.

Perfect courage is to do without witnesses what one would be capable of with the world looking on. (From Rochefoucauld's Maximes)

She closed the screen and pressed her hand against her mouth, eyes shut tight.

"I owe you an apology, Mr. Michallat," she said aloud.

32

The Temporary City had a much more permanent appearance to it now. The coming and going of transports and combat craft picked it out from a great distance, like the telltale procession of rockvelvets seeking a corpse.

Aras suppressed his Targassati aversion to objects that imposed on the natural landscape. This was a necessary reinforcement; he just wished it could have looked more *balanced*. He walked into the command center of the base and found not only Mestin but also her daughter Nevyan directing operations.

Aras still thought of Nevyan as an *isanket,* a little girl, a matriarch-to-be. The grim concentration on her face said otherwise. Aras caught Mestin's eye and his unspoken question must have been visible.

"She has to learn her duties sometime, and now is as good a time as any," Mestin said, and left her daughter tapping three-dimensional plans and re-routing vessels with elegant hand movements. "I see the isenj have told all creation about *c'naatat.*"

"It was never a secret."

"Why has the *Actaeon* demanded Shan Frankland?" There was nothing by way of transmissions that escaped Mestin's intelligence net. "This is not about the bezeri-killer any longer, I suspect."

Aras steeled himself to lie by omission. "They think she has access to *c'naatat,* because they believe it to be medical technology. They have no idea it occurs naturally. Their logic says that if it is technology, then they can acquire it."

"Are they serious about taking her?"

"At the moment."

"If they attempt to, then they must learn that we mean what we say." Mestin glanced back over her shoulder to check on Nevyan. "Personally, I would destroy all the *gethes* now and have done with it, but Fersanye and Chayyas believe it will do little to stop them coming in the long term, and so we should use the opportunity to find another, more lasting barrier."

Aras held out a human data chip to Mestin. "This is a recording of a conversation between Eddie Michallat and Shan Frankland."

"And he gave you this." Mestin stared at it and turned it in her fingers. "Why?"

"He says *Shan Chail* knows many more ways to fight small wars against certain types of human than we do. And I agree with him. Knowing their minds will be far more significant than technical intelligence."

"Everything will have a use," said Mestin. "I do not like change, but change is coming. Bring *Shan Chail* here until the *gethes* have left. I want no mistakes."

Aras worried at the prospect of having Shan kept at close quarters with wess'har even for a day or two. If he protested, it would draw attention. Lying was painful and difficult; he resolved to unlearn the skill as quickly as was practical. He would have to school Shan before she left.

Outside the air throbbed with the arrival of two more transports carrying personnel and equipment. Aras watched the smooth dark shapes for a few minutes and wondered what the bezeri would say about it all. It was part of the protection agreement, but it did not mean they would enjoy it.

He sat in the small surface skimmer for a few minutes, bobbing on the waves and waiting. A cluster of lights emerged from the depths. He took out his lamp and positioned over the brow of the vessel ready for a conversation.

Make them leave, said the first bezeri to reach the shallows. There was a great deal of green light in the words, a sure sign of anxiety. *Make them leave our world alone.*

We will, Aras signaled. *The* gethes *are leaving today and no others will ever be allowed to land again.*

There was a shimmer of blues at the far end of his vision. *What price will you be prepared to pay? When will you tire of this?*

Aras paused. It was the first time he had ever seen doubt expressed about wess'har commitment—or capability. The bezeri accepted their invincibility without question.

Whatever threatens you also threatens us, Aras replied. *We will not abandon you.*

The lights settled into a general haze of violets and ambers, and then sank rapidly into the depths. Aras flicked the skimmer into life and headed back to the island and Constantine. It was the first time the bezeri had taken their leave of him without a farewell.

"It's for the best," Shan told Josh. She stuffed her few possessions back into the grip and slung it across her back. "I want to keep you out of this."

She made her way up the stairs to the upper level of gal-

leries, Josh trailing behind her. On the way there seemed to
be far more colonists than she had ever seen underground
on a normal day. They were scared; perhaps they expected a
shooting match as the remnant of the mission withdrew. But
they showed no resentment of the trouble she had brought
to their world.

"One thing I forgot," said Shan. She fumbled in one of
the pockets of her waistcoat. An obliging colonist had altered all her clothes. "My tomatoes. Would you mind hanging on to them for me?" She pressed the container of
precious seeds into Josh's hand.

Aras was waiting for her at the top of the ramp. Behind
him were half a dozen wess'har males carrying metallic objects about thirty centimeters long, but nothing like his
gevir. Their vivid, finely draped clothing was as far from a
military uniform as she could imagine but they could only
be troops. She met their stares.

"Time to go," said Aras. "Tlivat will escort you to the
Temporary City."

"And what are you planning to do?"

"I shall ensure the *gethes* leave."

She knew better than to argue with Aras, and she knew
he would come to no lasting harm. She was already starting
to get used to the idea that he would always be around
whatever happened. Tlivat watched the rest of the wess'har
head off towards the camp and turned to Shan with a visible
sniff.

"You have no need to be afraid," he said. Whatever scent
she was exuding, he had not identified it as *c'naatat.* Perhaps they couldn't tell; maybe all alien things smelled the
same to them. They hadn't lived beside humans like Aras
had. She had no doubt that Aras would be in serious trouble
if—no, *when* the matriarchs discovered what she was. By
then, she hoped she would have made herself so useful to
them that they would understand Aras's rash gesture.

Tlivat had a surface vessel waiting on the beach. It was easy to forget Constantine was on an island. The sea was a calm dark gray, reflecting an overcast sky, and an occasional flash of brilliantly colored lights caught her eye as she helped him push the vessel into the shallows. It rocked alarmingly as she stepped in, and she reminded herself that she could not drown, even if she could not swim. There was now no real reason to learn anyway.

Tlivat set the skimmer towards the mainland and leaned back in the stern, his hands on a console that had emerged gracefully from the keel of the craft like a rapidly growing plant. A small pod of bezeri trailed them. Shan wondered if the mother of the dead child was among them.

Tlivat tilted his head. "They are curious."

"They know me as the bearer of bad news," said Shan.

He made a pointing gesture at her chest. "Your pocket is flashing."

"Oh. Thanks." Shan had disoriented herself, imagining the world as the bezeri saw it with these odd rigid creatures coasting along overhead in the upper reaches of their atmosphere. *We're birds,* she thought. She pulled out her swiss and checked to see what it had gathered for her.

It was a message from Eddie. Shame: she really should have made time to say goodbye and apologize for having such a low opinion of him. It wasn't personal. She had a low opinion of most humans, and maybe that was why he thought La Rochefoucauld was apt for her.

Shan, it read. *I think you need to see this, for all sorts of reasons. Call it a selection from the cutting-room floor.* That was it, apart from a large video file accompanying it. Of course: her embarrassingly frank interview about Green Rage. *What a nice bloke,* she thought. *A gentleman.*

She braced herself in the skimmer as best she could to avoid being thrown around by the larger waves. Tlivat was not a conversationalist. She occupied herself by checking the functions on her swiss, and then she decided to relive the interview with Eddie.

The screen of the swiss spread into a picture. But it wasn't the scrubby grass around the camp, or a close-up of her. It was hard to see what it was at first, just a mass of gray and off-white shapes, but then the shot pulled back in a series of jerks and she realized she was looking at a planet from high orbit. She had only just started to work out what the colors were when the screen split into two, one side showing a ussissi with a hearing device draped over its head, and the other an isenj, fidgeting on a padded bench.

It was an interview all right, but it wasn't hers. And it told her more than she had wanted to know about what happened to *c'naatat* prisoners of war.

Shan shut the swiss and put it back into her pocket. She would be far more patient with Aras in future, she decided. All the way to the Temporary City, she fought to clear images of horror from her mind.

If her own *c'naatat* had really cared for her welfare, it would have allowed her to get obliviously drunk.

"Don't worry, they don't expect you to shoot her," Barencoin said. Qureshi pulled a face and went on cleaning her rifle.

Lindsay didn't much care if they had to shoot Shan or not. Eddie kept telling her she was making a big mistake, but orders were orders, and she had no problem complying with this one.

The camp was closing down. Bennett, Hugel and Champciaux were crating up essential kit. Mesevy had been pottering around in the greenhouses for a while, salvaging plants and photosynthetic panels for the colony. Whatever they left behind the colonists would recycle in that conscientious smug way of theirs.

"Let's get it over with," said Chahal.

None of them appeared to have much enthusiasm for the task. Lindsay tried to loom over them, Shan-style. It hurt her afresh each time when she realized just how many mannerisms she had picked up from the woman.

"What's your problem with this?" she asked quietly. "You're not afraid of a hard target. Come on."

The marines looked at her. "We're supposed to detain her, not shoot her," said Barencoin. "And I don't fancy pulling this off in the colony. It's a rabbit warren. Loads of civvies around. No, I think we should call it off."

"And if she's what they say she is, it wouldn't matter what we pumped into her," Qureshi said. "I didn't join up to mess around with things like this. She's not a threat, not if she's holed up here."

"Did you hear me? We have our orders. Front up and earn it, people."

There was a long pause. *They would have been out the door by now if Shan had given the order,* Lindsay thought. But they stood up and slung their rifles on their webbing, although their expressions were unmarinelike in their sullen acceptance of the command.

"Ma'am, I think you should stay out of this," Barencoin said. "It's too personal for you."

"You saying I can't carry out my duty?"

"Yes, ma'am, I think I am. We don't blame you. It's terrible what you've been through, with David—"

"She can save lives, and she knows she can." Lindsay knew what she would have done in the same position. There was no question. It was as clear to her as the time she had given Hugel back the sub-Q that was meant to abort her child. "She gets what's coming to her. That's our job. We defend and protect human life above all else. We put our own kind first, before aliens, before animals, before plants and pretty views. Is that understood?"

Their faces told her it was not. But they tightened their

helmet straps and waited. Barencoin looked embarrassed.
They would have stood there a lot longer if a distinctive
quiet rush of air hadn't made them all look towards the
deckhead.

"Wess'har," Chahal said, and they sprinted outside into a
compound already ringed by wess'har troops. They were
shockingly alien in the flesh, so unlike the familiar burly
Aras that they were genuinely frightening. None of the
team had seen one before but it was clear who they were,
and they were extraordinary. Their faces were animal and
unfathomable; their weapons were not. One stepped forward. Either it recognized Lindsay, or it was looking for the
likely alpha female. She remembered that much of what
Shan had told her.

"You will leave," it said. The voice had many levels and
notes to it, but it was perfectly clear. "You will all go to
your shuttle and we will escort you into a docking orbit
with your *Actaeon* vessel. Then you will all return to your
home and you will not set foot on Bezer'ej or Wess'ej at
any time."

Lindsay tried to judge how much trouble they might be.
Shan said they didn't bluff. They were absolutely literal.
There was an unspoiled plain that had once been an isenj
city as proof of that.

"We won't leave without Shan Frankland," she said, ignoring what her guts were telling her. "We have orders to
detain her. You understand orders, don't you?"

The wess'har didn't even blink. Their flower-irised eyes
were unpleasantly compelling. "You will leave without
her."

"We can't do that."

"Then you will die. Those who wish to go may leave
now." The wess'har stepped back; Aras walked through
their line and stood within two meters of Lindsay. She had

seen him many times but this was different. It was personal. She stared at him and tried to hate him.

He seemed immune to her hostility. "Commander, Shan Frankland is now in the Temporary City. There is nothing you can do to retrieve her, except perhaps get killed." He had such kind eyes, sad as a dog's, in that curious hard face. "Make your choice."

"I will not leave without her."

"And we do not negotiate."

Lindsay still had her hand on her rifle, although she was well aware that it was pointless. "I didn't expect you to help," she said. "But I expected Shan to. She'll answer to Earth authorities."

"I think not." He stepped forward again, and this time he was inches from her, huge and suddenly menacing. "Understand this. If you knew what sort of life you coveted for your son, if you realized what my condition truly meant, then you would thank her. If she had tried to use it to cure your son, I would have had to destroy every one of you, and I would have done so. The end would be the same. The intervening detail of your small expectations of each other doesn't concern me. Now go."

Lindsay realized she had stepped back from him. Eddie, Hugel, and Champciaux were looking bewildered with their grips in their hands. The wess'har troops raised what looked like musical instruments, like sections of horns, beautiful golden curved objects. The open ends each pointed straight at one of the mission team.

"You go or you die," said the wess'har.

Eddie spoke up. "Commander, we're the ones with the stone axes here. Let's be smart for once and leave."

Lindsay looked over her shoulder at her marines. They were all combat troops, and she wouldn't have thought of any of them as cowards. She knew they would take on any-

thing if she ordered them to. But their hands were at their
sides. If she was going to die, she would probably be doing
it alone.

"Let's go home, ma'am," Qureshi said.

It was one promise Shan hadn't kept. She said she would
get them all home in one piece. It was up to Lindsay to take
on that promise now.

It was hardly the best evening for a baptism. The sky was
clear as glass, but there was a biting wind from the sea.
Only the fading roses and violets of the sunset gave any impression of warmth.

Shan and Aras stood on the top of the cliff and looked
down on to the beach where a large crowd of the colonists
had gathered. The assembly seemed a cheerful one. Several
of the colonists held what looked like bath towels. Mesevy,
draped in a shapeless off-white shift that reached her an-
kles, picked her way down the beach to the water's edge
with Josh and Sam.

"Bloody mad in this weather," said Shan, and noted that
all three of them flinched visibly as they waded into the water to waist height. Josh and Sam stood either side of Mesevy and looked as if they were reciting something while
she listened, her eyes closed. Then they each placed an arm
across her back and dipped her backwards into the sea, im-
mersing her totally for a few seconds before pulling her
back upright again. She stood soaked, hair flattened to her
head, gasping. Shan couldn't hear what was being said, but
she heard the "amen" from the crowd.

"So that's a baptism," said Aras.

"Never seen that before," Shan said.

And neither had the bezeri. As Shan looked farther out to
sea, she could see scatterings of light, blue and gold, flick-
ering and shimmering just beneath the surface. The bezeri
were watching the humans. It was unusual to see them so

near the surface lately; their dread of invaders had driven them deep.

"What do you reckon they're thinking?"

Aras considered the lights for a while and moved his head slightly as if reading aloud to himself. "Some of them are asking whether the humans are trying to breathe under water. They're debating whether to try to bring Mesevy to the surface if she gets into difficulty."

Shan smiled. "Have you explained baptism to them?"

"There's never been an adult baptism here before."

"I never thought of that."

"I explained that the water cleanses the human's soul. The bezeri wanted to know if the soul-dirt that was washed off would pollute their environment."

The crowd on the shoreline broke up and began moving back up the beach. Shan knew now what the big towels were for. Mesevy was wrapped tight in them, shivering.

"Your technology is pretty good, isn't it?"

Aras nodded. "You say so."

"Can you do selective memory wipes?"

"No."

"I was just hoping," she said. "There are so many things I'd rather forget. I seem to be remembering more than ever lately. I thought it was the SB."

"That's the wess'har in you. Our recall is complete."

"And what's the human in you, then? What do you get from us?"

"Restlessness," Aras said. "A need for solitude occasionally. And maybe that strange ability to know one thing and yet want to believe another. What do you call it? Faith."

They lapsed back into silence. It wasn't the baptism she had been waiting to watch. Close to the horizon she could see a very bright object, an artificial star she had watched on many nights until its orbit took it out of view. *Thetis* was still on station and waiting for rendezvous with *Actaeon,* it-

self a brilliant point of light nearby. Eventually the two stars
merged.

"There we go," said Shan. If she needed confirmation
that she was never going home, this was it. By the time the
ships parted again, they would be below the level of the
horizon and she would not see the sudden nova of energy as
Thetis turned and began its acceleration toward home.

"Your people are unwise to take isenj to Earth. You will
regret it."

"Unfortunately, I think we're going to get along with
them just fine."

"A mistake. I assure you."

"We all do unwise things."

"You still think I was a fool to infect you."

"Well, I don't think we'll have long to wait before the
matriarchs find out about it. They won't think it's too
clever."

Now that the baptism party had moved on, they scrambled down the slope to the beach. She could manage it in
wess'har time now, or at least in Aras-time. Neither gravity
nor variable oxygen hindered her. It was still an unsettling
prospect to wake each morning and wonder what might
have changed in her body. When the fear took her, she remembered the wonder of seeing polarized light and blues
beyond the scope of her human genes. Aras assured her she
would get used to it in time. Her only problem would be if
she refused to let go of the past.

And there was a lot of that to let go.

The retreating tide had left rock-pools, worlds in their
own right. She squatted down and stared into one to see
what life stirred in it when her shadow darkened the water.
There was a flurry of movement. Sand churned up, and then
the miniature universe was still again.

I am a world too, she thought. *C'naatat* only wanted the
best for its environment, for her. It wanted a stable colony,

just like the settlers of Constantine. *I'm not carrying a disease. And a world has responsibilities.*

On the shoreline, claret-colored weeds washed out in strands like hair. She stepped round the fronds with care, for there might have been a smaller world within them as well. A movement caught her eye, the last bezeri patrol sinking into the depths, trailing blue and green lights.

She looked into another pool. *I was eight years old, exploring the beach.* There were no crabs or limpets or razor shells here: pulses of light shimmered intermittently, the telltale signs of a glass-clear sea creature sheltering in the red weed. She hadn't thought of those childhood seaside holidays in years. It was as if the sudden separation from humanity had opened up a well of memories to cushion her against the unknown.

Shan took the azin-shell map carefully from Aras. It hinged open: the sand and fragments compressed within it shivered a little, as fragile as the ecology of the world itself. Carefully, she took a little vermilion powdered glass between her fingertips and let it fall slowly in an ellipse a little way from the shoreline—the settlement of Constantine. *It was the summer before the Alum Bay cliffs sank into the sea,* she thought. *I filled a glass lighthouse with layers of colored sands so the holiday would live forever.* Then she trailed the glass-powder round the very edge of the map, and shut it tightly again.

She waded into the shallows and left it where the bezeri could see it. She hoped they would understand that she was telling them she was enforcing an environmental protection zone, although they would not understand what EnHaz was.

All they really needed to know was that Superintendent Shan Frankland, Environmental Hazard Enforcement, had changed her mind about early retirement.

"Come on, home," she said, and took Aras's arm. "Borscht on the menu tonight. Can't wait."

On the patch of land that had once been the *Thetis* base camp there were marks on the grass like a floor plan, but all traces of the construction had already been picked clean. In the coming weeks, wess'har eco-tech would quietly erase all evidence that humans had ever been there and reclaim the ground for the wild.

The *gethes* had left no more lasting physical impression on Bezer'ej than the isenj had. Some things could be put back together again as if nothing had happened: but she wasn't one of them.

She glanced down at her hands.

Yes, they were definitely claws.